P9-DFZ-392

Praise for *New York Times* bestselling author Lori Foster

"Count on Lori Foster for sexy, edgy romance."

—Jayne Ann Krentz, *New York Times* bestselling author, on *No Limits*

"A sexy, heartwarming, down-home tale that features two captivating love stories… A funny and engaging addition to the series that skillfully walks the line between romance and women's fiction."

—*Library Journal* on *Sisters of Summer's End*

"Foster fills her scenes with plenty of banter and sizzling chemistry."

—*Publishers Weekly* on *Driven to Distraction*

Praise for *USA TODAY* bestselling author Joanne Rock

"Joanne Rock's sweet and sexy story pulled my heartstrings and pushed my hot buttons from the start…. Multileveled, and even fast paced…[*Dances Under the Harvest Moon*] delivers the couple to a well-deserved HEA."

—*Smart Bitches Trashy Books*

"Fast paced, attention grabbing and embroiled in scandal!… I recommend this book and this series in general to anyone who likes a power-driven story of lies and intrigue that revolve somewhat around a scandal in Hollywood. Looking forward to more to come!"

—*Thoughts of a Blonde* on *The Rival*

BREAKING HIS RULES

NEW YORK TIMES BESTSELLING AUTHOR
LORI FOSTER

Previously published as *Morgan*
and *His Accidental Heir*

Recycling programs
for this product may
not exist in your area.

ISBN-13: 978-1-335-40643-9

Breaking His Rules
First published as Morgan in 2000. This edition published in 2021.
Copyright © 2000 by Lori Foster

His Accidental Heir
First published in 2017. This edition published in 2021.
Copyright © 2017 by Joanne Rock

This edition published by arrangement with Harlequin Books S.A.

For questions and comments about the quality of this book,
please contact us at CustomerService@Harlequin.com.

Harlequin Enterprises ULC
22 Adelaide St. West, 40th Floor
Toronto, Ontario M5H 4E3, Canada
www.Harlequin.com

Printed in U.S.A.

CONTENTS

Lori Foster is a *New York Times* and *USA TODAY* bestselling author of more than one hundred titles. Lori has been a recipient of the prestigious *RT Book Reviews* Career Achievement Award for Series Romantic Fantasy, and for Contemporary Romance. For more about Lori, visit her website at lorifoster.com.

Books by Lori Foster

HQN

Road to Love

Driven to Distraction
Slow Ride
All Fired Up

The Summer Resort

Cooper's Charm
Sisters of Summer's End

Body Armor

Under Pressure
Hard Justice
Close Contact
Fast Burn

The Ultimate series

Hard Knocks (prequel ebook novella)
No Limits
Holding Strong
Tough Love
Fighting Dirty

Visit the Author Profile page at Harlequin.com for more titles.

MORGAN

Lori Foster

Prologue

It was one of those sweltering hot weekend mornings when a man had nothing better to do than sit outside in his jeans, feel himself sweat and wait for a breeze that wouldn't come. The sky was the prettiest blue he'd ever seen, not a single cloud in sight. He loved days like this, and looked forward to viewing them from his own house once he finished it. If all went well, it would be ready for him to move in by the end of summer.

Morgan Hudson tilted his chair back and closed his eyes. Everyone was gone for the day, and the house seemed strangely quiet, not peaceful so much as empty. He hoped he didn't feel that way when he got moved in. Living with three brothers and a teenage nephew got a man used to chaos, especially with *his* brothers.

Sawyer, the oldest, was the only doctor for miles around, and he had patients coming and going through the back office attached to the house all day long—sometimes even through the night. It was one reason the brothers had all hung around together for so long. Sawyer was an excellent father, but when Casey was little, they'd all pitched in to cover dad duty so the rigors of med school, and later being the town doc, didn't overwhelm him. It had been a pleasure.

Jordan, his younger brother, was a vet, and that meant the house and yard were always filled with stray animals. Morgan didn't mind. More often than not he got attached to the odd assortment of mangy, abandoned or just plain homely critters. 'Course, he didn't tell Jordan that.

Gabe, the youngest brother, was a rascal, with no intention of settling down anytime soon. And why should he when half the female populace of Buckhorn County, Kentucky would be bereft if he ever did? The women had spoiled Gabe something awful, and he indulged them all. Gabe just plain loved women, young and old, sweet or sassy. And they loved him back.

Casey, Sawyer's son, was constant chatter. He was at that awkward age of sixteen, half man, half kid, when females fascinated him, but then, so did driving and stretching his independence. Casey, as well as the brothers, was thrilled when Sawyer decided to marry again, adding a female into the masculine mix. The adjustment to Honey Malone had gone surprisingly smooth.

Morgan smiled. Damn, but he liked Honey. Mostly because the woman had snared his brother with a single look. Sawyer had fought it, Morgan'd give him that, but it hadn't done him a damn bit of good. He'd gone head over arse in love with Honey almost from the first day. And once Casey had decided he loved her, well, that had put a bow on the package. Sawyer would do anything for that boy, so it was a good thing Casey had taken to Honey the way he had.

Morgan wanted to have a son just like Casey some day—if he ever found a woman he wanted to marry. At thirty-four, he figured he'd waited plenty long enough. He almost had the house done, and he sure as hell was settled enough now, despite what his brothers thought. He had a respectable job and plenty of money put away. It was time for him to get on with his life, his hell-raising days long over.

A bird landed on the porch, right next to where Morgan's bare foot was braced on the railing. He cocked an eye open, whistled softly to the bird, then watched it take flight again. Obviously the bird hadn't known he was human—or else it'd thought he was dead. With a grin, Morgan closed his eyes again. He was like that, so still sometimes it set people on edge. To Morgan, it was all about control, taking charge of his life and seeing that things fell into place. He had the future mapped out, and he had not a single doubt that things would be just as he wanted them. He controlled himself, he controlled his future.

Whenever possible, he controlled those around him.

The man was sound asleep when Misty pulled up in front of the huge, impressive log house. It seemed to go on and on forever, sprawling over incredibly beautiful land. On the way in she'd seen a lake surrounded by colorful wildflowers, an enormous barn and several smaller outbuildings. In the distance, sitting atop a slight rise, was another house, but apart from that, the home was isolated.

Honey had told her a little about the property, but mostly she'd talked of her marriage. Sawyer, her husband-to-be, had rushed things through, and Honey was putting a wedding together in just under three weeks. It had taken Misty a few days to gather her things and join her sister so she could offer some last-minute help. The timing couldn't have been better, and Misty had given a silent prayer of gratitude that she actually had a place to stay for a short time. Otherwise, she'd have been homeless.

Honey had warned her that the testosterone level would be enough to strangle a frail woman, but still, Misty hadn't been prepared for the sight of the hard, dark man sitting on the porch. He wore tight faded jeans, the waistband undone—and nothing else. She gulped, seeing a flat, six-pack, slightly hairy abdomen.

Besides being massively built and layered in solid muscle, he was breathtakingly gorgeous. Not that it mattered to Misty, who was twice burned. She'd written men off, and they'd stay written off. But that didn't mean she couldn't look. And appreciate what she saw.

She inched closer, wondering exactly how to wake him or even if she should. She'd arrived a day early, so Honey might not be expecting her. But surely there was someone else in the house, and maybe if she knocked quietly…

She was right beside him, practically tiptoeing in her sandals, trying to decide what to do, when suddenly he opened his eyes.

Oh, Lord.

She felt snared, like a helpless doe in the headlights of a semi. She stared, swallowed and stared some more. The man seemed as surprised as she was, and then he suddenly moved, jerking upright. He lost his balance, and his chair went crashing backward with jarring impact.

The string of curses that emerged should have singed her ears, but instead it amused her. She smiled widely and leaned down to where he lay sprawled on the polished boards of the porch. "You all right?"

Still flat on his back, he ran one hand through his dark, wavy hair, eyes closed, and Misty had the distinct feeling he was counting to ten. When he turned his head to face her, she prepared herself for the impact of his gaze again.

It didn't help. The man had the most sinfully beautiful blue eyes she'd ever seen.

"Is there some reason why you're sneaking up on my porch?"

The chuckle came without warning. She was nervous, damn it, and she couldn't be. She didn't want Honey to know of her troubles, not when Honey had just found so much well-deserved happiness. Misty had already decided to act as if nothing had happened, to resolve her difficulties—*what an understatement*—on her own. Having the invitation to stay with Honey for a little while was a reprieve from heaven, and hopefully would give her a chance to get her bearings and make some very necessary plans.

"Now, I didn't sneak," she lied easily. "You were just snoring so loud you didn't hear me."

His blue gaze darkened to purest midnight. "I don't snore."

"No?"

"Any number of women can tell you so."

Uh-oh. She was on dangerous ground. This obviously wasn't the kind of man you could easily flirt with. He took things too seriously. And she sensed he wasn't exactly going to behave like a gentleman. Misty brushed her bangs out of her eyes and gave him a cocky grin. "I'll take your word for it. Must have been distant thunder I heard." She looked pointedly at the clear blue sky, and he scowled, quickly prompting her to add, "Did you break anything?"

Without her mind's permission, her gaze drifted over his big, hard, mostly bare body, and her pulse accelerated.

The man pushed himself into a sitting position off to the side of the chair. He let his arms dangle over his bent knees and narrowed his eyes in what she took to be a challenge. A very small, very sensual smile tilted his mouth. "You want to check me over to see?"

The idea of her hands coming into contact with all that exposed male skin made her fingertips itch. Distance became a priority, especially with the husky way he'd asked it. Misty came swiftly to her feet, but that just redirected his gaze to her legs, so close he could kiss her knee by merely leaning forward.

He looked as if he were considering it.

She quickly stepped back. Perspiration dampened her skin and caused her T-shirt to stick to her breasts. It had to be over ninety degrees, and the humidity was so thick you could choke on a deep breath.

Trying to lighten the suddenly charged mood, she asked, "How in the world can you sleep in this heat?"

He pushed himself to his feet and righted the chair. He was a good head taller than her, with sleek, tanned shoulders twice as wide as hers. She felt equal parts fascination and intimidation. She didn't like it. She would never let another man affect her in either way. When he looked down at her, his expression somewhat brooding, she gave her patented careless grin and winked. "Out all night carousing and now you're too exhausted to stay awake?"

He stepped forward, and she quickly stepped back— then had to keep stepping back until her body came into contact with the wood railing. He towered over her, not smiling, taking her in from head to toe. If Misty hadn't known for a fact that she had the right house, and if Honey hadn't assured her that all the men were beyond honorable, she'd have been just a tad more worried than she was. "Uh, is anyone else here?"

"No."

"No?" *Now* she was getting worried. "What about your brothers? And wasn't your mother supposed to be visiting, too?"

He frowned, but didn't back up a single pace. He was so close she could smell the spicy scent of his heated skin.

She held her breath.

"My mother had a slight emergency and she won't be able to make it after all. My brothers and my nephew are all in town together, enjoying a Saturday off."

They were alone! She could barely form a coherent sentence with him deliberately crowding her so. She had a suspicion that was why he did it. She swallowed and asked, "What about Honey?"

His gaze sharpened and his dark brows pulled down in a ferocious frown. "She's with them." He looked her over again, very slowly this time. To her, it seemed as if he was savoring the experience. Then he asked, "Just who the hell are you, lady?"

His expression was bland, but there was something in his tone, a mixture of heat and expectation. Misty bit her lip, then stuck out her hand, warding him off and offering a belated introduction. "Misty Malone." Her voice broke, and she had to clear her throat. "I'm Honey's sister."

His expression froze, then abruptly hardened as he stepped away without taking her hand. "Ah, hell." He glared an accusation, then added, "That wasn't at all what I wanted to hear."

Chapter 1

Just looking at her made him sweat.

And in the damned tux for his brother's reception, sweating was more than a little uncomfortable. Even the air-conditioning didn't help. He should look away, but he couldn't seem to drag his gaze from her. The sensuous way she moved, her deep black hair swaying to the music, looking almost liquid it was so silky, her husky laugh, all worked to make him crazy and put a stranglehold on his attention. Morgan loosened the tie around his throat and undid the top two buttons of his white shirt. But that didn't help the restriction of his pants, and he just knew if he started loosening them up, his new sister-in-law would have a fit. And he'd sooner kick his own ass than upset Honey.

"If you stare any harder, you're liable to set her on fire."

Morgan jerked, then turned to glare at Sawyer. "Aren't you supposed to be with your bride?"

"Jordan's dancing with her."

Great. Just great. After meeting Misty that first day on the front porch, Morgan had done his best to avoid her. Hell, he'd almost seduced his new sister-in-law's sister. And worse, she'd egged him on. What kind of woman did a thing like that?

He felt infuriated every time he thought about it. All his lauded control seemed to be paper-thin these days, especially with the way Jordan and Gabe adored the woman. They doted on Misty, every bit as fascinated as Morgan had been by her sensual looks and careless smile, only they seemed genuinely interested in her, and that really put a crimp in his mood.

Morgan didn't particularly like her. She was so brazen, so sassy and unrestrained, it was almost impossible not to be drawn to her on a sexual level. But where her sister was discreet and gentle, Misty was bold and outgoing. It was no wonder he hadn't figured out who she was on the spot; he'd expected the sister to be more like Honey, not the exact opposite.

With her come-on lines and lack of inhibitions, Misty could put any male on edge, and that wasn't at all the type of woman he was determined to be interested in these days. No, he wanted a woman like Honey, one he could settle down with, one that was as interested in becoming domestic as he was. Not that he wouldn't indulge in a little dalliance here and there before he found the wife, just not with Honey's sister. No way. That would be crossing the familial line.

Trying to sound disinterested rather than disgruntled, Morgan said, "I'm surprised Jordan could pull himself away from Misty. He and Gabe have been crowding her all night." Then he shook his head. "Hell, they've both been dogging her heels like lovesick puppies all week."

"And that bothers you, does it?"

Morgan snorted. "Hell, no. Except that she's a far cry from Honey and I don't want to see them get stuck in an awkward situation."

That made Sawyer laugh out loud. "Jordan and Gabe? I hate to break it to you, Morgan, but they're grown men and they've been handling their fair share of female companionship for some time now. Hell, Gabe started earlier than you did."

"He lied."

Sawyer laughed again. "Nope, I caught him at it, out in the barn that first time, so I know exactly how old he was."

Diverted for the moment, Morgan turned to Sawyer with a grin. "You're kidding?"

"Don't I wish. I think that's what started him on the path of debauchery."

Morgan chuckled at that. The youngest brother was a regular Lothario, to the delight of the female population of Buckhorn. "Details?"

Shrugging, Sawyer said, "The girl was four years older than him, and since then, it's like he's irresistible to women."

"Honey resisted him."

Sawyer's grin was very smug. "Yeah. I was glad to see it. Good for his ego."

"'Course, he wasn't really giving it his all, seeing as you'd already staked a claim." Before Sawyer could object to that, Morgan turned to Misty. "Does it amaze you how two sisters can be so damned different? I mean, Honey is just so kindhearted and innocent."

Sawyer had just taken a sip of his champagne, and he choked, but when Morgan gave him a suspicious look, he just raised his brows, as if encouraging Morgan to continue.

"Misty is…"

"What?" Sawyer seemed intent on digging in. "Sexy?"

"Hell, yeah, she's sexy. But then so is Honey."

Sawyer blinked at that, then frowned ferociously. "I'm not at all sure I like—"

"Oh, give it a rest, Sawyer. I'm not blind. And I just appreciate the fact she's so sexy—for you."

After downing the rest of his champagne in one gulp, Sawyer demanded, "Your point?"

Sawyer was being damn entertaining again, but Morgan couldn't take advantage of it because he couldn't pull his gaze away from Misty. Gabe had just swept her up into a new dance. She complained for just a moment about her feet, and Gabe, the rascal, merely went down on one knee and pulled her shoes off, tossing them aside. Misty seemed charmed, and they began a rather heated, intimate dance. The floor cleared to give them room, and Misty behaved totally uninhibited. Gabe was no better, showing off, making the women cheer, but that was his damned brother and he wasn't interested in looking at Gabe.

Misty was something altogether different.

Morgan had to grind his teeth together. "Will you just look at her?"

"I'd rather look at you looking at her. More amusing that way."

"It's like, Honey is so sweet and gentle, and Misty's

all spice and fire. What is it with her, anyway? Does she think she has to seduce every guy around her?"

"She's not seducing, she's dancing."

Morgan snorted. "The way she dances, it's the same damn thing."

Sawyer snickered. "For you, at least."

Just then, Jordan interrupted Gabe and stole Misty away. She laughed, as willing to partner him as Gabe, and Morgan nearly ground his teeth into powder. "It's not right, I'm telling you. She's playing with them both."

Deliberately adding oil to the fire, Sawyer said, "It seems to be a game they're enjoying." Then he clapped Morgan on the shoulder. "Relax, will you? She's just dancing, nothing more. Oops. Here comes Honey, so I better get this out quick. She's concerned because you're avoiding Misty. I was supposed to tell you to go dance with her."

"Ha." Morgan was positively appalled by that idea, but not for the reasons his brother would likely assume. "I'm not getting near her." He was afraid if he did, he'd explode. He couldn't recall ever wanting a woman quite the way he wanted this one.

She was staying with them at the house, so he saw her at breakfast, looking all sleepy but still full of smiles for his brothers. He saw her at bedtime, wishing everyone— but him—a good night's sleep. He even saw her in the afternoon, though he did his best to avoid it. She would be painting her toenails right out on the back patio, or puttering around the kitchen, giving the illusion of being domestic when he'd be willing to bet she didn't have a domestic bone in her entire lush little body.

It didn't matter what she did, he liked it—a little too much. And she knew it, which was why she avoided him as much as he did her. They were far too sexually aware of each other for comfort.

But it was all physical, and a fast, easy, physical relationship with his sister-in-law's sister would never do. Sawyer, damn him, had made the woman a relative with his marriage, and that put her off-limits for every single thing Morgan would like to do with her. And the things he'd like to do…

He almost groaned out loud. The vivid images of him and Misty together, naked, overheated, carnal, would amuse his brothers and shock the hell out of Honey. She was overprotective of Misty—why, he couldn't fathom. He had a feeling his sexual thoughts wouldn't shock Misty at all. He had the taunting suspicion she'd be with him every step of the way.

"Damn." Morgan felt the start of an erection and had to fight to control himself. Not easy to do when Misty was laughing and looking flushed from all that dancing. Jordan whirled her in a wide circle, and Morgan wanted to flatten him.

"Damn is right. You're in for it now."

Morgan turned to see what Sawyer was blathering on about and was met with Honey instead. She looked incredibly beautiful in her white wedding gown, her long blond hair loose and her face glowing. Morgan smiled at her. "Have I kissed the bride yet?"

"About a dozen times, I think." She grinned at him, and twin dimples decorated her cheeks.

"Morgan…" Sawyer's beleaguered tone didn't bother Morgan one whit. Annoying each other was the brothers' favorite pastime. And Sawyer, love-struck from day one though he fought it pretty damn hard, had made himself a prime target.

Honey laughed and patted her husband's chest. "Oh, Sawyer, relax. Your brother is just a big pushover."

Sawyer choked again.

Morgan, amused by her insistent misconceptions of him, grinned. Not another soul in Buckhorn, male or female, thought of him as a pushover—pretty much the opposite, in fact.

His grin fell flat with her next words.

"I want you to dance with Misty."

"Ah…"

"Morgan, it almost seems like you've been avoiding her. She told me just this morning at breakfast that you didn't like her."

They'd talked about him? Morgan wanted to ask exactly what had been said, but he didn't want to look too interested. "I don't dislike her."

"Of course you don't! But she thinks you do because you've spent so much time at work since she's been here, and you've barely said two words to her."

Morgan tugged on his ear, beginning to feel uncomfortable. He wanted to sock Sawyer, who stood behind his bride, smirking. "It's been really busy this week and being that I'm sheriff I can't just…"

"But you're not busy now. And look, she just finished a dance. It's the perfect time for the two of you to talk some more and get better acquainted."

Sawyer, ready to get back a little of his own, said, "Yeah, the timing is *perfect.* And with your, er, charm, you should be able to put her right at ease." Then he grinned, glancing at his wife. "You'd do that for Honey, wouldn't you, Morgan?"

Honey, playing along, gave him her most endearing smile.

He tried, but not a single rebuttal came to mind. "Well, hell." Morgan stomped away, resigned to his fate and unfortunately, in some ways, pleased to be forced into it. He saw Misty look up from across the room, as if she'd somehow sensed his approach. She did that a lot, seeming to know the second he entered a room. And then she'd get quiet and withdrawn—but only with him.

Her dark blue eyes, so bright and clear they still had the effect of making his heart skip a beat, widened. He saw her soft lips part, saw her cheeks darken with color. She turned, looking, he knew, for an avenue of escape. But she'd already been surrounded by every eligible bachelor in Buckhorn, and they were in no hurry to let her leave.

Morgan stopped right behind her. She didn't turn to face him, but she knew he was there; her shoulders stiffened the tiniest bit and her normally husky voice became a little bit shrill as she asked the men who would dance with her next.

Morgan looked at every man there, and he fashioned a grin. A very hard, unmistakable expression. Several of the men, eyeing him closely, began to back up, quickly making their excuses.

Morgan took advantage of their retreat. "I believe that'd be me, Malone."

She hated it when he called her by her last name. He'd found that out the first day they met. He'd been calling her by Malone ever since, because it helped to maintain the small distance necessary for his sanity.

"I don't think so, *Hudson*." She reached for Gabe's hand. He was one of the few men who wasn't intimidated by Morgan's darkest stare. In fact, Gabe looked highly entertained. He was a gentleman and would have assisted her, if Morgan hadn't beat him to it, reaching around her and snatching her slim fingers in his own before she could get a solid hold on Gabe. The reach brought his chest up flush against her slender back. He could smell her, warm woman and sweet sexiness. Her scent was like an irresistible tonic to him, and like any basic male animal, he reacted strongly to it. Her hair, so silky and luxurious, brushed his chin, and it was like having fire lick down his spine. He caught his breath.

They both froze.

Gabe chuckled. "You two going to stand there doing the statue imitation all night, or do you intend to dance? I have to tell you, Honey is frowning something fierce over the show you're giving the guests, and I think she's about to start this way."

Morgan drew in a deep breath, searching for control. "Get lost, Gabe."

"No way. I don't get to see you this rattled too often."

"I'm not rattled." He stepped back a safe distance but retained his hold on Misty. Trying to sound reasonable, rather than rattled, he said, "Your sister wants us to dance."

Misty's pink tongue darted out to lick nervously at her lips, and Morgan wanted to groan. He glanced at Gabe and saw that his brother was every bit as alert and fascinated as he was. *Damn.* He started backing out to the middle of the dance floor, tugging Misty along with him. Everyone could see she was a reluctant participant, and after the way she'd accepted every other partner, Morgan was peeved. "Come on, Malone. I won't bite you."

"Can I have that in writing?" Gently, she tried to disengage her hand. Morgan stared at her, refusing to let go and refusing to respond to her sarcasm.

She sighed. "Look, Morgan, this isn't a good idea."

Perversely, he asked, "Why not?"

"You don't like me! That was easy enough to figure out from the moment we met."

She was so…lovely, he couldn't help but study her face, the narrow nose, the high cheekbones, her small rounded chin. If he looked any lower, he'd never survive the dance, so he brought his gaze to hers. "I liked you well enough…at first."

"All right. Then from the moment I introduced myself. I have no idea what you've got against me, and to tell you the truth, I really don't care."

"You don't, huh?" It was amazing how she went straight to the heart of the matter. Most women wouldn't have been so bold.

He wondered if she'd be that bold in bed.

"No, I don't," she said. "Truth is, I'm not at all crazy about you, either."

The grin took him by surprise. Strangely, Morgan realized he was enjoying himself. Beyond being turned on, he felt challenged, and that didn't often happen with women anymore. "Why not?"

Before she could reply, the music changed, turned sultry. Misty gave such a heartfelt groan of despair, he chuckled. "Oh, no. I'm outta here." Again she tried to pull loose, but Morgan swept her closer and wrapped one arm around her waist.

Near her ear, he whispered, "Quit fighting me, Malone. It's only one dance." One dance that felt closer to foreplay. Just holding her was making him nuts, and this close, he could see a few damp, glossy black curls clinging to her forehead and temple. Her upper chest, visible over the scooped neckline of her maid-of-honor

gown, was dewy with perspiration. She was warmed up
and flushed all over. The vigorous dancing, he thought,
leaning subtly forward to breathe in her heated scent.
The thought of any other man in the room, especially his
damn younger brothers, being this close to her, being affected the same way, made him want to growl.

Misty frowned at him. "What's the matter with you,
anyway? You look like a thundercloud."

She pulled back, putting a few more inches between
their bodies, but Morgan could see the added color in her
cheeks and knew she was feeling the effects of the close-
ness, same as he was.

When he didn't answer, just continued to stare at her,
she sighed. "Don't pretend my honesty bothered you,
Morgan. I won't believe it."

Going for the direct attack, he surmised, and smiled.
"You haven't offended me." Then he made his own direct attack. "You wanna know what I don't like about
you, Malone?"

"No."

Her naturally husky voice dropped another octave in
her irritation. Where his hand rested on her back, he
could feel the satin of the dress, warmed by her body,
and the supple movement of her muscles. She was slim,
but still stacked like a Barbie doll, with lush breasts and
a narrow waist. Her legs seemed to go on forever, long
and sleek and sexy. Her bottom, though small, was perfectly rounded and just bouncy enough to make him catch
his breath whenever she walked away. He'd spent far too
many hours obsessing over her bottom.

And those breasts. He could spend at least an hour enjoying her just from the waist up. Unable to stop himself,
Morgan looked down at the pale, firm flesh and imagined

the formal dress around her waist, her breasts naked for him to see, to touch and taste, to enjoy. He groaned. It was almost too easy to imagine his mouth on her, considering how much cleavage was showing, more so than any of the other women in the wedding party, though they were all wearing similar gowns in different colors. With the shape of the neckline there was no way she could be wearing a bra, or at least, not much of one.

Almost burning up, he growled, "You're Honey's sister."

She blinked, wary surprise evident in her expression. "So?"

"That puts you off-limits. And I don't like it."

Her eyes widened. "Good grief! You make it sound like if you decided to...to—"

"Yeah, all that you're imagining and more."

Her breath caught, and she choked on her anger. "Like I'd be agreeable! Well, let me put your mind at ease here, Morgan. The answer would be no!"

Annoyed all over again, he said, "I'm not buying it, Malone. You flirt all the damn time. Not just when you talk, but when you move, when you eat." He looked at her breasts again, which were trembling with her ire. "Hell, even when you breathe."

His words made her sputter before she managed to spit out, "That's absurd!"

"Do you realize every guy here has been ogling your breasts?"

Her mouth dropped open, then abruptly snapped closed. "You're disgusting."

"I'm not the one showing so much skin."

Through her teeth, she ground out, "Every woman in

the bridal party is showing the same amount of skin, you idiot. Why don't you go lecture one of them?"

Easily, knowing it was true, he said, "None of them looks like you." Then he pulled her closer despite her slight resistance. "And I don't want any of them."

She looked flabbergasted. "Why, you…you arrogant bas—"

"Shh. Keep your voice down. I don't want your sister's reception ruined by a scene." She glared at him and her eyes looked hot enough to roast him, her cheeks rosy with color. He wanted to kiss her, but had at least enough sense to hold back from that.

Actually, Morgan wouldn't have been at all surprised if she'd socked him one, right there in the middle of the hall. And he was honest enough to admit he'd deserve it. He wasn't sure why he goaded her, but he couldn't seem to stop himself.

She huffed, then jerked against his arms. Very low, with clear warning, she said, "If you don't want me to cause a scene, then kindly get your paws off me and leave me alone."

With relish, he said, "Can't. Honey is determined to see us get acquainted."

She rolled her eyes. "Oh, for heaven's sake… I'll talk to her."

"Why bother?" He stared into her incredible eyes and felt a twisting in his guts as he muttered, "You won't be here much longer, and then it won't matter."

She quickly looked down and bit her lip.

Above the lust, suspicion blossomed. Morgan whispered, "Misty?"

Her gaze jerked to his face, and he realized he'd called her by her first name. Misty suited her, all dark and mysterious, except for those direct, intense blue eyes. "You *are* leaving soon, right?"

She swallowed, looking away once again. "I hadn't really thought about it."

Frowning, Morgan half danced, half steered them toward the patio doors. Misty didn't seem to realize his intent, she merely clutched at him to keep from losing her footing as he danced her first one way, then another, moving easily around the other couples.

When he opened the patio door and stepped outside, Misty started to hold back. Then he saw her square her shoulders and follow him. Evidently she'd decided they needed a showdown.

He thought she was exactly right.

He closed the door behind her, then said, "Come on."

The night was warm, heavy with humidity. Moonlight fell over her like a pale blush and formed a halo around her midnight hair. She tilted her head, ignoring his outstretched hand. "Where are we going?"

"Someplace more private. I know my brothers, and one or all of them will be out here in under two minutes to see what I'm doing."

"You won't be *doing* anything," she said.

He answered her with a shrug, then merely waited.

After a long moment, she sniffed, but took his hand and stepped cautiously forward. He realized then she was still barefoot. Irritation filled her tone when she said, "Obviously your brothers don't trust you any more than I do."

Morgan smiled in the darkness and stepped off the patio to head toward one of the gazebos decorating the back lawn of the town hall. "Oh, they trust me, all right.

They're just nosy as hell and can't ever pass up an opportunity to needle me."

Misty paused outside the ornate gazebo, staring at it
and breathing deeply of the scent of flowers, planted in
profusion around the white wood and trellis structure.
The entire county of Buckhorn was big on flowers. "I
love gazebos. I think they're so quaint."

Morgan opened the door and cautiously entered the
dim interior. "Yeah, I guess Gabe feels the same because
he built one—bigger and sturdier than this—down by
the lake at home."

"I saw it. Gabe really built that?"

"Yeah. He's a handyman of sorts, among other things."
The door banged shut behind them, sealing them inside
where the air suddenly crackled with awareness. Morgan refused to believe he was the only one who felt it.

Just enough moonlight filtered in to show the way to
the white bench seats lining the inside. He stared hard,
seeing the dull glimmer of Misty's eyes, the sheen of her
white teeth. "Would you like to sit down?"

"What I'd like is to find out what you want so I can
get back to my sister's celebration."

What he wanted? Now that was a loaded question.
From the second she'd taken his hand, he'd had a throbbing erection. Morgan seated himself, stretching out his
long legs on either side of her, caging her in. His eyes
quickly adjusted to the darkness, and her pale skin and
the light color of her dress made her visible. She didn't
so much as move a muscle. He crossed his arms and considered her. "You're different from Honey."

"Night and day," she admitted without hesitation, then
explained, "we're also very close. So what's your point?"

"I wouldn't want to see her hurt."

Misty stiffened again, but the rigid posture just caused her breasts to be more noticeable. "Anyone who hurt her would have to answer to me."

"Yet you think nothing of coming in here and flirting with my brothers, coming on to them—"

She suddenly inclined closer, and her voice was a near hiss. "I haven't *come on* to anyone! I danced, but then so did everyone else at the reception. It's what's expected at a—"

Morgan leaned forward and caught her shoulders in his hands, keeping her bent close. Her skin was silky and warm, and he flexed his fingers almost involuntarily. "You also parade around the house all day without a bra, and barefoot."

Her eyes narrowed, and he could feel her tremble. "It's ninety degrees outside, Morgan! Most every woman I've seen since I arrived has been wearing a sundress or tank top without a bra." She poked him in the chest, hard. "Maybe *you* should try wearing one to see how horribly uncomfortable they can be in this weather before you start judging me."

Morgan thought that was the most ludicrous thing he'd ever heard. He opened his mouth, but she quickly cut him off.

"And as for my bare feet, what of it? Don't tell me you have a foot fetish?"

He hadn't, not until he'd met her. He'd never even noticed a woman's feet before. But Misty had small, narrow feet, and she painted her toenails a bright cherry red. They looked sexy as hell, and every time he saw her pretty little feet, he imagined them digging into the small of his back while he rode her hard, making her scream with intense pleasure.

He also knew in his gut he wasn't the only male noticing. "You're entirely too comfortable around my brothers."

"Ha! I don't think it's your brothers you're worried
about at all."

Because that was so close to the truth, even if he didn't
want to admit it, Morgan slowly stood. Misty tried to
back up, but he had hold of her shoulders and she didn't
get far away from him. "You don't think so?"

She hesitated, going cautious on him now that he was
so close and towering over her. But then she lifted her
chin with her usual bravado. "No. I think it's…you."

He nodded, and his pulse thrummed in his veins.
"You're right. It is me. But it's also you."

"No, I—"

He stepped so close her back came up against the
smooth painted wall.

All the anger, all the frustration, abruptly shifted to
pure sexual tension. Morgan couldn't resist one second
longer. With his fingertips, he touched her cheek, then
her lips, gently, barely brushing, savoring her softness
and the way she trembled in response. Touching her felt
so right and made him feel downright explosive. She went
utterly still, not moving, not even breathing.

In a raw whisper, he said, "There is absolutely—" he
leaned closer "—no possible way—" her eyes drifted
shut and she panted for breath "—I'm feeling all this on
my own."

"This?" The word was a mere whisper, sighed against
his mouth.

"Lord, you make me hard, Misty." And then he kissed
her.

She held herself stiff for all of about two seconds before her mouth opened and her hands fisted on the lapels of his formal jacket. She moaned, a low, hungry, needy sound.

Morgan, who'd been successfully avoiding her for an entire week, was a goner.

Chapter 2

Insanity, Misty thought, feeling the hot delicious stroke of Morgan's tongue, the slide of his large rough hands down her spine. He had her pulled so close, their bodies were practically fused together. She hadn't expected this, hadn't known *this* even existed. Lord, the man knew how to kiss, knew how to move his hands and his legs and his…hips. Everything he did, every place he touched her, made her too hot, too hungry. Made her want more. And so far he hadn't even let his hands wander that far.

But no sooner did that thought filter into her fogged brain than one of those large hands came up over her rib cage to close on her breast.

Her nipples immediately drew tight, and she pulled her mouth away to gasp at the incredible sensations his touch caused.

He groaned harshly, and a rough tremble traveled through his big body.

Stunned, somewhat disoriented by the unbelievable intensity, Misty whispered, "No…"

At that single word, not even said with much conviction, he froze. His hand opened slowly, as if it took great effort to get his fingers to obey. With his face pressed to the place where her shoulder and neck met, he struggled for air, and every muscle—pressed so closely to her—stiffened.

Then he stepped away.

The air positively throbbed between them, but still, he'd stopped the second she'd asked him to. The significance of that didn't escape her; he was a remarkable man, very much in control of himself. Misty did her best to catch her breath, to stop staring at him in the darkness. She should leave, right now, but she couldn't seem to get her feet to move. Every nerve ending in her body was still alive in a way she hadn't known was possible.

"I won't apologize."

He sounded breathless, frustrated, on the verge of anger, and she swallowed hard, trying to calm her galloping heart. "I… I didn't ask you to."

Still without moving, he added, "This is going to be a problem."

Again, she asked, "This?"

Several beats of silence passed, then suddenly he moved away from her and he actually laughed. "Come off it, Malone. You felt it as much as I did." He turned back, looking for verification.

It she assumed was the incredible sexual pull. "If you mean…"

Through his teeth, he said, "I mean I touched you and you got so hot I feel singed. I kissed you and you sucked on my tongue and rubbed up against me and it was like throwing a match on gasoline. There's enough goddamned heat in this room to start a bonfire."

Misty sucked in her breath, shocked at the words, at the harsh vehemence of his tone, but unable to deny them. Part of her new determination in dealing with men was to be brutally honest—with herself and them. Sugarcoating things, *faking* things, had caused at least half of her present problems. Being too timid, too naive, had caused the other half. In order to get on with her life, she had to start facing things head-on.

A rough warning growl rumbled from deep in his throat. "Malone—"

"You're right," she hurried to assure him, unwilling to let him shock her with more of his brutal honesty. "And I'm sorry. You took me by surprise."

"Bull." He propped his hands on his hips and glared at her. "I've known from the day I met you how it'd be. Why the hell do you think I avoid you?"

Oh. That certainly explained a few things, she supposed. "I see. Well, I must not be as clever as you, because I thought you were a totally obnoxious, thoroughly unlikable jerk and I was thankful that you ignored me. I had no idea this—" she waved a hand, trying to come up with a word suitable to the loss of control and depth of sensation he'd sparked "—*chemistry* was between us. I wasn't even aware something like *this* existed."

He cursed again, but she didn't let him interrupt her. "Now that I do know, trust me, I won't let it happen ever again."

Morgan seemed to measure her words. And then she saw his eyes narrow, his expression darken. He looked at her breasts, and she knew her nipples were still painfully hard. Without a word, he reached out a hand and gently brushed the backs of his knuckles across one sensitive tip, gliding easily over the satiny material of the dress. Misty drew in a sharp breath and felt a small explosion of erotic stimulation throughout her body.

Morgan whispered, "Oh, it'll happen again, sweetheart, if you hang around. That's why you need to finish your little visit and hightail it out of town just as fast as you possibly can. My control only goes so far, and it seems you have no control at all."

The words were like a cold slap, reminding her of all her troubles, of how gullible she'd been, how utterly stupid.

She jerked away and bit her lip hard to keep herself from tearing up. No way would she let the big jerk see her cry. Much as she had hoped to regroup in Buckhorn, she could see that was now impossible. What she would do, she hadn't a clue. But he was right, leaving was imperative. She had absolutely no desire to get involved with a man again, for any reason. Especially not a domineering, bullheaded behemoth like Morgan Hudson, a man who didn't even like her, and in fact, seemed to disdain her.

Keeping her back to him, she drew a long, steadying breath. Then she reached for the door. "I'll leave first thing tomorrow morning." Despite her resolve, her voice quavered tenuously.

There was a slight pause. "Misty…"

He sounded uncertain, but she had no intention of discussing things with him. There was no one she could trust except Honey, and she wouldn't ruin her sister's current happiness for anything. After she got her life straightened out and made some plans that would hopefully carry her through the coming months, she could begin making confessions to her sibling.

The open door offered no relief from the heat; there wasn't a single breeze stirring. Misty stepped onto the dew-wet grass, then felt Morgan's hand settle on her shoulder. "Wait a minute."

She flinched at his tone but didn't bother trying to move away from him. Just that simple touch, his hand on her shoulder, made her acutely aware of him as a man. She almost hated herself. "What now?"

She turned to face him, trying to look irritated when she was actually breathless. The moonlight was brighter. She could see his every feature—the strong, lean jawline, the harshly cut cheekbones. He was by far the most impressive male she'd ever seen, but then, his brothers were nothing to sneeze at. There must have been a mighty impressive gene pool somewhere to create all that masculine perfection.

He stared at her, not answering at first. He shook his head, distracted, and just when he started to speak, another voice intruded.

"There you are."

Morgan looked up. "Casey. What in hell are you doing out here?"

Misty turned to see Sawyer's son. At sixteen, Casey already showed signs of his own masculine superiority. He was tall, nearly six feet, and had the bone structure that promised wide shoulders and long, strong limbs.

"Dad wanted someone to find you and haul you back inside."

Morgan shook his head. "And of course, you just naturally volunteered for the job."

Casey chuckled. "Actually, Uncle Jordan and Uncle Gabe beat me to it, and they did seem pretty anxious to come out here and fetch you in, but Dad told me to go instead, on account of he said you wouldn't slug me."

Morgan threw an arm around his nephew, held him in a brief headlock and then started them all toward the door. "Don't be too sure of that, boy. My affection for you is kinda thin at the moment."

With a laugh, Casey said, "I'm not worried. I can still outrun you."

"You think so, do you?"

"Yeah, 'cause I'm fast—and you're getting old." Casey ducked quickly under Morgan's arm and came to Misty's side. Walking backward, his grin wide, he said, "Dad also told me if you didn't want Honey to get after you, I should walk Misty in and you should come in after."

"He said all that, did he?"

"He said you wouldn't want to shatter Honey's skewed illusions, being as she doesn't know the real you, yet."

Casey was having a fine time of it, pestering his uncle. Misty smiled to herself, amused at their close camaraderie and a little wistful. Her own family consisted of Honey and her father, since her mother died when they were young. Her father had been overbearing and over-controlling, cold, without the foundation of love that would have made those personality traits more bearable. If it hadn't been for Honey, she didn't think her childhood would have been at all tolerable.

Casey seemed to have a fantastic family foundation. It was easy to see why Honey had fallen in love with the whole clan.

Morgan stopped just out of reach of the patio, still in the shadows where the lights didn't reach. "You go on in, Casey, and tell your dad I expect him to control his wife. We'll be there in just a moment."

"Dad said you'd say that, and then I was supposed to tell you he's sending Uncle Gabe and Uncle Jordan out in two minutes."

Morgan made a playful grab for Casey, but he jumped back, laughing. Holding up his hands, he said, "Hey, it was Dad, not me!"

Morgan reached for him again and Casey hurried to the door. After he opened it, he yelled back, "Two minutes, Uncle Morgan!"

"Damn scamp."

Misty was still smiling, though she felt great sadness inside. "You're all very close."

"We helped to raise him. Sawyer got full custody when Casey was just a little pup, and between raising him and finishing med school, he would have been frazzled for sure if we hadn't all pitched in. Not that it was a chore. Hell, Casey's always been a great kid, even if his sense of humor is sometimes warped."

Misty stared at him, dumbfounded. "*You* helped raise him?"

"Yeah, sure. Along with my mother and the others. What'd you think, that I was too reprehensible to be around a youngster?"

Actually that was exactly what she thought, but she kept the words to herself. "I was just…surprised. The idea of four men raising a baby…"

"Yeah, well, like I said, my mother taught us what we needed to know. But she felt real strong about Sawyer being involved as the dad, and that meant the rest of us just kinda chipped in. I was…let's see. Nineteen at the time. I'll admit, the diaper thing threw me for a while there, and having formula spit up on me wasn't exactly a treat." Then he grinned. "But the whole uncle bit really turned the girls on. Hell, every time I took Casey into town with me, they'd come on like a mob."

Misty rolled her eyes. "What a lovely image."

Morgan laughed, but then his laughter died. "Look, about what happened…"

"You already made yourself pretty clear, Morgan. I don't think we need to beat it into the ground. I said I'd leave in the morning, and I will."

He ignored that and sighed. "Malone, I care a lot about your sister. I wouldn't want her upset."

She could only stare at him. "You're worried I'll say something to Honey? What? Am I supposed to go tattle on you, is that it?"

Even in the dim light she could see the way he locked his jaw. "She wanted us to be friends."

"Good God!" she exclaimed, and when he frowned she added, "All right, forget the disbelief. For your information, I happen to love my sister."

"Glad to hear it."

"I wouldn't do *anything* to hurt her, and that includes disillusioning her about her new family." She poked him in the chest, her frustration level going right out the window. Her entire life was presently in the toilet, and Morgan Hudson was worried about her discretion? Ha!

"As far as I'm concerned, Honey can think we got along like best pals. But until I can get out of here tomorrow morning, stay the hell away from me."

She turned and stalked in, but at the door, she couldn't resist looking back one last time at Morgan.

He stood there in the moonlight, head tilted toward the dark sky, eyes closed, jaw clenched. His big hands were knotted into fists on his hips. Misty felt herself shiver, even though the evening was oppressively hot.

She knew then that he was right. Tomorrow morning she would leave Buckhorn behind. Hopefully, she'd think of somewhere to stay in the meantime.

She'd spent all her savings fighting the criminal conviction, and lost. She was homeless, out of a job and with no prospects.

And that was the least of her problems.

If Morgan hadn't been lying there awake, his body frustrated, his mind disturbed by sensual images, he might not have heard it. But he hadn't slept a wink all night, too busy remembering the sweet taste of Misty, the way she'd felt pressed against him. Perfect. Willing. *Hot.* Though his head told him things had ended when they should, his imagination had insisted on conjuring up a different ending to the tale, and he'd been rock-hard and hurting for more hours now than he cared to admit. It was like suffering the curse of wretched puberty all over again, and he had Misty Malone to thank for it.

The squeak came again, and Morgan recognized the sound as the porch swing that hung in the huge oak at the back of the house. Throwing off the sheet that covered him, he stalked naked to the open window and listened. His room was at one end of the house, opposite to Sawyer's and Casey's, with the entire living quarters in between so they all had privacy.

Morgan's bedroom faced the lake, as did Sawyer's. As did the porch swing.

Someone was out there and his gut instinct told him it was Misty. He felt it in his bones, by the way his heart beat faster, by the way his stomach knotted. Only Misty had ever had that intense effect on him, and he figured it was mostly because he had to deny himself. If she wasn't related by marriage, if he could have spent a long, hot weekend with her, indulging all his cravings, he'd be able to get her out of his system.

But he couldn't, and that was the only reason for his obsession. He was sure of it.

Morgan saw that the moon hadn't completely set, even while dawn was struggling to break. He glanced at the clock, surprised to see it was barely five-thirty. What was she doing up so early, hanging around outside? Looking for more ways to torment him?

It took him a mere two seconds to decide to go see her. He knew all the reasons he shouldn't, but something overrode them all, some basic need to spar with her one more time before the rest of the family would be there to pull him back.

He was still buttoning his favorite pair of worn, comfortable jeans, and wearing nothing else, when he stepped out of his room. At the last minute, he stopped, went back into his bedroom and then into his bathroom. He brushed his teeth, giving a disgusted glance at his morning beard and disheveled hair, then decided to hell with it and headed out. But when he passed the kitchen, he halted again and concluded a cup of coffee was definitely in order, if for no other reason than to help him get his bearings before facing her again. She threw him off balance with just a glance, and set his teeth on edge with blinding lust.

As he hurriedly measured the coffee, being careful to be quiet so he wouldn't wake anyone else, he thought about Misty and how she would look so early in the day, her dark hair still tousled, her eyes soft and warm. He imagined her still in her nightgown, something thin and slinky, and he almost dropped the carafe of water. The anticipation he felt was ridiculous, but real.

For at least a few hours this morning, he'd have her all to himself.

Jordan had an apartment above the garage and would be oblivious to anything and everything until at least ten o'clock. He liked to sleep late on the weekends, his only chance to catch up from his busy week.

Gabe might not even be back yet. He'd been surrounded by the single women of Buckhorn when last Morgan had seen him. But if he was home, his rooms in the basement would insulate him from the normal busy-house noises.

As for Sawyer, he was no doubt occupied with his bride. Morgan wouldn't be at all surprised if he didn't leave the bedroom all day. He grinned at that thought, remembering how Casey had told his father to feel free to linger, that he'd take care of all the chores for him.

Morgan was still grinning and feeling a little too anxious when he silently stepped outside with two steaming mugs of coffee. His bare feet didn't make a sound on the wet morning grass as he walked to the swing. It was a bit chilly, a heavy fog hanging over everything, which turned his first sight of Misty, her back to him, curled up on the swing, into a whimsical, almost ethereal picture. He was only two steps away from her when he heard her give a delicate sniff.

Everything masculine in him froze, and he experienced that incomparable dread men suffered when women turned to tears. He didn't know what to do. He strained to hear, hoping he'd misunderstood the sound, hoping she had a cold.

She sniffed again, then dabbed at her eyes with a wadded tissue. *Oh, hell.* Morgan felt a hard, curling ache around his heart and closed his eyes for a moment. The fact that her tears bothered him so much was a sure sign that things were out of control. Just physical attraction, he insisted to himself, despite his burgeoning sympathy and concern. Shoring up his nerve, he announced himself by clearing his throat.

Turning around so quickly she nearly upset the swing, Misty stared at him. She had glasses on, which he'd never seen before, and her hair was tied back with a plain elastic rubber band, long tendrils carelessly escaping. Even in the gray predawn light, he could see that she blushed.

Truth was, she looked like hell, and he hadn't thought such a thing was possible. Her nose was red and her eyes were hidden behind the reflection of the glasses. His simmering lust died a rapid death, not because of how she looked, but because he knew she was upset, and he was horribly afraid that *he* was the reason.

Not knowing what else to do, he held out one cup of coffee, for the moment ignoring her distress. "I heard the swing and figured you could use this."

She glanced at the cup as if it might hold arsenic. Morgan sighed. "It's coffee. Lots of sugar and cream. I figured since Honey drank hers that way, you likely did, too."

She took the cup, sipped, then quietly thanked him. Without another word, she turned her head to stare toward the lake, which could barely be seen through the fog. She had simply and plainly dismissed him. Her wishes couldn't have been any more clear than if she'd come right out and said, *Go away.*

Nettled, Morgan pretended not to notice.

He moved to sit beside her, never mind that there

wasn't really enough room. She quickly scrambled to get her legs out of the way, and it was then he noticed she was wearing a soft old cotton housecoat. No belt, just fat buttons all the way down the front. It looked loose and comfortable, like something that his sixty-year-old mother would wear when she wasn't feeling well. All the buttons were done up except the top one, and Misty clutched that small span of material together with a fist.

Morgan pushed a bare foot against the ground, making the swing sway gently, mindful of the coffee they each held. He kept his gaze on her profile. "You wear glasses."

She didn't answer him.

"I guess that answers the mystery of your big blue eyes, doesn't it? I always figured the color was a little too clear, a little too good to be real. Colored contacts?"

Her shoulders stiffened and she turned to him. Over the rim of the glasses, she glared and gave him a view of those perfect, clear, startling blue eyes, unadorned.

Morgan stared into her eyes, then whispered, "I guess I was wrong."

She turned away again, but muttered, "It's not the first time."

Ignoring that, he touched the rubber band sloppily knotted in her hair. "Rough night?"

One hand clutched the coffee mug, the other a damp tissue and the top of her housecoat. She hesitated, then slanted him another look over her wire-framed glasses. "If that's what you want to think, why not? I mean, you left before me, so it's entirely possible that once you were gone, I staged an orgy in that nice little gazebo you showed me."

Morgan sipped his coffee while keeping his gaze on her. His free arm rested over the back of the swing, his fingers almost touching her. *Almost*. "I somehow doubt your sister would have tolerated that."

She started to jerk to her feet, but Morgan caught her elbow. "No, don't let me run you off. I didn't come out here to harass you."

"No, you came to see if I was ready to leave. Well, don't worry. As soon as it's light, I'll get dressed and go. I packed last night so I could get an early start. I just wanted to watch the sunrise first."

Her words made him feel almost as bad as that time Jordan needed help treating an ornery mule and it kicked him in the gut, breaking two of his ribs. Morgan rubbed a hand over his chest, which didn't do a thing to help this particular ache, then muttered, "It's for the best and you know it."

"I'm not arguing with you, Morgan."

"Good, because I didn't come out here to argue."

"No? Then why?"

Hell, why *had* he come out? Whatever warped reasoning he'd used to justify his actions, he couldn't remember it now. Because he didn't have an answer, he tried changing the subject. "You look like you're…upset."

She shook her head in denial. "No, not at all."

But there was that tissue clutched in her hand, and her red nose and watery eyes. His conscience bothered him, and that had to be a first. In the normal course of things, he didn't bother with a guilty conscience. He was always rock certain of his decisions. "I don't have anything personally against you, Malone."

She snorted.

Morgan clenched his jaw, but he was determined to have his say. "It'll be best for all concerned if you leave soon."

She sighed, then turned to stare at him. "Yeah, well, you seem to be the only one who thinks so. Gabe spent half the night trying to talk me into hanging around, and Jordan even offered me a job."

In angry disbelief, he said, "You told them I asked you to leave?"

His anger didn't faze her. "No. But they knew I'd go sooner or later." Then she mumbled, "Though sooner seems to be on your personal agenda."

Morgan struggled to control his temper. "What did you tell Jordan?"

"That I'd think about it."

His muscles bunched in infuriated reflex. He wanted her gone. He did *not* want her hanging around his brother. "Like hell."

She shrugged nonchalantly, egging him on. She had a habit of doing that, deliberately pricking his temper—and his lust. Hell, half the time he was around her he didn't know for sure what he felt, just that he felt it too keenly and he didn't like it one damn bit.

Jealousy of his brothers was a unique thing, but he absolutely couldn't bear the thought of Misty being with one of them. Besides, he knew if she hung around, they'd eventually be involved, he had no doubt about that at all. Acting on gut instinct, he said, "Forget the job with Jordan. I'll pay you to go."

Her mouth fell open and she stared at him.

"How much do you want?" he asked, forcing the words out through his teeth.

"You're not serious."

"Why not?" He felt goaded and angry and out of control. He absolutely hated it. "You'd use Jordan, taking his infatuation with you to finagle a job. Well, why not use me instead? Hell, at least I know what I'm getting into. So name a price."

Her lips pinched shut, her eyes narrowed and an angry blush rose from her neck up. Then, as he watched, she gathered herself, and anger was replaced by deliberate belligerence. "Hmm, well now, I know what it was Jordan wanted in exchange for the job. But…exactly what would you expect in return for cash, Morgan? Or do I even need to ask?"

Her innuendo goaded his temper, but more than that, it stirred his desire for her, sending him right over the edge. He broke out in a sweat, his gut clenched, his body hardened. He reached for her, not even sure himself what he would do once he had hold of her. But she surprised him by her reaction. She leaped to her feet with a gasp. The coffee mug fell from her hand to the soft ground with a dull thud, spilling the coffee and rolling a few feet away. Misty covered her mouth with both hands. Her face was pale, and she swayed.

Morgan stood also and caught her to him, ignoring her feeble struggles. "Damn it, are you all right?" He shook her slightly, his alarm growing. "What the hell is wrong with you? Answer me, Malone."

Staring at him in horror, she opened her eyes wide and then pushed away, ran several feet to a line of bushes and dropped to her knees.

Morgan was dumbfounded. He started after her, but halted when he heard the unmistakable sound of retching. Never had he felt like such a complete and utter ass. He'd been harassing her again, when that hadn't been his intent at all. He'd argued with her after telling her he wouldn't. And she was sick. He made a false start toward her, then pulled back, as uncertain of what to do as he'd been on his very first date.

He'd hated the feeling then; at thirty-four, he hated it even more.

She probably drank too much last night, he thought, staring at her slim back as she jerked and shuddered. Some people just couldn't hold their liquor—though he didn't remember seeing her imbibe. Mostly she'd just danced and laughed and driven him crazy with an inferno of lust.

When she was done being sick, sitting there on her knees on the damp ground, her arms wrapped around her stomach, he inched closer. He felt totally out of his element, not quite sure what to say or do. But he knew he had to do something. She kept her back to him, no doubt mortified. He knew women could be unaccountably funny about such things. Finally, feeling like a fool, he knelt behind her. "You want me to go get you something to drink?"

She moaned and clutched herself a little tighter. "Just...go...away."

Morgan hesitated, then lifted one hand to her shoulder, gently rubbing. Touching her made *him* feel immeasurably better, whether it did anything for her or not. "I bet Sawyer has something he could give you for the hangover."

She laughed, a raw, broken sound that was close to a moan. "A hangover, Morgan? When I didn't drink a single drop?"

Way off base with that one, obviously. He nodded. "Okay, not a hangover."

She shook her head, and more silky strands of midnight hair escaped her rubber band to curl around her cheeks. A few tangled in the armature of her glasses, and he gently pulled them away.

Without looking at him, she said, "You always think the worst of me, don't you?"

He didn't know what to say to that.

"I should be used to it. God knows, men always… Oh, just go away." Her voice was thin, washed out; she sounded too tired to argue.

He couldn't stop his deep frown or his concern. "If you're sick, then—"

Her hands fisted on her thighs in a sudden startling display of frustration. Still without looking at him, she hissed, "Damn it, why can't you just leave me alone?"

He wouldn't let her rile him again. "Look, Malone, my mother would skin my hide if I left a sick woman wallowing out in the dew, without—"

"I am not sick!"

Her stubbornness annoyed the hell out of him, even as he continued to gently stroke her back. "Oh, then I'm hallucinating? That wasn't you just puking your guts up in my bushes? Because I have to tell you, Malone, if you're hoping to be a martyr to get my sympathy, it's not at all necessary. Hell, I already—"

She turned to him with a feral growl, momentarily startling him, then practically shouted, "I am not sick, you idiot! *I'm pregnant.*"

Chapter 3

Oh, God. Misty stared at Morgan, horrified by her statement, and ready to be sick all over again. She slapped a hand over her mouth and gulped air through her nose, determined to hold it back. She'd thought the fresh air would help, and it really had, but then Morgan had joined her....

She frowned, her queasy stomach almost forgotten. It was all his fault, and she said, without the demonic tone this time, "I don't suppose you'll just forget I said that?"

Dumbly, he shook his head, his eyes still wide, his jaw still slack. For once he wasn't scowling. He looked too stunned to scowl. "Uh, no. Not likely."

Her temper snapped. "Oh, of course not. That would be too easy, wouldn't it?" She frowned ferociously, wishing she could hit him over his hard head. "Well, it's none of your business, anyway. And if you tell my sister, I swear I'll make you regret it."

Morgan's expression hadn't changed. It was a comical mix of surprise, chagrin and helplessness. Something else, too, something bordering on anger, but she couldn't be sure. He blinked, but didn't say a word. With a sound of disgust, Misty rolled her eyes and started to get to her feet. "Look, I'm sorry about your bushes. Really. Do you think anyone will notice?" Before he could answer, she added, "But in a way, you're the one to blame. If you hadn't kept prodding me… But that doesn't matter now. I'm feeling much better, fine, in fact, so I'll just go get dressed and get on my way. Please thank your brothers for me. And tell Honey I'll be in touch."

She was rattled, which accounted for the way she was blathering on and on. She wanted to bite her tongue off. She wanted more coffee.

She wanted away from Morgan Hudson.

He'd slowly stood when she had, and now he stepped in front of her, blocking her attempt at a strategic retreat. "I don't think so, Malone. You're not going to make a confession like that and then just creep off."

She was too tired, too mind weary to deal with him now. As if speaking to an idiot, she said, "I didn't exactly have creeping in mind. I thought I'd dress, pick up my bags, walk out the front door and drive away. There's a big difference."

"You were crying. Your eyes are all puffy."

He said it like a heinous accusation. She waved a negligent hand, not about to explain herself to *him*. "Don't be silly. I always look like hell in the morning. Lucky for you, you won't have to get used to it."

She started around him again, and this time he picked her up. She would have screamed her head off, she was so exasperated, except she sure as certain didn't want the other brothers witnessing her this way.

Gabe was such a comedian, he'd probably start joking about the whole thing. And Jordan, with that mesmerizing voice Honey claimed could put a cow to sleep, would do his best to comfort her, which would make her cry again.

And Sawyer—she had no idea how he'd react to his new wife's sister showing up pregnant.

So instead of screaming, she held herself stiff and tried to ignore how easily Morgan carried her, his incredible strength, the delicious way he smelled this morning and her twinge of ridiculous regret when he sat her on the swing.

It had been so long since she'd been held, so long since she'd felt anything like caring or concern or gentleness, she was almost starving for it. Even Morgan's aggressive, demanding concern felt like a balm.

But she was also more savvy now, and she knew beyond a shadow of a doubt that Morgan Hudson was not a man to take comfort from.

"Uh, Morgan…"

Hands on his thighs, he leaned down in front of her until their noses nearly touched. "I'm going to go get you some juice. If you move so much as your baby toe before I get back, you won't be happy with my reaction. I mean it, Malone."

He looked more serious than she'd ever seen him. Not that she was afraid of him and his threats, but again, a ruckus might wake everyone else.

She turned her head away. "Bully."

"Damn right."

He sauntered off, but as if he hadn't trusted her to

stay put, he was back in less than a minute. Misty hadn't moved, only because she was so tired. For weeks now she'd been trying to come up with a solution, but the problems just kept adding up, and she hadn't a clue what to do. Finding a job was obviously top of the list. Then she could sell her car to make the first month of rent once she found a place she could afford.

Borrowing money from her father was out of the question. She wouldn't ask him for a nickel. They had never been close and she knew without approaching him what his reaction to her most recent problems would be. Probably even worse than his reaction to her pregnancy, which predictably had been disappointment. He'd give her money, but that's all he'd ever give, never understanding or emotional support. She had enough to deal with without his overwhelming condemnation on her shoulders.

No, she'd rather go it alone than go to her father.

She was still frowning, deep in thought, when Morgan handed her a tall, cold glass of orange juice. The juice looked wonderful, and she accepted it gladly. Sipping, she said, "I thank you—at least for the drink."

Morgan seated himself beside her and crossed his long arms over his massive chest. With his dark frown and set jaw, he looked belligerent and antagonistic. She didn't like his attitude at all.

She liked him even less.

Knowing he hated it when she acted brazen, and hoping he'd go away and leave her alone with her misery, she said, "You know, you really should show a little more decorum. Running around half naked is almost barbaric. Especially for a man built like you."

He blinked in surprise, and his brows smoothed out. "A man built like me?"

"Yeah, you know." She glanced at his hard, hair-covered chest, felt a shot of heat straight through the pit of her stomach and raised her brows. "All muscle-bound. You do that to attract the women? Because while I appreciate the sight of your sexy body, I'm not at all attracted."

He narrowed his eyes. "Are you trying to distract me, Malone?"

She sighed. "No, I'm being honest. You're an incredibly good-looking man, Morgan. And evidently a pushy one, too. But I'm not interested in any man, for any reason. I'm through with the lot of you—for good. Besides, I'm leaving today, and with any luck, you'll be long married with kids of your own and moved away before I ever visit again." She nodded at his chest once more. "You're wasting the excellent display on the likes of me."

"Oh, I don't know about that, considering most of what you just said was bunk. You are interested—at least in me." His voice dropped, and he looked her over slowly. She felt the touch of his gaze like a stroke of heat, from the top of her thighs to the base of her throat. "Last night proved that."

Misty swallowed hard, feeling a new sensation in her belly that wasn't at all unpleasant. "Last night was an aberration. I've had a lot on mind and you took me by surprise."

He let that slide without comment. "The part about me moving out is true enough, though. But I won't be far. The house on the hill? That's mine. It'll be ready to move into soon."

She couldn't see the house from here, but she remembered admiring it when she first arrived. It wasn't quite as large as this one, but it was still impressive. She wondered if he already had the wife picked out, too, but didn't ask. "Good for you."

Tilting his head, his look still far too provocative, Morgan said, "I'm curious about this professed disinterest of yours, especially considering your condition."

"My *condition?*" She hated how he said that—just as her father had, just as her fiancé had—with something of a sneer. She wanted the baby and she wouldn't apologize for having it, not to anyone, and certainly not to him. "It's not a disease, you know."

His gaze hardened. "When're you getting married, Malone?"

The words were casual, almost softly spoken, but they sounded lethal. And his stare was so intent, so burning, she looked at his chest instead of meeting his eyes. "None of your business."

"I'm making it my business."

The juice did wonders for settling her nausea and she finally felt more herself. Morning sickness was the pits, and she hoped she got past that stage soon, though now that the worst had happened and she'd been sick in front of Morgan, anything else had to be an improvement. "You do that a lot, do you? Butt in where you've got no business being? I bet that's why you took the position of sheriff. It gives you a legal right to nose around into other people's affairs."

He looked off to the distance, and Misty, following his gaze, saw that the sun was beginning its slow climb into the sky. It was a beautiful sight, sending a crimson glow across the placid surface of the lake, bringing a visual warmth that had her feeling better already. She sighed, knowing she'd never forget this place and how incredibly perfect it seemed.

Then Morgan spoke again, reminding her of a major flaw to the peaceful setting. Him.

"We can sit here until everyone else joins us if you want, but I got the impression you're keeping your departure a secret."

She sighed again, actually more of a huff. "You've got no right to badger me about something that is none of your damn business, Morgan."

"You're family now," he explained with a straight face. "That gives me all the rights I need."

Something that ludicrous deserved her undivided attention. She stared at him, almost speechless, but not quite. "*Family?* Get real."

He looked her over slowly, and she knew, even before he told her, that he was making a point. "Oh, you're family, all right, because if you weren't, we'd never have left that damn gazebo, that is, not until things ended in a way that we'd both have enjoyed. A lot."

The tone of his voice, both aggressive and persuasive, sank into her bones. Her stomach flip-flopped and her toes curled. Damn him, how could he do this to her now, when she'd just been sick, when she didn't like him, when he didn't much care for her? It wasn't fair that of all the men in all the world, Morgan Hudson had this singular effect on her.

But then, little in her life had been fair lately.

She shook her head, denying both him and herself. "You're twisting things around—"

"I'm stating a fact."

"The fact is that you want me as far from your family as you can manage!"

His shrug was negligent, but his gaze was hard. "As you pointed out, everyone else feels differently. Jordan even offered you a job."

"Which I refused."

His brows shot up. "You did?"

He sounded surprised, but then, she had been purposely harassing him by letting him think otherwise. That had been childish, and not at all smart. She sighed. "Of course I did."

"Why?"

Exasperated by his suspicious tone, she explained, "This'll be a shock, I'm sure, but I'm not the party girl you seem to think I am, Morgan. I realize both your brothers were likely just fooling around, but I don't intend to take any chances. I'm not interested in fun and games, and as I already told you, I'm even less interested in being serious with someone. I didn't want to accidentally encourage either of them, so I thanked Jordan for the offer, but declined, and I told Gabe I had other responsibilities and couldn't hang around any longer. So you can relax your vigil. Both your brothers are safe from my evil clutches."

He didn't react to her provocation this time, choosing instead to hark back to his earlier question. "When are you getting married?"

He wouldn't give up, she could tell. He looked settled in and disgruntled and determined. She was so tired of fighting men, her ex-fiancé, her ex-boss, even the damn lawyers and the judge. Maybe once she told Morgan everything, he'd be glad to be rid of her. She slumped into her seat, all fight gone. "I give up. You win."

He didn't gloat, and he didn't sound exactly pleased with himself. He was simply matter-of-fact in his reply.

"I always do." Then more quietly, "When are you getting married?"

"I'm not." She felt him studying her and she twisted to face him so she could glare right back. "I'm not getting married, okay? There's no groom, no wedding, no happily-ever-after. Satisfied now?"

There was a sudden stillness, then Morgan relaxed, all the tension ebbing out of him, his breathing easier, his expression less stern. She hadn't even realized he was holding himself so stiffly until he returned to his usual cocky self. He uncrossed his arms to spread one over the back of the swing, nearly touching her shoulder, and he shifted, all his big muscles sort of loosening and settling in.

In a tone meant to clarify, he asked, "You're *not* getting married?"

"What, do you want it written in blood? I'm not getting married. The very idea is repugnant. I have absolutely no interest in marriage."

"I see." The aggression was gone, replaced by something near to sympathy, and to Misty, that was even worse. "What happened to the father of the baby?"

Why not, she thought, fed up with fending him off. "He found out he was going to be a father and offered me money for an abortion." She wouldn't look at him. The humiliation and pain she'd felt that day was still with her. It had been the worst betrayal ever—or so she'd thought, until she'd lost her job. "I refused, he got angry, and we came to an agreement."

"What agreement?"

"I wouldn't bother him with the baby, and he wouldn't bother with me."

The swing kept moving, gently, lulling her, and though

Morgan was silent, it didn't feel like a condemning silence as much as a contemplative one. Finally he asked, "How long have you been sick in the mornings?"

"Only for a few weeks. And before you ask, yes, I'll tell Honey. But not now. She has a tendency to worry about me, to play the role of big sister even though I'm only a year younger than her. She's so happy with Sawyer now, she doesn't need to hear about my problems just yet."

His fingers gently touched her hair, smoothing it. It was clearly a negligent touch, as if he did it without thought. When she glanced at him, she saw he was watching her closely.

"Will the baby be a problem?"

"No! I want the baby."

His gaze softened. "That's not what I mean."

Lifting her chin, she said, "If you're asking me if I'll be a good mother, I hope so. I don't have much experience, but I intend to do my absolute best."

"No, I wasn't accusing you of anything or questioning your maternal instincts." He smiled slightly. "I just wonder if you know what you're getting into. Babies are a full-time job. How do you intend to work and care for it, too, without any help?"

She shook her head. Since she didn't even have a job at present, she didn't have an answer for him.

"Will you be able to get a leave of absence?"

The irony of that question hit her and she all but laughed. Instead, she turned her face away so he couldn't see how lost she felt.

Morgan touched her cheek. "Malone?"

"Isn't this interrogation about over?"

"I don't think so. So why don't you make it easy on yourself and just answer my questions?"

"Somehow I don't think this conversation is going to be easy on me no matter what I do."

He got quiet over that. "I don't mean to make things difficult for you."

"Don't you?"

"I didn't create this situation, Malone, and the attraction isn't one-sided. Will you at least admit that much?"

She didn't want to, but saw no point in denying it. "Yeah, so? I think the fact I'm pregnant and without a groom shows my judgment to be a bit flawed, so don't let it go to your head."

His large hand cupped the back of her skull, his fingers gently kneading. The tenderness, after his previous attitude, was startling. "Everyone makes a mistake now and then. You're not the first."

"Which mistake are we referring to? Me being pregnant, or my response to you?"

Again, he was quiet.

She decided to make a clean break, to finish her confessions and get away before she became morose again. She slapped her palms on her thighs, turned to him with a take-charge air and said, "Okay. You've worn me down. Besides, the sun is almost completely up. Everyone will be waking soon, and I hope to get out of here before that. I'd just as soon avoid the lengthy goodbyes if I can. So tell me, Sheriff, what other intrusive questions do you have for me before I'm formally dismissed?"

Again, he easily ignored her sarcasm. "How far along are you? You sure as certain don't look pregnant."

She laughed shortly. "Yeah, just think, if I did look

pregnant we probably wouldn't be having this conversation right now!"

"Malone?"

"Three months." She gave him a crooked grin. "From
what I understand, I may not start to show until my fifth,
maybe even my sixth month. By then, I'll be a distant
memory for you, Morgan."

"But you're sure you are—"

"Had the test, so yes, I'm sure. Besides, I feel the pregnancy in other ways."

His gaze went unerringly to her breasts, now thoroughly hidden beneath her sexless robe. Still, she practically squirmed with the need to shield herself with her
hands. She resisted the telltale reaction. "Yep, I'm bigger now," she said, doing her best to sound flippant, un-
affected. Trying not to blush. Her glasses slipped a bit,
and she pushed them back up.

"What about your job?"

Hedging, she asked, "What about it?"

"It occurs to me that I don't know all that much about
you."

Her eyes widened and she laughed. "Now there's a
revelation for you. Of course, anytime you don't know
something, you just fill it in with fiction."

He touched her cheek with the back of one finger and
his expression was regretful. "I admit to making some
pretty hasty assumptions. But you haven't helped, Misty,
coming on the way you did."

"I didn't—"

"Yeah, you did." He smiled just a little, making her
heart twist. "You flirt with everyone."

She sighed. "True enough. I was trying to act cheerful and worry-free so Honey wouldn't suspect anything. Maybe I overdid it just a bit."

"And maybe I want you bad enough that all you have to do is breathe and it seems like a seduction. At least to me."

Her gaze shot to his face; she was speechless.

"It's true, you know. I don't think I've ever wanted a woman the way I do you." His hand opened and his palm cupped her cheek. "Even now, with you looking like a maiden aunt and after you tossed your cookies in the bushes. Even knowing you're pregnant with another man's baby, I still want you."

She shook her head, words beyond her.

"I know. It's a damnable situation, isn't it?"

"No, it's not." She was resolute, driven by her emotional fear. "I'm leaving, this morning, right now if you'll just stop questioning me and let me leave without a fuss."

"It's not that easy, Malone, now that I know you're in trouble."

"Such an old-fashioned sentiment! Unmarried pregnant women are no longer in *trouble*. They're just…pregnant." She gave a negligent shrug.

"All right, if you say so." He looked far from convinced. "So quit hedging and reassure me. Where do you work?"

Knowing that, as sheriff, it would be easy enough for him to check, and not doubting for a moment that he probably would, she sniffed and said, "I only recently left Vision Videos."

"Vision Videos?"

"A small, privately owned video store. It's located in the town I…used to live in." She sincerely hoped he missed her small hesitation. The idea of being homeless was still pretty new to her. "It's very small scale, only three employees besides the owner, but the store did incredible business. He'd planned to open another location by the end of the summer and I was going to run it for him."

"But you're not now?"

"Now, I'm in the process of reevaluating my options."

He stared, and his softly stroking fingers went still. With disbelief ringing from every word, he said, "You're unemployed?"

"Momentarily, yes."

His eyes narrowed. "By choice? Because I'll tell you, if your boss fired you for being pregnant, that's against the law...."

"No, he didn't fire me for that."

Morgan's back stiffened, and his scowl grew darker. "But he did fire you?"

"Actually...yes."

"Why?"

"He...well, he accused me of doing something I didn't do."

"Damn it, Malone," he suddenly burst out, his irritation evident, his patience at an end. "It's like pulling snake teeth to get you to tell the whole—"

"All right!" She shot to her feet, every bit as annoyed as he was. Hands on her hips, she faced him. "All right, damn it. I was convicted of stealing from him. Three hundred dollars. But I didn't do it, only they believed that I did!"

Morgan stood, too, and now he looked livid. "They?"

She waved a hand. "The owner, the lawyer I had to hire, the despicable judge. Everyone."

Very slowly, Morgan reached out and took hold of her shoulders. "Tell me what happened."

Misty had no idea if he was angry with her or the situation. She tried to shrug his hands away, but he held on. Her temper was still simmering, though, and she was in no mood for his attitude, so she jerked away and then sat on the swing, giving a hard kick to make it move. Morgan grabbed the swing to stop it and sat beside her. "I'm waiting."

She crossed her arms over her breasts. He made her feel vulnerable and defensive when she had no reason to feel either one. "Not long after I found out I was pregnant and Kent, my ex, bailed out, I was at work and the cash came up short. The woman who'd worked before me had signed out and made her deposit, so the money had to have been taken during my shift. Only I didn't take it and I don't know where it went. I was in the bathroom—" She glanced at him. "Pregnant women spend a lot of time in the bathroom."

He made a face. "Go on."

"Anyway, there was no one in the store, so I made a quick run to the bathroom, and when I came back out, my boss and his girlfriend were just coming in. He was royally ticked that I'd left the counter, even after I explained that the store was empty and that I'd hurried. We argued, because he said I'd missed too much work lately, as well. See, I'd come in late twice, because of the morning sickness. Anyway, he was in a foul mood and being unreasonable, to my mind. I'd never been late or missed work before. Not ever. That's why he was going to make me a manager of the new store, because I was a good worker and dependable and all that."

"Get to the point, Malone."

She wanted to smack him. Instead, she said, "He checked the drawer and found out the money was missing. I still can't believe he accused me of stealing it. I'd been working for him for two years. I did everything, from inventory to decorations to promotion to sales to orders. I'm the one that helped that business do so well! I thought he trusted me."

"He called the cops?"

"Yes." The police had arrived, and she now knew firsthand the procedure used for thiefs. She shuddered with the memory, which wasn't one she intended to share with Morgan. "To make a long story short, the lawyer I hired said they had a good case against me. I was the only one in the store at the time the money was taken, and they found out I was pregnant, that the father of the baby had taken off. They painted me a desperate woman, with plenty of motive to take the money. He suggested I plead guilty to save myself a bundle in lawyer fees and court costs. I… I refused. So my lawyer suggested that I go with a trial to the bench, since that would get it over with quickly."

"I gather that wasn't the best decision possible?"

She shook her head. "A jury might not have been so autocratic or sexist."

"Sexist?"

"Yes. The judge was a stern-faced old relic who saw me as a femme fatale just because I'm young and I don't exactly look like a college professor."

One brow shot up, and his mouth quirked. "You mean because you're sexy as hell and he noticed?"

"That's not funny, Morgan."

"No, it's not. Sorry."

He still looked amused, though, which annoyed her

to no end. The judge's reaction to her had been salt in the wound. She could still remember how exposed she'd felt, standing before him.

She looked away and said quietly, "He gave me six months probation, made me pay back the three hundred dollars I hadn't even taken, as well as court costs and legal fees, then finished up with a scathing lecture about my responsibilities and morals and hoping I'd learned my lesson." She snorted. "The lesson I learned was that men see things one way, which is seldom the right or honorable way, and they sure as hell can't be trusted."

"Misty…"

"Don't use that tone on me, Morgan Hudson. You got what you wanted, all the nitty-gritty details. Well, now I'm done. I want to get out of here. I need to go find a job, and I'm just plain not up to fighting with you anymore, so if you'll excuse me—"

"No."

"No?" Incredulous, she turned to face him. "What do you mean, no?"

He stood, then caught her arm and pulled her to her feet. Still holding her, his gaze intent on her face, he said softly, "I mean you're not going anywhere, Malone. You're going to stay right here."

Chapter 4

Morgan stared at Misty, knowing that despite her outraged frown, there was no way he could let her go, not now. Her shoulders felt narrow and frail beneath his big hands, and he wished like hell she looked pregnant, so she'd be easier to resist. But she didn't. She looked soft and sexy, even with a red nose and those hideous glasses. He wanted her more than ever, but that was beside the point.

At least she wasn't planning on getting married. Though it wasn't any of his damn business, the very idea had set his teeth on edge. She could certainly do better than settling for some clown who didn't want his own child. He swore to himself that was the only reason it bothered him. Then he called himself a fool.

"You can't be off on your own right now. You said it yourself, you don't have a job, and you're sick."

She gave him a blank stare, as if he was a stranger.

"Damn it, Misty, you know I'm right!"

"I know you're nuts, that's what I know." He made a grumbling sound, and she said in exasperation, "It's morning sickness, Morgan, that's all. I'm fine the rest of the time. I'm perfectly capable of finding and working a job. Pregnant woman do it all the time, you know."

Actually, his mind was buzzing with possibilities. If she stayed—and she would because he didn't intend to give her a choice—he could give her a job. He'd long since figured they needed someone to answer the phones at the office, but more often than not folks just called him directly. It was a small county, and the crime level was amazingly low, so he'd been in no rush to hire a new deputy. But a secretary of sorts, someone to keep track of his schedule and forward calls and take notes, that'd be a blessing.

He'd put off the hiring for some time now. He hadn't really wanted anyone else mucking around his offices. But now...

He eyed her belligerent expression and winced. Better to tell her about the job later, when she wasn't so annoyed with him. He gave her a slight shake. "So what do you intend to do?"

"I intend to punch you in the nose if you don't stop manhandling me!"

His fingers flexed on her shoulders, very gently, and he saw her eyes darken. He hadn't hurt her, would never deliberately hurt her. No, her complaint was for an entirely different reason. "Manhandling, huh?" he asked softly. "And here I thought I was being all that was considerate and caring."

She bit her lip in indecision, then resolutely shook her

head. "Not likely, Morgan. You're up to something, I just haven't figured out what yet."

Her opinion of him was far from flattering, with good reason, he supposed. He dropped his hands and turned to think, only to hear her stomping away. He caught the back of her robe and drew her up short. "Whoa. Now where are you off to? We have to finish discussing this."

Through gritted teeth, she said, "There's no *we* to it, and there's nothing to discuss." She swatted his hands away and jutted her chin toward him. "I'm going in to shower and dress, and then I'm leaving. You won't have to worry about me at all, and your precious brothers will be safe from my lascivious tendencies."

Damn it, she was trying to make him feel guilty—and succeeding. "You let me think the worst about that, Malone. Admit it."

"You always assume the worst," she argued. "I'm not responsible for the way your mind works."

"No, you're not. But in a way, it is your fault." She looked ready to erupt, so he added, "I get around you, Malone, and I can barely think at all, much less with any logic. In case you haven't noticed, I've got the hots for you in a really bad way."

Her face went blank for a split second, and he braced himself for an attack. Then suddenly her mouth twitched, and she burst out laughing. "Is that your way of saying you're sorry?"

Hearing her laugh was nice, even if she was laughing at him. "I suppose you think I owe you that much?"

"Nope." Her glasses slid down her nose and more hair escaped the rubber band. She looked disheveled and vulnerable and so damn female he felt rigid from his neck all the way down to his toes. "I don't think you owe me a darn thing, Morgan, except to butt out of my business."

Shrugging in apology, he whispered, "I can't do that."

"You," she said with emphasis, "have no choice in the matter."

"I can help you, Malone."

"You want to help?" She turned away from him, then said over her shoulder, "Leave me be."

Why, Morgan wondered as she stalked away, would she steal money from an employer, but not take money from him when it was freely offered? Especially considering the situation she was in. And not only had she refused the money, she'd been downright livid over the idea. Somehow it didn't fit, and he damn well intended to find out what was going on.

Later. Right now he was busy plotting. She had turned down the money, but maybe she'd accept his help in other ways once he talked her into staying. He wasn't raised to turn his back on a woman in her predicament, especially considering that she *was* part of the family. Whether she liked it or not, that excuse was good enough for him.

He picked up the coffee mugs and her empty juice glass, then headed into the kitchen. He had a few things to take care of before she finished showering, so he might as well get to them. First was that ragtag little car of hers. Removing a few spark plugs ought to do the trick. Getting his brothers out of bed would be a little harder, considering the night they'd all had, but they would rally together for a good cause, and he definitely considered Misty Malone a good cause. Given how all his brothers had doted on her the past couple of weeks, he had no doubt they'd feel the same.

Twenty minutes later, Morgan was sitting at the

kitchen table with a bleary-eyed Casey when Misty walked in. The others hadn't quite made it that far yet, but Morgan knew they'd present themselves shortly.

Casey, with his head propped in his hand, glanced at her and yawned. "Morning, Misty. What're you doing up so early?"

Misty stopped dead in her tracks. Her hair was freshly brushed and twisted into a tidy knot on the top of her head that Morgan thought made her look romantic and amazingly innocent. Her glasses were gone—thank God—and she no longer had a red nose. She wore a yellow cotton camisole with cutoff shorts and strappy little sandals and she looked good enough to eat.

Morgan drew in a shuddering breath with that image and steered his wayward thoughts off the erotic and onto the essential.

Rather than answer Casey, her accusing gaze swung toward Morgan and there was murder in her eyes. He grinned. He'd rather have her fighting mad than looking morose any day. Leaning against the counter with his arms crossed over his chest, Morgan said, "What's with the suitcase, Malone?"

Casey, who hadn't noticed the luggage yet, sat up straight. His gaze bounced back and forth several times between the suitcase and Misty's face, and he looked more alert than he had only five seconds ago. "You're not leaving, are you?"

Misty ground her teeth, then whipped around to face Casey with a falsely bright smile plastered in place. "'Fraid so, kiddo. I have things to do. But I did enjoy my visit. Tell your dad thanks for me, okay?"

She started to move, but Casey jumped up, looking panicked, and all but blocked her way. "But Dad'll kill

me if you leave without saying goodbye! I mean, Honey
will be upset and that'll upset Dad. Just hang around
for breakfast, okay?" He glanced at Morgan for backup.
"Tell her, Uncle Morgan. Shouldn't she stay and have
breakfast?"

Morgan nodded slowly. "I do believe you're right,
Casey."

"Ah, no... It's better if I—"

The kitchen door swung open and Jordan dragged
himself in. He was wearing a pair of unsnapped jeans
and scratching his belly while yawning hugely. His hair
was still mussed and he looked like he could have used
another six hours of sleep, at least. The last Morgan had
seen him last night, three of the local women were trying
to talk him into taking each of them home. It was a hell
of a predicament for his most reserved brother.

Morgan had not one whit of sympathy for him.

Because Jordan had taken the path from the garage—
where he kept his apartment—to the kitchen, the bottoms
of his feet were wet. When he saw Misty packed up and
ready to go, he nearly slipped on the linoleum floor in
his surprise.

Morgan caught him, then pushed him upright. If Jordan knocked himself out, he'd be no help at all.

In his usual mellow tones, Jordan asked, "What's
going on here?" He dried his feet on a throw rug while
quietly studying everyone in turn.

Morgan feigned a casual shrug. "Misty says she's leaving."

Casey crossed his arms, ready to add his two cents'
worth. "She's not even going to tell anyone goodbye."

Looking from Casey's disapproving face to Misty's
red cheeks before finally meeting Morgan's gaze, Jordan

frowned. Not a threatening frown, as Morgan favored, but rather a contemplative one. Jordan was no dummy and caught on quickly that this was the reason he'd been summoned from his bed. He fastened his jeans now that he knew there was a lady present, then took several cautious steps forward, making certain not to slip again. Holding Misty's shoulders, he asked softly, "What's wrong, sweetheart? Why are you sneaking off like this?"

Morgan didn't like his brother's intimate tone at all. And he sure as hell didn't like Jordan touching her. He glowered at Misty as he said, "I don't think she wanted anyone to know she was going."

Jordan glanced at Morgan, then crossed his arms over his chest and regarded Misty with quiet speculation. "Is that true?"

After a long, drawn out sigh, Misty dropped her heavy bag and propped her hands on her hips. "I'm not sneaking, exactly. You all knew I was going to be leaving today."

Gabe spoke from the doorway where he'd negligently propped himself, unnoticed. "Not true." He gave Morgan a look, then came into the kitchen and dropped into a chair with a theatrical yawn. He, too, was bare-chested, but he wore loose cotton pull-on pants. "You said you couldn't stay, Misty, but you didn't say a damn thing about taking off today at six-thirty in the morning. Hell, the birds aren't even awake yet, so I'd definitely call that sneaking. What's up, sweetheart?"

Misty looked ready to expire. Morgan took pity on her and pulled out a chair. "Why don't you at least sit down, Malone, while you do your explaining?" He reached for her arm, but she sidestepped him. Breathing hard, she glared at them all, then said, "I'm leaving, that's all there is to it. I'm already packed and I want to get an early start. I'm not good at long goodbyes, so…if you'll excuse me?"

She picked up her bag and headed for the door. Her car was parked at the side of the house, close to the back door. There was a flurry of arguments from Casey, Jordan and Gabe, but Morgan had expected no less of them. It was why he'd so rudely dragged them out of their warm, comfortable beds. Unfortunately, Misty wasn't going to be swayed by them.

She stormed out of the house in righteous fury, and they all trailed behind, talking at once. Morgan listened to their arguments for why she should stay and even commended his brothers for making some good points.

Misty did an admirable job of ignoring them.

When Jordan realized how serious she was, he took the suitcase from her hand while stabbing Morgan with curious looks, as if waiting for *him* to stop her somehow.

Morgan almost laughed. He'd known there was no way he'd be able to bring her around. If he wasn't missing his guess, he was the biggest reason she was so set on going. That was why he'd pulled the spark plugs, as insurance until he got her over her pique and could make her see reason.

After Jordan stowed her suitcase in the backseat, he reached for Misty and pulled her into a fierce hug. To Morgan, seething at the sight of Misty snuggled up against Jordan's bare chest, the embrace didn't look at all familial. He was just about to tear them apart when Jordan leaned back the tiniest bit to look at her.

"Where will you be staying?" Jordan asked. "Is there a number where we can call you?"

Misty appeared stumped for just a moment, which made Morgan very suspicious, then she brightened. "I'm sort of moving around at the moment. But I'll let you know when I get settled, okay?"

Morgan continued to study her. It was amazing, even to him, but he could read her like a book, and he knew without a doubt she didn't have any place to stay. He wanted to throttle her, and he wanted to hold her tight.

Gabe stepped up next for his own hug, and he even dared to kiss her on the cheek, lingering for what Morgan considered an inappropriate amount of time. Morgan gave serious thought to throwing Gabe back into the basement. "If you change your mind," Gabe said, "promise you'll come back."

"I promise. And thank you."

Casey shook his head. "My death will be on your hands, because Dad is still going to kill me."

Morgan silently applauded Casey's forlorn expression, but Misty didn't buy it. She actually grinned. "Your father wouldn't hurt a hair on your head, and you know it! Now give me a hug." With a crooked smile, Casey obeyed.

And even that made Morgan grind his teeth. Casey was a good head taller than Misty with shoulders much wider. Morgan didn't like it at all. Hell, so far they'd all touched her more than he had!

Misty didn't even bother looking at Morgan. He crossed his arms and waited until she'd gotten behind the wheel and pulled her door shut, then he leaned back against a tall oak tree. He considered himself patience personified.

Jordan stepped up to him with an intent frown. It was unlike Jordan to be so disgruntled, and Morgan raised a taunting brow. "Sorry to see her go?"

Jordan didn't rile easily. "You got me out of bed just

to tell her goodbye? I figured you'd stop her somehow. Honey's going to be damn upset when she finds out we let her leave."

Morgan eyed his brother a moment longer, decided he didn't see any signs of lovesickness, and turned to stare at Misty. "She's not going anywhere."

Misty gave one final cheery wave to them all and turned the key. The engine ground roughly, whined, but didn't quite turn over. Frowning, she tried again. The car still wouldn't start.

Satisfied, Morgan watched Gabe saunter over to him, Casey at his side. "You tinkered with her car?" He sounded faintly approving. Gabe was the mechanic and handyman in the family. If he'd thought of it or had had time, he likely would have done the same.

Morgan gave him a wounded look. "Now, would I do a thing like that? I'm the law around here, Gabe, you know that. Tampering with a car is illegal." He looked at Misty with a smile. "I'm sure of it."

Grinning, Gabe went to the driver's window and tapped on it. When Misty rolled down her window, he said, "Doesn't sound like she's going to start, hon."

Misty dropped her head onto the steering wheel and ignored Gabe, ruthlessly twisting the key once again. She looked so forlorn that Morgan almost couldn't stand it. He wanted to lift her out of the car, hold her, tell her everything would be okay. He wanted, damn it, to take care of her. To protect her.

Because she was family.

Because she was a woman in need.

Because it was the right thing to do.

Not because he cared for her personally. Wanting a woman and caring for her were two different things, and he was never one to confuse the issues. Yes, he wanted her, more so now than ever, which seemed odd in the extreme. But he could deal with that. What he couldn't deal with was the idea of her running off with no place to go, and the fact that she'd be alone at a time when she needed family most.

So maybe she'd gotten into some trouble? He wasn't completely convinced yet. But even if it was true, everyone made mistakes, and being a pregnant, unmarried woman was as good a reason for theft as any he'd ever heard. He didn't approve, but he did understand. She was still young, only twenty-four, and she'd found herself in a hell of a predicament.

From the sound of it, she'd more than paid for the crime, not only financially, but emotionally, as well. He didn't blame her for not wanting to own up to it if she was guilty. Few people tended to brag about their bad judgment.

Convinced that he was still in control of things, including his own tumultuous emotions, Morgan walked over to the car and opened the back door. He lifted out her bag then nudged Gabe aside. He pulled her door open and cupped his free hand around her upper arm. Gabe stood there grinning at him, while Jordan and Casey watched with satisfaction.

"C'mon, Malone," Morgan said. "Sitting out here moping isn't going to solve anything."

She smacked her head onto the steering wheel again. "I can't be this unlucky."

Morgan hesitated, but he knew damn good and well he'd done the right thing. He'd needed to buy some time to undo the damage he'd inflicted with his insistence that she should leave. Later, she'd thank him. "Rattling your brains won't help. Come inside and we'll figure something out."

She leaned back in the seat and stared at him. "I hope you're happy now."

His smile was only fleeting before he wiped it away. "I'm getting there." He urged her out of the car and kept hold of her arm even as they walked back in. He was pleased that she didn't pull away from him. That surely showed some small measure of trust, didn't it?

Unfortunately, something he *hadn't* figured on happened: they found Sawyer and Honey smooching in the kitchen, wrapped up together in no more than a sheet.

Morgan halted abruptly when he saw them, which caused Misty to stumble into his side and Jordan to bump into his back. Like dominoes toppling one another, they all ended up crammed into the tiny doorway, gawking.

Misty groaned at the sight of her sister, then turned her face into Morgan's side. "I'm cursed."

At her softly spoken words, Honey jerked away from her husband, looked up, then blushed furiously. "Oh, Lord." She clutched at the sheet, pulling it up to her throat and all but leaving Sawyer buck naked. "It's barely six-thirty! We thought everyone was still in bed!"

Sawyer grabbed for an edge of the sheet to retain his modesty in front of Misty, then turned to frown at his brothers. "What the hell is going on?" He noticed the suitcase Morgan held, and his expression altered. "You going somewhere, Morgan?"

Standing on tiptoe, Casey attempted to see over Morgan's shoulder, then stated, "Misty was going to leave, but Morgan stopped her."

Sawyer glanced at his wife, then blinked at his son. His confusion was amusing, if unfortunate. "Leave where?"

"I don't know." Casey gave an elaborate shrug. "Home, I guess, though she said she's in the middle of moving somewhere and she'd have to tell us where exactly after she got settled. I tried to stop her, Dad, honest, but she was determined—"

Morgan felt Misty tremble and said, "That's enough, Case." Then to Sawyer: "Just a misunderstanding. What are you two doing out here? We thought you'd…sleep in…till at least noon."

Grinning like a rogue, Sawyer announced, "We needed nourishment."

Honey turned bright pink and elbowed her husband, who grabbed her and kissed her hard on the mouth. Morgan couldn't help but smile at them. Though Sawyer had fought it hard, he was so crazy in love with Honey, it was fun to watch them.

Morgan wanted a relationship like that. Then he thought of Misty beside him, the exact opposite of her sister, and he scowled.

Jordan shoved his way past the others. "If you two newlyweds want to go back to bed, I'll bring you a tray in just a few minutes. Coffee and bagels?"

"Perfect." Sawyer tried to turn Honey around, but she wasn't budging.

"Misty?" Honey looked oblivious to Sawyer's efforts. "You were going to leave without telling me?"

There was no mistaking her hurt, and although Morgan wouldn't have put Misty through such an ordeal, he decided it was probably best to get it all out in the open at once. The sooner Misty got through it, the sooner she could understand that she didn't need to leave.

He was surprised and pleased when he felt Misty's hand slip into his, and he squeezed her fingers tight, then answered for her. "Well, she's not going anywhere right now because her car won't start. You don't have to worry."

Honey's brows shot up. "Her car won't start?" She sent a suspicious look at Gabe. "Did you tamper with her car like you did mine?"

Gabe straightened from his sleepy, slouched position and crossed his heart with dramatic flair. "Never touched it. Hell, I just got up. I'm not awake enough to be playing with engines."

Jordan spoke before Honey could turn her cannons on him. "Same here. I didn't even know she was planning to leave until I saw her with her suitcase."

Misty stared at her sister, and Morgan could feel her tensing. "They tampered with your car?"

Honey shrugged. "I wanted to leave, because I thought I was intruding and putting them all in danger. But they weren't worried, and they thought it'd be better if I stayed here with them. They knew I couldn't very well leave without transportation, so they kept my car disabled. I thought Gabe was fixing it for me, but instead he was making sure it wouldn't run if I tried to sneak off." Honey smiled at her husband, then added, "Their intentions were good, so I forgave them."

Misty pulled her hand away and slowly turned to glare at Morgan. Her eyes were dark with accusation and anger. "Did you?"

Shrugging, he said, "You didn't exactly leave me a lot of choice."

Her gasp was so loud she sounded as if someone had pinched her. She drew back her arm and slugged him in the stomach, gasped again, then shook her hand and glared at him. "How dare you!"

He tried to rub the sting out of her hand, but she held it protectively away from him. Morgan frowned at that. "You wouldn't listen," he said by way of explanation. He was more than a little aware of their rapt audience, but saw no way around it. Damn it, she was Honey's sister, and she'd been preparing to slip off without a job, without money....

He'd never heard a woman growl so ferociously before. Everyone was frozen, silent. Misty looked as if she might hit him again, then thought better of it. Her expression was angry but resolute. "Fine. I'm calling a cab. He can take me to the bus station."

Morgan glared at her. "Don't push me, Malone."

"You've done all the pushing, you—you...!"

"Bastard?" he supplied helpfully.

She growled again. "Fix my car!"

"No." He crossed his arms over his chest.

Sawyer, ever the diplomat, cleared his throat. "Uh, Morgan..."

Still matching Misty glare for glare, Morgan shook his head. "She can't leave, Sawyer, all right?"

"Why?"

Gabe spoke. "If she's that set on going—"

"I'd prefer she stay, too," Jordan added, "but—"

Morgan closed his eyes, trying to think of some way around the problems. Nothing too promising presented itself. When he met Misty's gaze this time, he knew she could read his purpose.

"Don't you do it, Morgan," she warned.

He touched her cheek and gave her a small, regretful smile. "I'm sorry, sweetheart." Then he turned to everyone else and announced, "I don't want her to go, because she's pregnant."

The reaction wasn't quite what he'd expected. Honey's mouth fell open, Gabe and Jordan both became mute, Casey's neck turned red, and Sawyer leaned on the counter with a sigh, holding tight to his share of the sheet.

Misty went ahead and hit him again. He took hold of her hands before she hurt herself. This time she didn't pull away, but chose instead to stare at him with evil intent. He supposed she'd rather look at him than face everyone else. If he could have thought of a way to spare her, he would have.

Then Morgan realized no one was looking at Misty. They were all staring at him—with accusation. It was almost too funny for words.

"*I'm* not the father," he said dryly. "Hell, I've only known her a couple of weeks, if you'll recall."

Sawyer coughed. "That's actually quite long enough."

"In this case, it wasn't!"

Everyone relaxed visibly. Honey said to Morgan, "Well, of course she can't leave, you're right about that. Hang on to her until I get back, okay?" Then she took off like a shot, dragging Sawyer along with her, given that they shared the sheet and he didn't want to be left bare-assed.

Gabe sat down at the table and relaxed, at his leisure. "All this excitement has made me hungry. Jordan, if you're fixing breakfast, make some for me, too."

Jordan nodded and began pulling out pans. "Might as well skip the bagels and go for pancakes. Casey, Misty? Either of you hungry?"

Casey glanced at Misty, then pulled out his chair. "I'm always hungry. You know that."

Misty's eyes were wide, as if she'd been prepared for an entirely different response to his statement, maybe something more dramatic than an offer of breakfast. Did she think he and his brothers were ogres? Morgan almost smiled at her. Had she expected to be stoned? To receive a good dose of condemnation? He chucked her chin, then said gently, "Didn't I tell you it'd be all right?"

Misty didn't bother answering. She looked like she'd turned to stone. Morgan held her gaze, trying to think of some way to smooth things over with her. "I don't suppose you'll believe me when I tell you that wasn't intentional?"

Her eyes darkened to navy and her lips firmed.

"Okay, the car part was," he admitted, just to rile her. He couldn't bear seeing her look so lost. "And I admit I got Jordan and Gabe and Casey out of bed."

She mumbled under her breath, no doubt something insulting, but he just pretended he hadn't heard her. "I swear, I had no idea our newlyweds would be up. And I didn't plan to let the cat out of the bag about your pregnancy, either."

Her expression remained murderous.

Leaning close, crowding her against the cabinets so his brothers couldn't see her or hear him, Morgan whispered, "I have no intention of sharing your other secrets, so you can rest easy on that score, okay?" They were so close, her scent filled him with every breath he took. He braced his hands beside her hips on the counter; she braced her hands on his chest. She didn't quite push him away, and he saw her lips part. It amazed him the effect they had on each other. Even when she was likely thinking of ways to bring him low, she still responded to him. When they did finally come together—and he was certain it would happen sooner or later—he could only imagine how explosive it would be.

His heart thundered. "Misty?" She slowly looked up and met his gaze. "There's no reason for anyone to know about the rest unless you want to tell them, okay?"

Misty shivered, but before she could answer Honey came whipping into the room in her robe and skidded to a halt when she saw Morgan's nose practically in Misty's ear. "Hey, now, none of that. Get away from her, Morgan. I want to talk to my sister without you trying to intimidate either of us."

Morgan slowly straightened, wondering what Misty was thinking, if she'd believed him. "I've never intimidated you, Honey."

"Not for lack of trying." She caught Misty's arm and pulled her aside.

Morgan lifted the suitcase. "I'll just take this back to her room."

Misty shook her head to refuse him, while Honey gave him her sweetest smile. "Thank you, Morgan. Misty and I will be in the family room, talking."

"I'll call you when breakfast is ready," Jordan said, and Misty seemed unaware of the concern in his tone.

After the sisters left, Morgan felt both his brothers watching him. He turned to glare at them. "What?"

"Not a thing."

"Didn't say a word."

Casey made a show of studying a bird outside the kitchen window.

"Damn irritants," Morgan muttered. He lifted the suitcase and carried it out of the room. He knew his brothers each had at least a dozen questions, wondering what he was doing mixed up in the middle of Misty Malone's affairs, and why he was the only one privy to her startling news. But he wasn't about to betray her trust any more than he already had. They could just go on wondering.

When Morgan got to the room Misty had been using, he found the bed neatly made and everything very tidy. He pictured her sleeping in that bed last night, or rather, not sleeping. Just worrying. He'd told her she should leave, and this morning she'd been crying.

His stomach cramped and he idly rubbed his hand over it, but the ache continued. He could easily imagine what she'd been thinking, how she'd felt—how he'd made her feel—and he hated it. She probably hadn't slept at all last night, worrying about what she'd do, worrying about finding a job and about the baby.

A baby, a little person that would look like Misty, with dark hair and big blue eyes... He smiled at the thought, then caught himself and scowled.

What kind of job could a woman with a record get? He didn't know the terms of her probation—he'd have to ask her about that—but he knew it wouldn't sit well with an employer, especially not when she'd supposedly stolen from the last guy who'd hired her. Would she be able to earn enough to take care of herself and a baby?

She was certainly stubborn enough to make it work somehow, but she had a hard road ahead of her. And that route wasn't even necessary.

Morgan considered things for a moment, then came to some decisions. He opened her suitcase, emptied it on the bed, took the case to his room and shoved it under his bed. If she wanted to try sneaking out again, he wouldn't make it easy for her. At least until he knew she had a decent plan. Then, he told himself, he'd let her go.

He also intended to do a little investigating. Getting

the details of the theft wouldn't be hard, and then he'd make his own conclusions.

He felt like a warlord, holding her against her will, but damn it, it was only stubborn pride that had her wanting to leave in the first place. That and his big mouth. He had the feeling if he hadn't asked her about leaving, if he hadn't pushed her, she'd have stayed on for a while, using the time to make new plans. She had a lot to deal with, and until he'd started harassing her, she'd probably seen this as an ideal situation, a place to regroup and be with her sister without anyone knowing what had happened.

Except that she'd told him everything. He took immense satisfaction in that small success, discarding the fact that he'd bullied the information out of her. Misty wouldn't have told him if she hadn't trusted him at least a little.

He remembered stories of her father that Honey had shared. That man wasn't one to coddle or offer comfort, so Morgan had no doubt she hadn't even tried going to him for help. According to Honey, neither of them was overly close to the man, and with good reason.

Everything would work out, he was certain of it.

On his way to the kitchen Morgan passed the family room and was brought up short by a disgruntled, *"He hates me."*

Morgan stalled, his heart jumping, his muscles pulled tight. He waited, eavesdropping like a maiden aunt to hear what Honey would say in reply.

Her soft voice was soothing, just as Morgan had known it would be. "Morgan doesn't hate you, Misty. He kept you here because that's just how they all are. They're a little on the gallant side, and Morgan wants to protect you."

There was a rough, disbelieving laugh. "Right. If you say so."

Morgan could tell she didn't believe her sister and he pulled his hands into fists. Even his toes cramped. Hate her? Hell, no. What he felt was as far from hatred as it could get, and a whole lot steamier than that cold emotion. He wanted to devour her, to make love to her for a week so he could get her out of his system.

He hated the effect she had on him, but he didn't hate *her*.

"I do say so," Honey insisted. "I know them all better than you do."

"It doesn't matter what Morgan thinks or how he feels about me, Honey. The point is, I didn't mean to intrude on you. The last thing you need right now is to start worrying about me."

"There, you see? I won't worry as long as you're around so I can see you're doing okay. Morgan probably knew that, too."

Morgan lifted his brows. Sounded good enough to him, though thoughts of Honey hadn't much entered into his mind while he was trying to think of ways to keep Misty around.

"But…" Misty floundered, then insisted, "I need to get back to work. I can't just stay here indefinitely."

Morgan hustled through the doorway before Misty could convince Honey that she should leave. He surveyed both women cozied up on the couch, and Misty's eyes widened in alarm.

There was no way for him to reassure her right now, so he didn't bother trying. He'd already given her his word that he wouldn't tell about her stint with the law. It wouldn't hurt her to trust him just a bit.

He got right to the point. "I heard you mention your job."

"Morgan." Her tone said she'd kill him if he said one more word.

The threat didn't worry him. After all, the woman had hurt her hand just smacking him in the stomach. And she had shared her secrets with him, which he chose to see as a sign of trust whether she realized it or not. "I have a solution."

Misty moaned again. He noticed she'd been doing a lot of that lately.

Undaunted, he held up his hands and pronounced, "You're going to come to work for me."

Misty stared at Morgan, wondering what he was up to now. Somehow, in the short time it had taken her to shower, he'd done something to her car so it wouldn't start, shaved so that he looked refreshed and ready to take on the day instead of looking like a dark savage, and he'd pulled on more clothes.

She was eternally grateful for the clothes part.

Even when he made her so mad she wanted to club him on top of his handsome head, she couldn't seem to ignore him. The man filled up the space around her with his size, his scent, his pushy presence. When he was there, he was really there, and she doubted any sane woman would be oblivious to him, especially not when he was flaunting his bare, muscled chest.

Morgan had the type of body that had always secretly appealed to her. He was tall and powerful and immeasurably strong—but he could be so gentle.

She shook her head. Just because he distracted her didn't mean she'd let him off the hook. What she'd most wanted *not* to happen he'd made sure *had* happened. Never mind that she was now in the situation she'd originally wanted, with a safe place to stay, close to her sister.

How the circumstance had come about was totally unfair—and all Morgan's fault. Honey deserved some carefree time, but now she'd worry endlessly. Honey had a horrible tendency to mother her, a habit she'd gotten into because their mother had died long ago and their father was so cold and undemonstrative. Though Honey was only slightly older, she'd taken the big-sister role to heart.

She'd have told Honey the whole story eventually, of course, because they didn't keep secrets from each other. But not now, not when Honey had just gotten married and found so much happiness. It wasn't fair to drop such a burden in her lap.

She should have choked Morgan instead of punching him in his rock-hard middle, she thought, surveying his dark frown. But judging by his thick neck, that wouldn't have done him much damage, either. The man was built like a pile of bricks and was just as immovable.

And now he'd offered her a job. Or more precisely, he'd demanded she take a job. *With him.*

He hadn't precisely told Honey that Misty didn't have a job anymore. No, he'd made it sound as if he was only offering her an alternative so she could stick around. Did that mean he'd been sincere when he'd promised not to tell anyone about the rest of her troubles? God, she hoped so. It was all too humiliating, and though she knew Honey would believe her innocent, she had no idea how the others would feel.

Being pregnant was one thing; she wanted the baby and couldn't really regret its existence. And the brothers had been very accepting about the whole thing—almost cavalier, in fact. But surely they wouldn't want a jailbird in their home. She felt sick at the idea of them finding out.

"I already have a job," she stated forcefully, when Honey gave her a nudge for sitting there and staring.

Morgan lifted one brow and proceeded to settle himself into the stuffed chair adjacent to the couch. Contrary to how Misty felt, he looked at his ease and without a care in the world. His dark blue eyes were direct, unflinching.

"Now Malone," he said easily, "you were just telling me that you hate that job, that you planned to look for something else. Why not look here, so you can be close to your…family?"

"I never—" Misty bit her lip, stopping her automatic protest in midsentence. How could she dispute his enormous lie without telling the actual truth? He'd cornered her, and he knew it.

After clearing her throat, she smiled sweetly. It always worked for Honey. "I never meant to imply *you* should give me a job."

Morgan waved his hand in dismissal. Apparently the big ape was immune to her smile. "Of course you didn't. I know that. You'd never hint around that way. You're much too…up-front and honest for that." His eyes glittered at her and he added, "But I want you to take the job."

She glanced at Honey, saw no help there and resolutely shook her head. "No."

"How can you refuse when you don't even know what the job is yet?"

Through set teeth, she growled, "What is the job?"

Morgan actually smiled, which put her even more on edge. "I need an assistant. Someone to act as sort of a secretary and a dispatcher, when necessary. No, don't look like that. You won't need special training. Buckhorn is a small county and we do things just a bit differently. You'd need to take calls, keep track of where I am and forward on the important ones, but make notes for the ones that can wait. Mostly just for mornings and afternoons. Your evenings will be free, and just think, you can spend more time with Honey."

Honey leaned forward in her seat, already excited by the prospect. "Morgan, that's a great idea!" To Misty, she said, "It only makes sense, Misty, for you to be with family now. This is no time to let your pride get in the way."

"Of course it isn't," Morgan agreed.

Honey sighed. "Didn't I tell you he was wonderful?"

Misty almost choked, especially when she glanced at Morgan and saw his amusement. She thought she might throw up again. She drew a deep breath and tried to sound reasonable. "I don't know anything about working for a sheriff…"

"I'll tell you everything you need to know, sweetheart."

There was only so much she could take and remain composed. "I am not," she said in lethal tones, "your sweetheart."

Honey patted her hand. "They all use endearments, so you might as well get used to it. I swear, at first I thought they knew my name before I'd even given it to them. Then I realized everything female is a sweetheart or a honey to these guys, even the hodgepodge of animals Jordan keeps around." Honey gave Morgan a fond smile. "They're very old-fashioned in a lot of ways."

Under her breath, Misty muttered, "You mean they're overbearing, macho, autocratic—"

"What's that, Malone? I couldn't quite hear you." Morgan looked ready to laugh.

"Not a thing." She stood, and both Honey and Morgan came to their feet, too, as if they thought she might topple over at any moment. Good grief, she wasn't even showing yet. "I'll think about the job, Morgan."

He gave her a slow nod, looking at her from his superior height in a way that made her feel downright tiny. "That's fine. But make it quick, okay? I need you to start tomorrow."

Her eyes widened. She didn't want to start tomorrow! She didn't want to start at all. If anything, she hoped to make some solid plans tomorrow that would appease everyone so she could be on her way. "But…"

"Will you, Misty? Please?" Honey hugged her close, and Misty had no choice but to return the embrace. Since meeting Sawyer, her sister was deliriously happy and she wanted everyone else to feel the same. Over Honey's shoulder, Misty glared at Morgan. He winked at her, the obnoxious brute.

Misty pushed her sister away slightly and drummed up a reassuring smile. "Why don't you go have breakfast with that new husband of yours? I want to discuss this… job, with Morgan."

"But you haven't even told me about the baby yet, or how far along you are, or anything!"

Misty thought about moaning again, but with Morgan watching her so closely, she held it in. To her surprise, he took Honey's arm and said, "One thing at a time, hon, okay? If she takes the job and sticks around, you'll have all the time in the world to chat."

It was obvious Honey didn't want to, but she finally agreed to leave. She gave Morgan a warning look on her way out that had Morgan chuckling in a deep rumble.

Misty saw nothing funny in the situation, but he didn't

give her a chance to light into him. No sooner was Honey gone from the room than he walked to her and said, "I told you I won't say a word about the job or the conviction. You have my word on that."

It was as if he'd deliberately taken away her steam. But Misty had more than one grievance and she was nowhere near ready to give up her anger. "Why should I believe you?"

His hesitation was plain before he lifted a hand and smoothed her cheek. He was so gentle, so warm, she couldn't get her feet to step out of his reach. "I didn't want to hurt you, Malone. You must know that."

She managed a rude laugh. "You couldn't hurt me."

Her disdainful tone never fazed him. His mouth tilted in a wry, regretful smile. "I think you're wrong about that. I think you've been through a hell of a lot and you're vulnerable right now."

Because he was right, she felt twice as determined to deny it. "Don't get all mushy on me, Morgan. My stomach can't take it."

He lifted his other hand so that he framed her face. "You're so tough, aren't you, Malone? Ready to take on the world all alone. I admire that kind of courage, you know."

"So my insults aren't having the desired effect, huh? You must have a thicker skull than I figured."

Morgan whistled. "You really are ticked, aren't you?"

"Ticked? I'm a whole lot more than *ticked*. What you did was reprehensible."

"What I did," he said, his thumbs gently smoothing her cheeks, "was try to keep you here since I was the one who had run you off."

Misty blinked at him. He felt guilty? Is that what this

was all about? Caught between disbelief and annoyance, she struggled with her fading anger. She really hadn't wanted to go, but neither had she wanted her personal business sallied about for the entire family to hear. Facing them again was going to be incredibly tough. She already knew there'd be dozens of questions, most importantly about the absent father.

As if he'd read her mind, Morgan made a tsking sound. "Come on, Malone, stop beating yourself up. There's no reason to be embarrassed, you know. My brothers won't judge you. If anything, they'll rightfully blame the guy who got you pregnant and then walked away. Like Honey said, we're old-fashioned about things like that. A guy should take responsibility for his actions."

She appreciated the sentiment, if not the interference. "Yeah, well, this guy didn't. And believe me, things are better with him out of the picture."

Morgan laughed. "I'm not disputing that. If he was around, I'd be tempted to beat him into the ground."

"Really?" That wasn't an altogether unpleasant thought. She'd felt the same many times after the way Kent had reacted to her news.

Morgan nodded, then said gruffly, "He hurt you. The least he deserves is a good beating."

Misty was speechless. Morgan had sounded almost like he cared, like he didn't despise her, after all. She said facetiously, "How...sweet of you."

Morgan's look was stern. "Look, Malone. The last thing you'd want is to be married to a loser."

"The last thing I want is to be married, period." Misty stared at his chest and muttered, "I've had my fill of dealing with men, thank you very much."

"I think you've just been dealing with the wrong men."

"Such an obvious truth." She looked at him pointedly.

He let her implication pass without comment, then leaned down until his forehead touched hers. She could feel his warm breath on her lips, his body heat seeping into her, his gentleness flowing over her. She sighed.

"It's also obvious," he said very softly, "that Honey loves you to death. Nothing will change that."

Oh, how could he make her feel like this when she was rightfully angry? "I know my sister loves me, Morgan. But telling her wasn't your decision to make."

"Maybe, but it was the right decision. You were just being stubborn, admit it."

"No, never."

He laughed. "At least this way you're with family, and I'm talking about all of us. We are family now, Malone, whether you like it or not. You don't have a job, you don't even have a place to stay."

Alarmed, she finally managed to dodge his soothing hands and move out of reach. She tried for a credible laugh, but it sounded more like a weak snicker. "Don't be ridiculous."

His eyes narrowed. "It's no good, Malone. I know you too well."

"You hardly know me at all!"

"But we're getting there." Then in a softer tone, "Just where the hell did you think you were going to go?"

The best she could come up with was a shrug.

"That's what I figured. So why not stay here?"

Misty felt like screaming in frustration. "For crying out loud, Morgan, you *told* me to leave!"

He shook his head. "Damn it, that was before."

"Oh, I see. A pregnant woman isn't so risky. You're no

longer worried that I'll seduce your brothers? After all, I thought that was your overriding concern."

Morgan leaned against the wall by the fireplace and crossed his arms over his chest. Misty recognized that stance and the accompanying expression all too well.

"No, my overriding concern was the chemistry between us. And your pregnancy doesn't change that much. You're still too damn sexy, and only a dead man wouldn't be tempted."

She wished she hadn't brought it up. "That's ridiculous."

He very slowly shook his head. "It's true. You have to know how gorgeous you are, how you make a man feel. But I have an idea on how to handle that."

The words, along with the way he'd looked at her as he spoke, made her skin flush and her belly tingle.

She didn't want to be attracted to him! He was arrogant and stubborn, but he was also very dedicated to his family, protective and so incredibly good-looking she imagined women had been chasing him for most of his life.

She mustered up a bored look to hide her reaction to him and asked, "So what's it going to be? Bundle me up in burlap? Paint a big red A on my forehead to ward off the innocent? What?"

"Nothing so drastic as that." He paused for a long moment, as if measuring his words, then he met her gaze and his eyes were hard...determined. "I'll just tell everyone that we're involved, so you're off-limits."

"What?"

He smiled at her reaction. "Believe me, Malone, that'll be enough to keep all other men away, which is what you wanted, right?"

Chapter 5

Morgan waited until Misty looked at him, then snagged her gaze and refused to let her look away. There was a soft blush to her cheeks that about drove him crazy. He had a gut feeling that blush was a combination of anger, embarrassment and excitement.

He understood the anger and wished for some way to spare her the embarrassment. The excitement he relished.

"It's a good plan, Malone."

"For me to pretend to…to be your…" Her stammering ceased, and she stared at him blankly.

"My woman. Yeah, that's the plan." He wanted to walk closer to her, to touch her again, but he didn't dare. She looked skittish enough to jump out of her skin if he even breathed deeply. "Here's how I see it," he said, trying to sound reasonable. "You do need a job, but it won't be easy to find one without employers knowing you were convicted of stealing from the last place you worked. And once they know that, they'll be reluctant to hire you, right?"

"Maybe."

"And you're still on probation?"

She nodded hesitantly. "For a few more months."

"That's what I figured."

She gulped, and her hands fisted. In shame? In regret? He just didn't know, but he hated to see her feel either emotion. He intended to do what he could about her conviction as soon as possible. But for now, he had other things to contend with. "The job I'm offering gives county wages, which aren't great but neither are they piddling. And the fact you worked for a sheriff's office will have to look good on your résumé, and to your probation officer."

She didn't appear quite convinced. She stared at her feet in deep concentration.

A niggling sense of panic seeped in. Misty had been very clear about her feelings on involvement of any kind. The only way Morgan could see around that was to wrangle his way into her life. Keeping her here, hiring her on, showing her she could trust him and rely on him was part of a great plan. He'd just have to make damn sure it worked. "As I said, it's not a hard job—"

Her head shot up and she glared at him. "I'm not afraid of hard work."

"I didn't mean that." Sometimes Morgan wished he was as good at soothing frazzled nerves as his brother Jordan. Jordan could talk the orneriness out of a mule, whisper a baby bird to sleep. He was one hell of a vet, but his talents carried over to people, as well. Morgan, on the other hand, usually relied on rigid control to get his

way. He managed things, taking on other people's problems and resolving them so they didn't have to worry.
Most people appreciated that.

Only it didn't work with Misty. She bucked him at
every turn, refusing to accept what he was best at offering.

"All I meant," he continued, "is that you could easily
do the job. You don't need any special training or skills.
And by accepting it, you can stay here indefinitely, which
rids you of the cost of room and board."

She was already shaking her head before he'd finished.
"I can't just stay here free, Morgan."

He straightened. "Why the hell not? You hadn't been
in a hurry to leave until I prodded you along."

"That's not entirely true." She looked flabbergasted
by his persistence, but he'd be damned if he'd back off.
"Sure, I had hoped to hang out for a week or two more
while I figured out what to do next, but then I'd have
left. I never intended to stay here any longer than that."

He scowled at her. Everything had changed the moment she'd dropped to her knees in front of those bushes.
She *should* stay, which meant he no longer had to fight
himself for wanting her to stick around.

She'd said she wasn't as outgoing as she'd pretended.
He wasn't buying that for a single second. She might not
be such a real flirt, only using that as a way to cover her
worries. But she was brazen and outrageous and beautiful. She was also strong and proud, qualities he'd always
admired in men and women alike. But for right now, he
wished she wasn't quite so proud.

"Honey wants you to stay." That was the only argument he could think of that might convince her. Telling her *he* wanted her to stay didn't seem to be such a

great idea. She'd ask him why, and beyond telling her he wanted to ravish her senseless, he'd have no excuse. Even knowing she was pregnant by another man, now that she'd admitted she wouldn't be marrying that man, hadn't dampened his lust. In fact, he admired her courage, which seemed to add a keen edge to his feelings.

In a mumble totally unlike her usual decisive tone, Misty said, "My sister is new here. This is Sawyer's house and—"

"Honey is new, but permanent. She can invite anyone here that she wants." Misty had a lot to learn about them, first and foremost what *family* meant. When Honey became Sawyer's wife, she became an equal member of that family.

Actually, Morgan thought, smiling a little inside, she'd been an accepted member of their family as soon as they'd all realized Sawyer loved her.

"But Sawyer might not care for—"

"Sawyer will love having you here. But truth is, the house belongs to all of us. My father built it back when he and my mother were married. When she and Gabe's father retired, they decided to move to Florida, and we took over the upkeep of the house. Since grown men need some privacy, Gabe converted the basement into an apartment, and Jordan did the same with the rooms over the garage."

She looked him over as if trying to figure him out. "But you still live in the house."

"Yeah." He could see the questions in her eyes and grinned. "I don't, however, bring women here for overnight, if that's what you're asking. Casey is almost sixteen now, and *he* thinks he's all grown up, but I still wouldn't flaunt lovers in front of him. I remember being sixteen.

Guys that age don't need any help in the raging hormone department."

She looked startled for a moment, then frowned. "Being raised in a house full of males must be ideal for a boy his age."

Morgan shrugged. "We've done the best we could. But I know Casey loves the idea of having Honey around. Just as he'll love the idea of you sticking close, too."

"I don't know, Morgan. I mean, the others…"

"It won't be a problem. The only problem would be if I let you get away."

She still didn't look convinced, then she harked back to what he'd said earlier. "Gabe is your half brother?"

Morgan grinned, suddenly knowing how he'd reassure her. "Come here, Malone. I have a nice long tale to tell you."

She snorted at that, but she did go ahead and seat herself—in a chair so he couldn't sit beside her. He chose the couch, and realized they'd switched positions from earlier. He couldn't remember ever grinning so much, but damn, she amused him with her constant advance and retreat. She was a mix of bravado and prudence, and he realized it was a potent combination, guaranteed to drive any man crazy.

"My father died when I was just a baby." Her eyes widened and he laughed. "I know. Tough to imagine me as a squalling infant, huh?"

"The squalling part I can believe, but the idea of you ever being little boggles the mind. You're just so—" her gaze skimmed his chest, his shoulders, then down to his thighs "—massive now."

Because he had her attention, Morgan settled back and stretched out his long legs, then laced his fingers together on his stomach. Misty swallowed and slowly closed her eyes, so she didn't see his grin. "I was still little when my mom remarried and had Jordan. But things didn't work out and she divorced him."

Her eyes snapped open. Looking more fascinated by the moment, Misty said, "After she had Gabe, you mean?"

"Nope." He laughed outright at her confusion. "My father died in the war. He was my mother's first real love, and she had a hard time getting over him. Then she met Jordan's father. She was lonely and she had two sons to raise. She thought she loved him and married again. But not long after that he lost his job and started to drink. Things went from bad to worse. It wasn't easy for her to work a job, care for three kids and put up with the small-town stigma of being a divorced widow with three sons."

"I don't imagine it would be." Misty picked at a thread on her shorts, then admitted, "Even in this day and age, being a single mother has its problems. Not to mention being a mother of three. She must have a lot of courage."

He said softly, "You have your own share of courage, sweetheart. Deciding to have the baby shows a lot of guts and determination."

She changed the subject, or rather got it back on track. "Do you remember much of Jordan's father?"

"Not really. I was only two when she married him, and I've never heard my mother complain much about those times. All she says is that he gave her Jordan, so she doesn't regret a moment of it. But I've lived here my whole life and lots of people talk, mostly about how strong she was and how she'd gone off men completely after losing one and divorcing another." He watched her closely. "I guess sort of like you claiming you don't want anything to do with men now. A woman gets hurt like that, and it's hard to ever trust again."

He stared at her until she slowly lifted her gaze to meet his.

"I'm not hurt, Morgan. I keep telling you that. I'm just a little wiser, is all. My priorities right now are a job and security for the baby. I don't need a man for that."

But he wasn't just any man, and he damn well wanted her to realize it. He went on with his story as if he hadn't been sidetracked. "You know what I do remember? Sitting with her in the evening and reading books, coloring pictures or sometimes making cookies. She worked damn hard, but she was never too tired to talk with us or to give us hell if she caught us fighting."

Misty gave him a pointed look. "Us, meaning *you* most likely. Somehow I don't see the others getting into as much mischief as you likely did."

Morgan shrugged. "True. I've always been a bit of a hell-raiser—something Mom claims I inherited from my father's side of the family, though I've seen her riled a few times so I'm not buying it. As to the others, Sawyer's always been serious and a bona fide overachiever. There aren't too many men I know who could have cared for a baby and finished up med school without missing a beat. Even with our help, he had his hands full, but he never complained."

Misty sighed. "Sawyer is the exception. Most men would run from that kind of responsibility."

For some reason that observation irritated Morgan beyond all reason. "You haven't known enough good men to make that judgment."

Her laugh was a little sad. "That's true enough, I suppose." Then she smiled at him, a real smile that affected him like a stroke in just the right place. "I think it's wonderful that you're all so close. My father isn't that way at all. If it wasn't for Honey…"

"I know. She's told me a lot about him, and about how close you both are because of it." Morgan wished she'd open up a little with him, but her smile was gone and she now had that closed look on her face that he recognized all too well. He said carefully, "Being that you are so close, aren't you just a bit pleased by the idea of having her nearby?"

She ignored his question to ask one of her own. "So what about Gabe? I gather he wasn't found under a rock?"

"Sometimes I wonder. But my mother is still married to Brett Kasper, and he's Gabe's father."

She studied him closely. "You all look different, but I never realized…. I mean, well, you and Sawyer do have similar looks, except that you're an imposing hulk and he's not."

"Gee thanks."

She waved that away. "You have the same dark hair, and there's something about the shape of your jaws. Stubborn, you know?"

"I've heard that, yes."

"But now Gabe, with that blond hair and those incredible electric blue eyes—"

"Malone," he said in warning.

"And Jordan has brown hair and green eyes and his voice is so—" she shivered "—seductive."

"You're pushing me again, Malone."

Misty started laughing, and Morgan realized she'd been deliberately baiting him. He smiled with her. "Do I need to start worrying about my brothers' virtue again?"

"Ha! None of you have any virtue left, and you know it."

"Not true. Virtue and chastity are not the same thing at all."

She chuckled again, shaking her head in feigned disbelief. Whether she realized it yet or not, she liked him, and she'd like being with him. Morgan spoke his thoughts aloud without even thinking about it. "Hearing you laugh is much nicer than hearing you cry."

Just like that, she stiffened up on him. Color darkened her cheeks, and her eyes narrowed. "If you hadn't been sneaking around this morning, you wouldn't have been subjected to hearing me cry."

Embarrassing her hadn't been his intent. He lowered his voice to a soothing growl. "I wasn't complaining, Malone, except that I don't like seeing you unhappy."

She sat forward, her brows lifted in mock surprise. "Oh, I see. That's why you announced to everyone that I'm pregnant, because you thought it would somehow make me happy?"

"No. But I knew going off on your own wouldn't make you happy, either. If anything, it would've made you more miserable."

"I am *not* miserable."

He raised his hands in surrender. "I stand corrected. And before you run away in a huff, do you want me to tell you the happy ending to my mother's story?"

"With your idea of *happy,* I'm not at all sure."

In a persuasive tone, he suggested, "Try trusting me just a little, Malone."

"No, never."

She was determined not to give an inch, and it frustrated him beyond measure. "You're awfully fond of that particular saying."

"Only when I'm around you."

He gave a drawn-out sigh at her stubbornness, then went on. "It took a long time, and Brett Kasper had to work real hard to get around my mother's resolve after losing one man and divorcing another, but he finally won her over. You never saw a more dedicated man than Brett. When my mom gave him the cold shoulder, he cozied up to us boys instead. Mom didn't stand a chance."

"You mean he manipulated events like you're trying to do with me?"

"Whatever works, Malone." When she growled, he gave her a small smile. His mother had supposedly been as against involvement as Misty, but she'd gotten turned around by the right man. He liked to think the same could be true of Misty. "I'll have you know, they've been married for some time now. You'd have met them at the wedding except Brett had a few health problems and couldn't travel, and my mom wouldn't leave him. He's okay now, nothing serious, but the doc still wants him to rest and Sawyer seconded that, so they missed the wedding. As soon as they can, though, they'll come for a visit."

"She sounds…incredible."

"She's as stubborn as a pit bull when you get her nettled, which luckily doesn't happen often. But for the most part, she's a woman who likes to laugh and isn't afraid to show how much she cares. She's going to love Honey. She's been waiting for one of us to give her a daughter by marriage. I think she's hoping for lots of granddaughters, too." He grinned. "She says I was such a trial, she's ready for something easier—like girls."

"I can believe that!"

Morgan leaned forward and caught her hand. "Do you see the point, Malone? You aren't the first person to make a mistake, but in time, you'll forget your reservations about men."

She started to speak, but he cut her off, already knowing what she would say. Her insistence that she wanted nothing to do with men was almost more than he could take. "So what do you say we join the others?"

She closed her eyes and groaned. "I don't know. The thought of facing your brothers again is enough to make my stomach jumpy."

Morgan considered that, then shrugged. "So don't face them. At least, not for long, and not today. Tell me you'll take the job, then we can go into town and get things set up for you. It's a good excuse and you can have a few hours to get used to the idea before sitting down with them all at dinner tonight. I can show you around town, and all in all, we can waste most of the day."

She bit her lip while scrutinizing him. "You don't have anything else you need to do?"

"Nope. Sunday is my day off. If anything comes up, someone will call, otherwise I'm free."

She still hesitated. "I don't know. It seems pretty fishy to me that this job just suddenly came available."

He still held her hand, and now he smoothed her knuckles with his thumb, marveling at how such a stubborn and defensive woman could feel so soft and delicate. He could just imagine those small hands on his body, and it made him crazy. He cleared his throat. "The job was always there, only I didn't want to hire anyone for it."

"Why?"

"Too many women were applying just to get close to me." She laughed hilariously and he waited, pretending to be affronted. When she finally quieted, he cocked a brow. "It's true. I'm considered something of a catch, only I'd rather do the catching for myself."

"That's right. You said you're looking for a wife."

Her bald statement gave him pause. She didn't seem particularly bothered by the idea. "Not actively," he muttered, "just giving it some thought." The idea of a wife wasn't something he wanted to discuss with Misty, especially since he'd all but forgotten that plan since meeting her. She kept him far too preoccupied for rational contemplation of the future. "And the last thing I need while I'm trying to work is a woman who's set on seducing me."

"I suppose if she breathes, you'd consider it a come-on?"

"Ah, you have no faith in me, Malone. I told you, the effect you have is totally unique. Contrary to your dirty little mind, I don't run around jumping every woman in the area. Hell, I have to live here, and I'm the sheriff—a respected position, you know. I have to set an example." He squeezed her hand. "Unfortunately I can't seem to remember that around you."

His honesty had her pink-cheeked again. He loved how she blushed, how her eyes turned bluer and her lips pressed together in a prim line. She was bold, and she gave as good as she got, but any talk of intimacy flustered her.

Damn, but he wanted to kiss her silly.

"If all that's true, Morgan," she fairly sputtered, "if I really affect you like that, why in the world would you want me around the office?"

"Because it solves a dilemma for both of us." He used his in-command tone, the one that made people sit up and take notice of his official position as sheriff. "You need a job, and I need a worker who won't be jumping my bones, interfering with my schedule and causing a scandal. You've made it pretty clear you plan to resist my bones, so…" He didn't admit his hope that her resistance wouldn't last long. "It's an ideal trade-off."

She considered that for a long moment, then finally nodded. "Okay. I can try the job, I suppose. On one condition."

The restriction in his chest immediately lightened, though he hadn't even noticed how tight it felt until she said she'd stay. "Let's hear it."

"I want you to fix my car. I will not be left here without transportation."

She stared at him defiantly until he nodded. "I can do that, but I have a condition of my own."

"Why am I not surprised?"

He tugged her slightly closer, holding her gaze. "I want your promise that if you decide to leave, you'll tell me."

Her eyes narrowed. "You can't keep me here against my will, Morgan."

"I'm all too aware of that unfortunate fact. And I won't even try. But if you decide to leave I want to know it."

"I wasn't really sneaking this time—"

"Malone."

"Oh, all right. I promise. But fix my car today."

He nodded. "And my other suggestion?"

"What other suggestion?"

He looked at her mouth, so sweetly lush and very kissable, then at her full breasts pressing against the pale yellow camisole—just as kissable. He saw how she tucked her long slender legs beneath her, how smooth her thighs were, lightly tanned. Even her shoulders were sexy, making his tongue nearly stick to the roof of his mouth. "I'll stake a claim for all to see, and that'll keep interested males at bay."

Dark lashes swept down over her eyes to avoid his gaze. She subtly tugged her hand away from his and stood. "I don't know, Morgan."

He got up and stood very close behind her. "We will be involved, Malone, in an arrangement." She stiffened and he caught her shoulders before she could move away. "The type of arrangement is nobody's business but our own. I'm not coercing you into bed."

"As if you could."

"Is that a challenge?"

"No!"

He smiled at her anxious tone. "We'll be partners of a sort. You said you were through with men."

"Completely."

"Well, pretending to be mine ought to take care of other men hitting on you, and I'll have some much needed help at the office."

She shook her head while he stared at her nape, exposed by her upswept hair. He imagined kissing her there, watching her tremble. He couldn't push her now or she'd walk out the door, and she was right, there wasn't a damn thing he could do to stop her.

"That attitude is archaic, Morgan."

His newfound possessive streak was archaic, but he was dealing with it. Barely.

He rubbed her shoulders, relishing the warmth of her skin. His thumbs brushed the back of her neck to the base of her skull, lulling her, soothing her. "Look at it this way, Malone," he added in a whisper, "all your problems will be temporarily solved. And if you think this would be hard on you, just think of what it'll do to me."

"What?"

She sounded intrigued, and he hid his smile. "I want you, so you can figure it out, I'm sure. Given that you seem to take sadistic delight in making me miserable, the idea ought to appeal to you."

The torment would be worthwhile, he thought. He could spend a good deal of his time shoring up their ruse by getting closer to her. He knew, even if *she* didn't, that they'd eventually end up in bed. The chemistry between them was just too strong, no matter how hard she tried to deny it.

And he was tired of even trying.

With a wide, impish smile, she turned to face him. "Well, since you put it that way..." She patted his chest. "Making you miserable does hold a certain attraction."

He caught her hand and flattened it against his body. "So you agree?"

"You've convinced me."

Morgan stared at her, his heart thumping so heavily in his chest he thought for sure she'd felt it. He leaned toward her and saw her eyes widen. "Why don't we seal it with a kiss?"

Misty braced herself for a sensual assault. The memory of his last kiss in the gazebo was still fresh in her mind. But instead of being overwhelmed, she felt Morgan's mouth, warm and dry, brush very lightly over her own. She opened her eyes slowly and looked at him. His dark blue eyes were filled with heat, but also with tenderness, and she almost melted.

For a man of his size, he could sometimes be so remarkably gentle. She gave him a slight smile that he returned.

"Am I interrupting?"

They both jumped apart, she in guilty surprise, Morgan with a curse. He turned to face Jordan, leaning in the doorway with a contented smile.

Jordan tipped his head. "Breakfast is getting cold."

"Did you ever hear of knocking?"

"What fun would that be?"

Morgan turned his back on his brother and faced Misty. His wide shoulders completely blocked her from Jordan's view. Using the edge of his hand, he tipped up her chin, then asked, "What's it to be, Malone? Breakfast with the family, or do you want to go into town?"

"I'm not really hungry." She saw Morgan's understanding and quickly added, "I'm not being a coward. I really just don't have an appetite. I'll go in with you, though. No reason you should do without food, and I have to face them all sooner or later. It might as well be now."

"Get it over and out of the way, huh?"

His frown was back, but she had no idea why. "Something like that."

He glanced at Jordan over his shoulder. "We'll be right there."

Accepting the dismissal, Jordan chuckled and ambled off. The moment he was gone, Morgan framed her face and kissed her again. Before she could say much about it, if indeed she could have gathered her scattered wits to offer a protest, he took her hand and hustled her from the room.

Everyone was in the kitchen when they strolled in, still hand in hand. Like the audience at a Ping-Pong match, all eyes moved in unison to their entwined hands, to their faces, then to each other. Brows climbed high.

Morgan shook his head. "The lot of you remind me of monkeys in a zoo—not you, Honey. The masculine lot."

Honey frowned. "Is everything okay, Misty?"

"Everything is fine." She tried subtly to take her hand from Morgan, but he wasn't letting go, and shaking him off might bring on more speculation. She knew he intended to announce their involvement, but did he mean to do it right now? At this rate, no announcement would be necessary!

There was no way she could continue to stand there and let everyone stare at her with concern. She had to get hold of herself and the situation. She glanced at Sawyer, then Jordan and Gabe. "Morgan insists it'll be all right if I stay here for a little while longer—"

"Absolutely."

"Of course!"

"You know you're welcome here."

Misty smiled at their combined assurance and even felt a little teary over it. "That's very generous of all of you."

Sawyer, with his arm draped over the back of Honey's chair, said, "You're family now, Misty. Family is always welcome for as long as they want to be here. Remember that, okay?"

Honey squeezed him in a tight hug. "Didn't I tell you they were all incredible?"

Gabe laughed. "Nothing incredible about welcoming beautiful women into your home." He eyed their clasped hands and added, "In fact, if you want some privacy, Misty, I have extra room in the basement." He bobbed his eyebrows at her.

Jordan looked mildly affronted. "I was going to offer to share my apartment with her. With Morgan always looming over her, it's for certain she won't get any peace and quiet around here."

Casey, looking like an imp, turned to the side to face

his uncles and said, "Hey, if you guys have extra room, I'll move in with you."

Sawyer reached over and clapped his laughing son on the back. "They'll both strangle you for that, Case." Then to Morgan: "Stop letting them bait you. You look ready to do bodily harm, and then what will Misty think of you?"

"She'll think I'm possessive."

"And you have the right to be?"

"Damn right." Morgan released her hand and put his arm around her, hauling her up so close she felt her ribs protesting. "We've come to an agreement."

She gave Honey a helpless look, but Honey just rolled her eyes, as if she'd expected nothing less from Morgan.

In between bites of pancake, Gabe asked, "Is the baby's father aware of this *agreement,* or is he likely to show up here anytime soon, demanding to know what's going on?"

Jordan scoffed. "If he has any sense, he'll show up. I know I would. 'Course, I wouldn't have let her get away in the first place." Then he eyed Morgan, and added, "Not that it's likely to do him any good if he does come here."

Misty had never felt so overwhelmed in her life. Not only did they seem to accept her pregnancy without hesitation or condemnation, but they also championed her and complimented her and apparently welcomed her involvement with their brother. There were no prying questions.

She was totally speechless.

Morgan was not. "He's out of the picture, and I say good riddance. But if he does ever show his face here, believe me, I'd love to have a minute or two alone with him."

"He doesn't know where I am," Misty pointed out.

Morgan gave her a level look. "Perhaps you could tell him."

"Oh, for heaven's sake." Honey shook her finger at Morgan. "You're always looking for a reason to pound on somebody."

"Sometimes you don't have to look for a reason."

Honey turned to Misty. "Don't pay any attention to his threats. It's like a dog growling, all for show. He's actually very sweet."

A round of masculine grunts disputed Honey's description. Obviously nobody else thought Morgan to be sweet.

"He is!" Honey protested. "At least, once you get to know him better—" She stopped and laughed. "But I guess you know him well enough already, huh?"

Morgan paid them no mind. "I think I do a pretty good job of not pounding on people most of the time, which is why I was elected sheriff." He grinned. "Total control of my temper."

"As I remember it," Jordan said, "it was your ability to take control of everyone else that gave the townsfolk assurance you could handle just about any situation."

"I don't seem to have control over your mouth, brother."

"No." Jordan chuckled. "But then, I've been fighting with you all of my life and lived to tell about it."

"Can we get back to the subject at hand?" Gabe asked. "What's this agreement you two have? I'm dying of curiosity."

Misty held her breath, uncertain as to what Morgan might come up with by way of explanation. None of them seemed particularly surprised that they were supposedly involved, which to her was no less than amazing.

All they'd done since they first met was antagonize each other. Or at least that's all any of his family had seen. If anything, they should have believed that they despised each other. But of course, his brothers knew Morgan better than she did, and maybe grousing and growling was part of his normal temperament.

Heaven knew, he seemed to wear a perpetual frown when he wasn't laughing with her or trying to kiss her. She glanced at him and saw that indeed, his brows were pulled down and his expression was dark. It irritated her. She moved away from his side and gave him a look to let him know that if he spelled out their agreement completely, there'd be hell to pay.

To her surprise, he laughed, then kissed her loudly, right there in front of everyone. "Quit scowling, Malone. You're going to get wrinkles."

"Yeah. Or worse, you'll start looking so forbidding, we'll confuse you with Morgan." Gabe ducked when Morgan reached for him, then laughed as he resettled himself in his seat and went back to work on his pancakes.

"Misty is going to help me out around the station."

Sawyer sat back in his seat. "I thought you didn't want to hire a woman because she might get ideas."

"In this case, it's a moot point. The ideas are mutual." He looked at each brother in turn. "Any objections?"

Jordan lifted his glass of milk and said mildly, "With the two of you competing for the darkest frown, who would dare?"

Casey stood and took his empty plate and glass to the dishwasher. "I think it's great. So can I be excused? I want to go into town today."

Sawyer glanced at his son. "A date?"

"Sorta."

Morgan snagged Casey and roughed up his hair. "You're taking after your uncle, boy."

With a twinkle in his eyes, Casey asked, "Oh, yeah? Which one?"

Gabe held out his arms. "If she's gorgeous, then obviously me!"

Honey reached over and slapped Gabe's arm. "Thanks a lot!"

The moment Misty had dreaded seemed to have come and gone without much notice. She was a tad bemused at that.

"No offense, Honey," Gabe said after blowing her a kiss, "but you're married into the family now so I can't make lecherous jokes about you."

Still holding Casey in a way that made Misty wistful over the easy familiarity, Morgan said, "We can give you a ride. Misty and I are going into town ourselves."

Misty, a little surprised that he'd even suggest it, thought she'd have a slight reprieve from Morgan's isolated attentions until Casey shook his head. "Thanks, but I'd rather ride Windstorm. Jordan said she needs the exercise and I was planning on cutting across the field."

Morgan explained to Misty, "Windstorm is a new horse. Jordan brought her home not too long ago."

"I'm meeting up with friends, then we're all going to the lake for a little while."

"Anybody I know?" Morgan asked.

Casey struggled to hide his grin. "Just some girls, mostly."

Sawyer took one look at his son's innocent expression and groaned. "Lord, he is like Gabe."

At that, Casey laughed. "We're just going to swim. We won't get into any trouble."

Gabe sent mock glares around the room. "I didn't always get into trouble, you know."

"Just often enough," Jordan said with a raised brow, "to keep everyone on their toes."

Sawyer raised a hand. But before he could interject anything into the conversation, Honey stood and took Casey's arm.

"Never mind your overbearing, interfering uncles." She slanted her gaze toward Gabe. "You're *nothing* like them, except for the good looks, of course. Go and have a good time, but be careful, okay?"

Casey lifted her off her feet in a bear hug. "I'll be home by three o'clock."

"That's fine." And once he left the room, she glowered at Sawyer. "Quit comparing him to your disreputable brothers. You'll put ideas in his head."

"Would you all quit talking about me like I was the scourge of the area? Disreputable, indeed."

Honey pointed at Gabe. "And proud of it, from what I can tell."

To Misty's surprise, Sawyer didn't look at all put out by Honey's audacity toward his son. Instead, he grinned. "You're turning into a rather ferocious mother hen."

"Oh, no," Misty said, "she's always been that way. Even when she was just a little girl."

There was a round of laughing comments on that, all teasing Honey until she blushed.

Morgan pulled up a chair next to Misty and propped his head on his fist to stare at her. "You look a little numb, sweetheart. You okay?"

She shook her head, watching Sawyer nuzzle on

Honey, then Jordan and Gabe roughhousing. She didn't know what to think. "The way you all carry on, it amazes me, and now here I am right in the middle of it."

Honey's lips curled into a big smile. She said to the brothers, "It takes some getting used to, since we were from such a small family. And all our meals were very formal. No one gathered in the kitchen just to chat, and there was never this much joking around."

"I wasn't complaining," Misty said, not wanting them to misunderstand. "It's…nice."

"Of course it is." Honey cuddled against Sawyer's side, and he kissed her ear. "You know, you can't get around it, so now I just chime in, too. You'll get used to it."

Misty hadn't planned on being around long enough to get used to them. But now she was having fun. It had been a while since she'd felt the honest urge to laugh.

Morgan nudged her. "You want some pancakes or do you still want to head straight to town?"

Misty thought about it. Most of her anxiety was gone, and her stomach was starting to rumble. There was still a platter of lightly browned pancakes sitting in the middle of the table, with warmed syrup and soft butter beside it.

She grinned at Morgan, feeling more at ease than she had in ages. "Let's eat."

Chapter 6

It was almost an hour before they finally left the house. Though she'd never have imagined it, she'd enjoyed breakfast immensely. No one said too much about her pregnancy other than to try to force an extra pancake on her along with a tall glass of milk. And no one pressured her for information on the father of the baby. They seemed to simply accept that she was there, unmarried, and that they wanted her to stay.

True to his word, Morgan played the part of an interested party, holding her arm, opening the door for her. But then she thought about how all the brothers did the same, for both her and Honey, and she realized Morgan likely wasn't playing at all. He was flat-out mannerly, no way around it, and she had to admit she rather liked it.

"Are you sure I don't need to change clothes?" She wore her camisole and cut-offs, but Morgan had insisted she looked fine. The way he'd stared at her, though, giving her such a slow, thorough perusal, made her uncertain. She wore what most women wore on such hot days, but they were going to his office, and she'd likely meet a few townspeople.

"You look sexy as sin, which makes me nuts wanting to take you, but I can handle it. When you actually work tomorrow, you'll need to wear something more... conservative. Maybe jeans and a plain blouse or something. And definitely a bra. I won't get any work done if I know you're not wearing a bra."

Morgan took three more steps before he finally realized she'd stopped. He turned to face her, hands on his hips in an arrogant pose. He lifted one brow. "What's the problem now, Malone?"

As if he truly didn't know. Amazing. Even more amazing was that she felt equal parts furious and aroused. After all the condemnation she'd received from men of late, his open admiration was a balm, whether she admitted to liking it or not.

It was unnerving that of all the men she'd ever known, this particular man could make her feel such depths of excitement at such a rotten time. She didn't want to want him. She didn't want to want any man, but definitely not one who was so bold and...potent. There'd be no way to control Morgan Hudson, or to control her own erratic heartbeat in his presence.

"If this is going to work," she said, carefully enunciating each word, hoping to hide her trembling, "you have to stop being so...outspoken."

"Getting to you, is it?"

He blocked the sun with his big body, leaving long shadows to dance around her. "Annoying me, actually."

His slow smile was provoking. He strolled over to

stand directly in front of her. "Is that why you're all flushed?" he asked. His gaze dropped to her chest and he groaned. Misty looked down, and she wasn't surprised to see that her nipples were pressed hard against the soft material of her camisole. She ached all over, and she couldn't stop her body from reacting.

Desperate, she turned to leave, and Morgan gently clasped her shoulders, halting her. They stood silent, motionless, for several heartbeats and then he sighed. "Give me a break here, Malone. I'm doing my best."

His best to seduce her? His best was actually pretty darn good. She turned slowly to face him and stared him in the eye, refusing to let him intimidate her.

Morgan hesitated, then ran a hand over his face in frustration. He ended with a rough laugh, taking her off guard. "You want the truth?"

"No!"

"I'm not used to women pushing me away."

"Oh, please." But she could easily believe it. Morgan had an incredible body, sensual eyes and a devastating smile that he generally hid behind a frown. She imagined any woman he looked at was more than willing to look back—and more.

"I've never known such a contrary woman," he muttered. "You want me, but you keep saying no. You make me crazy, Malone."

He looked so endearing, as if he were baring his soul, she had to fight to keep from smiling at him. She huffed instead. "You were crazy long before I stepped into the picture."

"Nope. I was in control, one hundred percent. Now I'm walking around with a semierection."

She gave a groan of frustration. "That's exactly what

I'm talking about, Morgan. Your…masculine discomfort is of no concern to me."

"Well, it should be since you're the cause." She would have groaned again, but Morgan added, almost to himself, "You've shot all my well-laid plans to hell."

Misty sputtered, both hurt and insulted. It was the hurt that made her sarcastic, because she knew exactly what plans he referred to. "Please, don't let me get in your way! I'll even help in the wife hunt if you want." He looked surprised, then disgruntled.

"No." He leaned over her. "I don't need your help."

"Why not? Tell me what qualities you're looking for and I'll keep my eyes open."

Morgan leaned closer, then lifted her chin with the edge of his fist. "Right now, I don't want a wife. I want you. And if you were honest, you'd admit you want me, too."

She met his gaze just as intently, determined to make him understand before she broke down and proved him right. "Sorry, Morgan, but I've sworn off men."

His hand opened, cradling her face. "That's the hell of it, Malone. You're not giving me a chance." His gaze touched on her everywhere—her eyes, her lips, her breasts. His thumb moved softly over her bottom lip. "It could be perfect, sweetheart. I'd make sure of it."

Misty wondered if she looked in the dictionary for the word *temptation* if it would feature a picture of Morgan Hudson. She could feel herself shaking inside, could feel her nerve endings all coming alive at his sensual promise—a promise she felt sure he could keep. The man was as seductive and searing as the bold stroke of a warm hand.

Wanting to give him equal honesty, she wrapped her

hand around his wrist and shared a melancholy smile. "I have no doubt you…know what you're doing, Morgan. But I already feel a little used. I don't relish feeling that way again."

His fingers slid over her head to the back of her neck, cupping her warmly. "Oh, babe." His fingers caressed, kindled. His sigh was warm, his words soft. "I would never hurt you."

When she started to speak, he hushed her. "No, don't give me all your arguments. You'll make me morose."

She laughed at that. Morgan was so brutally honest, so different from the other men she knew. He didn't try to whitewash what he wanted, which was sex. He made it clear he intended to find a wife soon and that she didn't fit the role—a fact she knew only too well. He kept her aware of what he thought about things, and while she did consider him far too forward and pushy, it was nice not to have to guess about ulterior motives and hidden agendas.

Compared to Kent, a man who'd sworn undying love then dropped her the moment he found out she was pregnant, Morgan's honesty was refreshing. It was still alarming, but she'd trust it over insincere promises any day.

He released her, then rubbed the back of his neck. "You should know I'm not going to quit trying. I figure sooner or later I'll wear you down and you'll admit you want me."

"Why don't you try holding your breath?"

He wagged a finger at her. "Play nice, Malone."

"But you're the one who told me I could make you miserable, right? That's why I agreed to this farce in the first place."

She grinned at him, which made him laugh and shake his head. "Witch."

Misty wasn't offended. Somehow he'd made the name sound like an endearment.

He took her hand and started them on the way again. "Speaking of this farce... I should also point out that the job has nothing to do with your continued rejection." He glanced at her. "I'm not going to fire you if you keep saying no. I won't like it, and I'll do my damnedest to change your mind, but the job is yours as long as you're fulfilling it."

"No blackmail, huh?"

"No. I just wanted to make sure we understood each other."

For some reason, she'd never once doubted that. The way Morgan interacted with his family, treating Casey almost like a son, Honey like a sister, she knew he was too honorable to try forcing her hand. And he'd already proven that night in the gazebo that all it took was a soft, simple no to make him back off. She wasn't afraid of him. She was only afraid of herself when she was with him.

She was still pondering that when Morgan opened the garage door and she got a good look at the official car he expected her to ride in.

She backed up two steps. Granted it wasn't a typical law enforcement vehicle, but it had the lights on the roof and the word Sheriff emblazoned on the side in yellow and blue. Memories flooded back, and she winced.

To stall, she asked Morgan, "What type of sheriff are you?"

He looked up, saw her expression, then glanced at the shiny black four-wheel-drive Bronco. "Just a regular run-of-the-mill county sheriff, why? You don't like my transportation?" He wore a devilish grin.

"I've never seen anything like it." She walked around

the truck, looking at it from all angles. "I thought offi-
cials drove sedans, not sport utility vehicles."

"It's for off-road driving, but there's no sport to it.
There're a lot of hills in these parts. And though we don't
have much in the way of big crime, just about anything
that happens involves those damn hills. Last fall, a little
girl got lost and we spent two days on foot looking for
her. A four-wheel-drive would have made all the difference on some of the off-road searches. After that, the
townsfolk got together and donated the Bronco."

Misty felt a little sick as she asked, "The child?"

"I found her curled up real tight under an outcropping
of rock." His hands curled into fists and his jaw locked.
"Her father had given up looking and was back at the
station, drinking coffee and letting people dote on him."

He sounded thoroughly disgusted, not that Misty
blamed him.

"Sawyer had rounded up about fifty people and we'd
been at it all day and through the night. When I found
her late the following afternoon, she was terrified, cold
and crying for her daddy."

Misty put her hand on his arm, aware of the bunched
muscles and his tension. Knowing Morgan as well as she
did now, she could imagine how difficult that would have
been for him, trying to console a child, hurting when that
wasn't possible. "Her father should have been with you."

"He was a damn fool, visiting these parts and camping
out when he didn't have a clue as to what he was doing.
The weather was too cold for it and he didn't exactly pick
the best spot to pitch his tent. The little girl wandered off
because he wasn't watching her close enough."

"But she was all right?"

"Other than being a little dehydrated and scared silly,

she did great. Cutest little thing you'd ever seen. About five years old." His eyes met hers, diamond bright, and he added, "I know if it had been my kid, I wouldn't have quit looking until I found her."

"I think," Misty said, studying his intent expression, "you wouldn't have let her out of your sight in the first place."

Morgan kissed her nose. "No, I wouldn't have."

Misty wondered if he'd slept at all during those two days, and seriously doubted that he had. She gave him a tremulous smile. The man was proving to be entirely too easy to like.

Morgan stared at her mouth, groaned, then pulled the door of the Bronco open. "Let's go, Malone, before I forget my good intentions."

She clasped a hand to her heart. "You have good intentions? Toward me? I had no idea."

Suddenly his eyes narrowed. "Why are you stalling? What's up?"

"Don't be ridiculous." She eyed the truck again, then with a distinct feeling of dread, hefted herself into the seat. Morgan gave her a long look before he slammed the door.

When he climbed in on his own side, he said, "You wanna tell me about it?"

"I have no idea what you're talking about." She stared with feigned fascination at the control panel, the radio. Behind her was a sturdy wire-mesh screen separating the cargo area from the front seat—for prisoners, she knew. Unable to help herself, she shuddered.

Morgan started the engine, then reached for her hand. "When you were arrested, they cuffed you?"

"I don't want to talk about that." She tried to pull away,

but he held her hand tight and rubbed his thumb over her knuckles. He did that a lot, grabbing hold of her and not letting her go. This time she appreciated the touch. She curled her fingers around his.

"I imagine you were," he said, speaking about the arrest in a matter-of-fact way. "It's pretty much policy these days, for safety reasons."

She chewed her lip, then slowly closed her eyes, giving up. "It was the most degrading moment of my entire life. It was bad enough when Mr. Collins accused me of stealing the money, and I couldn't believe it when he actually called the cops."

"Mr. Collins?"

"My boss at Vision Videos. I kept thinking somehow things would get straightened out, that they'd realize there'd been a mistake."

"They didn't find the money on you?"

"No, because I didn't have it." She glared at him, then asked, "You think I'm guilty, don't you?"

Morgan was silent as they pulled onto the main road. He drove with one hand, still holding on to her with the other. Finally he muttered, "To be honest, I have serious doubts."

"Really?"

He glanced at her. "But if you did do it, I'd understand, okay?"

There was that damn honesty again; he wasn't convinced of her innocence, but he'd allow for the possibility. She almost laughed. For a man who wanted to get intimate with a woman, he wasn't going about it in the usual way—with lies and deceptions that would soften her up. "Even the lawyer I hired didn't believe me, not really."

"The evidence must have been pretty strong."

"Yeah, the fact that I'm a pregnant, supposedly desperate female was proof positive that I'd steal from a man I'd worked with for two years, even though I'd never been in trouble before in my life."

"Your boss knew you were pregnant?"

"Morning sickness kind of gives you away. That and the fact that I suddenly had more nights free." Misty was only vaguely aware of the beautiful scenery as they drove down the long road. The sun was bright, the day hot, but the air-conditioning in the truck had her feeling chilly.

Or maybe it was the dredging of memories that made her feel so cold inside. "I wasn't dating Kent anymore, and I knew that with the baby coming I needed to save up more money, so I'd offered to work more overtime." She slanted Morgan a look. "That made me seem guilty, too, by the way. My boss said small amounts of money had been missing several nights in a row, which was the first I'd heard of it, but he claimed that was why he'd come in unexpectedly to check on me that day, and found the money missing."

"When exactly did this all take place?"

She told him the exact day she'd been arrested.

Morgan surprised her by lifting her hand to his mouth and then turning it to gently kiss her palm. "I wasn't thinking. I didn't mean to make you uncomfortable riding with me."

Misty held her breath as his mouth moved against the sensitive skin of her palm. That, added to the gentle way he had of speaking to her sometimes, left her feeling vaguely empty and jumpy inside.

She swallowed hard. "After everything I've been through, it's silly to let a little ride get to me. But you just can't imagine what it was like. There were tons of people gathered outside the video store when I was arrested. They led me out in handcuffs and I just wanted to die. I thought I'd be glad to get in the car, where people couldn't see me, but instead, it seemed we hit every red light and folks in the other cars would stare."

Morgan slowed for a deer that ran across the road, distracting Misty for the moment. He spoke quietly, holding her hand on his thigh. "Sweetheart, people are always going to stare at you, no matter what, because you're beautiful. That's something you just ought to get used to."

Laughing helped to wash away the melancholy. "You may find this hard to believe, Morgan, but no one has ever carried on so much about my looks. Honey was the one the guys were always after. Men prefer blondes, you know."

"Sawyer certainly does." He turned to give her a lazy grin. "But I'm not Sawyer."

"You've got me there."

"You know what I prefer?"

She started whistling, which only made him chuckle. "I prefer dark-haired women with long, sexy legs and incredible…"

"Morgan—" she warned.

"—smiles." He laughed at her expression. "Such a dirty mind you have, Malone. What did you think I was going to say?"

She reached over and smacked him for that, then couldn't help laughing again. "I figure I'm only slightly better than average-looking—and I'm giving you the slightly better based on all this praise you've heaped on me lately."

He didn't look at her, just made a sound of disagreement. "You can ask any man and he'll tell you the same.

Hell, just hearing you talk makes me hard, even when I don't like what we're talking about."

Of course she looked, then immediately jerked her gaze away. "If you don't stop being so shameless—" She sighed, unable to think of a threat that might carry any impact. It annoyed her that he'd once again gotten her to stare at him in a totally inappropriate way.

"You'll what? No, don't answer that. And for your information, I can't seem to help it."

She tugged her hand free, tucking it close so he couldn't retrieve it. "Keep your lips to yourself. That might be good for starters."

"Malone, I swear, one of these days you're going to take back those words."

She laughed again. "You're incorrigible."

"And a distraction?"

She blinked, realizing that he had, indeed, distracted her. She nodded, giving him his due, but felt it necessary to point out the obvious. "My ride then was a little different. I was in the back, handcuffed, and the officers were in uniform—and armed."

Morgan grinned at her. "The county insists the Bronco is partly for my personal use, sort of a perk, so you're not the first woman to be seen in it."

"Did I ask for that information?"

"I just wanted you to know that if anyone stares this time, it'll be with a different kind of curiosity. And I do wear a uniform when I'm on duty, which I'm not right now. As to being armed, it's a habit." He made that statement, then shrugged.

"What do you mean?" Misty turned slightly in her seat to face him. "You carry a gun around with you?"

"All the time."

Once again she looked him over, then cocked an eyebrow. "Must be a good hiding place."

"Want to search me, Malone?"

Yes, but she wouldn't tell him that. "I'm waiting."

"You're no fun at all, but we'll work on that." He leaned down and lifted the hem of his jeans. "Ankle strap. I wear a belt holster when I'm on duty."

She'd seen him in uniform, and the sight had been impressive indeed. He looked nothing like Andy Griffith, that was for sure. When Morgan got decked out in his official clothes, he looked like a female fantasy on the loose. His shirt fit his broad shoulders to perfection, and his slacks emphasized his long, strong legs. The holster around his waist gave an added touch of danger to his dark good looks.

She imagined the females of Buckhorn County would continue to elect him sheriff just to get to see him in uniform each day.

Not that he didn't look great today in his jeans and soft T-shirt.

Misty eyed the small handgun in a leather holster. It was attached to an ankle cuff with a Velcro strap. Despite herself, she was fascinated. "Do the good citizens of Buckhorn know about that gun?"

"You kidding? They insist on me holding up my image. Why, if they thought I wasn't armed, they'd be outraged. They each consider me their own personal sheriff, you know."

"Especially the women?" *Ouch.* She hadn't meant to say that.

Morgan gave her a knowing look, but thankfully didn't tease her. "Men and women alike, actually. Half my job is spent letting them bend my ear and reassuring them that the corruption of outside communities hasn't infiltrated yet."

"If corruption hasn't infiltrated, then why do they want you to carry a gun?"

He shrugged a massive shoulder. "I told you. Image." Almost as an afterthought, he added, "And I have had occasion to use it now and then."

He had her undivided attention. "You're kidding?"

"Nope. Being that we're a small town, a few of the more disreputable sorts thought it'd be the ideal hideout. To date, I've apprehended an escaped convict, caught a man wanted for robbery, and another for kidnapping."

Her eyes were wide. "Did you…shoot anyone?"

His hands tightened on the wheel. "The kidnapper, in the knee. The son of a bitch held a gun to a woman. He's lucky that's all I did to him."

Misty fell back in her seat, amazed. "I never would have imagined." Morgan seemed dangerous in many ways, and he certainly held his own when it came to taking charge of any situation. But she'd never imagined him being involved in a possibly lethal situation. He could have been killed! "This is incredible."

Again, he shrugged.

"What would the good citizens think if they knew you were consorting with a known criminal?"

"You?"

"Do you know any others?"

"Sure." He didn't allow her to question that. He gave her a speculative look, then suggested, "You could get your name cleared, you know."

"I don't see how that's possible." She bit her lip. "Once something is on your permanent record…"

"I could get it taken care of. It's a lot of legal jumble,

and I can explain it later, but if you really didn't take the money…"

Misty felt her heart beating faster. "I didn't take the money." She waited for his reaction, her breath held. She wanted Morgan to believe her. It had suddenly become important to her, and not just because he wanted to help.

Seconds ticked by, and then he nodded. "I'll see what I can do."

He said nothing else, and that, she supposed, was that.

They reached the center of town, which was really no more than a narrow street full of buildings. Misty hadn't paid much attention to it when she'd been at the hall for Honey's wedding. She'd still been too nervous about Morgan and too excited for her sister. But now she had the chance to take it all in, and she wasn't going to miss a single thing.

There were two grocery stores at opposite ends of the street, a clothing store that looked as if it had been there for over a hundred years, a diner and a hairdresser, a pharmacy… She eyed the pharmacy as they drove past, wondering how awkward it might be to get her prenatal vitamin prescription filled; she'd run out of them yesterday.

One thing she didn't see was a bus station, and she wondered just where the nearest one was. After her comment earlier that she'd take a bus home, she felt rather foolish to realize there wasn't a bus around. You'd think one of the brothers could have mentioned that fact to her.

There were people sitting outside their shops, others lounging against the wall or standing close chatting. There were even some rocking chairs sitting under canopied overhangs, to invite loiterers.

"This is like going back in time," she murmured as

they drove to the end of the street then turned right onto a narrower side street. There were a few houses, a farm with some cattle moving around, and a funeral parlor, which was easily the biggest, most ornate structure she'd seen so far. Then Morgan pulled into the circular drive of a building that looked like an old farmhouse. It was two stories with a grand wraparound porch, white columns in the front and black shutters at every window.

"Why are we stopping here?"

"This is my office, darlin'." He chuckled at her as he drove right up close to the front door and stopped. The double doors wore a professional sign that read: Enter at Right. Evidently that didn't apply to the sheriff.

Morgan parked and turned off the engine. "The station used to be by the county courthouse, farther into town, but it was too small so years ago, long before I was elected, they moved it here. Makes for a bit of whimsy doesn't it?"

Morgan climbed out, and at that moment two men came around from the side of the house to greet him. "Hey there, Morgan! Didn't expect to see you today. Anything wrong?"

Morgan frowned, as if surprised to see them. "Nope, no problems. I was just showing the lady around." He opened Misty's door and handed her out of the vehicle. Close to her ear, he said, "Two of the biggest gossips around. They weren't supposed to be here today, but that never stopped them before. And since they're here, we might as well take advantage of it."

Misty leaned away to look at him. "I don't understand."

"Anything they see makes the rounds of Buckhorn

faster than light. This'll be a good place to start letting folks know you're off-limits."

Misty froze just as her feet touched the ground. Surely, Morgan didn't mean to do anything in front of these nice old men! But then she met his hot gaze and knew that was exactly what he intended.

She started to shake her head but he was already nodding. And darned if he wasn't smiling again.

Chapter 7

All it took, Morgan thought as he watched Misty's eyes darken and her lips part, was a nice long look from him. She could deny it all she wanted, but her hunger was almost as bad as his own. When he felt it, she felt it, and right now was proof positive.

Well aware of Howard and Jesse closing in behind him, their curiosity caught, he leaned down and kissed her. It was a simple soft touch. He brushed his mouth over hers, once, twice. She drew a small shuddering breath, and her eyes slowly drifted shut, but she didn't stop him. No, she'd raise hell with him after, he had no doubt of that, but for now, she was as warm and needy as he. Her small hand fisted in his shirt, trying to drag him closer, proved it.

"Misty?" He whispered her name, watching the way her eyelashes fluttered.

"Hmm?"

His own smile took him by surprise. All his life people had teased him about his ferocious frowns, but something about Misty made him feel lighthearted, joyful deep inside. He touched the tip of her nose. "Sweetheart, we have an audience, or I'd sure do better than one measly peck, I promise."

Her eyes flew open, then widened. She peeked around his shoulder cautiously, saw the two men, and her own version of a fierce frown appeared. Her fisted hand released his shirt, and she thumped him in the chest. "Of all the—"

Morgan grabbed her hand, threw one arm around her shoulders and turned, taking her with him to face Howard and Jesse. "I thought I told you two not to work on the weekend."

"Nothing better to do today. We figured we'd get it done and out of the way."

Morgan gave Jesse a good frown to show him what he thought of that, but he knew better than to start debating with him now. "So how's the work going?"

Jesse nodded quickly, a habit he had when he was nervous, and being around women always made him nervous, especially the really pretty ones. "It's getting there. I'll have the lot of it cleared out by midweek." Though he spoke to Morgan, his eyes didn't leave Misty's face.

Howard scratched his chin, watching Misty with acute interest. "It's looking real good."

Amused by their preoccupation, Morgan nudged Misty slightly forward and said, "This is Honey's sister, Misty Malone. She's here for an extended visit and she'll be helping out around the station. Misty, this is Jesse and Howard."

Both men did a double take at that announcement,

but Morgan ignored their reactions, knowing why they looked so shocked. They'd obviously jumped to the wrong conclusion. He hid his grin and decided to explain things to them later.

Jesse tipped a nonexistent hat and muttered, "Nice to meet you."

Howard stuck out his hand, realized it was covered with dirt and pulled it back before Misty could accept it. With an apologetic shrug, he explained, "I've been digging out the weeds. Messy work, that. Nice to meet you, Miss Malone."

Misty smiled. "Call me Misty, please. What exactly are you doing back there?"

It was Jesse who answered. "There's been a ton of weeds growing in the gully out back for as long as the sheriff's been stationed here. It draws mosquitoes and gnats and it's just plain ugly. Morgan wants us to clear them out and plant a line of bushes instead. We don't have the bushes in yet, but we will soon."

"I love outdoor work." Misty stepped away from Morgan and headed to the side of the house to check their progress. "I used to work with my father's gardeners when I was younger. It's hot work, especially on a day like today. But I always preferred that to being cooped up inside."

Morgan could just picture her as a little girl, hanging out with the hired help because her daddy ignored her and she had nothing better to do. It made his stomach cramp.

Howard nodded. "Know what you mean. Fresh air is good for you. I used to farm in my younger days. There's nothing like it."

She went around the corner of the house, Howard and

men time and again to bring a cooler with drinks, they never remembered to do it.

Misty was more restrained, using the edge of her shorts to clean the top of the can then opening it cautiously and sipping. It was so hot and humid outside that the little wisps of her hair escaping her topknot had begun to curl around her face.

She squinted against the sun, wrinkling her small nose, and smiled at him. "The bushes will look great once they're in. It'll make the yard looked bigger, too, without the tall weeds breaking up the length."

Morgan nodded, content just to look at her and drink his soda and enjoy the feel of the sunshine.

He loved the old farmhouse—and had since the moment he'd been elected and moved his things into the desk. He forced his gaze away from her and surveyed the back porch. "She's a grand old lady, isn't she?"

"She's beautiful." Misty, too, looked at the porch with the turned rails and ornate trim. "You don't see that kind of detail very often anymore."

"It's solid." Morgan finished off his cola, then crushed the can in his fist. "This house is partly what inspired me to build my own home. I was forever doing improvements to the station and finally decided I needed my own place to work on. But even with my house almost complete, I still love it here."

"Somehow, I think it suits you. Especially because you're in charge."

"It does," he agreed, ignoring her teasing tone. "You want to see inside where you'll be working?"

"Sure." She turned to the men and smiled. "Howard, Jesse, it was nice meeting you."

They each nodded, ridiculous smiles on their faces.

Morgan could only shake his head in wonder. Was no
man immune? As they walked through the back door, he
saw her smile and raised a brow in question.

"They're very sweet."

He gave her an incredulous look. "Uh-huh. You go
right on wearing those rose-colored glasses, sweetheart."

She gasped at him in disapproval. "You're such a
cynic. They're very nice men who are working hard for
you. I'd think you'd appreciate that a little."

Morgan led her into his office, which had once been
the dining room. It had a large white stone fireplace, now
filled with lush ferns instead of burning logs. He'd had
the arched doorway framed and fitted so he could close
the door for privacy. He'd never needed or wanted that
privacy more than now.

He propped his shoulders against the mantel. "Jesse
was picked up for fighting two weekends ago. He broke
two pool sticks and several lights after a man accused
him of cheating at a game. Jesse wouldn't cheat, but he
does have a terrible temper."

Misty stared at him in blank surprise.

"Now Howard, he's cooler than that. You won't catch
him causing a brawl."

"You're dying to tell me, so spit it out." She mimicked
his stance, leaning against the opposite wall.

Grinning, Morgan said, "He slipped into the theater
without paying—five times in a row. He loves the movies, but says the prices have gotten too high. Arnold kept
kicking him out and Howard kept creeping back in. No
one would have known, but during the last movie, he
tried stealing a bite of popcorn from the woman sitting
next to him."

"And she complained over that?"

Morgan winked at her. "The woman was Marsha Werner, and he'd recently broken off a relationship with her and was, I imagine, trying to worm his way back into her good graces. She wasn't impressed, so she raised a ruckus and I finally had to arrest him. But it was Marsha who came and bailed him out, so who knows what's happening there?"

Misty tried to stifle a smile. "It's a little hard to imagine him in a relationship."

"That's only because you haven't met Marsha. Things soured between them when she wanted to get married, but they were a good couple, like the best grandma and grandpa you'd ever met." Morgan watched her smile widen and added, "Marsha's real fond of the movies, too, but as she continually explains to me in rather loud tones, she's an upstanding citizen and she pays for her entertainment."

Misty lost control of her twitching smile and laughed out loud. Morgan watched her, seeing the way the heat and humidity outside had made her shirt stick to her breasts. She'd smell all warm and womanly now if he could just get close enough to her to nuzzle her soft skin.

"So what kind of sentence did each of them get?"

He held her gaze and murmured, "Community work. That's why they're fixing the yard. I bought the bushes and they agreed to do the work. In addition, of course, Jesse had to promise to stay out of the pool hall for a month, and Howard had to pay for the movies he'd seen."

"Ah. They considered that a terrible punishment?"

"Not the yard work, but the other, yeah. With any luck, it'll make an impression this time. But I hate to see them in any real trouble. They're both pushing seventy, and even though they get around well enough to get into mischief, they don't mean any real harm. I think they're just lonely and a little bored, more than anything else."

She twisted her mouth in a near grimace, then asked, "When you arrested them…"

"No, I didn't handcuff them," he answered gently, able to read her train of thought. It hurt him to see her so hesitant, to know that her own memories ate at her. He'd fix things for her one way or another, he vowed. "I didn't stick them in back of the Bronco, either. They both rode up front with me. That way, I could give them a stern talking-to during the ride. They hate that."

Misty smiled at him for a nearly endless moment, then turned up her can of soda and finished it off. She set the can on his desk. "I'm impressed, Morgan."

"With what?"

"Your compassion. And the fact that you obviously have a soft side, which you hide pretty well, by the way."

He wasn't at all sure he wanted her noticing his soft side, not that he had one, anyway. He frowned at the mere thought.

Misty gave a loud sigh. "Now what are you scowling about? I insult you and you laugh, I compliment you and you start glowering at me."

Morgan didn't move. She had an impish look about her that intrigued him. "Come closer and I'll tell you why I'm frowning."

"Oh, no, you don't."

"Afraid of me, Malone?"

She made a rude sound, refusing to be drawn in by his obvious challenge. "Not likely. You're as big as an ox and built like a ton of bricks, but you don't beat up on women."

He made his own rude sound. "That's not what I

meant, and you know it." He lowered his voice to a suggestive rumble. "You're afraid if you get too close, you won't want to move away again. But this is my office and I don't do hanky-panky here. At least, not any serious hanky-panky. So you're safe enough."

"And what constitutes the serious stuff?"

He looked at her breasts and felt his heartbeat accelerate. "Anything below the waist?"

She swallowed and he could see the thrumming pulse in her throat. "Howard and Jesse are right outside."

"Not for much longer. I only let them work for a few hours a day, mostly in the morning because the afternoon heat is too much for them."

"Then why have them doing that job at all?"

She was bound and determined to distract him, so Morgan let her. The last thing he wanted was for her to be wary of him. "Their pride is important to them, and to me. Already they've told anyone who'd listen that I've given them such a hard, impossible job, then they come here and have a great time futzing around, proving that they can do it. In fact, they complain about the short days I insist on, because Jesse used to be in construction and Howard was a farmer. They say they're used to the heat, but—" He realized he was rambling and ground to a halt.

"You're pretty wonderful sometimes, Sheriff, you know that?"

He unfolded his arms, letting them hang at his sides. In a rough whisper, he said again, "Come here."

She took one step toward him, then halted. "This is crazy."

Morgan nodded in agreement. Crazy didn't even begin to describe the way she made him feel.

She looked undecided and he held his breath, but she

turned away. She pretended an interest in the office. Her voice shook when she started talking again. "This is your desk?"

She picked up a framed school picture of Casey and studied it.

"You know it is. My office is the biggest room. The cells are in the basement, though they seldom get used—and yes, I'll take you on a tour in a bit. The kitchen has been rearranged into a lobby of sorts, and there's always coffee there for anyone who wants it. The family room faces the kitchen through open doorways across the hall, and that'll be where you work. There's a lot of office equipment in there. I'll have my deputy, Nate Brewer, show you where he keeps things and how to use the file system. The upstairs has been turned into conference rooms for different community events."

He watched her inch closer to him to look at a plaque hanging on the wall. Not wanting to scare her off now that she was almost within reach, he said, "That's my mission statement."

"Mission statement?"

"My intent for holding office as sheriff. The community got to read it prior to the election." He was thankful she didn't read the whole thing. His patience was about run out and he just wanted to taste her.

"You had the plaque made?"

"Nope. The advisory board did." He saw her start to ask and said, "They're a group of citizens that bring concerns to me. Sort of a community awareness system."

She leaned closer to the plaque. "It says here that you founded the advisory board during your first term in office."

He shook his head. "I was the one who suggested

a voice in the community, so they'd all feel more involved in decisions. But they're the ones who organized the board and set up the structure for it. Now they have these big elections to decide who gets to serve in the various advisory board positions."

She moved closer still, examining a trophy on the mantel beside him. Morgan tried to block it with his shoulders, but she inched around him until she could see it clearly. "What's this for?"

Feeling uncomfortable with her inquisition, Morgan cleared his throat. "That was given to me by the student council at the high school."

"It says, outstanding community leadership."

"I know what it says, Malone." He glared, but she glared right back, and he gave up with a sigh. "I started a program where the students can interact with the elders in the community, helping out with chores and such. I'd hoped to give the kids some direction and the elders some company, that's all. But now participation is recognized by the governor for qualifications to state scholarships."

She looked at him. "That's remarkable."

Morgan shifted to face her, determined to satisfy her curiosity so he could get her mind on more pleasurable topics. "Naw. The students took it a lot further than I did, making it a hell of a program. That's why I thought it deserved to be brought to the governor's notice."

She glanced at the writing on the base of the trophy. "It says here that you help supply scholarship funds, as well."

Morgan rubbed his ear and bit back a curse. "Yeah, well, that's just something I sort of thought would help...."

Misty reached up and took his hand, enfolding it in both of her own. Her blue eyes were filled with amusement and something else. He was almost afraid to figure out what. "Don't be modest, now, Sheriff."

"I'm not!"

"And don't be embarrassed, either."

He gave her his blackest scowl. "That's just plain fool-ish. Of course I'm not embarrassed. No reason to be. It's all just part and parcel of my job."

Misty shook her head as if scolding him, and it ran-kled. "I can't quite figure you out, Morgan."

Slowly, so she wouldn't bolt, he slipped his hand free and trailed his fingers up her bare arm to the back of her neck. He'd always loved the feel of women, the smooth-ness compared to a man's rough angles. But for whatever reason, he loved the feel of Misty more.

Just touching her arm made his heart race, his groin throb. He could only imagine how it would be once he had her naked beneath him, able to touch and taste and investigate every small part of her. He shook with the thought.

Goose bumps appeared where he'd touched her, and she gave a small shiver. "I'm as clear as glass, sweet-heart." He was aware of how husky his voice had gone, but damn, he felt like he was burning up. Gently rub-bing the back of her neck, he urged her a tiny bit closer, then closer still. He stared at her thick eyelashes, resting against her cheeks, at the warm flush of her skin. "I'm just a man who wants you."

She answered in a similar husky whisper. "*That* part has been plain enough." Staring at his throat, her small hands restless, she refused to meet his gaze. "It's the rest that confounds me."

"But anything else is unimportant." And then he kissed her.

* * *

Misty knew her joke about making Morgan miserable had backfired in a big way. She was the one suffering, not him. She realized she actually liked the big guy, and almost cursed. He was so cavalier about all he did, all the responsibility he accepted.

And she seemed to have no control around him at all. He was just so big and so strong and so incredibly handsome. But it was more than that.

Morgan was a nice man.

He was also an honorable man who took his job very seriously and cared about people, not just the people he called family, but all the people in his community. Like an overlord of old, he felt responsible for their safety and happiness. And that made him almost too appealing to resist.

A soft moan escaped her when Morgan touched his mouth to hers and she felt his tongue teasing her lips.

"Open up for me, Malone."

Her hand fisted in his shirt over his hard chest. She felt the trembling of his muscles, the pounding of his heartbeat—and her lips parted.

Morgan let out his own groan only seconds before his tongue was in her mouth. She'd never known kissing like this, so hot and intimate and something more than just mouth on mouth. Maybe it was because Morgan was unique, but being kissed by him seemed more exciting than anything she'd ever done.

Beneath her fingers she could feel his labored breaths, and she opened her palm, amazed by the way his hard muscles shifted and moved in response to her touch. She felt powerful—no man had ever made her feel that way before.

As if he'd known her thoughts, he caught her other hand, which had been idly clasped at his waistband, and dragged it up to his chest. "Damn, I love it when you touch me."

Misty tucked her face beneath his chin and tried to take a calming breath. Instead, she inhaled his hot male scent and renewed desire. Rather than pushing his advantage, Morgan looped both arms around her and rocked her gently.

"It's almost too much, isn't it?" he growled against her temple.

Words were too difficult, so she nodded, bumping his chin. She felt like crying and hated herself for it. She'd never been a woman who wept over every little thing, so she assumed it must be the pregnancy making her so weak.

Then again, Morgan wasn't a little thing. He was a great big hulking gorgeous thing, and how he made her feel was enough to shake the earth.

His fingertips smoothed over her cheek. "I'm trying to give you time, sweetheart. I know you've been through a lot and until this morning, I've done nothing but push you away. But it's not easy." He gave a shaky laugh and admitted, "It's damn near impossible, if you want the truth."

His words prompted a new thought, but there was no way she could look him in the eyes right now. Morgan would see everything she felt and he'd stop trying to be so considerate. If he pushed even the tiniest bit, she'd give in to him and she knew it. As much as she wanted him, she didn't know if it was the right thing to do. She needed more time.

Hiding her face close to his chest, she did her best

to sound casual when she spoke. "It was a rather quick turnaround for you."

"No." He kissed her ear, then nipped her lobe, making her jump. "I wanted you something fierce the first second I saw you. I just figured it'd be too complicated if we got involved."

"Because you're looking for a wife?"

He stiffened slightly, then deliberately began rubbing her back. "Because you're Honey's sister, so you were off-limits for a fling."

It felt like her heart broke, his honest words hurt so much. Her throat was constricted, and she swallowed hard so he wouldn't know how strongly he'd affected her. "But now, since it's obvious what type of woman I am, my relationship to Honey no longer matters?"

"What the hell are you talking about?" Morgan tried to tip her back to see her face, but she held on to him like a clinging vine and he finally quit trying. His mouth pressed warmly to her temple and his arms tightened. "I don't think you're easy, Malone, if that's what you're getting at."

"No?" She forced herself to unclench his shirt. The man would wear wrinkles all day thanks to her. And his brothers would probably take one look at him and know why. "I'm pregnant, with no husband, no job. I'm a convict, for crying out loud. What's your definition of easy?"

He took her off guard, thrusting her back a good foot with his hands wrapped securely around her upper arms. His scowl was enough to scare demons back to hell. Misty held her breath, not afraid of him physically, really, but very uncertain of his mood.

He started to say something, then paused. "Damn it,"

he growled, "don't look at me like that. I would never hurt you."

She nodded. "I know it."

"Then why are you shaking?"

"*You're* shaking me."

He looked poleaxed by that observation, then dropped his hands to shove them onto his hips in a thoroughly arrogant stance. Misty wrapped her arms around herself and watched him cautiously.

He didn't apologize. "And you deserve it, too."

"For asking a question?" Now that he wasn't touching her, she could regain her edge.

"For suggesting something so stupid." He took a quick step toward her, leaned down in a most unnerving way and practically shouted, "I do not think you're easy!"

Misty blinked.

"Hell, woman, you're about the most difficult female I've ever run across. You fight me at every damn turn."

For some reason, Misty felt like smiling. She bit her lip, knowing Morgan wouldn't appreciate it one bit. "That's not true."

"No? I go crazy for you, and you ignore me, then flirt outrageously with every other male in the county."

That got her good and mad. "I did no such thing! And you ignored me first." She hadn't meant to bring that up; it made her sound spiteful, as if she'd ignored him to get even. She frowned at him for making her say too much.

"I tell you to leave, you argue about it. I all but beg you to stay, you argue about it."

"I did not argue about leaving."

"You got snide, I remember that well enough." He rubbed his neck and groaned. "Hell, it was all I could do to keep my hands to myself, to put up with having you in the house until Sawyer's wedding, and you just kept sniping at me, and for some fool reason that only made me want you more."

"How could I have ignored you and sniped at you at the same time? That doesn't make sense, Morgan."

His eyes narrowed. "You'd snipe with silence, by being there, making me want you, then chatting with one of my disreputable brothers as if I wasn't in the room when I knew damn good and well you were aware of me. Admit it, Malone."

This time she gave in to the grin; she couldn't help herself. "Admit I was aware of you? Sure. You're a mite hard to miss, Morgan, being so big and all."

He took another step toward her, and she backed up. In soft tones that sounded like threats rather than compliments, he said, "I admire your pride, sweetheart, I really do. But that pride is misplaced when you cut off your nose to spite your face."

"What is that supposed to mean?"

"It means you wanted to stay here, but stubbornly refused just because I'd been a pigheaded fool and asked you to go."

"I agreed to stay, Morgan," she said, feeling it necessary to point that out.

"And you refused a good job, just because you thought it was created for you."

"Uh… I took the job, too, remember?"

"I remember that I had to practically get down on my hands and knees, as well as resort to every lamebrained scheme around, to get your agreement! And you dare to say I think you're *easy?*"

"Will you stop shouting at me?"

He halted. Misty had her back to a bookcase, and Morgan was only a scant inch away. "Yeah, I'll stop shout-ing. As long as you promise to never again put words in my mouth."

Because he looked so sincerely put out over it, she agreed. "I'm sorry."

With his hands on the bookshelf level with her head, he caged her in. "Listen good, Malone, because I don't want to have to repeat this." His gaze dipped to her mouth, then came back to her eyes, pinning her motion-less. "I do not think you're easy. I think you're a beautiful woman who got involved with the wrong guy and ended up in some trouble because of it. And no, I'm not talk-ing about the pregnancy, because you're right, that's not real trouble. If you want the baby, then everything else will work itself out. I was talking about being blamed for the theft."

He drew a long breath, then squeezed his eyes shut. "And I'll have you know that even arguing with you makes me hot. I'm so damn hard right now I could be considered lethal."

A startled laugh burst out of her, making Morgan scowl all the more. She looked at his face, then doubled over in laughter, making an awful racket but unable to help herself.

Morgan waited patiently, crossing his arms over his chest and blocking her so she couldn't move away. His reaction made her laugh harder, and she fell against him until he was forced to prop her up.

When she finally quieted, Morgan was rubbing her back and smiling at her. "You want to tell me what brought that on?"

"You're priceless, Morgan."

"How so?"

He was such a reprobate. She smiled at him as she explained, aware of his hands drifting lower, almost to her behind. "You have absolutely no consideration for my modesty or my sensibilities. You talk about the most personal things—"

"Like what?"

"Like the fact you seem to have a problem with control."

He shook his head very slowly. "Not usually. Everyone will tell you I maintain absolute control."

She quirked a brow and stared at his fly.

With a grin, Morgan said, "That's an aberration, an involuntary reaction that can't be controlled around you."

She almost started laughing again. "Well, whatever it is, you show no hesitation in talking about it, shocking me all the time, embarrassing me."

His hands slid over her bottom completely, and he lifted her to her tiptoes so she fit against him. She caught her breath as his voice went husky and deep. "I want you to know how much I want you, sweetheart."

Contentment swelled inside her. She knew it was dangerous to make herself vulnerable to him, but at the moment, she was too touched to care. "That's just it," she said softly, "you show no hesitation about making me blush, but you're so considerate of my feelings otherwise. Thank you."

Morgan's fingers contracted on her backside, caressing and exciting. "You want to know how you can thank me?"

Misty was ready to start laughing again when a tentative knock sounded on the door. She jumped, bumped her head on the bookcase, then shoved him away. "Good grief, my first time in your office and look what happens."

With a wry look, Morgan turned and headed for the door. "Unfortunately, not a thing happened." He stepped into the hallway. Misty went to the office door to peek out and see who it was. When she saw Howard and Jesse stomping to remove the dirt from their boots, she stepped out to greet them.

"Are you all done for the day?"

Jesse shook his head. "Just taking off for lunch. Is this your first day?"

"No, Morgan was just showing me around today. I'll start tomorrow."

Jesse frowned at Morgan. "How long does she have?"

Misty didn't understand the question, and Morgan didn't help by grinning at her. "I'm not sure yet. What do you think?"

"I think it'd be nice to keep her on for good, but I don't suppose that'd be fair."

Howard agreed. "Can't imagine what she could've done—not that I'm prying, you understand. But to be here in the first place…"

Misty frowned in confusion. "I'm here because Morgan said he needed someone to answer the phone and take messages."

Jesse nodded. "That's a fact. Just about every day one woman or another comes here insisting just that. But I always wondered if it's really work they have on their minds." He gave her an exaggerated wink. "Ought to put an end to that now, what with Misty here, though."

"That," Misty said while trying to hide her annoyance at the thought, "is entirely up to Morgan."

"Yes, it is," Morgan agreed, smiling at her, "but it so happens I think Jesse is right. One female in the office is more than enough."

Misty clamped her lips together to keep from replying.

Morgan looked disappointed at her restraint. He turned his attention to the men. "You both have lunch with you?"

"Naw, we're going to the diner. Ceily promised me meat loaf today."

He glanced at his watch. "Is the diner open yet?"

"She'll slip us in through the kitchen."

Howard added, "You take it easy on the little lady, now, you hear?"

"I should explain something, here, guys—" Morgan began, and Misty knew he was going to blurt out something stupid, about how they were involved.

She rushed to his side and nudged him playfully with her shoulder, trying to act like a pal instead of an almost lover. "Morgan is a big pushover. Don't you worry, I can handle him."

Both the men stared at her in awe. Morgan rumbled, a sound between a laugh and a growl. "Malone—"

"Behave, Morgan," she snapped, giving him a telling look before forcing a smile on the men. "They're hungry. Let them go eat."

"But—"

Misty ignored him. "Run on, now. You both look famished to me. Everyone knows big healthy men need to eat a lot to keep up their strength. Especially when they're working as hard as you two are."

Jesse and Howard puffed up like proud roosters.

Misty waved them off, and after Morgan had shut the door, he said with amusement, "You certainly wrapped them around your little finger."

She didn't appreciate that comment at all, considering she'd barely managed to keep him from embarrassing her again. "They're very sweet men."

Morgan choked on a laugh. "They feel the same way about you. That's why they were trying to find out why you're here."

She didn't understand his humor at all. "Is it so uncommon for you to hire someone?"

Morgan pursed his mouth, but ended up chuckling anyway. "Actually, yeah, it is. And Malone, they don't think you were hired."

"What's that supposed to mean? Do they think I coerced the job out of you? I swear, Morgan, if people are going to talk because I'm working here..."

He leaned a shoulder against the wall, and even though his mouth wasn't smiling, she saw the unholy glint in his blue eyes. "Oh, they'll talk, all right. You see, at this moment Jesse and Howard are probably telling anyone they can find that you're serving out your time working here—same as they are."

She felt her eyes nearly cross. "That's ridiculous!"

Shrugging, he said, "That's usually why I bring someone in underfoot. Because they got into mischief and have to do community work."

"But..." She couldn't think of anything to say, then her temper flared. "You could have set them straight!"

"I believe I tried to. But you were too intent on telling them how you could handle me to let me finish."

Misty moaned and covered her face. "So now, even though no one here knows I was actually arrested, they're all going to think the same about me anyway."

Morgan pulled her hands down and kissed the end of her nose. "Let me show you around the office, explain your duties, then we'll go to the diner and set them straight."

"We will?"

He brushed his thumb over her bottom lip. "Believe me, Malone, no one is going to have any doubts as to why I'm keeping you close, I promise. So quit your worries."

Misty followed him into the office, but his promise, and the way he'd given it, left an empty ache inside her.

Morgan was slowly getting under her skin, and that left her feeling far from reassured.

Chapter 8

"Ouch." Misty bumped her head as she knelt and crawled beneath the desk. "You're sure she went under here?"

Jordan sounded slightly strangled as he said, "Yeah, she's under there."

In the farthest corner, against the back wall, Misty saw a curled calico tail. "Ah, I see her. She's a little thing."

"I found her abandoned." Anger laced Jordan's tone, and that was unusual because Misty had never heard this particular brother sound anything but pleasant. "I brought her home to heal, and your sister sort of bonded with her. Usually she's in bed with Honey, but today, well, I think she knew it was a day for shots and that's why she's running from me."

Misty bumped her head again when she tried to look at Jordan. All she could see was his feet. He'd been chasing the cat to take it to his clinic when they'd run into each other in the hallway. The cat had scurried away while Jordan kept Misty from falling on her behind.

Misty had been hoping to leave the house before Morgan. According to Honey, he'd been looking for her last night and had been disgruntled when he couldn't find her. But she wasn't yet ready to tell him where she'd been. Dodging him this morning was the only way she could think of to buy herself some time.

"So do you like your new job?" Jordan asked her as she crawled deeper beneath the desk.

"Actually, I do." She reached out her hand and the small cat, hissing at her, managed to inch a little farther away.

"That's good. I gather Morgan is behaving himself?"

"Morgan is Morgan. He never really behaves. You know that."

"Uh, yes, I see your point."

Morgan was the most forward, outspoken man she'd ever known, but he kept her smiling and sometimes even laughing. And he always made her very aware of her own femininity. The man could scorch her with a look, and in the short time she'd spent with him, she'd become addicted to the feeling.

But the entire week had been a series of near misses. Though she worked in his office, he was seldom there. She'd had no idea he kept such a horrendously busy schedule. After hours wasn't much better. When Morgan was free, she was gone. When she was free, Morgan got called away. His plan to make them look like a couple wasn't quite working out as she'd assumed. She hated to admit it, even to herself, but she'd been looking forward to his outrageous pursuit. And she missed him.

Jordan coughed suddenly, then suggested, "Uh, maybe you should just come on out of there?"

"No, I've almost got her. She's worked herself into a tiny little ball. Let me just scrunch in here a bit more."

"No, wait. I'll pull the desk out."

Misty was sure she heard repressed laugher in Jordan's voice, but the sound was muffled because most of her upper body was wedged into the seating area of the desk. "No, if you do that she'll just run off again. At least this way I have her cornered."

Jordan made a strangled sound.

"What?"

"Never mind."

Misty tried wiggling her fingers at the cat. She had hoped to be gone already, out the door before Morgan awoke. Working with him was more enjoyable than she'd thought it would be. She liked getting to know everyone in the town, and it was so obvious to her how they all adored their sheriff. He was treated with respect and reverence and a bit of awe.

"So your arrangement with Morgan is working out?"

She snorted, wondering which arrangement Jordan referred to. The work or the personal relationship. "Yes, things are fine. Although Morgan does like to complain a lot."

"Well, as to that," Jordan said cautiously, "I think he complains because things aren't going quite the way he planned."

"Things aren't going quite how I planned, either." She laughed, then added, "Morgan gripes because it's a habit, just like scowling at everyone." Misty thought of all she'd learned about Morgan in the past week, how he reacted with the various community members who liked to stop by and offer suggestions or complaints or idle chitchat. His patience was limitless, and why not? He usually controlled everything and everyone without anybody even realizing it. He was careful not to offend, strong and supportive, understanding. But the final word was his, and they all respected that about him. In fact, she often got the impression that they brought their minor gripes to him so he *would* take charge, saving them the hassle.

Overall, she admitted he made a pretty wonderful sheriff.

"You know, Jordan, Morgan would like the world to think he's a real bear, but Honey's right. Deep down he's just a big softy."

There was a choked laugh, then a loud thump. Jordan cursed under his breath.

"Now don't tease, Jordan. You know I'm right. Even though you all harass each other endlessly, you know your brother is pretty terrific."

Jordan's voice was lazy. "I think you and Honey are sharing that particular delusion. She's as misguided about him as you are." Then: "Just think. With you two singing his praises, Morgan will be known as a real pussycat in no time at all."

Laughing, Misty said, "I wouldn't go that far!"

Her laugh startled the cat, and when she tried to run, Misty reached out and scooped her up. "I've got her." She started crawling backward, inching her way out. The cat didn't fight her. Instead, it purred loudly at the attention.

Misty held the small calico close to her chest and scooted until she bumped into a pair of hard shins. Startled, she turned and looked up to see what Jordan was doing, and was met with Morgan's blackest look. He had his big feet braced, his hands on his hips and his jaw locked. He didn't move.

Jordan stood behind him, grinning.

For some fool reason, Misty felt her face heating. How long had he been there? What had she just been saying about him? She pulled her gaze away from his and frowned at Jordan. "You could have warned me."

"Warned you about what?" Jordan asked innocently.

Morgan reached down and caught Misty's elbow. "Come on, Malone, quit abusing my brother."

Judging by the way Jordan rubbed his shoulder, Misty had the suspicion Morgan had already done enough abusing, but she had no idea why. Jordan didn't seem bothered by it, though. He looked entertained. She frowned at Morgan. "What do you want?"

He didn't appear to like her question. "We need to get to work."

Misty stood, attempting to ignore Morgan's nearness and Jordan's attentive presence. "We've got a few minutes."

Crossing his arms over his chest, Morgan said, "Is that so? Then why were you trying to hightail it out of here so early?"

She couldn't very well explain with Morgan's brother standing there, so she turned to Jordan and handed him the cat. "Hang on to her this time."

"Thanks, sweetie." Jordan leaned forward and kissed her cheek, grinned at Morgan one more time, then left them. Misty could hear his soft crooning voice as he spoke with the cat.

She had a feeling Jordan had kissed her just to provoke Morgan, and seeing the way Morgan clenched his jaw, it must have worked. They stared at each other for a long, silent moment. Finally, Morgan shook his head. "You've been avoiding me all week."

"That's not true! We've just had conflicting schedules, that's all."

"Your only schedule is working with me. Yet I haven't had one single second alone with you. That's avoidance."

She didn't want to admit that she'd missed him, too, or that she did, in fact, have another schedule. "It's not my fault that you work all the time."

"I knocked at your door at six yesterday." His gaze softened. "I expected to find you in bed still, all warm and sleepy. But you were gone already."

Misty wondered what he would have done if he'd found her in bed, and the thought wasn't at all repulsive. She cleared her throat. "Maybe it was a good thing I wasn't there."

"There you go with those lecherous thoughts again, Malone. I was just going to offer to take you to breakfast."

She winced at the very idea. "If you'll recall, Morgan, mornings are a little rough for me. I like to walk down and sit by the lake. The fresh air settles my stomach some."

He scowled over that, and his voice sounded gruff, more with concern than annoyance. "I'd forgotten. Has the morning sickness been bad?"

Oh, when Morgan was being so sweet, it was all she could do to resist him. She wasn't even sure she wanted to anymore. Thoughts of being with him had consumed her lately. When he was around, she could barely take her eyes off him, and when he wasn't, her thoughts centered on him.

Misty realized he was watching her, and she coughed. "Actually," she said, deciding to give him a small truth, "it's been better lately. Usually, as long as I don't eat, my stomach settles down fairly quick."

"So you've been skipping breakfast?"

"I was never much for big morning meals, anyway."

His frown was back, more intense than ever. "You weren't at dinner last night, either." He looked her over, then shook his head. "You know how important it is for you to eat properly right now. "

"I have enough mothering from Honey. You don't need to start, too." And before he could protest that, she added, "Besides, I'm not starving myself. I ate in town last night."

He went still, then he flushed and growled, "With who?"

This was exactly the subject Misty had hoped to avoid, but now it looked as if she had no choice but to tell him. Exasperated, she pushed past him and headed down the hall. Morgan followed. "If you must know," she said over her shoulder, "I was working."

"You got off work at three o'clock, Malone. I watched you leave."

Yes, he had. She shivered just remembering. Morgan had been watching her with a brooding frown as she'd gathered her things. He was stuck talking with an elderly woman who claimed her neighbor mowed his grass too early in the morning to suit her. Misty had known by the look on Morgan's face that his patience was about at an end. If she hadn't been required to be elsewhere, she very well might have hung around just to see what he'd do. "I left the station at three o'clock. But then I went to the diner."

"To meet someone?"

Her temper snapped. Did he always have to think the worst of her? "That's none of your concern."

She kept walking, but he had stopped. She didn't mean to, but when she turned to face him and saw his expression, her heart almost melted. He looked angry and frustrated and…hurt.

She'd never thought she'd see a look like that on the inimitable sheriff's face.

She didn't like it at all.

She stomped down the hall to glare at him, thrust her chin up and said, "No, I wasn't meeting anyone. I went there to work."

His confusion was almost laughable. "You're working at the diner? Since when?"

"Since yesterday. Ceily hired me." His mouth opened and she said, "Before you ask, yes, I told her about my record."

"Misty." He said her name so softly, like a reprimand, and she felt a lump gather in her throat. He took both her arms, his thumbs rubbing just above her elbows. "I hadn't even thought of that."

"Bull. You had that look on your face."

"What look?"

"The one that's full of doubt."

"That was just me trying to figure you out." His mouth tipped in a small smile. "What did Ceily have to say?"

"I told her the truth, that I was innocent but couldn't prove it, and that the whole thing had cost a lot so I needed to save up more money now. She believed me." Misty twisted her hands together, once again caught in a worry. Ceily was a very pretty, petite woman with long, golden-brown hair and big brown eyes. She looked to be around Gabe's age. She'd been very warm and welcoming to Misty from the onset. "She didn't strike me as the type to carry tales. She even warned me about telling any secrets to Howard or Jesse. She said they're both horrible gossips."

Morgan laughed. "She would know. Jesse is her grandpa."

"I hadn't realized. They don't look anything alike."

"Considering Jesse is old and cantankerous and Ceily is young and cute, I'm not surprised you didn't see the family resemblance. But you're right about Ceily, she doesn't gossip. You don't have to worry about that."

Without meaning to, Misty frowned at him. "You know her well?"

He shrugged. "As well as I know anyone here. Ceily and Gabe went through school together, and she used to hang out at the house when they were younger. They're both water fanatics. She's a good kid."

Misty relaxed the tiniest bit. It appeared her secrets were safe with Ceily, which had been her only concern.

Morgan asked, "Do you mind telling me how you figure on doing both jobs?"

"I knew you wouldn't understand," she muttered. He was strong and capable and respected…and it would have been so easy to lean on him and let him help her, to follow suit with the entire town and let Morgan handle her problems. But she wanted to regain what she'd lost on her own. It was the only way she could think of to restore her self-respect.

He let her go reluctantly and fell into step beside her as she headed for her room. "Tell me what I don't understand, babe."

She shook her head. "What I do for you can barely be considered part-time, Morgan. It's only six hours a day."

"I didn't want you to overdo."

Why, oh, why, did he have to say things like that? "I'm not breakable, you know."

"I would never suggest such a thing." He kept pace with her easily, then paused when she reached her door. "No one would ever doubt your strength or determination, Malone. If that's what this is about…"

Flustered, Misty shrugged. "There's no reason I can't work for the diner in the evenings, right? Ceily agreed to put me on at four. That gives me time to grab a bite to eat and then get in four or five more hours. Last night, I made fifty bucks in tips. It's a good job."

Morgan propped his hands on his hips, dropped his head forward and paced several feet. When he finally faced her again, he looked grim. "I'm going to let all that go for now."

"How magnanimous of you."

He didn't appreciate her dry wit. "I want to talk to you about something else. Will you ride into work with me?"

She regretted the need to refuse him. "I can't. I'll be going to the diner again after we finish at the station. I'll need my car to get home."

"I'll pick you up when you get off."

"That doesn't make sense, Morgan. You never know when you might get a call, and I don't want to interrupt things for you."

He did a little more jaw locking. Misty wondered why he didn't have a perpetual headache.

"All right. Then let me take you to my house tonight. I've been wanting to show it to you, anyway."

The idea was tempting. From afar, his house looked wonderful. It wasn't quite as large as the house he shared with his brothers, but it had just as much character. The exterior appeared to be cedar, and few of the mature trees had been displaced during the building. Every morning when she went to the lake, she looked at his house. Its position on the hill would prove a stunning view. "Why do you want to go there?"

He shrugged. "I just want your opinion, to see if you like it. No other woman has seen it yet, except for Honey. But the two of you are so different, I thought it'd be nice to get your reaction, too. The house will be done before much longer. Gabe works on it off and on, and I get up there whenever I can. All the major stuff is done, now it just needs the finishing touches."

Misty chewed her bottom lip. She wasn't stupid; she knew if she was alone with Morgan for any length of time, they'd probably end up making love. She'd honestly believed no man could ever tempt her again, but she hadn't counted on a man like him. She'd thought him incredibly sexy from the moment she saw him, and since then, she'd also discovered what a wonderful man he was, inside as well as out.

He was always honest with her, and she knew deep in her heart she'd never meet another man like him. She was through with lasting relationships, and as soon as she could save up a little money, she was going to move away. By the time she returned for a visit, Morgan might well be married and on his way to having his own children.

She shook her head, saying mostly to herself, "I don't know...."

His hands cradled her face. "I won't lie to you, Malone. I want some time alone with you. I want to be able to talk to you without one of my damn brothers nosing in, or someone at the station staring at us." He looked at her mouth. "And I want to kiss you again. We've barely seen each other all week. At this rate, no one is going to believe we're involved. Already I've had people questioning our relationship."

He said the last with a growl, and she almost laughed at him. "What people?"

His frown deepened. "No one you need to know about. I made it clear you weren't free—like we agreed, right?"

"Uh, right." Morgan was in a very strange mood, she decided. It was almost as if he was…jealous.

"It's Nate's fault. He's running around telling people we hardly talk, much less act involved."

"Nate, your deputy?"

"Yeah." Morgan looked suspicious. "And that reminds me, has Nate been flirting with you?"

Startled, Misty shook her head. She'd met Nate her first day on the job. He was a good-looking young man, not a whole lot taller than she was, with brown hair and green eyes and full of smiles. He'd asked her to lunch during her break, but she'd declined, choosing instead to eat at her desk—an apple and a peanut-butter sandwich she'd packed. After that, Nate usually brought a bagged lunch, too, and visited with her while they ate.

Morgan generally had appointments during that time and ate on the road. The amount of community work he did astounded her.

Morgan gave her a long sigh. "Are you sure?"

She scoffed at him. "He's only a boy, Morgan."

"He's twenty-two years old, Malone, old enough to be my deputy, and only two years younger than you." Morgan's tone was exasperated. "Would you even realize it if Nate *was* flirting?"

"Well, I assume so."

Morgan put one arm on the wall beside her head. "For

some reason, I think you're just oblivious to the way you affect men."

"Maybe that's because, so far, you're the only one claiming to be affected. That only makes you the oddity, Morgan, not the norm."

He didn't look at all insulted by her comment. His large hand spread out over her middle, making her suck in her breath as a shock of awareness rolled through her. His fingertips, angled downward, nearly touched her hipbones. His palm was hot and firm against her.

Very softly he asked, "Now, how can that be true, when I know for a fact at least one other man chased you down? You didn't get pregnant all by yourself."

She couldn't reply. So many feelings swamped her at once, it was difficult to sort them out. In the past, every relationship she'd shared had started because she wanted someone to call her own, because she'd believed women were supposed to share their lives with men. It wasn't because she found a man irresistible and craved his company.

She no longer felt she needed or wanted a man in her life, and she'd decided she was better off on her own. But how she felt around Morgan was so different from those other relationships. She *did* crave him, and ignoring Morgan was like trying not to breathe—impossible.

By reflex, she put her hand over his, intending to pull it away, but instead, she held it tighter to her. "Kent... Kent was like most men, saying the right things to get my attention. I wanted to believe that he cared, so I did. But he never really wanted me, not like—" She stammered into silence and blushed.

Morgan gave her a satisfied smile. "You mean, like I do?"

How could he expect her to answer that? "All he really wanted," she said, ignoring his question and her embarrassment, "was the convenience of being with one woman. He never really cared about me."

"He was obviously a goddamned fool."

She looked up at him, then felt snared in his gaze. "Men flirt by nature. It doesn't mean anything. And it doesn't matter who the woman is or what she looks like."

"There's flirting, and then there's flirting." Morgan gave her a small smile. "You can believe I've never disabled another woman's car, or dragged her into a gazebo."

Misty managed a laugh. "No, probably it was the women dragging you into private places."

Morgan's fingers on her abdomen began a gentle caress that made it difficult for her to remain still. "Let's try this from another angle, okay? Forget Kent—he's not worth mentioning. And he's hardly a good example of the male species. Agreed?"

"Agreed."

"So. Has Nate been hanging around your desk? Talking to you a lot? Has he asked you out?"

She could barely think with his palm pressed so intimately to her body. Her khaki slacks weren't much of a barrier. And she could feel his breath on her cheek, could smell the delicious scent of cologne and soap and man. His wrist was so thick where she held him, her fingers couldn't circle it completely. "Um, yes, yes and no."

He nuzzled his nose against hers. "Yes and no what?"

"Yes, he talks with me, and yes, he stops by my desk. Just about everyone who comes into the station does."

Morgan dropped his forehead to hers. "I need to put a paper sack over your head. I hadn't realized it, but I'd have been better off hiding you away here at the house."

Misty couldn't help but smile. "No, he hasn't asked me out. He invited me to lunch once, but that hardly counts as a date. That was just a friendly visit between employees. I think he gets lonely at lunchtime, because now he usually eats at the station with me."

Morgan looked at her like she was a simpleton. "He's *flirting,* Malone."

"No, he's not."

Morgan drew an exasperated breath and shook his head at her. "I'm going to put a stop to it."

"Jesse and Howard are always there. And don't you dare suggest they're flirting, too."

He tipped his head back and groaned. "I'm surprised every single male in the area isn't there hanging on your damn desk. From now on, I'm going to make sure I'm around to take you to lunch. And stop shaking your head at me!"

"Morgan, you're being unreasonable." But deep inside, she was pleased by his jealousy. She had to admit that maybe, just maybe, she was fighting a losing battle.

"I want to make sure you eat right."

"Uh-huh. I can tell that's your motivation." Misty quit denying him. "If you want to take me to lunch, that's fine with me."

"Then it's settled." Triumph shone in his gaze. "And about damn time, too."

"You know, Morgan, if everyone found out I was pregnant, that'd likely put an end to any interest—imagined or otherwise."

Morgan kissed her brow, then her nose. "Don't count on it. It didn't do a damn thing to make me want you less."

He was about to kiss her again, and she was about to

let him, when Sawyer emerged from his bedroom and glanced at them.

"A little rendezvous in the hall?" he asked.

Misty felt like kicking Morgan. How did she always end up in these awkward situations when he was around? "Did we wake you?"

"Nope, I had early appointments this morning. The honeymoon is over now that a flu bug has started making the rounds."

That sounded innocuous enough, and Misty sighed. "Well, I need to get going, anyway. I was just on my way out."

Morgan tipped his head. "Didn't you need something from your room?"

She closed her eyes. She'd come to her room just to escape him, but she wouldn't admit that in front of Sawyer, who showed no signs of giving them any privacy. With a weak smile, she said, "Whatever it was, I've forgotten."

She darted around Morgan and made a beeline past Sawyer. She was almost out of hearing range when Sawyer said, "You've got her on the run, Morgan. I just wonder if that was your intent."

Morgan glared at his brother. "I know what I'm doing."

"And what exactly is that?"

They both left the hall in the direction of the kitchen. The smell of coffee was tantalizing, and Morgan needed a shot of caffeine to boost him. Unfortunately, Jordan was still there, the cat on his lap.

"You," Morgan said, effectively distracted, "were ogling Misty when I walked in."

Jordan shrugged, then said to Sawyer, "She'd climbed

under the desk to get the cat for me." His grin was un-holy. "She has a damn fine bottom."

Morgan felt ready for murder. "Keep your eyes off her bottom."

"Why? You sure didn't." He rubbed the cat and said in an offhand way, "Sawyer, I meant to mention it to you earlier. I think there's something wrong with Morgan."

Sawyer filled his coffee cup then sank into a chair. He blew on the coffee to cool it, showing no interest in Jordan's gibe.

Which of course didn't stop Jordan. "Yep, I think he must be sick. Half the time I see him, he's got this glazed look in his eyes. And once or twice, I've actually caught him smiling."

Sawyer laughed. "No! Morgan smiling? That's absurd."

Morgan came half out of his seat, and Jordan held up a hand, grinning. "No, don't throttle me. I'm on my way out the door right now. I just hung around to tell you... goodbye." He stood, the cat tucked under his arm, and grabbed his keys hanging by the door. "I'll see you all later."

As the door closed behind him, Morgan muttered, "Good riddance."

"Quit being such a grouch, Morgan. I survived, so I'm certain you will, too."

"Survived what? I don't know what you're talking about."

"Falling in love." Sawyer added quickly, "No, don't give me all your excuses. I've heard them all and even made up half of them. It'll do you no good."

Morgan felt like an elephant had just sat on his chest. He wheezed, then managed to say, "I am not in love."

"No? Then what would you call it? Lust?"

"What I'd call it is no one's business but my own."

"I think Honey might disagree with you there. She loves her sister more than you can imagine. I think they spent the longest time with no one but each other. Right now, Honey's convinced you're an honorable, likable gentleman. But if you hurt Misty, she'll take you apart. And I can tell you right now, there's not a damn thing I could do about it."

"I keep telling you that you should control your wife."

"Spoken like a true bachelor."

"Besides, I'd never hurt Malone."

"Oh? You think having an affair with you won't hurt her? She's been through enough, Morgan. Did you know she went to her father and he offered not an ounce of comfort? Honey told me about it. It seems he was more disappointed with her than anything else."

Which, Morgan assumed, pretty much guaranteed she wouldn't bother him with her arrest and conviction. She'd known without asking that her father wouldn't assist her, or even take her side. Morgan shook his head, feeling that damn pain again. Misty had come to the only person she could really count on: her sister. And thank God she had.

Sawyer frowned at him. "She needs some stability, Morgan, not more halfhearted commitments."

Morgan downed half his coffee, burned his tongue and cursed in the foulest of terms. Sawyer never said a word. "Look, Sawyer, she doesn't want a commitment, all right? She told me that herself. She's sworn off men."

"Hate to break it to you like this, Morgan, but you're a man."

"That's not what I meant! What we feel—well, it's mutual. Only she doesn't want to get overly involved." Almost as an afterthought, he added, "Any more than I do."

"I thought you wanted to get married?"

He shook his head, wondering if Sawyer was rattling him on purpose. "I want a wife like Honey."

Sawyer spewed coffee across the table. Morgan gave him a look then handed him a napkin. "I said a wife *like* her, not Honey, herself. I want someone domestic and settled and sweet...."

"You don't think Misty fits the bill? What, she's not sweet? She's got a nasty temper?"

"I never said that," he ground out between clenched teeth. He thought Misty Malone was about the sweetest woman he'd ever met, even if her temper rivaled his own. Or maybe because of her temper. He almost grinned. "You keep forgetting, Misty doesn't want to get married. She's told me that plain as day."

Suddenly Sawyer's eyes widened. "Good God. You're afraid."

Morgan slowly stiffened, and he felt every muscle tense. In a low growl, he asked his brother, "Are you deliberately trying to piss me off?"

Sawyer waved a hand, dismissing any threat. "You're afraid you'll ask her and she'll turn you down."

Even his damn toes tensed. "You're a doctor of medicine, Sawyer, not psychology. There's a good reason for that, you know."

Sawyer started to laugh. "I don't believe this. Women have been chasing you for as long as I can remember, and now here's one you've got cornered, keeping her as close as you can get her, but you're afraid of her."

"Honey's not going to like you much with a bloody nose."

Morgan hadn't actually raised a hand in anger toward any of his brothers since his early teens. He assumed that was why Sawyer so easily ignored his warning.

Sawyer was still laughing, and Morgan decided it was time to change the subject. "She's taken another job."

That shut him up. "Misty quit working for you?"

"No, she took a second job. But should she be doing that in her condition?"

"Her condition isn't exactly debilitating," Sawyer pointed out, then with curiosity: "What job did she take?"

"She's working at the diner." Morgan knew he sounded disgruntled, but damn it, he didn't want her working two jobs. And he sure as certain didn't want her out there where anyone and everyone from town would be able to look her over. The woman didn't know her own appeal. Before she'd even be aware of it, she'd find herself engaged again. Morgan wasn't about to let that happen.

"From what she said, I gather she plans to work there an additional six or so hours, all in the evening. I think it's too much."

Sawyer frowned in thought. "She's a healthy young woman, and her pregnancy is still in the early stages, so it probably won't bother her right now. But when she gets further along, there's a good chance her ankles will swell and her back will hurt if she stays on her feet for that long."

"Maybe you should try talking to her." Morgan thought it was a terrific idea, and his mood lightened. "You're a doctor. She'd listen to you."

"I'm not *her* doctor, so it's none of my business. Come to that, it's none of your business, either."

"Hmm. She hasn't mentioned seeing a doctor at all. And shouldn't she be taking vitamins or something?"

Sawyer gave it up. "Why don't you ask her about it. I can give her the vitamins, but she should have regular checkups with an obstetrician. Being she's new in the area, I could recommend someone." As an afterthought, Sawyer asked, "How far along is she?"

"I think she said around three months. Why?"

Sawyer finished his coffee and stood. "No matter." He looked his brother over carefully. "I've got to get to work. Are you going to be okay?"

Morgan immediately frowned again. "I'm fine, damn it."

"Just asking." He turned to go, but hesitated. "Morgan? At least think about what I said, all right? If you wait too long to figure things out, you could blow it. And I can only imagine what a miserable bastard you'd be in that case."

Morgan watched him go, thinking that marriage had made Sawyer more philosophical than usual. Then he thought of Misty at the office, with Nate and Jesse and Howard all sucking up to her. He saw red.

Howard and Jesse were old enough to be her grandfathers, and she was right when she said Nate wasn't much more than a kid.

It was a sad day when he got jealous over the likes of them, but Morgan admitted the truth—he *was* jealous. Viciously jealous. He didn't want anyone looking at her, because he knew good and well that any red-blooded male, regardless of his age, would be thinking the same erotic things he thought.

Jealousy was new to him. He'd been dating women since before he was Casey's age, and never once experienced so much as a twinge. If a woman wasn't interested, he moved on. If she was, they set up ground rules and had some fun. The twist with Misty was that she was interested, but she'd rather deny them both because she'd been burned and she didn't want to get *involved*. Morgan had thought that the promise of an uninvolved relationship might suit her, but so far she'd turned that down, too.

Was Sawyer right? Was Misty only trying to protect herself from being hurt again? He knew having a record wasn't something she'd ever be able to accept, so he'd set things in motion on that front. He didn't believe she was guilty, but he had a hunch who was. He'd hired a few men to check into it, and now it was only a matter of waiting to see if he was right.

Maybe once that was taken care of, she'd stop holding back on him. If he could only get her to see how good things would be between them… What? He'd get her to marry him?

Morgan thought about that, then nodded. Life with Misty would be one hell of a wild ride. He grinned with the thought. She was spicy and enticing and sweet and stubborn, and he wanted her so bad he couldn't sleep at night.

Morgan stood and picked up his hat, then snatched his keys from the peg on the wall. It was well past time he got a few things clear with her. Tonight, when he took her to his house, he'd stake a claim. He'd show her that they were a perfect match and when she got used to that, he'd reel her in for the permanent stuff.

In the meantime, he'd shore up his cause by showing her how gentle and understanding he could be. He'd even make a point of not frowning and maybe, just maybe, she'd stop fighting him so hard and then he could quit feeling so desperate, because he sure as certain didn't like the feeling one damn bit.

Chapter 9

Morgan's better intentions were put on hold when he found a woman with a car full of kids and a flat tire waiting on the side of the road. She'd been on her way home from grocery shopping when the tire blew. Unfortunately, her spare wasn't in much better shape. Morgan called in to Misty, told her why he'd be late and asked her to postpone his morning meeting with the town trustees.

She'd sounded a little frazzled when he called, but he didn't have time to linger and find out why. He bundled the woman, her children and her flat, as well as her worthless spare, into the Bronco and drove to her house. The kids, ranging in age from one year to twelve, had screamed and yelled and generally enjoyed the excitement of being in the sheriff's car. Morgan wondered if he ought to make that a regular part of the Blackberry Festival. He and his deputy could take turns giving the kids a ride around the town square.

His thoughts wandered from that as the woman tried to thank him in her driveway, obviously embarrassed that her children were loud and that he'd had his day interrupted. Personally, Morgan thought the kids were pretty cute, three of them girls, the youngest two boys, and he told her so even as he juggled a bag of groceries and a tiny three-year-old. The mother had positively beamed at him then.

All in all, they'd acted like children, which they were, so he saw no reason for her to be uncomfortable about a little noise.

After Morgan helped her get her groceries inside, he called Gabe. His brother met him at the garage where they got both tires repaired. After they'd driven back out to her car and changed the tire, Gabe drove the woman's car to her house while Morgan took the Bronco. Finally, they both went back to the garage.

"I appreciate your help, Gabe. Could you believe those tires she's driving on? And with five kids in the car." Morgan shook his head, wondering if there was any way he could help her. She and her husband were both hard workers, but her husband had suffered an illness and missed a lot of work in the past year.

Gabe rubbed the back of his neck. "What's her husband do for a living?"

"He's a carpenter, I think."

"Maybe we could barter with him. You still need some trim put on the back deck, and if he could—"

Morgan grinned. "—do the work on a weekend, I could give them some tires." He clapped Gabe on the back, almost knocking him over. "Hell of an idea."

Gabe shifted his shoulder, working out the sting of his brother's enthusiasm. "If you want, I could get hold of the guy, tell him I'm not able to do the trim and see if he'd be interested. It'd probably sound more authentic coming from me."

Morgan started to clap him again and Gabe ducked away. "I'll take that as your agreement and get in touch with him tomorrow. I'll let you know what he says."

Morgan left Gabe with a smile on his face. But when he pulled into the station, Ms. Potter, the librarian, hailed him. She wanted to know if he'd agree to take part in their annual read-a-thon, where a group of leading citizens would each pick a day to read to the preschoolers and anyone else who wanted to listen in. Morgan agreed, though it wasn't one of his favorite tasks. The books for that age group tended to rhyme, and his tongue always got twisted.

Next it was two shop owners who wanted to know if he was going to have the county take care of a massive tree limb that was likely to fall on their roofs if a storm hit. Morgan eyed the tree, agreed it needed a good trimming and made a note to get hold of the maintenance crew.

By the time he finally walked into the station he was hot and sweaty and frustrated. He looked forward to seeing Misty, to reassuring her, showing her what a great guy he could be and that she could trust in him. Little by little, he'd win her over. Then he'd talk to her again about her avoidance of commitments.

He walked into chaos.

The noise had reached him even before he opened the door. Laughter. Lots of male laugher and music and a banging noise. Morgan frowned and headed directly for the small desk that Misty occupied during her work hours. He found her sitting there—not in the chair, but on the edge of the desk, her long legs bare, crossed at the ankles. Casey was there, too, with a couple of his pals, and they had evidently supplied the music that was blasting from a portable CD player. Howard had pulled Misty's chair to the side of the desk and was seated in it. Jesse had his bony butt propped on the arm of the chair. Nate stood in front of Misty, dancing while she cheered him on.

Her tailored slacks had been replaced with shorts. Her white blouse was gone in favor of a loose T-shirt. She was barefoot, and of all damn things, she was licking an ice-cream cone.

Morgan saw red.

No one had noticed him, and he watched silently while his temper seethed. When Nate made a turn, Misty shook her head, swallowed a large lick of ice cream and then handed her cone to Casey. Casey, the traitor, just laughed and held it for her.

Misty stood in front of Nate and executed the dance step herself.

Lord, she looked sexy.

Morgan glanced around at the other men in the room and saw his thoughts mirrored on all their faces. The last thin thread of his control snapped. "What the *hell* is going on here?"

His roar effectively stopped the dance. Nate nearly jumped out of his skin, Casey quickly handed Misty back the cone, and both Howard and Jesse jerked to their feet. The loud banging noise continued.

Morgan stalked into the room. His gaze slid over Misty, then shifted to Casey. "Turn that damn music off."

One of the kids with Casey hurried to obey. Nate stepped forward. "Uh, Morgan, we were just—"

Morgan cut him off with a glare. Nate stammered for a moment, then clicked his teeth together and went mute.

With a sound of disgust, Misty stepped forward. "For heaven's sake, Morgan. Stop trying to terrorize everyone."

Morgan stared at her and silently applauded her courage. No one else in the room would have dared call him to task. She obviously didn't realize quite how angry he was.

Her hair was mussed, her skin dewy, her eyes bright. She looked like someone had just made love to her. And she dared to stand there giving him defiant looks in front of everyone.

"Is this what I pay you for, Malone? To have a party?"

Her eyes narrowed. "We weren't having a party. If you'll just listen…"

The T-shirt clung to her damp skin, emphasizing her breasts and distracting him. Her cuffed walking shorts showed off her long, sleek legs. A pulse tapped in his temple, making his head swim. "Employees of this office," he said succinctly, "do not traipse around dressed like that."

She took a step closer to him and stared up, her brows beetled. "I had to change."

His gaze dropped to the large cone she held, now dripping on her hand. "Nor do they eat ice-cream cones during business hours."

"Morgan." She said his name like a growl.

He ignored the warning, too angry to care that now she was angry, too. "I pay you to work, to answer the phone and take messages. It's little enough to expect that you might take those duties seriously."

Casey groaned, then mumbled, "Now you've done it."

Morgan paid no attention to his nephew. He was too

fascinated by the way Misty's eyes darkened, turning midnight blue.

She went on tiptoe. "I'll have you know, I've worked my butt off today!"

He leaned to look behind her. "Looks to me like you've got plenty of ass left."

Her gasp was almost drowned out by the groans of the spectators. Misty turned around and snatched up a stack of notes scattered over the desk's surface. "These," she said, slapping them against his chest one by one, "are from your various girlfriends hoping for a date tonight." They fluttered to the floor to land around his feet. "They've been calling all day, tying up the damn phone."

"Malone—"

"And they were rather persistent that you reply right away." She gave him a sarcastic-sweet smile. "Before I leave, I'll be sure to let them all know you're most definitely free!"

"Malone…"

"And this," she said, throwing a yellow bill at his face, "is for the plumber, because everything backed up and soaked the floor. If it wasn't for Howard and Jesse helping me mop we'd still be six inches under."

He started to get a little worried. "Uh, Malone…"

"And that constant banging you hear," she practically yelled, "is the repair man working on the cooling system. In case you missed it, it's about ninety degrees in here."

So that was why she was all warm and damp. Not because she'd been playing so hard? His brow lifted, but she wasn't through yet. Morgan was aware of Howard and Jesse trying to slip out unnoticed. Casey's two friends had already slunk as far as the door. Nate was open-

mouthed beside him, not moving so much as a muscle.
Casey, the rat, whistled.

"And finally," Misty snarled, in a voice straight out of
a horror movie, "this is the first break I've had all day.
The flooding water ruined my lunch, and with no air-conditioning I was too hot to eat, anyway, so Nate got me an
ice-cream cone to tide me over until dinner. But since you
don't think I should be eating it, why don't *you* take it!"

And with that, she aimed the damn thing like a mis-
sile, ice cream first, into the middle of his chest. Morgan gasped as the chill hit him, then made a face when
he felt the first sticky dribble soak under his collar and
mingle with his chest hair.

Casey stopped whistling. "Uh-oh. The fat's in the fire
now."

Howard and Jesse ran out the door, slamming it behind them.

Nate made a strategic turn and crept out.

Like a stiff, well-trained soldier, Misty tried to troop
out after him. Morgan caught her by the arm, pulling
her up short. "Oh, no, you don't." A clump of ice cream
dropped to the floor with a plop. He dragged Misty closer.

He hated to admit it, but her temper turned him on.

He had an erection that actually hurt it was so intense,
and every muscle in his body was pulled taut against the
need to take her. He stared at her, aroused by the glit-
ter in her eyes, by the way her chest heaved. "I think we
should share the cone, Malone."

Misty reared back, but he caught her other arm, pulling her up close. She stared at his chest, covered in goo,
and her lips twitched.

"You think it's funny?" But he fought his own smile.
No, life with Misty would never be mundane.

"I think you got what you deserved." Her bare heels slipped on the floor as she tried to dig in. She giggled as another plop of ice cream fell loose. "Morgan, no! I mean it, Morgan. Don't you dare—"

Her words ended in a gasp of outrage as he squished her up against his chest. "Cold, isn't it?"

She tried to twist free, which only made her breasts slip and slide over his chest. Morgan groaned.

"You..." she started to say breathlessly.

Morgan kissed her. It was a funny kiss, since she was struggling so hard against him, but laughing, too, and they had the damn cone crunching between them, the ice cream fast melting with their combined body heat.

Casey cleared his throat. "I'll be on my way now. See you both later. No need to see me off."

Morgan lifted his head. "Get out of here, will you?"

Casey laughed. "I'm going, I'm going."

Morgan watched as Casey dragged his gawking friends out the door and quietly closed it behind them. Misty tried again to pull loose, and he tightened his hold. "Oh, no, you don't. I have a few things to say to you."

She twisted in his arms, realized she couldn't get free, and stopped squirming. "What?"

He kissed her again. Then against her lips, "I'm sorry."

"You should be."

"Mm." With her mouth open he deepened the kiss, tasting her, making love to her. He groaned when the banging noise suddenly stopped.

As he gasped for breath, she muttered, "You ruined my T-shirt. Now what am I going to wear to work?"

Morgan cradled her head in his palms and asked, "You were going to go to the diner dressed like this?"

"I'm perfectly decent, Morgan, so don't start again."

"Dear God, you'll start a riot."

"It was your plumbing that ruined my other clothes. Casey was nice enough to bring these to me when I called."

"I'll run home and get you something else, okay?"

When she hesitated, he waggled her head. "Have some pity on me, Malone! I'm not used to being jealous, and it's taking some getting used to here."

"You really were jealous?"

"What did you think? That I just enjoy making an ass of myself?"

She mumbled, "Well, you do it often enough." Then she glared at him. "You have some explaining to do, insulting me like that in front of everyone."

He swallowed hard, still very aware of her soft body lined up along the length of his. "You're not going to quit on me, are you, just because I yelled a little?"

"I can't." She gave him a sad smile. "I need the job."

Morgan kissed her again, this time gently, because he hated to hear that, to be reminded of her position. "I'm sorry."

"For embarrassing me?"

"Yeah, though you didn't seem all that embarrassed to me. More like raging mad."

"True. On top of everything else, I was suffering my own share of jealousy. I mean, *eight* calls from women, Morgan."

"You were jealous?"

She frowned at him. "That, and annoyed. You have very pushy girlfriends."

He tried to look innocent. "Some of them are probably just friends."

"Probably? You don't know?"

He bit his lip, then chuckled. "It doesn't matter any-more, anyway. I swear. Now tell me you forgive me."

"Are you sorry for what you said?"

"About your sweet tush? Hell, no. You do have a great—"

"Don't say it, Morgan!" She laughed. "And about ru-ining my clothes?"

"Come into the bathroom and I'll help you clean up." Then he frowned. "I gather we do have running water now?"

"Yes, but I can clean up without your help. You," she said, pointing to all the paper littering the floor, "have a lot of calls to return."

Morgan looked down and saw that he'd stepped all over the message slips.

"You know, Morgan, it suddenly occurs to me." Her frown was back, her mouth set in mulish lines. "You're running around insisting every male in the area believes we're involved, even to the point of putting on this cave-man routine. But there seems to be an awful lot of fe-males who don't know a thing about it."

"I've been too busy mooning over you to give other women a thought. And that includes thinking about them long enough to update my status from available to un-available."

He loved how quickly her moods shifted, from mad to playful, from brazen to shy. Right now she looked un-certain. She stared at his chocolate-covered chest. "Are you considered unavailable now?"

Morgan tipped her chin up. "For as long as you're will-ing to put up with me."

She stared at him a moment, then pulled him down for a hungry kiss. Her hands were tight on his shoulders,

her mouth moving under his. Morgan felt singed. It was
the very first time she'd ever initiated anything, and he
wanted so badly to strip her naked and sate himself on
her, he was shaking with need.

A sudden hum and the kick of cool air let him know
the repairs on the system were complete. And just in the
nick of time. A few more seconds and he'd have burned
up.

"Tonight, will you let me make love to you, Malone?"

She touched his mouth, gave him a small smile, then
nodded. "I do believe I'd like that."

His heart almost stopped. He reached for her, but the
repairman gave a brief knock and stepped in.

"All done." He drew himself up short as Morgan
stepped away from Misty and he got a good look at the
ice cream mess on their clothes.

Morgan grinned. "Just leave me a bill."

Chapter 10

It seemed to be Morgan's day for chaos.

The rain was endless, coming down in sheets, and he was relieved and thankful when he saw that Misty's car was already parked around back by the kitchen door, as was her habit. He'd worried endlessly about her driving home in the pouring rain. She'd worked all day and had to be exhausted. He'd hoped to follow her home, then immediately sweep her off to his house. But then he'd gotten held up and the storm had started. He put the truck in Park, close to where she'd left her car. Normally he would have driven the Bronco into the garage, but he wanted to be as close to the back door as he could, so Misty wouldn't have as far to run in the rain.

He sighed as he picked up his small bundle in the front seat beside him, wrapping his rain slicker around it to keep it dry, then dashed the few feet through the downpour.

The kitchen door opened before he reached it, so he figured someone had been watching for him. Unfortunately, it wasn't Misty. No, she was engaged in what appeared to be a heated argument with Sawyer. It was Honey who had opened the door.

He kissed her cheek to thank her, then turned to see what the hell was going on.

Misty went on tiptoe and said to Sawyer's chin, "If you don't take the money, I can't stay!"

Sawyer threw his arms into the air, spotted Morgan and let out a huge sigh of relief. "She's worse than Honey, I swear."

Rain dripped down the end of Morgan's nose. His shirt stuck to his back. He glanced around the kitchen and asked, "Where's Jordan?"

Sawyer looked surprised by his question, then said, "In his rooms, why?"

Slowly, so as not to startle the creature, he unwrapped his burden. A fat, furry, whimpering pup stared at them all, then squirmed to get closer to Morgan. He said to Honey, "Can you get me a towel? I found the damn thing under the front steps of the gym. He's been abandoned awhile, judging by how tight his rope collar was."

Morgan was still so angry he could barely breathe. Cruelty to an animal sickened him, and it was all he could do to hold in his temper, but he didn't want to scare the poor pup more than it already was.

Sawyer picked up the phone and called Jordan while Misty inched closer. Her eyes were large, and she was looking at him in that soft, womanly way she had. He'd get her alone tonight if he had to carry her through the damn storm.

Honey skittered into the kitchen with a towel.

The back door opened, and both Gabe and Jordan came in. They wore rain slickers that did little enough to keep them dry. Jordan was all business, taking the pup without asking questions, ignoring his own damp hair and shirt collar. Gabe shook his head. "It looks pretty young. What kind of dog do you think it is?"

Jordan murmured to the frightened animal as he gently toweled it dry. "A mixed breed. Part shepherd by the looks of him, maybe with some Saint Bernard. He'll be big when he's full grown." Jordan investigated the pup's throat and scowled where the too-small rope collar had rubbed off much of the fur. "I'll need my bag."

Gabe turned to the door. "I'll get it." He pulled the hood of his slicker over his head and stepped into the rain without hesitation.

Misty started unbuttoning Morgan's shirt as if she did so every day. "You'll catch a cold if you don't get some dry things on."

Sawyer nodded. "Go change, Morgan. And take Misty with you. Maybe you can talk some sense into her."

Morgan stood still while Misty peeled off his wet shirt. "What have you been up to now, Malone?"

Sawyer didn't give her a chance to answer. He waved a few bills under Morgan's nose. "She wants to pay for staying here."

Morgan scowled. "I thought we had all that resolved."

Taking his hand, Misty tugged him from the room. "I won't be a freeloader. If I stay I have to contribute. I've been eating here almost every day...."

Morgan allowed her to lead him away from the others, but the second they were out of sight he pulled her around and pinned her to the wall, then gave her a deep, hungry kiss. Against her lips, he whispered, "Damn, I missed you."

She looped her arms around his neck and smiled. "I was starting to wonder. I thought you'd be home hours ago."

"I had to do a class, and one of the women got hurt, and then I found the pup." He groaned. "God, it's been a hectic day."

He knew his wet slacks were making her damp, too, but he couldn't seem to let her go. He'd thought about her all day long.

"What kind of class?"

Oh, hell. He hadn't meant to say that. He took her hand and now it was he leading—straight into his bedroom. He closed the door and turned the lock. "Let me change real quick and we'll run up to the house. I'll drive you straight into the garage so you won't get wet."

"Morgan." She crossed her arms and leaned against his door while he hunted for a towel to dry himself. "What class?"

Trying to make light of it, he said, "I teach some of the women self-defense two Fridays of the month. Especially the women who work as park guides for the mountain trails. Sometimes they end up alone with a guy, so they need to know how to defend themselves."

Eyes soft and wide again, Misty asked, "You said one of them got hurt?"

"Yeah, but not in the class. I'm careful with them, and the high school gym lets us use the mats. But she slipped on the front steps when she was leaving and twisted her ankle. She couldn't drive, so I took her to the hospital and then had to go fetch her husband because they only have the one car and it was still at the high school. The only good part is that I found the pup when she fell. If I hadn't bent down to lift her, I'd never have heard it whimpering."

"So you bundled them both up and did what you could?"

"Don't get dramatic, Malone. Anyone would have done the same."

"Obviously not, or that poor little puppy wouldn't have been there in the first place." She sauntered over to him and touched his bare chest, smoothing her hands over his wet skin. "I don't think you control things so much as you try to take care of everyone."

Morgan kicked off his wet shoes even as he bent to kiss her again. Her hands on his flesh were about to make him nuts. "Let me change," he growled, "so we can get out of here."

She nodded and stepped away, then sat on the edge of his bed. If she had any idea what that did to him, seeing her there, she wouldn't have dared test his control. Morgan opened a drawer and pulled out dry jeans and socks. He was just about to unzip his slacks when she asked, "Morgan, am I just another person you're trying to take care of?"

He halted, unsure of her exact meaning, but angry anyway. "You want to explain that?"

She shrugged, then quickly looked away when he jerked his pants open. Hands clasped in her lap, she said, "You wanted me gone until you thought I needed to stay. And you not only try to coddle me, you said you're trying to prove me innocent of stealing. I just wondered if I was… I don't know. Another project of sorts. Like the scholarship at the school, the puppy you just brought home, that other woman you helped today."

"What other woman?"

"Gabe told me about the woman with the flat. He said you do stuff like that all the time."

She looked at him with deep admiration again, when what he wanted was something altogether different. "Gabe has a big mouth."

His dry jeans in place, Morgan sat beside her on the bed. He bent to pull on socks and shoes, his thoughts dark. He could feel her looking at him as he hooked his cell phone to his belt and clipped his gun in place.

"You might as well save it, you know."

Startled, Morgan glanced at her. "Save what?"

"The look. I'm immune to it. You're not nearly as much of a badass as you let everyone believe. Ceily told me you haven't even been in a fight in ages, and the last one was over too quick to count."

Displeasure gnawed at his insides. "You were talking about me with Ceily?"

"Oh, quit trying to intimidate me." She waved a hand at him. "You got a reputation when you were a hotheaded kid, but even then, you were never a bully. I've heard plenty, and any fights you got into were because you were defending someone else. The last fight was in a bar in the neighboring town. Ceily said some guy tried to drag his girlfriend out of there and you stopped him. Rather easily, as a matter of fact, which I suppose only added to your reputation, right?"

Morgan decided that when he got hold of Ceily he'd strangle her. "Did she also tell you how that woman was most…grateful?"

Misty snorted. "Yeah, she did. But that's not why you did it, so don't even bother running that by me. You're the sheriff now because you hate injustice and abuse and you take a lot of satisfaction in setting things right and taking care of others. Admit it."

The hell he would. His reputation had worked to his advantage for most of his life, and he'd damn well earned it. He pulled a loose black T-shirt over his head then twisted to face her. "You still going to the house with me?"

Her dark, silky hair swung forward and hid her profile as she stared at her hands. She looked a tiny bit nervous. "If you want me to."

Morgan caught her chin and turned her face toward him. "What do *you* want?"

She bit her lip, took a deep breath, then smiled. "To be with you."

His heart punched up against his breastbone and his vision blurred. He stood up before he decided to forget about the tour and took her right now. They needed privacy, not for what he wanted to do, but for all the things he wanted to say. "C'mon."

Her hand caught securely in his, he led her out of the room. She looked cuddly in a soft, oversize sweatshirt and worn, faded jeans. Unfortunately, she wore sneakers, but he'd keep her feet dry. He looked forward to holding her close. When they got into the kitchen, everyone leaned over watching Jordan and the pup. Now that it was dry, the dog resembled a round matted fur ball with a snout and paws. A stubby tail managed to work back and forth, and it gave a squeaky bark at Morgan.

Morgan grinned. The dog was incredibly cute in an ugly, sort of bedraggled way. "Is it going to be okay?"

"*It* is a *he,* about three months old, I'd say, and yeah, he'll be fine. He just needs to be cleaned up and loved a little."

Morgan nodded. It was obvious the poor thing had been abandoned, and if he ever found out who'd done it, a very hefty fine would be presented. "I'll keep him. I was thinking of getting a dog anyway, for when I move into the house. This one'll do as well as any." At his pronouncement, Misty squeezed his hand.

Honey predictably grumbled about him moving out. She protested any time he mentioned it, saying she wanted him to stay, then went on to tell him how wonderful his house was and offered to help him decorate. He adored her.

Jordan watched as Morgan pulled two raincoats off the hooks. "I can keep him with me tonight if you want, since you appear to have plans to brave the storm again."

"Misty hasn't seen my house yet."

The brothers all grinned and cast knowing looks back and forth.

Sawyer handed Morgan the money Misty had tried to give him. "Make her take this back."

Misty held up her hands, palms out. "I can't continue to eat here if you won't let me pay for my share of the food and stuff. That's just tip money—I can afford it. Honest."

Sawyer's eyebrows shot up. "Tips? You made this much in tips already?"

"According to Ceily," Morgan grumbled, "every male that came in wanted to show her his gratitude, even if he hadn't done a damn thing for him. She said Misty kept the restaurant packed most of the night."

Misty blinked at him. "You talked to Ceily? When?"

He flicked the end of her nose. "Before I came home. She felt the need to page me and let me know how…successful you were. She even suggested she might want to lure you away from the station so you could work more hours for the diner. She claims she wouldn't even need to show up with you there drawing in customers and raking in the dough."

Gabe laughed, Jordan bit his lip and Sawyer rolled his eyes. Morgan didn't think it was the least bit amusing. "I told her you were going to continue working for me. That's right, isn't it, Misty?"

Her eyes narrowed. "As long as you all let me pay my way."

She was the most cursed stubborn woman he'd ever met. He caught her chin on the edge of his fist. "Most of the time, the food is *given* to us."

With a wholly skeptical look, she murmured, "Uh-huh."

"It's true, damn it. Sawyer barters with his less fortunate patients. Hell, he gets paid more often with food than with money. That's why we're always overloaded with desserts and casseroles."

"You're serious?" When he nodded, she said, "I had no idea."

Sawyer looped one arm around Honey and added, "I have vitamins I can give her, too, so she won't have to go to the pharmacy, but of course she refused them."

And Honey piped in, saying, "I know for a fact she's embarrassed about getting them in town. Everyone will know she's pregnant if she does. Make her accept them, Morgan."

Morgan took one look at Misty's inflexible expression and laughed out loud. Were they all under the misguided notion that he had some control over the woman? Hell, she butted heads with him more than anyone else!

Knowing it would only prompt her stubbornness more, he said, "Yeah, sure, I'll take care of it."

Her brows snapped down, her mouth opened to blast him with invective, and Morgan kissed her—a quick, grinning smooch. She gave him a bemused look, and he dropped the coat over her head, then lifted her in his arms.

She fussed and wriggled, but he contained her with no effort at all and when she saw all the brothers watching intently, she made a face at them, but at least stopped struggling. "You have the worst habit of hauling me around."

"I don't want your feet to get wet going out."

"Oh."

Sawyer said, "Finally, he's listening to me."

Honey acted as if it was all par for the course. "Here, Misty, I packed a basket so you could both eat. I doubt if either of you have had dinner yet. Take your time. You'll love Morgan's house and maybe the rain will have stopped by the time you head back."

Morgan watched Misty balance the large basket with one arm while looping the other around his neck. "Don't wait up for us," he said to the room at large.

He darted out the door and made his way cautiously to the Bronco. Misty opened the car door, and he slid her inside. The rain wasn't coming down quite so fiercely now, and Morgan hoped Honey was right, that it would stop soon. Too many wrecks happened in weather like this, and he didn't look forward to his evening getting interrupted. Already his anticipation was so keen he had to struggle for breath. He was semihard and so hot the windows started to steam the second he got behind the wheel.

"Will you accept the vitamins?" He drove from the

driveway to the main road, hoping the conversation would work as a distraction. "Sawyer offered them because he wants to, you know."

With her arms around the basket, she grumbled, "He offered because I'm Honey's sister."

"Bull. If you'd just stumbled into our lives the way Honey did, he'd do the same. Sawyer cares about people and likes doing what he can. It has nothing to do with you being related. Except that he takes it more personal when you refuse."

She shook her head. "All right, fine. I'll take the vitamins, but I insist on paying my own way. I won't be swayed on that. Regardless of where the food comes from, I'm still staying there and taking up room."

Morgan smiled at her. "Stubborn as a mule." He pulled up in front of his garage and hopped out to open the door, then drove inside. "I'm going to have the driveway poured soon, and then we'll install a garage door opener, but that's stuff I can take care of after I move in."

Misty didn't wait for him to open her door after he'd turned off the engine. She hefted the heavy basket in her arms and climbed out. "I want to see the outside of the house, too. From down the hill, it looks gorgeous."

Morgan felt like a stuffed turkey, he puffed up so proud. "Let's go through the inside first and maybe the rain will let up." He opened the door leading into the house and reached in for a light switch. The first-floor laundry looked tidy and neat, a replica of the one in the house where he'd grown up, with pegs on the wall for wet coats and hats, a boot-storage bench and plenty of shelving. "All the fixtures aren't up yet, but there's plenty of light."

He turned to look at Misty and caught her wide-eyed

expression of awe as she stared from the laundry room into the kitchen. "Oh, Morgan."

Like a sleepwalker, she went through the doorway and turned a circle. "This is incredible."

The kitchen had an abundance of light oak cabinets, high ceilings with track lighting and three skylights. Right now, the rain made it impossible to see anything but the blackness of the sky, but Morgan knew on a sunny day the entire kitchen would glow warmly, and in the evening, you'd feel like the stars were right on top of you.

"C'mon. I'll show you around." He took the basket from her and set it on the counter.

She kept staring at his cathedral ceilings. "I love the design. It's like you're in a house, but not, you know? Everything is so open."

"I don't like closed-in spaces." He laced her fingers with his own and said casually, "I figure it's easier to keep an eye on kids when they aren't behind doors getting into mischief. Other than the four bedrooms and the two baths, all the doorways are arches."

She stalled for a moment inside the dining room. He turned to look at her, and she shook her head. "How many kids do you plan on having?"

He held her gaze and said, "Three sounds about right. What do you think?"

Her fingers tightened on his and she said quietly, "I think I'll worry about raising this one before I even contemplate adding any more."

He wanted to tell her she didn't have to worry, that she wouldn't need to raise the baby on her own, but he had to bide his time. He didn't want to scare her off. "I don't have the dining-room furniture yet. I'm still working on that."

She went to a window and looked out. "The view of the lake is gorgeous."

"Yeah. Back here in the coves the lake is almost always calm, not like farther up where all the vacationers keep it churning with boats and swimming and skiing. It's peaceful, nothing more disturbing than an occasional fishing boat."

"I bet in the fall it's really something to see."

"Yeah. And in the winter, too, when everything is iced over. I figure I'll need to hire someone to keep all the windows clear, but what's the point of living on a hill with great scenery if you can't see it? The view from the master bedroom is nice, too." He slipped that in, then added, "The deck runs all the way around the house."

The next room was the living room and he watched her inspect his choice of furniture, wondering if she'd like it.

"Everything looks so cozy, but elegant, too."

Morgan rubbed the back of his neck. When he'd chosen the blue-gray sofa and two enormous cranberry-colored chairs, elegance hadn't entered his mind. It was the saleslady who'd suggested the patterned throw pillows to "pull it all together." He'd been going strictly for comfort. The softness and large dimensions of the furniture had appealed to him. "I'm glad you like it."

"You could fill this place up with plants. You know, like you did around the fireplace at the station."

Morgan watched her closely as he admitted, "One of the women I used to see on occasion brought in those plants. I'd never have thought of it. It's the cleaning lady that keeps them watered and healthy."

She sent him a narrow-eyed look over the mention of a girlfriend. "Well, I can just imagine a lot of plants really blending in here. With the stone fireplace and the light from the windows, it'd be great. What do you think?"

"I think maybe you should help me pick some out."

She blinked at him in surprise, then smiled. "I'd love to."

Satisfied on that score, he took her hand and continued on the tour. He opened the first door they came to. "This is the hall bath."

Misty stuck her head in the door, and her mouth fell open. "It's...decadent."

Grinning, Morgan gently shoved her the rest of the way in. "Yeah. I kinda like it. Other than my bedroom, it's my favorite room. It turned out just the way I wanted."

Morgan watched her run her hand over the creamcolored tiled walls, the dual marble vanity. A large, raised tub took up one entire corner, looking much like a small pool. You could see the water jets inside the tub, and all the fixtures were brass. There was a skylight right above it and a shelf surrounding it for lotions and towels and candles—things he'd noticed Honey was partial to, so he assumed other women would be, too. In the adjacent corner was a shower with two showerheads, one on either side of the stall.

Honey was a hedonist when it came to her baths—the woman could linger for hours. He'd assumed most women were the same, but Misty tended to take quick showers, just as he did. He frowned with that thought, until he considered showering with her, and then his breath caught. He eyed the shower. It was plenty big enough to make love in....

"It's beautiful, Morgan."

He shifted his shoulders, trying to ease the sexual

tension that had invaded his muscles. "I still have to get towels and stuff, but I figured there was no rush on that."

Tentatively, without quite looking at him, she said, "I could help with that, too, if you want."

Morgan stared at her, then swung her around and gave her a hard, quick kiss. "Thanks," he said in a gruff tone, his throat raw with some unnamed emotion that he didn't dare examine too closely. It was based on sexual need, but there was a lot of other more complicated stuff thrown in that he didn't understand at all.

Misty looked at his mouth, drew a slow, broken breath and then licked her lips. Morgan was a goner. Backing her into the cool tile wall, he took her mouth again, this time more thoroughly, then didn't want to stop kissing her. She felt perfect, tasted perfect. She made him feel weak when that had never happened before, but she also made him feel almost brutal with driving need. He wanted to devour her, and he wanted to cherish her.

She arched against him and he cupped her rounded backside with a groan. "Damn, Malone."

In a husky, laughing tone, she asked, "Are you ever going to use my first name?"

She sounded a bit breathless, and he forced himself to loosen his hold. Sawyer was right; she'd been through a lot, and even the strongest woman in the world needed time to adjust. "Malone suits you. It sounds gutsy and sexy and a little dangerous."

She allowed him to lead her from the room, but she asked, "Dangerous? Me?"

With his arm around her shoulders, his heart still galloping wildly, he steered her to the first empty bedroom. "To my libido, yeah."

The first three bedrooms were empty, but still Misty

oohed over the tall windows and the ultrasoft carpet and the oak moldings. Morgan felt as if he might explode by the time he got her to his room. There were no curtains yet on the French doors that flanked the tall windows, almost filling an entire wall. The doors led to a wide, covered deck. The overhang wasn't quite sufficient to shield them from the wind, and the rain blew gently against the glass. "Let me show you something."

Without hesitation she came into the room and went to the wall of windows with him. "Look at the lights on the lake. Isn't it beautiful?"

She stared into the darkness for long minutes, then finally nodded. "Yes."

"I've always enjoyed the lake, the way sunlight glints on every tiny ripple, and how the evening lights along the shore turn into colored ribbons across the water. Even on stormy days, it's great to watch. The waves lap up over the retaining wall and every so often the lake swells enough to cover my dock. The fish get frisky on those days and you can see them leaping up into the air and landing again with a splash. On my next day off I'll take you boating and we can swim in the cove. Would you like that?"

She continued to gaze into the rainy night. "I've always loved being outdoors, and around water. When I was younger, we had a sailboat. My dad would take us out about twice a year, but mostly he used the yacht for entertaining his guests or business associates."

Morgan hugged her from behind, knowing her relationship with her father had been far from ideal. "I don't have a yacht, but I think you'll like our boat. Or rather boats—we have three. An inboard for waterskiing, which Gabe uses more than anyone else. He's as much fish as man. And a fishing boat with a trolling motor, which is so slow you could probably paddle faster. And a pontoon. My mother bought the pontoon and left it here, but whenever she visits she takes it out."

Misty leaned her head back to look at him. "I didn't know you had a gazebo."

The gazebo was only barely visible in the darkening sky, a massive shadow on the level ground fifteen feet off the shore of the lake. He'd had electricity run down there so a bug light could hang inside the high ceiling, though it wasn't lit now.

Morgan kissed her temple and looped his arms around her middle so that his hands rested protectively over her belly. "I had Gabe build it for me." His fingers contracted the tiniest bit, fondling her gently.

She sucked in her breath, and her hands settled over his. "When?"

In a hoarse tone, he explained, "After that night I kissed you at the wedding. In the gazebo."

She twisted in his arms. "But…you'd asked me to leave then."

He searched her gaze. There was no accusation there, just confusion. "I wanted you to stay." Very gently, he pulled her closer. "Damn, I wanted you to stay."

Her smile was shaky, and then she touched the side of his face. "I have to tell you something about me."

Morgan leaned forward and nuzzled the soft skin beneath her chin. He felt wound too tight, edgy and aroused and full to bursting. He tasted the silky skin of her throat, her collarbone. He didn't say anything, waiting for her to continue.

He felt the deep breath she took. "You're a special treat for me, Morgan."

He grinned at that and continued to put soft, damp kisses on her throat, beneath her chin, near her shoulder. He felt her tremble and held her closer.

"I want you to understand what this means to me."

He leaned back to look at her. She appeared far too serious and solemn to suit him.

"I know that an unwed pregnant woman sort of gives the impression of being experienced—"

"Damn it, Misty, I didn't—"

She pressed her fingers to his mouth. "Just listen, okay?" He nodded reluctantly and she continued. "Truth is, I haven't had much experience at all. Back in high school I got very curious, and we experimented a little. Very little, actually. Things didn't last long with him, but it was no big heartbreak."

Very carefully, Morgan pulled her earlobe between his teeth. She shuddered.

"And then there was Kent. I'd only been with him a few times, but we were careful. It's just that the condom broke—"

He squeezed her tight, cutting off her spate of confessions. "Enough."

Jealousy washed through him. The idea of her with a kid in high school was bad enough; his brain nearly overflowed with visions of her being groped in the backseat of a car, making him hazy with anger. But to think of her as a grown woman with a man she'd thought she loved... A man who had gotten her pregnant, then turned away from her. He could barely tolerate the idea.

"I don't need to have an accounting for past lovers, Malone." He growled those words against her ear, then added, "I don't care about any of that."

She wriggled loose so she could see him. "But that's

just it. I don't have much of an accounting to give. Not because I'm so particular, and not because I think it's wrong. It's because no one ever really made me want him. Not the way you do."

Emotion nearly clogged his throat. Morgan hugged her right off her feet. "You don't have to worry, baby. I'll take care of you. I won't hurt you."

She pushed against his shoulders. "Morgan, you don't understand."

Morgan lowered her to the floor with him so that they faced each other on their knees. Misty's eyes were dark and wide and even in the dim light he could see her excitement. He slipped his hand under the hem of her sweatshirt and stroked her bare waist. Very softly, he said, "Explain it to me, then."

Morgan hoped she was about to give him a clue to her feelings. She hadn't balked at the idea of helping him decorate, but neither had she seemed to realize why he wanted her help. And his comment about kids had gone completely over her head: in order for him to have those three kids, he'd need her cooperation, because no other woman would do.

She hesitated, her chest rising and falling in fast breaths, then she blurted, "I want to get my fill of you."

A wave of lust washed over him, making him tremble. That was not what he'd been expecting, or even hoping for. *But it might do.*

"You're so open about sex and how you feel," Misty explained, "that I don't have to worry about my old inhibitions or any of that stuff. I don't have to worry about what you'll think of me, or if I'll offend you." She touched his face with a trembling hand. "I want to do everything to you that I've been imagining doing. I want to let go completely."

Morgan swallowed hard, struggling to come up with a coherent reply.

It wasn't necessary. Misty launched herself at him, her hands holding his ears while she kissed him hungrily. He felt her small tongue in his mouth, felt her sharp little teeth nip his bottom lip. With a harsh groan, he rolled to his back, keeping her pinned against his chest, and she touched him all over, her hands busy and curious and bold.

He thought of all the things he'd meant to say to her, but at the moment, none of them seemed important.

Morgan made a sound somewhere between a groan and a laugh. She didn't care if she amused him. "I've wanted you for so long," she told him between kisses. "It's awful to want someone that bad."

"Tell me about it." He worked her sweatshirt up until he could pull it over her head. She lifted her arms to help him, not feeling a single twinge of shyness. Not with Morgan.

As soon as the shirt was out of the way, Morgan reached for her. His hands were so large and rough and hot, and she moaned as he cuddled her breasts in his palms. His thumbs stroked over her nipples and she felt wild at the sweet ache his touch caused. "This is almost scary."

"No." Morgan brought her back down for another kiss, but she dodged him.

"I want your shirt off, too." He was such a big hulk that there was no way she could get his clothes off him without his cooperation. She slid to the side and tugged his shirt free of his jeans. Morgan curled upward, making the muscles in his stomach do interesting things, and he threw the shirt off. She'd seen his chest many times, but now was different. Now she was allowed to touch and taste and have her way with him.

Misty attacked the snap on his jeans.

"Slow down, babe."

"No, I don't want to. I kept telling myself I couldn't do this, but then I realized there was no way I could *not* do it. I want you too much. I doubt I'll ever meet another man who makes me feel this way."

"Damn right you won't." Morgan caught her hands and pulled them away from his zipper. "Kiss me again."

She gladly complied. And while she was kissing him, licking his mouth, tasting his heat and feeling the dampness of his tongue, the smoothness of his teeth, Morgan rolled her to her back. The plush carpeting cushioned her.

"I don't want to hurt you, Malone."

She pulled him closer, breathing deeply of his scent. "You won't."

"The baby…"

Everything seemed to go still with his words. Morgan loomed over her, heat pulsing off him, his dark blue eyes burning hot, his hair mussed. There was so much concern and tenderness in his gaze that she felt tears well in her eyes. Misty touched his cheek, then his wide, hard chest. She let one finger drift over a small brown nipple and heard his sharp intake. "I want you naked, Morgan."

His head dropped forward and he labored for breath.

"You won't hurt me, I promise." She watched the way his wide shoulders flexed, how the muscles in his neck corded. "I've been thinking about this all day, and if I'm going to do this—"

His gaze snapped to hers. *"You are."*

"—then I want to do everything. Why take a risk un-less you make it worthwhile?"

The look on his face was almost pained before he de-liberately wiped it away. "I'm not a risk, babe."

Misty didn't want to tell him that he was the biggest risk she'd ever taken. She loved him so much, even more than she desired him. Around him her heart felt vulner-able and soft and a little wounded because she wished so badly she could have met him months ago. He could break her so easily.

She shook her head, willing to tease him to chase her dark thoughts away. This wasn't a time for wariness, but a time to break free. "I've never had an excellent lover, Morgan." She slipped her fingers down his side, over his hip. "I want you to be excellent."

His teeth flashed in the darkness and his hand smoothed over her hair, then tucked it behind her ear. "You know how to put on the pressure, don't you?"

"Are you intimidated?"

He snorted. After staring at her for a long moment, he shifted to sit up. His gaze strayed to her body again and again while he pulled off his shoes and socks and laid his cell phone aside. "So you want to see all of me?"

"Yes."

"Should I turn on some lights?"

Misty laughed. How she could recognize humor while burning up with need was amazing. Morgan made her hungry, and he amused her, and he made her feel special and cherished in so many ways.

But then, he did that for a lot of people.

"With no curtains on the windows?" she asked. "Don't you think that might be unwise? What if someone is out there and they see you prancing around in the buff?"

He chuckled, but the sound was strained as he stared at her breasts. "I don't prance, Malone. And there's no one out there on a night like this."

She pretended to consider his offer, then said, "No, let's leave the lights off." She'd definitely be more daring without too much illumination. She needed the shadows to enjoy herself fully. At least this first time.

Morgan shrugged. "Whatever you want."

"That's the spirit." Her laugh ended on a gasp when he came to his knees and carefully pulled down his zipper, easing it around a rather large, hard erection. She didn't want to laugh now. No, she just wanted to watch. And touch.

And taste.

Without any signs of modesty, Morgan slowly shucked his jeans and underwear down his hips, then sat back and pulled them the rest of the way off. "Now you," he rumbled, and leaned forward to do the job himself.

Misty stared at his naked body and felt the warmth build beneath her skin, felt her womb tighten, her breasts ache. His hips were a shade lighter than the rest of his sun-darkened skin, the flesh looking smooth and hard, taut with muscle. Crisp, curling hair covered his chest and tapered into a downy line on his abdomen. She felt a little lecherous eyeing his swollen erection and wondered how it would feel to touch him there.

Belatedly, Misty remembered that she wanted to be a full participant, not a passive one. She toed off her sneakers, then came up onto her elbows as Morgan worked the button of her pants loose and started on her zipper. "Would you rather I strip? It'll be easier."

Morgan froze for a heartbeat, then shook his head. "I'd

never live through it. The fact you're not wearing a bra is already more than any man should have to deal with."

"You *wanted* me to wear a bra."

His hand opened over her belly and caressed her lightly, smoothing over her skin, dipping quickly into her belly button, then sliding beneath her open jeans to palm her buttocks. She reached for his erection and wrapped her hand around him.

He was hard and hot and silky. He flexed in her hand, and she tightened her hold.

With a groan, Morgan hooked his fingers into the waistband of her jeans. His voice was gravelly and low when he spoke. "Unveiling you slowly would have been better for my system. Saving me the shock, you know?"

Misty ignored his words, enthralled with the velvety feel of him. "Do you like this, Morgan?" She squeezed him carefully, heard his rough gasp. "You'll have to give me some direction, okay?"

He had her jeans as far as her knees and he paused to tilt his head back and suck in deep breaths. "Harder."

Misty's heartbeat drummed at his growled command. She tightened her hand and stroked him again. "Like this?" she whispered.

Morgan suddenly caught her wrist and pulled her hand away. "I'm sorry, but I can't take it." He kissed her knuckles and placed her hand next to her head on the floor. "You need to do some catching up, sweetheart, so keep those soft little hands to yourself for a few minutes, okay?"

Nodding, Misty lifted her hips so he could pull her jeans the rest of the way off. Morgan pushed them aside, and immediately bent down to kiss the top of her right thigh. "Damn, you smell good," he muttered as he nuzzled her hipbone, her belly, leaving warm damp kisses on her skin.

Misty shifted, not sure if she should protest or not. He'd taken the lead, but she loved how he looked at her, the husky timbre of his voice.

"Open your legs."

"Morgan..."

"Shh. Trust me, okay?"

It seemed as though her heartbeat shook her entire body. Around her nervousness, her excitement, she whispered, "I do trust you. I always have."

Morgan looked down at her, making her feel exposed and agitated and eager. He wedged her thighs apart and settled between them. He stared into her eyes and cupped her breasts. His solid abdomen pressed warmly against her mound, making her arch the tiniest bit. Her thighs were opened wide around his waist.

Misty nearly choked on a deep breath when he lowered his head and sucked one nipple deep into his mouth. Her back arched involuntarily, but Morgan took advantage of the movement to slip his arm beneath her, keeping her raised for his mouth. He shifted to her other breast, making her moan with the sharp tingle of a gentle bite.

"I could spend an hour," he whispered, "just on your breasts."

Misty tangled her fingers in his hair. "I told you I wanted to do some things."

"We'll take turns."

He went back to her nipple, and true to his word, he seemed insatiable, tasting her, licking her, sucking her deep. Each gentle tug of his mouth was felt in her entire body. His tongue was both rough and incredibly soft on her aroused flesh. When he finally lifted himself away from her, she could barely keep still. Her nipples were swollen and wet, and she covered them with her own hands, trying to appease the throbbing ache.

Morgan growled at the sight of her touching herself and began kissing his way down her abdomen. When he reached her belly, he paused, then rested his cheek there. "I can't believe there's a baby in here," he whispered. "You're so slim."

Misty choked on an explosion of emotion, so touched by the way he accepted her and her condition. "I… I'm bigger than I used to be. I've gained seven pounds." It amazed her that he didn't seem the least put off by her pregnancy. Kent had been disgusted and repulsed by the idea, but Morgan seemed more intrigued and concerned than anything else.

He placed a gentle kiss on her navel, then slipped his hands under her thighs and opened her legs wide. "Bend your knees for me, sweetheart. That's it. A little wider."

She felt horribly exposed with her legs sprawled so wide, his warm breath touching her most sensitive flesh. He was looking at her, studying her, and it embarrassed her even as it excited her almost unbearably.

Knowing what would happen, overcome with curiosity and carnal need, Misty dropped her head on the carpet and stared at the heavily shadowed ceiling.

The first damp stroke of his hot tongue felt like live lightning. She jerked, but he held her still and licked again. She groaned. Morgan used his thumbs to open her completely and tasted her deeply, without reserve.

"Oh, God."

"So sweet," he murmured, and anything else he said was lost behind her moans.

She couldn't hold still, couldn't think straight. His

fingers glided over her wet swollen tissues, dipping inside every now and again, but not enough to make the building ache go away. His tongue did the same, lapping softly, then stabbing into her.

"Morgan, please..."

"Tell me if I hurt you," he murmured hotly, and even his breath made her wild.

But then she gasped as he began working two fingers deep into her. Moving against him, she tried to make him hurry, tried to make him go deeper.

"You're so tight," he murmured and she heard the repressed tension in his voice.

"Morgan."

His mouth closed over her throbbing clitoris, sucking gently while his fingers stroked in and out, and she was lost. She cried out, thankful that they were alone, that he'd had the sense to insure their privacy, because she wanted to yell, needed to yell. Nothing had ever felt like this, so powerful and sweet and so much pleasure it was nearly too much to bear.

Morgan moved up over her, settling his hips gently against hers. His hands cupped her face until her eyes opened. "I'm going to come into you now."

"Yes."

"Tell me if I—"

"You won't hurt me." If he didn't get on with it, she might be forced to rape him. A gentle pulsing from her recent climax still shook her, but she wanted more, she wanted it all, she wanted Morgan.

"Put your legs around me."

As soon as she'd gotten her shaky limbs to work, he smothered her mouth with his own and pushed cautiously into her. Her body bowed, trying to accommodate him, then wilted as he sank deep, entering her completely. His raw groan echoed her own.

A moment of suspended pleasure and building anticipation held them both, then he began moving in deep, gentle thrusts. He stayed slightly propped up on his elbows rather than giving her his weight. Misty tried to protest, wrapping her arms tight around him and doing her best to bring him to her.

"No, sweetheart. I'm too heavy," he panted, his jaw tight, his shoulders bunched. His eyes blazed at her and he kept kissing her, as if he couldn't get enough; deep, hungry kisses and gentle, tender kisses.

Even now, he was being so careful with her. Her heart swelled painfully. "Please, Morgan."

He squeezed his eyes shut, his jaw clenched, and the sight of him, so strong, so powerful and so gentle, added to the physical pleasure and made her climax again with a suddenness that took her breath away. She strained against him, her thighs tightening, her fingers digging into his powerful shoulders. The second her muscles tightened around his erection, Morgan cursed, then gave up the struggle.

He allowed her to pull him down and pressed his face into her throat, hugging her closer still, his big body straining and shuddering as he came.

For long moments he rested against her, dragging in air, his body gradually relaxing. She felt him kiss her throat...and she felt his smile.

Misty squeezed him again. She didn't know what she had expected, but the contentment, the happiness, the peace nearly overwhelmed her. "That was wonderful," she whispered to him, needing to say the words. "You were wonderful."

As though it took a great effort, Morgan slowly struggled up onto his elbows and smiled down at her. "So you're satisfied?"

She bit her lip, then slowly shook her head. "No, never."

Morgan blinked at her, then threw his head back and laughed. "Damn, Malone, I never thought I'd like hearing those two words leave your lips."

She touched his mouth with a finger. She no longer vibrated with need, but the curiosity was still there, and the love. "What you did to me, Morgan? I want to do that to you, too."

Morgan jerked. He breathed deep and he cursed and he shuddered. Finally he just laughed again, the sound low and rough. "From the moment I met you I knew on a gut level exactly how things would be with you."

"Did you?" When Morgan smiled, he made her want to smile, too.

"Yeah. Why do you think I've been going so crazy? I'm glad to see I wasn't wrong."

He rolled onto his back so that she was perched above him. His grin was so wicked and so lecherous, she almost blushed. "Now," he said.

And before she could ask him, "Now what?" his cell phone rang.

Chapter 11

It was almost two in the morning by the time he got home, and he felt exhausted down to his soul. A three-car mishap had dragged him out of Misty's arms. Luckily no one was seriously hurt, but he was still pissed off. A few idiots from the next county over drank too much and tried joyriding over their deeper roads. They'd taken out not only a length of fence along Carl Webb's property, but they'd also knocked over a telephone pole. Cows had wandered loose in the road and into the neighboring field, Carl had been infuriated—and rightfully so—and many people had been without phone service.

In the pouring rain, it was damn inconvenient trying to sort everything out. One of the fools had a concussion, the other a broken nose. Morgan thought they deserved at least that much, though they'd both whined and complained endlessly.

He hadn't had a chance to say anything to Misty. He'd made love to her, and he'd made her laugh, but he hadn't told her that he wanted her to stick around as a permanent member of the family. He hadn't told her that he wanted her to be with him forever.

And she hadn't said a thing about how she felt, other than that she'd enjoyed making love with him. That was just dandy, but it wasn't enough. Not even close.

He kicked off his muddy boots just inside the kitchen doorway and made his way through the silent house to his room. His wet clothes went into a hamper and a warm shower helped to relieve his aching muscles, but not his aching head. He needed some sleep, but as he threw back the top sheet, the thought of climbing into his big bed all alone didn't appeal to him one bit. He glanced at the door, thought of Misty all warm and snuggled up in her own bed, and it felt like that fat elephant was on his chest again.

He stood there undecided, at the side of the bed for a full three minutes before cursing and pulling on underwear. Grumbling all the way down the hall, he got to Misty's room and started to knock, then changed his mind. The doorknob turned easily and the door swung open on silent hinges. He could barely see Misty curled on top of the mattress, her room nothing but shifting moon shadows as the trees swayed outside with the wind. But he could hear her soft, even breathing. She was likely exhausted and he promised himself he wouldn't keep her awake, but he wanted to hold her and there was no longer any reason to deny himself.

When he stood next to her bed she shifted and yawned, then opened her eyes to look at him. Immediately she sat up, shoving her silky hair out of her face. "Morgan? What's wrong? Did you just get in?"

Her normally deep voice was even rougher with sleep, and sexy as hell. "Yeah." He bent and scooped her out of the bed, lifted her up against his bare chest, and started out of the room. She had on a thin knee-length cotton gown, and her warm, sweet scent clung to her skin, making him regret his resolve to let her rest.

She tucked her face under his chin. "Where are we going?"

"To my room. I want to hold you while I sleep."

She made a soft, humming sound of pleasure and curled closer. As he toed her door closed from the hallway, he heard another door open. He turned, Misty held tight in his arms, to see Casey leaving the bathroom.

Casey blinked, then quickly averted his gaze. "I didn't see a thing."

"Make sure you don't repeat a thing, either."

Casey waved him off, too sleepy to care. Misty groaned. "How do you always embarrass me like this?"

"Why would you be embarrassed?" He went down the hall to his room and once inside he nudged the door closed. He didn't immediately put her in the bed; he liked the feel of her in his arms, the trusting way she accepted him.

"What will Casey think?"

"That I've got too much sense to sleep alone with you nearby." When she didn't comment on that he turned her slightly to see her face. Her eyes were closed, her expression relaxed. Not really wanting to, he gently lowered her to the mattress and climbed in beside her. "Sleep, sweetheart. We'll talk in the morning."

Before he could pull her against him, she had her arm around his waist, her head on his shoulder and one thigh covering his. And damn, it felt right. He wanted to sleep this way every night for the rest of his life.

Misty kissed his chest. "I'm awake now, you know."

Her voice was even huskier, and he eyed her in the darkness. "Shh. Don't tempt me. It's late and we both need some sleep." And he fully intended to explain a few things to her before he made love to her again.

Her soft little hand slipped down his stomach, making him suck in a deep breath. "Malone," he growled in warning. "Behave yourself."

She sat up, and he expected her to start arguing. He grinned, wondering what she would say, if she'd come right out and admit that she wanted him enough to force the issue.

Instead, she shifted around, and when she curled up against him again, she was naked. She shimmied onto his chest, cupped his face in both hands and said teasingly, "Don't make me get rough with you, Morgan."

He stroked the long, silky line of her back to her lush bottom and gave up. "All right, but be gentle with me. I've had a trying night." She laughed at that, her first kiss kind of ticklish and silly. But he had both hands on her bottom now and the second his fingers started to explore she groaned, and for the next hour neither one of them thought of sleep.

Morning sunlight nearly blinded him when he heard Misty's soft, pain-filled moan. He immediately sat up to look at her. She had both hands holding her middle, her mouth pinched shut and her eyes closed. She looked pale. He said very quietly, "Morning sickness?"

She gave a brief nod. "It hasn't been this bad lately. But I don't usually wake up with a hairy thigh over my belly, either."

"Oh. Sorry." Morgan shifted away from her, trying not to shake the bed overly, then said, "Don't move. I'll be right back." When she didn't answer, he said, "Malone?"

"All right."

He pulled on jeans and darted into the kitchen. Honey was there, and Casey and Gabe. They all smiled at him and treated him to a round of inanities. He grumbled his own greetings, then stuck bread in the toaster and water on to boil. He glanced at Casey, who pursed his mouth, silently assuring Morgan he hadn't said a word about Misty.

Not that it mattered now, anyway. The world would soon know how he felt about that woman.

"What exactly are you doing?" Gabe asked as Morgan dug out a tea bag. Everyone in the family knew for a fact he wasn't a tea drinker.

"Misty has morning sickness. Mom said nibbling on dry toast and sipping sweet hot tea before she got out of bed would help."

"Ah."

Honey started to rise from her chair. "If Misty's sick—"

Gabe caught her arm, earning Morgan's gratitude. "It's nothing Morgan can't handle. Isn't that right, Morgan?"

"It's under control." He set the toast and tea on a tray and left the room. He heard Gabe chuckling, then some whispering, but he didn't care. He was going to ask Misty to marry him, so they could gossip all they wanted.

Misty was still flat on her back in the bed when he reached her side. "I have a remedy here. First, nibble a few bites of toast…that's it. No, don't argue. I promise, it'll help."

Crumbs landed on her chest, and he brushed them away. He imagined he'd have to change his sheets more often if this ritual continued, though his mother had claimed the morning sickness usually didn't last that long. Generally not past the first trimester, and Misty should be about through that.

"Now some hot tea."

"I hate tea."

"Tough. It'll help. And I made this real sweet."

She sipped carefully while he held her head, then sighed. "Not bad."

After several minutes of repeating the procedure, she cautiously sat up and smiled. "You're a miracle worker. I won't even need to sneak off to the lake."

Morgan smoothed her hair, thinking she was about the most precious-looking woman first thing in the morning, with her eyes puffy, a crease on her cheek from the pillow. He frowned at himself. "If you ever do want to go to the lake, let me know and I'll keep you company, okay?"

Instead of answering him, she asked, "You've taken care of a lot of pregnant ladies, huh?"

"No, you're my first. Why?"

"How'd you know the toast and tea would help?"

She was naked under the sheet, which barely kept her nipples concealed. Now that she no longer felt sick, talking required major concentration on his part. "I asked my mother."

She jumped so hard she spilled her tea. Yep, his sheets were in for a lot of washing.

He eyed the spill on the top sheet and started to pull

it away from her before she got soaked, but she gripped it tightly to her chin and glared at him. "You did what?"

She sounded like a frog. "I asked my mother. I figured she had four kids so she had to have had morning sickness, right? She told me what worked for her. And by the way, she sends her love."

Misty pulled her knees up and dropped her head. "I don't believe this," was her muffled complaint.

Morgan smoothed her hair again. He loved her hair, shiny black and silky. Between the two of them, they'd likely have dark-haired children. He wondered if their eyes would be dark blue like his, or vivid blue like Misty's. It didn't matter to him one whit. "Will you marry me, Misty?"

She jerked upright and thwacked her skull on the headboard. With a wince, she rubbed her head, then eyed Morgan. "What did you say?"

Damn. Morgan took in her expression of stark disbelief and faltered. Her eyes were narrowed, her pupils dilated. Her soft mouth was pinched tight.

And he was hard again.

"I said," he muttered through his teeth, "will you marry me?"

"Why?"

Morgan stiffened, and he knew his damn face was heating. He hadn't blushed since sixth grade! "What the hell do you mean, *why?*"

She didn't blink, didn't look away from him. As if talking to a nitwit, she asked slowly, "Why do *you* want to marry *me?*"

A knock on the door saved him from trying to give a stammering reply. He sure as hell hadn't expected her to answer his proposal with an interrogation. He gave her a glare, waited until she'd pulled the sheet higher, then called out, "Come in."

Gabe stuck his head in the door. He kept his gaze resolutely on Morgan, and not on Misty. "You have a phone call."

"Take a message."

"Uh, Morgan, it's from out of town. I think you'll want to take it."

He could tell by Gabe's tone who the caller was. Hating the interruption, even while he was relieved by it, he stood. "I'll be right back."

Misty nodded, her face almost blank.

He put his hands on his hips. "We'll finish this conversation when I get off the phone."

"All right."

She sounded far from enthusiastic, and he wanted to demand to know how she felt, but knew he'd do better to bide his time. Patience, more often than not, wasn't his virtue.

He didn't look at her again as he left the room.

Twenty minutes later he was lounging against the wall outside the hall bathroom when Misty finally emerged, fresh from her shower. She put on her brakes when she saw him and stared at him warily without saying a word.

Morgan noticed her wet hair, her pink cheeks, her bare feet. She had on a T-shirt and loose cotton drawstring pants. "You going somewhere?"

"I have to be at the diner in about an hour."

He wanted to curse, to insist she skip work today, but he knew without even asking that he'd be wasting his breath. The woman was bound and determined to make all the money she could. Well, that'd be over with soon enough.

"All right. Then I guess we ought to get right to it."

"You're going to tell me why you want to marry me?"

There was no one else in the hallway, but he'd definitely prefer more guaranteed privacy. He took her arm and led her to his room. When he closed the door, he leaned against it and watched her. "Do you remember a woman named Victoria Markum?"

Misty backed up until her knees hit his mattress, then dropped onto it. "Yes. She was Mr. Collins's girlfriend."

He nodded. "Well, I hired some people to talk to her."

She frowned in confusion. "You hired people?" At his nod, she asked, "But why?"

"To prove your innocence. And don't give me that look, Malone. I didn't tell you because I didn't want you to start squawking about me spending my money. This is something I wanted to do, all right?"

"I'll pay you back—"

"The hell you will." Morgan went to her and sat beside her, then took her hands. "Can't you just accept that I care and I want to help?"

She searched his face for a long time before she grudgingly said, "Thank you. I don't know what to say."

"You could ask me what I found out."

"All right." She bit her lip, her face filled with anxiety. "I hope, judging by the way you're acting, it's good news?"

"As a matter of fact, it is. You see, Malone, I believed you when you said you hadn't taken the money. That meant someone else did, of course. I wondered if perhaps Ms. Markum might have done it."

Misty squeezed his fingers; her hands were ice-cold. "I never even considered that. I kept wondering if someone had managed to slip into the store and open the register while I was in the restroom, or if maybe the money had just been miscounted, but... Victoria didn't seem like a thief to me. She was... I don't know. Too ditzy. And I think they were planning on getting married, so she'd have been sort of stealing from herself, right?"

Morgan held both her hands between his own to warm them. "Actually, they were planning on marrying, or at least, Ms. Markum was. But we found out that Ms. Markum and your boss had a falling out. He, it seems, took the money she'd been holding for him in her own savings account, and ran with it, so she was more than willing to talk to us. It didn't even take much prodding, from what the investigator told me. You see, she didn't steal the money...but he did."

"What?"

"Collins had been skimming from himself. Ms. Markum may be a ditz, but she has facts and dates and exact amounts that should corroborate her testimony. All we need to do now is contact your lawyer, who can file for a motion for the first trial to be declared a mistrial, based on the new evidence. The second trial should be scheduled quickly, probably within a month, because they won't want you serving more of a sentence than you've already had to."

She shook her head. "It can't be that easy."

"Actually it is." He smiled, trying to reassure her. "Well, you'll have to see the judge again, of course, but this time I'll be with you."

She stared at him in amazement, her bottom lip starting to quiver.

"Now, Malone," he said uneasily, "don't cry. I can't stand it."

Big tears welled in her eyes anyway. "I can't believe you did this for me."

He pulled her close and kissed the tip of her nose, which was starting to turn red. "I want you to be happy."

She launched herself against him, knocking him back on the bed. She kissed his face, his throat, his ear. Morgan laughed even as he felt himself harden. There was no way Misty Malone could crawl all over him without turning him on. He caught her mouth and held her still for the deep thrust of his tongue, but pulled back slowly before he completely lost control.

He held her head to his shoulder and smiled. "That's one problem taken care of."

She squeezed him tight. "You are the most amazing man."

Laughing, Morgan growled, "So you keep telling me. Now answer my other question. Will you marry me?"

She went still. Very slowly she raised her face. "You still haven't told me why you want to marry me."

Because he'd had a few minutes to come up with a reply, he said easily, "You're sexy and beautiful."

Her smile was radiant. "You're sexy and beautiful, too, but that's not a good reason to tie yourself to someone for life."

He snorted at her compliment. "We have great sex together. Hell, I still feel singed."

Her smile melted away and her eyes darkened. "Me, too. It was the most incredible thing. I'd never imagined sex could be like that." She brushed a kiss over his jaw, then added, "But we don't have to get married to have great sex. For as long as I'm here, I'm willing, Morgan."

His stomach started to cramp. She wasn't saying yes, and in fact, she was making a lot of excuses to cancel out every reason he gave her. But there was one reason she couldn't refute. "You're pregnant."

"The baby isn't your responsibility."

"It is if I want to make it my responsibility."

"Oh, Morgan. You're not thinking straight. You can't really want to be a fill-in for another man's child."

"The baby will be mine if you marry me."

She touched gentle fingers to his mouth and her expression was one of wonderment. "You say that now because you're feeling protective of me, just like you feel about everyone. But I don't need you to take care of me, Morgan. I can take care of myself, and the baby."

Morgan moved swiftly, rolling her beneath him before she could draw a deep breath. "Let me tell you something, Misty Malone. What you know about men doesn't add up to jack. And for your information, I don't care that the baby isn't mine. It's yours, and that's all that matters to me."

She shook her head, making him curse. He caught her hands and raised them over her head. "I'm going to tell you a little story."

"I have to be at work soon."

"Tough. Don't rush me." She wisely didn't push him on that score. Morgan drew a deep breath, then admitted, "Sawyer isn't Casey's natural father."

Misty's eyes widened and her mouth opened twice before she sputtered, "That's ridiculous!"

"No, it's true. If you want all the details, you can ask Honey. I'm sure Sawyer told her the whole story."

"But…" She searched his face, then looked away. "She's never said a word."

"Likely because it doesn't matter. Not to Sawyer, and sure as hell not to the rest of us. No one could love that boy more than we do. Sawyer knew all along that Casey wasn't his. But he'd been married to Casey's mother, and she didn't want him. So he brought Case home, a squalling little red-faced rodent, and we all went head over heels. Hell, a baby is a baby. It doesn't matter who planted the seed. All that matters is who loves him and cares for him and shelters him. I want to do that with you, Misty." He swallowed hard, his hands gripping her shoulders. "Marry me."

He could feel her shaking beneath him, saw the tears gathering in her eyes. She bit her lip and sniffed.

"Malone?"

"I… I can't."

Never in his life, Morgan thought, had anything hurt so much. He'd been in brawls, he'd been injured by cars and animals. He'd had broken limbs and a broken nose and more bruises than he could count. But nothing had ever hurt like this.

He stared at Misty, not wanting to believe that she'd refused him. She'd told him all along that she didn't want commitment, that she was through with involvement. But he hadn't believed her, not really. He hadn't *wanted* to believe her.

His head throbbed and his blood boiled. He wanted to rage, he wanted to shout. But he'd made a big enough fool of himself already.

He rolled to the side of the bed and stared at the ceiling. He started to ask her why, but wasn't at all sure he wanted to know the answer. Misty scampered off the bed, and her bare feet made no sound on the carpet. His door closed very quietly.

By the time he followed her, she'd already left for work.

Gabe gave him a questioning look, but Morgan didn't even bother to acknowledge him. He left for work and didn't come home until late that night. He didn't see Misty at all.

Misty was sitting by the lake when Honey found her. She glanced at her sister, shielding her eyes from the sun. "Hey. What's up?"

"That was my question." Honey lowered herself onto the edge of the dock beside Misty. She pulled off her sandals and dangled her feet in the water. "Morgan has looked like a thundercloud all day, growling at everyone, ready to spit nails. We're all avoiding him. The only one not afraid is the puppy."

Misty looked at the dark lake water and promised herself she wouldn't cry. "The dog has really taken to him, then?"

"Amazing, isn't it? Do you know what he named that little wad of fur? Godzilla. And the dog seems to like it."

Misty summoned up a smile, when in truth, it was all she could do not to bawl like a baby.

Honey made an exasperated sound. "So Morgan is more feral than ever and you're so morose the sun won't even shine on you. What's going on?"

Misty turned her face away, resting it on her bent knees. Hoping Honey couldn't hear the strain in her voice, she said, "Nothing. I just wanted some peace and quiet."

"Funny. That's just what Morgan said."

"Oh?"

"Yeah. He sent Gabe and Jordan running, and Sawyer was ready to hit him in the head, but I insisted he talk to me. He won't growl at me, you know. I think he's afraid it'll break me or something."

Funny. Morgan had never hesitated to shower her with his bad moods, not that she'd minded. He hadn't scared her at all, because she'd seen through him.

Honey cleared her throat. "He told me he just wants to finish up the house so he can get moved out. He's been spending every spare minute up there." Honey hesitated, then said with a dramatic flair, "Tomorrow he's moving in."

Her stomach cramped, because she knew she'd chased him away, but what else could she do? Marry a man who didn't love her?

"I hate to see him go," Honey admitted softly. "The house won't seem the same without him."

Misty didn't reply to that. What could she say? She'd barely seen Morgan in two days. Even today, at the station, he'd not taken much notice of her. When he had looked at her, his expression had been flat. There'd been no teasing, no lust, no tenderness, none of the things she was used to and that she had begun to expect. Oh, he'd still been courteous, telling her to go to lunch, to take her time, to make sure she ate right. It was as if what had been between them was no longer there.

Misty couldn't bear to think about that, so she decided to do something she should have done already. "I have a confession."

Honey's arm slipped around her shoulders. "I'm still a good listener, you know."

"You're going to be angry," Misty warned her.

"I doubt it."

But when Misty explained all about the theft, how she'd been found guilty, Honey was absolutely livid. Not at Misty, so much, but that her boss had dared to accuse her and that the judge hadn't believed her.

It took some fast talking on Misty's part to make Honey understand that all was well now, or at least on the way to being well, thanks to Morgan, and to explain why she hadn't told her sooner.

"So Morgan is the one that got it all straightened out?"

Misty nodded, once again confounded by his generosity. "He's pretty wonderful, isn't he?"

"*I've* certainly always thought so."

She'd always thought so, too, but what she felt wasn't enough to make a marriage work. Misty heaved a sigh. "I have to leave tomorrow morning. I might be gone overnight. I'm not sure."

Honey stiffened. "Leave where?"

"My lawyer needs to see me. There're some things that have to be done to set up the new trial. Everything should go well, so I'm not worried about that. I already told Ceily, and I told Nate. I know I should have told Morgan that I wouldn't be in, but I just couldn't. Things aren't great between us right now."

Very gently, Honey asked, "Why not?"

Misty squeezed her hands into fists. "He asked me to marry him."

There was a moment of stunned silence, then Honey gasped theatrically. "Well, that bastard! How dare he?"

Shaking her head at her sister's mocking outrage, Misty said, "You don't understand."

"I understand that you love him, sis. Isn't that what's most important?"

"No." Misty dropped her feet into the water with a splash, then watched the ripples fan out until they disappeared. "What's important is that two people love each other. But Morgan doesn't love me. He likes to take care of people, and he thinks I need a husband because I'm pregnant. You've said yourself how old-fashioned he is. But that's not good enough anymore. I've learned a lot through all this, most importantly that you can't cut corners. If there isn't love, then there's nothing."

"And you think Morgan doesn't love you?"

Misty lifted one shoulder, not sure what to say. "I asked him why he wanted to marry me. He gave me a lot of good reasons, but not once did he say he loved me."

"So ask him outright."

Misty stared at her, appalled. "I can't do that!"

"Why not?" Honey kicked her feet, too, splashing them both. "Morgan is a hardheaded man. Actually, he's just hard, period. All over."

"I know, I know." Misty hadn't been able to sleep at night, remembering how wonderfully hard Morgan was. She loved everything about him, but she was crazy nuts about his big, solid body. And after only making love with him twice, she was addicted. She didn't think she could have ever gotten enough of him.

"Hard men are usually sensitive men."

Misty snorted over that bit of nonsense. "Morgan is about as blunt as they come. He always tells me what he's thinking or feeling, even if it embarrasses me to death."

Honey looked at the sky and pondered that. "Well, then, don't you think you owe him the same courtesy?"

She shuddered at just the thought. "I'm a horrible coward. Morgan's made it clear from the first that he's attracted to me. But that's all."

"How can you say that?" Honey frowned at her. "Morgan's done everything he could to keep you close by. He even made up that ridiculous story about the two of you having an agreement."

"You knew that wasn't real?"

Honey smiled. "It was plain on your face."

Bemused for a moment, Misty wondered if all his brothers had known he was just making up their involvement. Then she shook her head. "It doesn't matter. He kept me here because he was trying to take care of me— whether I wanted him to or not. He does that for everyone, Honey." She turned to face her sister, wanting her to understand. "Morgan is about the most giving, caring man I've ever met. That's why being a sheriff is so perfect for him. He loves taking care of other people's problems. He's a natural caregiver—though he'd choke if he heard me say that, and probably frown something fierce. He tries to hide his gentleness behind a big tough exterior."

Honey waved that away. "I know. But still—"

"No. If he loved me, surely he would have said so."

"Will you at least think about it? Maybe he's not quite as tough or as confident as you think he is."

The idea of Morgan being insecure would take some getting used to, but to appease her sister, she agreed to think it over. What would Morgan say if she blurted out that she loved him? Would he be embarrassed? Would he lie and say he loved her, too, just to keep her from embarrassment? She closed her eyes, not sure at all what his reaction would be.

"I was looking for you for another reason, too."

Honey's serious tone pulled Misty out of her contemplation. "What's wrong?"

After a deep breath, Honey said, "Father wants to visit us. He called a few minutes ago."

That was the very last thing Misty had expected to hear. Incredulous, she stared at her sister. "You must be kidding."

"Unfortunately…no."

Misty narrowed her eyes. "He wants to come here? To Kentucky?"

"Yes. That's what he said. I'm supposed to call him back and tell him when it'd be convenient."

A summons from her father wouldn't have thrown her so badly. But a visit? It didn't make any sense. Unless… "What are we being accused of now? Is he mad about something?" Then a horrid thought intruded. "Oh, God. He found out I'd been arrested, didn't he?"

"I don't think so. Actually, he told me he wants to meet my husband. Sawyer is afraid he's going to bring up his will again, and you can just imagine how that'd go over."

Misty nodded. All her life, her father had claimed to want a son to carry on the family name. Since their mother had died without giving him one, he'd decided that Honey, as the oldest child, would have to supply a husband to fill the role of masculine heir.

Sawyer had flatly refused to accept anything from him. And their father had been peeved ever since. He hadn't even attended the wedding.

"Father said he was intrigued by the notion of men

who would blindly turn down money and power. When I mentioned to him that he should have come to the wedding, he actually said he regretted missing it. Can you believe that?"

"Uh…no."

Honey softened her tone. "He also said he was worried about you."

"Since when?" Misty couldn't help but feel bitter over her last conversation with her father. He'd been very disappointed that she'd gotten pregnant, and he hadn't bothered to try to hide that disappointment.

"Here's what I think." Honey pulled her feet from the water and stood, then looked at Misty. "I think I'm so happy that I don't mind hearing him out, seeing what he has to say. Sawyer told me that not everyone is as capable of expressing love as we are. He asked me about Father's upbringing, our grandparents, and you know, I think he might be on to something there. Father was always a cold, detached man, just as his parents were and as they expected him to be. After Mom died, he was all alone. That couldn't have been easy for him, Misty. I'm not saying we have to be all loving and hugging." She shuddered, then laughed. "That would be too weird after all this time. But I'd at least like to make my peace with him. And you're going to be giving him a grandchild. Maybe he'll look at things differently, but either way, I want to know that I gave our relationship every chance."

Honey walked away, leaving Misty to think things over. True, her father had never been the type to hug or even give a quick compliment. But he'd made certain they were always well dressed and well fed, and they'd never wanted for anything material. Just the fact that he wanted to meet Sawyer and the brothers showed a bending on his part, a sort of olive branch. She supposed it wouldn't hurt to listen to him.

As she walked up to the house, dodging stones on the ground and the occasional bee feasting on clover, she smiled. She couldn't begin to imagine her father's reaction to the brothers. They were overwhelming and dominating and they spoke their minds without hesitation.

Her father would be in for a surprise.

Early the next morning, Morgan stared at his bedroom ceiling, a habit that had replaced sleeping in the past few days. No matter how hard he worked, no matter how he exhausted himself, he couldn't sleep. He was so damn tired he could barely see straight, but when he closed his eyes, all he could think of was Misty.

Hell, even with his eyes open, she was all he could think of. He alternated between fantasies of making love to her until she begged him to marry her and throttling her for turning down his proposal in the first place. Not that he would ever really hurt her, he thought with disgust. Hell, no.

There was one bright side to all his recent labors; his house was done. He could now move in and live in comfort—and solitude. But he didn't want to. He'd come to think of the house with Misty in it. Without her, it didn't seem complete no matter what he did to it.

Sawyer was right, he was a miserable bastard. He never should have given in to his needs. He should have avoided her instead of finding out for a fact how sweet she was, how right it felt to be inside her, holding her, talking with her, loving her. Now she was still here, a damn relative, and he had to look at her and know she was close, but she didn't want him.

He closed his eyes and groaned.

Two seconds later his bedroom door flew open and bounced off the wall. Morgan leaped out of bed, automatically reaching for his gun. The overhead light came on, nearly blinding him in the gray morning shadows, but showing his brother's angry face clear as day. Sawyer stalked in, grabbed Morgan's discarded jeans and flung them at him.

"Get dressed."

Morgan began pulling on his pants without hesitation. It wasn't often Sawyer issued commands that way. "What's wrong?"

"You blew it, that's what."

He stumbled, his jeans only to his knees. "What the hell does that mean?"

"It means Misty is gone."

Forget the elephant, it felt like his heart was smashed flat. Wheezing, a little light-headed, he asked, "Gone where?"

Sawyer jutted his chin toward Morgan and growled, "She *left,* Morgan. What did you expect her to do with you moping around, ignoring her, acting like she didn't exist? I thought you loved her!"

Morgan dropped onto the edge of the bed. "I asked her to marry me," he said, feeling numb. "She turned me down."

"You must have misunderstood."

Sawyer and Morgan both turned to see Jordan standing in the doorway. Morgan shook his head. "No, I asked and she flatly refused."

Jordan crossed his arms over his chest and frowned. "I can tell she cares about you."

Gabe walked in. "She's crazy about him, if you ask me."

"Oh, for the love of—" Morgan stood and finished pulling on his pants. "If that's true, why wouldn't she marry me?"

Honey pushed Gabe out of her way and glared at all of them. "Because she said you didn't love her."

"What?"

"She said you were just trying to take care of her, but without love, it wasn't worth it."

Morgan cursed so viciously that Gabe backed up and Jordan rolled his eyes. Sawyer pulled Honey protectively to his side. "Get a grip, Morgan. Are you going to go after her or not?"

His head shot up. "Go after her? When did she leave?"

Honey tapped her foot. "About two minutes ago."

Before she had finished, Morgan had snapped his jeans, shoved his gun in his pocket and started out of the room. But his brothers had all congregated inside, blocking his path at the end of the bed, so he bounded over it instead, bouncing on the mattress as he dodged past them. He ran out the doorway, not bothering with a shirt or shoes. Gabe trotted after him, waving a shirt. "Wait! Don't you want to finish dressing?"

Morgan ignored him, but he couldn't ignore the loud guffaws from his other brothers. He snatched his keys from the peg by the back door and ran into the yard.

"Damn irritants," he muttered, then winced as his bare feet came into contact with every sharp stone on the dew-wet grass. He slipped twice, but within thirty seconds he had the Bronco out, lights flashing and sirens blasting. When he caught up to her…

Morgan filled the time it took to get to town by plotting all the ways he'd set her straight.

She was in front of the sheriff's office when he spotted her. She slowed when she noticed his flashing lights, and after a few seconds she pulled over.

Unfortunately, Ceily was just coming to the diner to start preparing the food, and she paused on the front stoop to watch as Morgan climbed out of the Bronco and slammed the door. Nate was at the station already, and he and Howard and Jesse also walked out to see what was happening. It wasn't often that Morgan pulled anyone over with so much fanfare.

By the time he'd circled the front of the Bronco, Misty had already left her car. She gaped at him, then demanded, "What in the world is wrong with you? Has something happened?" She gazed at him from his shaggy hair, his bare chest, to his naked feet.

Morgan stomped up to her, ignoring the sting to his feet and the way the sidewalk was quickly beginning to crowd with curious onlookers. He hooked his hand around the back of her neck and drew her up to her tiptoes. "Where in hell do you think you're going?"

She blinked at him. "I have to meet with my lawyer today."

Morgan prepared to blast her with his wrath—and then her words sank in. "You're not leaving?"

"Leaving, as in for good?"

He nodded.

"Why would you think that?"

He seriously considered going home and choking Sawyer. But first, he had a few things to straighten out. "You should have told me you were leaving."

"You," she said, beginning to show her own pique, "haven't shown the slightest interest in talking to me lately!"

"Because I asked you to marry me and you had the nerve to say no."

A loud gasp rose from their audience.

Morgan pretended he hadn't heard them. "Do you know how many other women I've asked to be wife? Do you? *None!*"

"Well, I'm honored," Misty sneered, then poked him in the chest and her own voice rose to a shout. "But I'm not marrying a man who doesn't love me."

He sputtered in renewed outrage. *"Who the hell says I don't love you?"*

Misty caught her breath, panting, then said with deep feeling, her gaze intent, *"Who says you do?"*

Morgan growled, ran a hand roughly through his hair, then he picked her up. He held her at eye level and said, "Damn woman, I asked you to marry me! Why would I do that if I didn't love you?"

Someone on the sidewalk—it sounded like Ceily—called out in a laughing voice, "Yeah, why would Morgan do that?"

Morgan jerked his head around to face them all. "Can't you people find something to do?"

"No!" was the unanimous retort.

Morgan growled again. "Nate, arrest anyone who doesn't scatter."

Nate promptly looked dumbfounded. "Uh…"

Misty regained his attention by saying softly, "You just

want to help me, like you helped that woman with the flat tire, and the dog, and the school kids and the elderly."

Morgan walked to her car and plunked her down gently on the hood. He braced his hands on either side of her hips, then leaned in so close his nose touched hers. "Listen up, Malone. I didn't ask the damn dog to marry me. I didn't ask Howard or Jesse to marry me."

Jesse shouted, "He's speakin' the truth there."

Misty opened her mouth twice before she got words to come out. She spoke so softly, Morgan could barely hear her. "You said…you said you were looking for a wife."

He gave a sharp nod. "You."

"But…" Her voice faded to a shy whisper. "You said you wanted three children."

"Three total." His hand covered her belly, and he smiled. Breathing the words so no one else would hear, he explained, "This one and two more. I was trying to hint to you that I'd be a good father."

"Oh, Morgan." She cupped his face, and tears filled her eyes. "I already know you'd be an excellent father."

He straightened and put his hands on his hips. "I swear, if you start crying again, Malone, I won't like it." He drew a breath and added, "Hell, it just about kills me to see you unhappy."

She sniffed loudly. "I'm very happy."

"So you won't cry?"

"I won't cry."

A fat tear rolled down her cheek, making him sigh in exasperation. The woman was forever turning him in circles. But since she seemed in an agreeable mood for a change… "Tell me you'll marry me."

She nodded. "I'll marry you."

She started to put her arms around his neck, but he

held her off. "Not so quick, Malone. I told you I love you. Don't you have something to say to me?"

With everyone on the sidewalk cheering her on, she grinned around her tears and said, "Morgan Hudson, I love you so much it hurts."

He scooped her into his arms for a fierce hug, then turned to the crowd, laughing out loud. "You heard her. Consider me an engaged man." Then to Misty, "Damn. Do you think we have time for me to go home and get dressed before we go see your lawyer? I'd probably make a better impression that way."

Epilogue

Morgan hauled Misty into his lap after her father had left. She protested, saying, "No, Morgan, I'm too fat now!"

Three months had passed. She was rounded with the child growing inside her, but still so sexy he could barely keep his hands off her. Every day he loved her more.

He kissed her cheek and smiled. "I promise to bear up under the weight."

Honey, a little subdued and cuddled up against Sawyer's side, said, "Misty, you look wonderful. Not at all fat."

Gabe laughed. "When I start looking like you two did, you'll have to give me some pointers so I can find my own beauty."

Sawyer blinked. "I wasn't looking. That's why Honey sort of...blindsided me." Honey playfully punched him for that remark, making Sawyer laugh.

Shrugging, Morgan added, "I wasn't looking, either."

The feminine weight in his lap gasped over his statement. "What an outrageous clanker! You even told me you wanted a wife."

Morgan shook his head. "That was just lip service. Sawyer seemed so tamed, I thought I should give it a try, too. But I wasn't putting much effort into it, not until I saw you."

Gabe nodded. "As I said, they're both gorgeous."

"Looks don't matter, Gabe." He tilted Misty's chin up and kissed her lips. "It was Misty's mouthy bluster that reeled me in."

Gabe made a face. "You can say that *now.*"

Jordan shook his head. "Your day will come, Gabe."

"Ha! But not before yours, old man. If we're going in order, you're doomed."

Jordan made a face at him. "If you keep using words like doomed, Misty or Honey are going to flatten you."

Casey flopped down on the sofa. "So, Dad, what do you think about me visiting Mr. Malone?"

Morgan hid a smile. Mr. Malone had surprised them all. True, the man was so rigid he bordered on brittle. But he had made the effort to unbend a little more on each visit. His first had been horribly strained, but with all the ribald teasing going on, he could hardly stay puckered up indefinitely. This time, he'd actually kissed each daughter's cheek.

And rather than trying to offer his money to Sawyer again, he'd asked—actually *asked*—if he could put a good portion of it in a trust for the baby. Morgan and Misty had discussed it, then agreed, as long as equal money was put in for each child either of the sisters had.

That had settled one problem, but then the man had fixated on Casey. All along, he'd seemed very impressed by Casey's manners, his maturity, and within a few hours of this visit, he'd damn near adopted him as a pseudo heir. None of them were overly pleased by it, especially not Honey, but when the man had invited Casey to visit, to look over his enterprises, Casey had shown some interest.

Sawyer pursed his mouth, then hugged Honey closer so she wouldn't protest. Morgan knew Honey hated to let Casey out of her sight. She had a hard time thinking of him as a young man, despite the fact he was exactly that. "I suppose we could all make a trip up there. If after that you want to hang around for a short visit, it'd probably be all right."

"Great." Casey didn't seem overly enthusiastic either way, and when he said he had a date, Morgan understood why. The male brain had a hard time focusing when females were being considered.

They all watched Casey leave with indulgent smiles. Seconds later, Honey and Sawyer left to begin dinner. Jordan had a few calls to make, and when Morgan started kissing his wife, Gabe left the room whistling.

"You about ready to head home?" Morgan asked.

"I thought we were staying for dinner."

"We'll come back," Morgan promised, then gave her a lecherous grin. He picked her up in his arms and suffered through her complaints.

"I'm too heavy now for you to keep doing this!"

Morgan just grinned at her. "Do you know, you're the only one who's ever doubted my strength."

"That's not true." She kissed his chin. "I just like to match it."

* * * * *

Joanne Rock credits her decision to write romance after a book she picked up during a flight delay engrossed her so thoroughly that she didn't mind at all when her flight was delayed two more times. Giving her readers the chance to escape into another world has motivated her to write over eighty books for a variety of Harlequin series.

Books by Joanne Rock

Harlequin Desire
Dynasties: Mesa Falls

The Rebel
The Rival
Rule Breaker
Heartbreaker
The Rancher
The Heir

Texas Cattleman's Club: Inheritance

Her Texas Renegade

Visit the Author Profile page at
Harlequin.com for more titles.

HIS ACCIDENTAL HEIR

Joanne Rock

For Barbara Jean Thomas,
an early mentor and role model of hard work.
Thank you, Barbara, for teaching me the value
of keeping my chin up and having faith in myself.
During my teens, you were so much more than a
boss—you were a friend, a cheerleader and
a sometimes mom on those weekend trips
with the crew. I'll never forget my visit to
New York to see Oprah, courtesy of you!
Much love to you, always.

Chapter 1

"Rafe, I need you in the Antilles Suite today." Maresa Delphine handed her younger brother a gallon jug of bubble bath. "I have a guest checking in who needs a hot bath on arrival, but he isn't sure what time he'll get here."

Her twenty-one-year-old sibling—who'd recently suffered a traumatic brain injury in a car accident—didn't reach to take the jug. Instead, his hazel eyes tracked the movements of a friendly barmaid currently serving a guest a Blackbeard's Revenge specialty drink on the patio just outside the lobby. The Carib Grand Hotel's floor-to-ceiling windows allowed for views of the tiki bar on Barefoot Beach and the glittering Caribbean Sea beyond. Inside the hotel, the afternoon activity had picked up since Maresa's mad dash to the island's sundries shop for the bath products. All of her runners had been busy fulfilling other duties for guests, so she'd made the trip

herself. She had no idea what her newest runner—her recovering brother who still needed to work in a monitored
environment—had been doing at that hour. He hadn't answered his radio and he needed to get with the program
if he wanted to remain employed. Not to mention, Maria
might be blamed for his slipups. She was supporting her
family, and couldn't afford to lose her job as concierge for
this exclusive hotel on a private island off Saint Thomas.

And she really, really needed him to remain employed
where she could watch over him. Where he was eligible
for better insurance benefits that could give him the long-
term follow-up care he would need for years. She knew
she held Rafe to a higher standard so that no one on staff
could view his employment as a conflict of interest. Sure,
the hotel director had approved his application, but she
had promised to carefully supervise her brother during
his three-month trial period.

"Rafe." She gently nudged her sibling with the heavy
container of rose-scented bubbles, remembering his
counselor's advice about helping him stay on task when
he got distracted. "I have some croissants from the bak-
ery to share with you on your next break. But for now, I
really need help. Can you please take this to the Antilles
Suite? I'd like you to turn on the hot water and add this
for a bubble bath as soon as I text you."

Their demanding guest could stride through the lobby
doors any moment. Mr. Holmes had phoned this morning, unsure of his arrival time, but insistent on having a
hot bath waiting for him. That was just the first item on
a long list of requests.

She checked her slim watch, a gift from her last employer, the Parisian hotel where she'd had the job of her
dreams. As much as Maresa loved her former position,

she couldn't keep it after her mother's car accident that had caused Rafe's head injury almost a year ago. Going forward, her place was here in Charlotte Amalie to help with her brother.

She refused to let him fail at the Carib Grand Hotel. Her mother's poor health meant she couldn't supervise him at home, for one thing. So having him work close to Maresa all day was ideal.

"I'll go to the Antilles Suite." Rafe tucked the bubble bath under one arm and continued to study the barmaid, a sweet girl named Nancy who'd been really kind to him when Maresa introduced them. "You will call me on the phone when I need to turn on the water."

Maresa touched Rafe's cheek to capture his full attention, her fingers grazing the jagged scar that wrapped beneath his left ear. Her mother had suffered an MS flare-up behind the wheel one night last year, sending her car into a telephone pole during a moment of temporary paralysis. Rafe had gone through the windshield since his seatbelt was unbuckled; he'd been trying to retrieve his phone that had slid into the backseat. Afterward, Maresa had been deeply involved in his recovery and care since their mother had been battling her own health issues. Their father had always been useless, a deadbeat American businessman who worked in the cruise industry and used to visit often, wooing Maresa's mother with promises about coming to live with him in Wisconsin when he saved up enough money to bring them. That had never happened, and he'd checked out on them by the time Maresa was ten, moving to Europe for his job. Yet then, as now, Maresa didn't mind adapting her life to help Rafe. Her brother's injuries could have been fatal that day. Instead, he was a happy part of her world. Yes, he would forever cope with bouts of confusion, memory loss and irritability along with the learning disabilities the accident had brought with it. Throughout it all, though, Rafe was always... Rafe. The brother she adored. He'd been her biggest supporter after her former fiancé broke things off with her a week before their wedding two years ago, encouraging her to go to Paris and "be my superstar."

He was there for her then, after that humiliating experience. She would be there for him now.

"Rafe? Go to the Antilles Suite and I'll text you when it's time to turn on the hot water." She repeated the instructions for him now, knowing it would be kinder to transfer him to the maintenance team or landscaping staff where he could do the same kinds of things every day. But who would watch out for him there? "Be sure to add the bubbles. Okay?"

Drawing in a breath, she took comfort from the soothing scent of white tuberoses and orchids in the arrangement on her granite podium.

"A bubble bath." Rafe grinned, his eyes clearing. "Can do." He ambled off toward the elevator, whistling.

Her relief lasted only a moment because just then a limousine pulled up in front of the hotel. She had a clear view out the windows overlooking the horseshoe driveway flanked by fountains and thick banks of birds-of-paradise. The doormen moved as a coordinated team toward the vehicle, prepared to open doors and handle baggage.

She straightened the orchid pinned on her pale blue linen jacket. If this was Mr. Holmes, she needed to stall him to give Rafe time to run that bath. The guest had been curt to the point of rudeness on the phone, requiring a suite with real grass—and it had to be ryegrass only—for his Maltese to relieve himself. The guest had also ordered a dog walker with three years' worth of references and a groomer on-site, fresh lilacs in the room daily and specialty pies flown in from a shop in rural upstate New York for his bedtime snack each evening.

And that was just for starters. She couldn't wait to see what he needed once he settled in for his two-week stay. These were the kinds of guests that could make or break a career. The vocal kind with many precise needs. All of which she would fulfill. It was the job she'd chosen because she took pride in her organizational skills, continually reordering her world throughout a chaotic childhood with an absentee father and a chronically ill mother. She took comfort in structuring what she could. And since there were only so many jobs on the island that could afford to pay her the kind of money she needed to support both her mother and her brother, Maresa had to succeed at the Carib Grand.

She calmed herself by squaring the single sheet of paper on her podium, lining up her pen beside it. She tapped open her list of restaurant phone numbers on her call screen so she could dial reservations at a moment's notice. The small, routine movements helped her to feel in control, reminding her she could do this job well. When she looked up again—

Wow.

The sight of the tall, chiseled male unfolding himself from the limousine was enough to take her breath away. His strong, striking features practically called for a feminine hand to caress them. Fraternizing with guests was, of course, strictly against the rules and Maresa had never been tempted. But if ever she had an inkling to stray from that philosophy, the powerful shoulders encased in expensive designer silk were exactly the sort of attribute that would intrigue her. The man towered over everyone in the courtyard entrance, including Big Bill, the head doorman. Dressed in a charcoal suit tailored to his long, athletic frame, the dark-haired guest buttoned his jacket, hiding too much of the hard, muscled chest that she'd glimpsed as he'd stepped out of the vehicle. Straightening his tie, he peered through the window, his ice-blue gaze somehow landing on her.

Direct hit.

She felt the jolt of awareness right through the glass. This supremely masculine specimen couldn't possibly be Mr. Holmes. Her brain didn't reconcile the image of a man with that square jaw and sharp blade of a nose ordering lilacs for himself. Daily.

Relaxing a fraction, Maresa blew out a breath as the newcomer turned back toward the vehicle. Until a silky white Maltese dog stepped regally from the limousine into the man's waiting arms.

In theory, Cameron McNeill liked dogs.

Big, slobbery working canines that thrived outdoors and could keep up with him on a distance run. The long-haired Maltese in his arms, on the other hand, was a prize-winning show animal with too many travel accessories to count. The retired purebred was on loan to Cam for his undercover assessment of a recently acquired McNeill Resorts property, however, and he needed Poppy's cooperation for his stint as a demanding hotel guest. If he walked into the financially floundering Carib Grand Hotel as himself—an owner and vice president of McNeill Resorts—he would receive the most attentive service imaginable and learn absolutely nothing about the establishment's underlying problems. But as Mr. Holmes, first-class pain in the ass, Cam would put the staff on their toes and see how they reacted.

After reviewing the Carib Grand's performance reports for the past two months, Cameron knew something was off in the day-to-day operations. And since he'd personally recommended that the company buy the property in the first place, he wasn't willing to wait for an overpriced operations review by an outside agency. Not that McNeill Resorts couldn't afford it. It simply chafed his pride that he'd missed something in his initial research. Besides, his family had just learned of a long-hidden branch of relations living on a nearby island—his father's sons by a secret mistress. Cam would use his time here to check out the other McNeills personally.

But for now? Business first.

"Welcome to the Carib Grand," an aging doorman greeted him with a deferential nod and a friendly smile.

Cam forced a frown onto his face to keep from smiling back. That wasn't as hard as he thought given the way Poppy's foolishly long fur was plastering itself to his jacket when he walked too fast, her topknot and tail bobbing with his stride and tickling his chin. It wouldn't come naturally to Cam to be the hard-to-please guest this week. He was a people-person to begin with, and appreciated those who worked for McNeill Resorts especially. But this was the fastest way he knew to find out what was going on at the hotel firsthand. He'd be damned if anyone on the board questioned his business acumen during a time when his aging grandfather was testing all his heirs for their commitment to his legacy.

The Carib Grand lobby was welcoming, as he recalled from his tour six months ago when the property had been briefly shut down. The two wings of the hotel flanked the reception area to either side with restaurants stacked overhead. But the lobby itself drew visitors in with floor-to-ceiling windows so the sparkling Caribbean beckoned at all times. Huge hanging baskets of exotic flowers framed the view without impeding it.

The scent of bougainvillea drifted in through the door behind him. Poppy tilted her nose in the air and took a seat on his forearm, a queen on her throne.

The front desk attendant—only one—was busy with another guest. Cameron's bellhop, a young guy with a long ponytail of dreadlocks, must have noticed the front desk was busy at the same time as him, because he gestured to the concierge's tall granite counter where a stunning brunette smiled.

"Ms. Delphine can help you check in, sir," the bellhop informed him while whisking his luggage onto a waiting cart. "Would you like me to walk the dog while you get settled?"

Nothing would please him more than to off-load Poppy and the miles of snow-white pet hair threading around his suit buttons. Cameron was pretty sure there was a cloud of fur floating just beneath his nose.

"Her name is Poppy," Cameron snapped at the helpful soul, unable to take his eyes off the very appealing concierge, who'd snagged his attention through the window the second he'd stepped out of the limo. "And I've requested a dog walker with references."

The bellhop gave a nod and backed away, no doubt glad to leave a surly guest in the hands of the bronze-skinned beauty sidling out from her counter to welcome Cameron. She seemed to have that mix of ethnicities common in the Caribbean. The burnished tint of her skin set off wide, tawny gold eyes. A natural curl and kink in her dusky brown hair ended in sun-blond tips. Perfect posture and a well-fitted linen suit made her look every inch a professional, yet her long legs drew his eye even though her skirt hit just above her knees. Even if he'd been visiting the property as her boss, he wouldn't have acted on the flash of attraction, of course. But it was a damn shame that he'd be at odds with this enticing female for the next two weeks. The concierge position was the linchpin in the hotel staff, though, and his mission to rattle cages began with her.

"Welcome, Mr. Holmes." He was impressed that she'd greeted him by name. "I'm Maresa. We're so glad to see you and Poppy, too."

He'd spoken to a Maresa Delphine on the phone earlier, purposely issuing a string of demands on short notice to see how she'd fare. She didn't look nervous. Yet. He'd need to challenge her, to prod at all facets of the management and staff to pinpoint the weak links. The hotel wasn't necessarily losing money, but it was only a matter of time before earnings followed the decline in performance reviews.

"Poppy will be glad to meet her walker." He came straight to the point, ignoring the eager bob of the dog's head as Maresa offered admiring words to the pooch. Cameron could imagine what the wag of the tail was doing to the back of his jacket. "Do you have the references ready?"

"Of course." Maresa straightened with a sunny smile. She had a hint of an accent he couldn't place. "They're right here at my desk."

Cameron's gaze dipped to her slim hips as she turned. He'd taken a hiatus from dating for fun over the last few months, thinking he ought to find himself a wife to fulfill his grandfather's dictate that McNeill Resorts would only go to the grandsons who were stable and wed. But he'd botched that, too, impulsively issuing a marriage proposal to the first woman his matchmaker suggested in order to have the business settled.

Now? Apparently the months without sex were conspiring against him. He ground his teeth against a surge of ill-timed desire.

"Here you go." The concierge turned with a sheet of paper in hand and passed it to him, her honey-colored gaze as potent as any caress. "I took the liberty of checking all the references myself, but I've included the numbers in case you'd like to talk to any of them directly."

"That's why I asked," he replied tightly, tugging the paper harder than necessary.

He could have sworn Poppy slanted him a dirty look over one fluffy white shoulder. Her nails definitely flexed into his forearm right through the sleeve of his suit before she fixed her coal-black eyes on Maresa Delphine.

Not that he blamed Poppy. He'd rather be staring at Maresa than scowling over dog walker references. Being the boss wasn't always a rocking-good time. Yet he'd rather ruffle feathers today and fix the core problems than have the staff jump though the hoops of an extended performance review.

Cameron slid the paper into his jacket pocket. "I'll check these after I have the chance to clean up. If you can have someone show us to our room."

He hurried her on purpose, curious if the room extras were ready to go. The bath wasn't a tough request, but the flowers had most likely needed to be flown in. If he hadn't been specifically looking for it, he might have missed the smallest hesitation on her part.

"Certainly." She lifted a tablet from the granite countertop where she worked. "If you can just sign here to approve the information you provided over the phone, I'll escort you myself."

That wasn't protocol. Did Ms. Delphine expect additional tips this way? Cam remembered reading that the concierge had been with the company since the reopening under McNeill ownership two months ago.

Signing his fake name on the electronic screen, he fished for information. "Are you understaffed?"

She ran a pair of keycards through the machine and slid them into a small welcome folder.

"Definitely not. We'll have Rudolfo bring your bags. I just want to personally ensure the suite is to your liking." She handed him the packet with the keys while giving a nod to the bell captain. "Can I make a dinner reservation for you this evening, Mr. Holmes?"

Cameron juggled the restless dog, who was no doubt more travel-weary than him. They'd taken a private jet, but even with the shorter air time, there'd been limo rides to and from airports, plus a boat crossing from Charlotte Amalie to the Carib Grand since the hotel occupied a small, private island just outside the harbor area in Saint Thomas. He'd walked the dog when they hit the ground at the airfield, but Poppy's owner had cautioned him to give the animal a certain amount of rest and play each day. So far on Cam's watch, Poppy had clocked zero time spent on both counts. For a pampered show dog, she was proving a trouper.

As soon as he banished the hotel staff including Maresa Delphine, he'd find a quiet spot on the beach where he and his borrowed pet could recharge.

"I've heard a retired chef from Paris opened a new

restaurant in Martinique." He would be spending some time on that island where his half brothers were living. "I'd like a standing reservation for the rest of the week." He had no idea if he'd be able to get over there, but it was the kind of thing a good concierge could accommodate.

"I've heard La Belle Palm is fantastic." Maresa punched a button on the guest elevator while Rudolfo disappeared down another hall with the luggage. "I haven't visited yet, but I enjoyed Chef Pierre's La Luce on the Left Bank."

Her words brought to mind her résumé that he'd reviewed briefly before making the trip. She'd worked at a Paris hotel prior to accepting her current position.

"You've spent time in Paris, Ms. Delphine?" He set Poppy on the floor, unfurling the pink jeweled leash that had matched the carrying case Mrs. Trager had given him. He'd kept all the accessories except for that one— the huge pink pet carrier made Cam look like he was travelling with Barbie's Dreamhouse under his arm.

"She's so cute." Maresa kept her eyes on the dog and not on him. "And yes, I lived in Paris for a year before returning to Saint Thomas."

"You're from the area originally?" He almost regretted setting the dog down since it removed a barrier between them. Something about Maresa Delphine drew him in.

His gaze settled on the bare arch of her neck just above her jacket collar. Her thick brown hair had been clipped at the nape, ending in a silky tail that curled along one shoulder. A single pearl drop earring rolled along the tender expanse of skin, a pale contrast to her rich brown complexion.

"I grew up in Charlotte Amalie and worked in a local hotel until a foreign exchange program run by the cor-

porate owner afforded me the chance to work overseas."
She glanced up at him. Caught him staring.

The jolt of awareness flared, hot and unmistakable.
He could tell she felt it, too. Her pupils dilated a fraction, dark pools with golden rims. His heartbeat slugged
heavier. Harder.

He forced his gaze away as the elevator chimed to announce their arrival on his floor. "After you."

He held the door as she stepped out into the short hall.
They passed a uniformed attendant with a gallon-sized
jug stuffed under his arm, a pair of earbuds half-in and
half-out of his ears. After a quick glance at Maresa, the
young man pulled the buds off and jammed them in his
pocket, then shoved open a door to the stairwell.

"Here we are." Maresa stepped aside so Cam stood
directly in front of the entrance to the Antilles Suite.

Poppy took a seat and stared at the door expectantly.

Cameron used the keycard to unlock the suite, not sure
what to expect. Was Maresa Delphine worthy of what the
company compensated her? Or had she returned to her
hometown in order to bilk guests out of extra tips and
take advantage of her employer? But she didn't appear to
be looking for a bonus gratuity as her gaze darted around
the suite interior and then landed on him.

Poppy spotted the patch of natural grass just outside
the bathroom door. The sod rested inside a pallet on car-
peted wheels, the cart painted in blues and tans to match
the room's decorating scheme. The dog made a break
for it and Cam let her go, the leash dangling behind her.

Lilacs flanked the crystal decanters on the minibar.
Through the open door to the bathroom, Cameron could
see the bubbles nearing the edge of the tub, the hot water
still running as steam wafted upward.

So far, Maresa had proven a worthy concierge. That was good for the hotel, but less favorable for him, perhaps, since her high standards surely precluded acting on a fleeting elevator attraction.

"If everything is to your satisfaction, Mr. Holmes, I'll leave you undisturbed while I go make your dinner reservations for the week." She hadn't even allowed the door to close behind them, a wise practice, of course, for a female hotel employee.

Rudolfo was already in the hall with the luggage cart. Cameron could hear Maresa giving the bellhop instructions for his bags. And Poppy's.

"Thank you." Cameron turned his back on her to stare out at the view of the hotel's private beach and the brilliant turquoise Caribbean Sea. "For now, I'm satisfied."

The room, of course, was fine. Ms. Delphine had passed his first test. But was he satisfied? No. He wouldn't rest until he knew why the guest reviews of the Carib Grand were lower than anticipated. And satisfaction was the last thing he was feeling when the most enticing woman he'd met in a long time was off-limits.

That attraction would be difficult to ignore when it was imperative he uncover all her secrets.

Chapter 2

As much as Maresa cursed her alarm clock chirping at her before dawn, she never regretted waking up early once she was on the Carib Grand's private beach before sunrise. Her mother's house was perched on a street high above Saint Thomas Harbor, which meant Maresa took a bike to the ferry each morning to get to the hotel property early for these two precious hours of alone time before work. Her brother was comfortable walking down to the dock later for his shift, a task that was overseen by a neighbor and fellow employee who also took the ferry over each day.

Now, rolling out her yoga mat on the damp sand, she made herself comfortable in child's pose, letting the magic of the sea and the surf do their work on her muscles tight with stress.

One. Two. Three. Breathe.

Smoothing her hands over the soft cotton of her bright pink crop top, she felt her diaphragm lift and expand. She rarely saw anyone else on the beach at this hour, and the few runners or walkers who passed by were too busy soaking up the same quiet moments as she to pay her any mind.

Maresa counted through the inhales and exhales, trying her damnedest to let go of her worries. Too bad Cameron Holmes's ice-blue eyes and sculpted features kept appearing in her mind, distracting her with memories of that electric current she'd experienced just looking at him.

It made no sense, she lectured herself as she swapped positions for her sun salutations. The guest was demanding and borderline rude—something that shouldn't attract her in the slightest. She hated to think his raw masculinity was sliding under her radar despite what her brain knew about him.

At least she'd made it through the first day of his stay without incident. But while that was something to celebrate, she didn't want her brother crossing paths with the surly guest again. She'd held her breath yesterday when the two passed one another in the corridor outside the Antilles Suite, knowing how much Rafe loved dogs. Thankfully, her brother had been engrossed in his music and hadn't noticed the Maltese.

She'd keep Rafe safely away from Mr. Holmes for the next two weeks. Tilting her face to the soft glow of first light, she arched her back in the upward salute before sweeping down into a forward bend. Breathing out the challenges—living in tight quarters with her family, battling local agencies to get her brother into support programs he needed for his recovery, avoiding her former fiancé who'd texted her twice in the last twenty-four hours asking to see her— Maresa took comfort in this moment every day.

Shifting into her lunge as the sun peeked above the horizon, Maresa heard a dog bark before a small white ball of fluff careened past her toward the water. Startled by the sudden brush of fur against her arm, she had to reposition her hands to maintain her balance.

"Poppy." A man's voice sounded from somewhere in the woods behind the beach.

Cameron Holmes.

Maresa recognized the deep baritone, not by sound so much as by the effect it had on her. A slow, warm wave through the pit of her belly. What was the matter with her? She scrambled to her feet, realizing the pampered pet of her most difficult guest was charging into the Caribbean, happily chasing a tern.

"Poppy!" she called after the dog just as Cameron Holmes stepped onto the beach.

Shirtless.

She had to swallow hard before she lifted her fingers to her lips and whistled. The little Maltese stopped in the surf, peering back in search of the noise while the tern flew away up the shore. The ends of Poppy's glossy coat floated on the surface of the incoming tide.

The man charged toward his pet, his bare feet leaving wet footprints in the sand. Maresa was grateful for the moment to indulge her curiosity about him without his seeing her. A pair of bright board shorts rode low on his hips. The fiery glow of sunrise burnished his skin to a deeper tan, his square shoulders rolling with an easy grace as he scooped the animal out of the water and into his arms. He spoke softly to her even as the strands of

long, wet fur clung to his side. Whatever he said earned
him a heartfelt lick on the cheek from the pooch, its white
tail wagging slowly.

Maresa's heart melted a little. Especially when she
caught a glimpse of Cameron Holmes's smile as he turned
back toward her. For a moment, he looked like another
man entirely.

Then, catching sight of her standing beside her yoga
mat, his expression grew shuttered.

"Sorry to interrupt your morning." He gave a brief
nod. Curt. Dismissive. "I thought the beach would be
empty at this hour or I wouldn't have let her off the leash."
He clipped a length of pink leather to the collar around
Poppy's neck.

"Most days, I'm the only one down here at this time."
She forced a politeness she didn't feel, especially when
she wasn't on duty yet. "Would you like a towel for her?"

The animal wasn't shivering, but Maresa couldn't
imagine it would be easy to groom the dog if she walked
home with wet fur dragging on the ground.

"I didn't think to bring one with me." He frowned,
glancing around the deserted beach as if one might appear. "I assumed towels would be provided."

She tried not to grind her teeth at the air of entitlement.
It became far easier to ignore the appeal of his shirtless
chest once he started speaking in that superior air.

"Towels are available when the beach cabana opens at
eight." Bending to retrieve the duffel on the corner of her
mat, she tugged out hers and handed it to him. "Poppy
can have mine."

He hesitated.

She fought the urge to cram the terry cloth back in
her bag and stomp off. But, of course, she couldn't do

that. She reached toward the pup's neck and scratched her there instead. Poppy's heart-shaped collar jangled softly against Maresa's hand. She noticed the "If Found" name on the back.

Olivia Trager?

Maybe the animal belonged to a girlfriend.

"Thank you." He took the hand towel and tucked it around the dog. Poppy stared out of her wrap as if used to being swaddled. "I really didn't mean to interrupt you."

He sounded more sincere this time. Maresa glanced up at him, only to realize how close they were standing. His gaze roamed over her as if he had been taking advantage of an unseen moment, the same way she had ogled him earlier. Becoming aware of her skimpy yoga crop top and the heat of awareness warming her skin, she stepped back awkwardly.

"Ms. Trager must really trust you with her dog." She hadn't meant to say it aloud. Then again, maybe hearing about his girlfriend would stop these wayward thoughts about him. "That is, no wonder you want to take such good care of her."

Awkward much? Maresa cursed herself for sticking her nose in his personal business.

His expression remained inscrutable for a moment. He studied her as if weighing how much to share. "My mother wouldn't trust anyone but me with her dog," he said finally.

She considered his words, still half wishing the mystery Ms. Trager was a girlfriend on her way to the resort today. Then Maresa would have to take a giant mental step backward from the confusing hotel guest. As it stood, she had no one to save her from the attraction but herself. With that in mind, she raked up her yoga mat and started rolling it.

"Well, I hope the dog walker and groomer meet your criteria." She stuffed the mat in her duffel, wondering why he hadn't let the walker take the animal out in the first place. "I'm happy to find someone else if—"

"The walker is fine. You're doing an excellent job, Maresa."

The unexpected praise caught her off guard. She nearly dropped her bag, mostly because he fixed her with his clear blue gaze. Heat rushed through her again, and it didn't have anything to do with the sun bathing them in the morning light now that it was fully risen.

"Thank you." Her throat went dry. She backed up a step. Retreating. "I'm going to let you enjoy the beach."

Maresa turned toward the path through the thick undergrowth that led back to the hotel and nearly ran right into Jaden Torries, her ex-fiancé.

"Whoa!" Jaden's one hand reached to steady her, his other curved protectively around a pink bundle he carried. Tall and rangy, her artist ex-boyfriend was thin where Cameron was well-muscled. The round glasses Jaden wore for affectation and not because he needed them were jammed into the thick curls that reached his shoulders. "Maresa. I've been trying to contact you."

He released her, juggling his hold on the small pink parcel he carried. A parcel that wriggled?

"I've been busy." She wanted to pivot away from the man who'd told the whole island he was dumping her before informing her of the fact. But that shifting pink blanket captured her full attention.

A tiny wrinkled hand reached up from the lightweight

cotton, the movement followed by the softest sigh imaginable.

Her ex-fiancé was carrying a baby.

"But this is important, Maresa. It's about Isla." He lowered his arm cradling the infant so Maresa could see her better.

Indigo eyes blinked up at her. Short dark hair complimented the baby's medium skin tone. A white cotton headband decorated with rosettes rested above barely there eyebrows. Perfectly formed tiny features were molded into a silent yawn, the tiny hands reaching heavenward as the baby shifted against Jaden.

Something shifted inside Maresa at the same time. A maternal urge she hadn't known she possessed seized her insides and squeezed tight. Once upon a time she had dreamed about having this man's babies. She'd imagined what they would look like. Now, he had sought her out to…taunt her with the life she'd missed out on?

The maternal urge hardened into resentment, but she'd be damned if she'd let him see it.

"Congratulations. Your daughter is lovely, Jaden." She straightened as the large shadow of Cameron Holmes covered them both.

"Is there a problem, Ms. Delphine?" His tone was cool and impersonal, yet in that awkward moment he felt like an ally.

She appreciated his strong presence beside her when she felt that old surge of betrayal. She let Jaden answer since she didn't feel any need to defend the ex who'd called off their wedding via a text message.

"There's no problem. I'm an old friend of Maresa's. Jaden Torries." He extended his free hand to introduce himself.

Mr. Holmes ignored it. Poppy barked at Jaden.

"Then I'm sure you'll respect Maresa's wish to be on her way." Her unlikely rescuer tucked his hand under one arm as easily as he'd plucked his pet from the water earlier.

The warmth of his skin made her want to curl into him just like Poppy had, too.

"Right." Jaden dropped his hand. "Except Rafe's old girlfriend, Trina, left town last night, Maresa. And since Trina's my cousin, she stuck me with the job of delivering Rafe's daughter into your care."

Maresa's feet froze to the spot. She had a vague sense of Cameron leaning closer to her, his hand suddenly at her back. Which was helpful, because she thought for a minute there was a very real chance she was going to faint. Her knees wobbled beneath her.

"Sorry to spring it on you like this," Jaden continued. "I tried telling Trina she owed it to your family to tell you in person, and I thought I had her talked into it, but—"

"Rafe?" Maresa turned around slowly, needing to see with her own eyes if there was any chance Jaden was telling the truth. "Trina broke up with him almost a year ago. Right after the accident."

Jaden stepped closer. "Right. And Trina didn't even find out she was pregnant until a couple of weeks afterward, while Rafe was still in critical condition. Trina decided to go through with the pregnancy on her own. Isla was born the end of January."

Maresa was too shaken to even do the math, but she did know that Trina and Rafe had been hot and heavy for the last month or two they were together. They'd been a constant fixture on Maresa's social media feed for those weeks. Which had made it all the more upsetting when

Trina bailed on him right after the accident, bursting into tears every time she got close to his bedside before giving up altogether. Had she been even more emotional because she'd been in the early stages of pregnancy?

"Why wouldn't she have called me or my mother?" Her knees wobbled again as her gaze fell on the tiny infant. Isla? She had Rafe's hairline—the curve of dark hair encroaching on the temples. But plenty of babies had that, didn't they? "I would have helped her. I could have been there when the baby was born."

"Who is Rafe?" Cameron asked.

She'd forgotten all about him.

Maresa gulped a breath. "My brother." The very real possibility that Jaden was telling the truth threatened to level her. Rafe was in no position to be a father with the assorted symptoms he still battled. And financially? She was barely getting by supporting her family and paying some of Rafe's staggering medical bills since he hadn't been fully insured at the time.

"Look." Jaden set a bright pink diaper bag down on the beach. Cartoon cats cartwheeled across the front. "My apartment is no place for a baby. You know that, right? I just took her because Trina showed up last night, begging me for help. I told her no, but told her she could spend the night. She took off while I was sleeping. But she left a note for you." He looked as though he wanted to sort through the diaper bag to find it, but before he leaned down he held the baby out to Maresa. "Here. Take her."

Maresa wasn't even sure she'd made up her mind to do so when Jaden thrust the warm, precious weight into her arms. He was still talking about Trina seeming "unstable" ever since giving birth, but Maresa couldn't follow his words with an infant in her arms. She felt stiff and awkward, but she was careful to support the squirming bundle, cradling the baby against her chest while Isla gurgled and kicked.

Maresa's heart turned over. Melted.

Here, the junglelike landscaping blocked out the sun where the tree branches arced over the dirt path. The scent of green and growing things mingled with the sea breeze and a hint of baby shampoo.

"She's a beauty," Cameron observed over her shoulder. He had set Poppy on the ground so he could get closer to Isla and Maresa. "Are you okay holding her?"

"Fine," she said automatically, not wanting to give her up. "Just…um…overwhelmed."

Glancing up at him, she caught her breath at the expression on his face as he looked down at the child in her arms. She had thought he seemed different—kinder— toward Poppy. But that unguarded smile she'd seen for the Maltese was nothing compared to the warmth in his expression as he peered down at the baby.

If she didn't know better—if she hadn't seen him be rude and abrupt with perfectly nice hotel staffers—she would have guessed she caught him making silly faces at Isla. The little girl appeared thoroughly captivated.

"Here it is." Jaden straightened, a piece of paper in his hand. "She left this for you along with some notes about the kid's schedule." He passed the papers to Cameron. "I've got to get going if I'm going to catch that ferry, Maresa. I only came out here because Trina gave me no choice, but I've got to get to work—"

"Seriously?" She had to work, too. But even as she was about to say as much, another voice in her head piped up. If Isla was really Rafe's child, would she honestly want

Jaden Torries in charge of the baby for another minute? The answer was a crystal clear *absolutely not*.

"Drop her off at social services if you don't believe me." Jaden shrugged. "I've got a rich old lady client paying a whole hell of a lot for me to paint her portrait at eight." He checked his watch. "I'm outta here."

And with that, her ex-fiancé walked away, his sandy-gold curls bouncing. Poppy barked again, clearly unimpressed.

Social services? Really?

"If only I had Poppy around three years ago when I got engaged to him," she muttered darkly, hugging the baby tighter.

Cameron's hand briefly found the small of her back as he watched the other man leave. He clutched the letter from Rafe's former girlfriend—Isla's mother.

"And yet you didn't go through with the wedding. So you did just fine on your own." Cameron glanced down at her, his hand lingering on her back for one heart-stopping moment before it drifted away again. "Want me to read the letter? Or would you like me to take Isla so you can do the honors?"

He held the paper out for her to decide.

She liked him better here—outside the hotel. He was less intimidating, for one thing.

For another? He was appealing to her in all the ways a man could. A dangerous feeling for her when she needed to be on her guard around him. He was a guest, for crying out loud. But she was out of her depth with this precious little girl in her arms and she didn't know what she'd do if Cameron Holmes walked away from her right now. Having him there made her feel—if only for a moment—that she wasn't totally alone.

"Actually, I'd be really grateful if you would read it."
She shook her head, tightening her hold on Isla. "I'm
too nervous."

Katrina—Trina—Blanchett had been Rafe's girlfriend
for about six months before the car accident. Maresa
had never seen them together except for photos on social media of the two of them out playing on the beach
or at the clubs. They'd seemed happy enough, but Rafe
had told her on the phone it wasn't serious. The night of
the accident, in fact, the couple had gotten into an argument at a bar and Trina had stranded him there. Rafe had
called their mother for a ride, something she'd been only
too happy to provide even though it was late. She'd never
had an MS attack while driving before.

Less than ten days after seeing Rafe in the hospital,
Trina had told Maresa through tears that she couldn't
stand seeing him that way and it would be better for her
to leave. At the time, Maresa had been too focused on
Rafe's prognosis to worry about his flighty girlfriend. If
she'd taken more time to talk to the girl, might she have
confided the pregnancy news that followed the breakup?

"Would you like to have a seat?" Cameron pointed toward a bench near the outdoor faucet where guests could
rinse off their feet. "You look too pale."

She nodded, certain she was pale. What was her
mother going to say when she found out Rafe had a
daughter? If he had a daughter. And Rafe? She couldn't
imagine how frustrated he would feel to have been left
out of the whole experience. Then again, how frustrated
would he feel knowing that he couldn't care for his
daughter the way he could have at one time?

Struggling to get her spinning thoughts under control,
she allowed Cameron to guide her to the bench. Carefully,

she lowered herself to sit with Isla, the baby blanket covering her lap since the kicking little girl had mostly freed herself of the swaddling. While she settled the baby, she noticed Cameron lift Poppy and towel her off a bit more before setting her down again. He double-checked the leash clip on her collar then took the seat beside Maresa.

"I'm ready," she announced, needing to hear whatever Isla's mother had to say.

Cameron unfolded the paper and read aloud. "'Isla is Rafe's daughter. I wasn't with anyone else while we were together. I was afraid to tell him about her after the doctor said he'd be…'" Cameron hesitated for only a moment "'…brain damaged. I know Rafe can't take care of her, but his mother will love her, right? I can't do this. I'm going to see my dad in Florida for a few weeks, but I'll sign papers to give you custody. I'm sorry.'"

Maresa listened to the silence following the words, her brain uncomprehending. How could the woman just take off and leave her baby—Rafe's baby—with Jaden Torries while she traveled to Florida? Who did that? Trina wasn't a kid—she was twenty-one when she'd dated Rafe. But she'd never had much family support, according to Rafe. Her mother was an alcoholic and her father had raised her, but he'd never paid her much attention.

A fierce surge of protectiveness swelled inside of Maresa. It was so strong she didn't know where to put it all. But she knew for damn sure that she would protect little Isla—her niece—far better than the child's mother had. And she would call a lawyer and find out how to file for full custody.

"You could order DNA testing," Cameron observed, his impressive abs rippling as he leaned forward on the bench. "If you are concerned she's not a biological relative."

Maresa closed her eyes for a moment to banish all thoughts of male abs, no matter how much she welcomed the distraction from the monumental life shift taking place for her this morning.

"I'll ask an attorney about it when I call to find out how I can secure legal custody." She wrapped Isla's foot back in a corner of the blanket. "For right now, I need to find suitable care for Isla before my shift at the Carib begins for the day." Throat burning, Maresa realized she was near tears just thinking about the unfairness of it all. Not to *her*, of course, because she would make it work no matter what life threw at her.

But how unfair to *Rafe*, who wouldn't be able to parent his child without massive amounts of help. Perhaps he wouldn't be interested in parenting at all. Would he be angry? Would Trina's surprise be the kind of thing that unsettled his confused mind and set back his recovery?

She would call his counselor before saying anything to him. That call would be right after she spoke to a lawyer. She wasn't even ready to tell her mother yet. Analise Delphine's health was fragile and stress could aggravate it. Maresa wanted to be sure she was calm before she spoke to her mother. They'd all been in the dark for months about Trina's pregnancy. A few more hours wouldn't matter one way or another.

"I noticed on the dog walker's résumé that she has experience working in a day care." Cameron folded the paper from Trina and inserted it into an exterior pocket of the diaper bag. "And as it happens, I already walked the dog. Would you like me to text her and ask her to meet you somewhere in the hotel to give you a hand?"

Maresa couldn't imagine what that would cost. But what were her options since she didn't want to upset her mother? She didn't have time to return home and give the baby to her mother even if she was sure her mother could handle the shocking news.

"That would be a great help, thank you. The caregiver can meet me in the women's locker room by the pool in twenty minutes." Shooting to her feet, Maresa realized she'd imposed on Cameron Holmes's kindness for far too long. "And with that, I'll let you and Poppy get back to your morning walk."

"I'll go with you. I can carry the baby gear." He reached for the pink diaper bag, but she beat him to it.

"I'm fine. I insist." She pasted on her best concierge smile and tried not to think about how comforting it had felt to have him by her side this morning. Now more than ever, she needed job security, which meant she couldn't let an important guest think she made a habit of bringing her personal life to work. "Enjoy your day, Mr. Holmes."

Enjoying his day proved impossible with visions of Maresa Delphine's pale face circling around Cameron's head the rest of the morning. He worked at his laptop on the private terrace off his room, distracted as hell thinking about the beautiful, efficient concierge caught off guard by a surprise that would have damn near leveled anyone else.

She'd inherited her brother's baby. A brother who, from the sounds of it, was not in any condition to care for his child himself.

Sunlight glinted off the sea and the sounds from the beach floated up to his balcony. The noises had grown throughout the morning from a few circling gulls to the

handful of vacationing families that now populated the
beach. The scent of coconut sunscreen and dense floral
vegetation swirled on the breeze. But the temptation of
a tropical paradise didn't distract Cam from his work
nearly as much as memories of his morning with Maresa.

Shocking encounter with the baby aside, he would
still have been distracted just remembering her limber
arched back, her beautiful curves outlined by the light of
the rising sun when he'd first broken through the dense
undergrowth to find her on the private beach. Her skimpy
workout gear had skimmed her hips and breasts, still
tantalizing the hell out of him when he was supposed
to be researching the operations hierarchy of the Carib
Grand on his laptop.

But then, all that misplaced attraction got funneled
into protectiveness when he'd met her sketchy former fiancé. He'd met the type before—charming enough, but
completely self-serving. The guy couldn't have come up
with a kinder way to inform her of her niece's existence?

On the plus side, Cameron had located some search
results about her brother. Rafe Delphine had worked at
the hotel for one month in a hire that some might view
as unethical given his relationship to Maresa. But his application—though light on work history—had been approved by the hotel director on-site, so the young man
must be fit for the job despite his injury in a car wreck
the year before. That, too, had been an easy internet
search, with local news articles reporting the crash and
a couple of updates on Rafe's condition afterward. The
trauma the guy had suffered must have been harrowing
for his whole family. Clearly the girlfriend had found it
too much to handle.

Now, as a runner for the concierge, Rafe would be directly under Maresa's supervision. That concerned Cameron since Maresa would have every reason in the world to keep him employed. As much as Cam empathized with her situation—all the more now that she'd discovered her brother had an heir—he couldn't afford to ignore good business practices. He'd have to speak to the hotel director about the situation and see if they should make a change.

The ex-fiancé was next on his list of searches. Not that he wanted to pry into Maresa's private life. Cameron was more interested in seeing how the guy connected to the Carib Grand that he'd come all the way to the hotel's private island to pass over the baby. That seemed like an unnecessary trip unless he was staying here or worked here. Why not just give the baby to Maresa at her home in Charlotte Amalie? Why come to her place of work when it was so far out of the way?

Cam had skimmed halfway through the short search results on Jaden Torries's portraits of people and pets before his phone buzzed with an incoming call. Poppy, snoozing in the shade of the chair under his propped feet, didn't even stir at the sound. The dog was definitely making up for lost rest from the day before.

Glimpsing his oldest brother's private number, Cam hit the button to connect the call. "Talk to me."

"Hello to you, too." Quinn's voice came through along with the sounds of Manhattan in the background—horns honking, brakes squealing, a shrill whistle and a few shouts above the hum of humanity indicating he must be on the street. "I wanted to give you a heads-up I just bought a sea plane."

"Nice, bro, But there's no way you'll get clearance to land in the Hudson with that thing." Cameron scrolled to a gallery of Torries's work and was decidedly unimpressed.

Not that he was an expert. But as a supporter of the arts in Manhattan for all his adult life, he felt reasonably sure Maresa's ex was a poser. Then again, maybe he just didn't like a guy who'd once commanded the concierge's attention.

"The aircraft isn't for me," Quinn informed him. "It's for you. I figured it would be easier than a chopper to get from one island to another while you're investigating the Carib Grand and checking out the relatives."

Cam shoved aside his laptop and straightened. "Seriously? You bought a seaplane for my two-week stay?"

As a McNeill, he'd grown up with wealth, yes. He'd even expanded his holdings with the success of the gaming development company he'd started in college. But damn. He limited himself to spending within reason.

"The Carib Grand is the start of our Caribbean expansion, and if it goes well, we'll be spending a lot of time and effort developing the McNeill brand in the islands and South America. We have a plane available in the Mediterranean. Why not keep something accessible on this side of the Atlantic?"

"Right." Cam's jaw flexed at the thought of how much was riding on smoothing things out at the Carib Grand. A poor bottom line wasn't going to help the expansion program. "Good thinking."

"Besides, I have the feeling we'll be seeing our half brothers in Martinique a whole lot more now that Gramps is determined to bring them into the fold." Quinn sounded as grim about that prospect as Cameron felt. "So the plane might be useful for all of us as we try to…contain the situation."

Quinn wanted to keep their half siblings out of Manhattan and out of the family business as much as Cameron did. They'd worked too hard to hand over their company to people who'd never lifted a finger to grow McNeill Resorts.

"Ah." Cam stood to stretch his legs, surprised to realize it was almost noon according to the slim dive watch he'd worn for his morning laps. "But since I'm on the front line meeting them, I'm going to leave it up to you or Ian to be the diplomatic peacemakers."

Quinn only half smothered a laugh. "No one expected you of all people to be the diplomat. Dad's still recovering from the punch you gave him last week when he dropped the I-have-another-family bombshell on us."

Definitely not one of his finer moments. "It seemed like he could have broached the topic with some more tact."

"No kidding. I kept waiting for Sofia to break the engagement after the latest family soap opera." The background noise on Quinn's call faded. "Look, Cam, I just arrived at Lincoln Center to take her out to lunch. I'll text you the contact details for a local pilot."

Cam grinned at the thought of his stodgy older brother so head over heels for his ballerina fiancée. The same ballerina fiancée Cam had impulsively proposed to last winter when a matchmaker set them up. But even if Cam and Sofia hadn't worked out, the meeting had been a stroke of luck for Quinn, who'd promptly stepped in to woo the dancer.

"Thanks. And give our girl a kiss from me, okay?" It was too fun to resist needling Quinn. Especially since Cameron was two thousand miles away from a retaliatory beat-down.

A string of curses peppered his ear before Quinn growled, "It's not too late to take the plane back."

"Sorry." Cameron wasn't sorry. He was genuinely happy for his brother. "I'll let you know if the faux McNeills are every bit as awful as we imagine."

Disconnecting the call, Cameron texted a message to the dog groomer to give Poppy some primp time. He'd use that window of freedom to follow up on a few leads around the Carib Grand. He wanted to find out what the hotel director thought about Rafe Delphine, for one thing. The director was the only person on-site who knew Cameron's true identity and mission at the hotel. Aldo Ricci had been successful at McNeill properties in the Mediterranean and Malcolm McNeill had personally appointed the guy to make the expansion program a success.

With the McNeill patriarch's health so uncertain, Cameron wanted to respect his grandfather's choices. All the more so since he still hadn't married the way his granddad wanted.

Cameron would start by speaking to his grandfather's personally chosen manager. Cam had a lot of questions about the day-to-day operations and a few key personnel. Most especially the hotel's new concierge, who kept too many secrets behind her beautiful and efficient facade.

Chapter 3

Seated in the hotel director's office shortly after noon, Cameron listened to Aldo Ricci discuss his plans for making the Carib Grand more profitable over the next two quarters. Unlike Cameron, the celebrated hotel director with a crammed résumé of successes did not seem concerned about the dip in the Carib Grand's performance.

"All perfectly normal," the impeccably dressed director insisted, prowling around his lavish office on the ground floor of the property. A collector of investment-grade wines, Aldo incorporated a few rare vintages into his office decor. A Bordeaux from Moulin de La Lagune rested casually on a shelf beside some antique corkscrews and a framed invitation from a private tasting at Château Grand Corbin. "We are only beginning to notice the min-ute fluctuations now that our capacity for data is greater than ever. But those irregularities will not even be noticeable by the time we hit our performance and profit goals for the end of the year."

The heavyset man tugged on his perfectly straight suit cuffs. The fanciness of the dark silk jacket he wore reminded Cameron how many times the guy had taken a property out of the red and into the ranks of the most prestigious places in the world. To have enticed him to McNeill Resorts had been a coup, according to Cameron's grandfather.

"Nevertheless, I'd like to know more about Maresa Delphine." Cameron didn't reveal his reasons. He could see her now through the blinds in the director's office. She strode along the pool patio outside, hurrying past the patrons in her creamy linen blazer with an orchid at the lapel. Her sun-splashed brown hair gleamed in the bright light, but something about her posture conveyed her tension. Worry.

Was she thinking about Isla?

He made a mental note to check on the sitter and be sure she was doing a good job with the baby. Little Isla had tugged at his heartstrings this morning with her tiny, restless hands and her expressive face. That feeling—the warmth for the baby—shocked him. Not that he was an ogre or anything, but he'd decided long ago not to have kids of his own.

He was too much like his father—impulsive, fun-loving, easily distracted—to be a parent. After all, Liam McNeill had turfed out responsibility for his sons at the first possible opportunity, letting the boys' grandfather raise them the moment Liam's Brazilian wife got tired of his globe-trotting, daredevil antics. Cameron had always known his father had shirked the biggest responsibility of his life and that, coupled with his own tendency to follow his own drummer, had been enough to convince Cam that kids weren't for him. And that had been before discovering his dad had fathered a whole other set of kids with someone else.

Before an accident that had compromised Cameron's ability to have a family anyhow.

"Maresa Delphine is a wonderful asset to the hotel," the director assured him, coming around to the front of his desk to sit beside Cameron in the leather club chairs facing the windows. "If you seek answers about the hotel workings, I urge you to reveal your identity to her. I know you want to remain incognito, but I assure you, Ms. Delphine is as discreet and professional as they come."

"Yet you've only known her for…what? Two months?"

"Far longer than that. She worked at another property in Saint Thomas where I supervised her three years ago. I personally recommended her to a five-star property in Paris because I was impressed with her work and she was eager to…escape her hometown for a while. I had no reservations about helping her win the spot. She makes her service her top priority." The director crossed one leg over the other and pointed to a crystal decanter on the low game table between them. "Are you sure I can't offer you anything to drink?"

"No. Thank you." He wanted a clear head for deciding his next move with Maresa. Revealing himself to her was tempting considering the attraction simmering just beneath the surface. But he couldn't forget about the gut instinct that told him she was hiding something. "What can you tell me about her brother?"

"Rafe is a fine young man. I would have gladly hired

him even without Maresa's assurances she would watch over him."

"Why would she need to?" He was genuinely curious about the extent of Rafe's condition. Not only because she seemed protective of him, but also because Maresa hadn't argued Trina's depiction of her brother as "brain damaged."

"Rafe has a traumatic brain injury. He's the reason Maresa gave up the job in Paris. She rushed home to take care of her family. The young man is much better now. Although he can become agitated or confused easily, he has good character, and we haven't put him in a position where he will have much contact with guests." Aldo smiled as he smoothed his tie. "Maresa feels a strong sense of responsibility for him. But I've seen no reason to regret hiring her sibling. She knows, however, that Rafe's employment is on a trial basis."

Aldo Ricci seemed like the kind of man to trust his gut, which might be fine for someone who'd been in the business for as long as he had, but Cameron still wondered if he was overlooking things.

Maybe he should confide in Maresa if only to discover her take on the staff at the Carib Grand. Specifically, he wondered, what was her impression of Aldo Ricci? Cameron found himself wanting to know a lot more about the operations of the hotel.

"Perhaps I will speak to Ms. Delphine." Cameron wanted to find her now, in fact. His need to see her has been growing ever since she'd walked away from him early that morning. "I'd like some concrete answers about those performance reviews, even if they do seem like minute fluctuations."

He rose from his seat, liking the new plan more than

he should. *Damn it.* Spending more time with Maresa didn't mean anything was going to happen between them. As her boss, of course, he had a responsibility to ensure it didn't.

And, without question, she had a great deal on her mind today of all days. But maybe that was all the more reason to give her a break from the concierge stand. Perhaps she'd welcome a few hours away from the demands of the guests.

"Certainly." The hotel director followed him to the door. "There's no one more well-versed in the hotel except for me." His grin revealed a mouth full of shiny white veneers. "Stick close to her."

Cameron planned to do just that.

"Have you seen Rafe?" Maresa asked Nancy, the waitress who worked in the lobby bar shortly after noon. "I wanted to eat lunch with him."

Standing beside Nancy, a tall blonde goddess of a woman who probably made more in tips each week than Maresa made in a month, she peered out over the smattering of guests enjoying cocktails and the view. Her brother was nowhere in sight.

She had checked on Isla a few moments ago, assuring herself the baby was fine. She'd shared Trina's notes about the baby's schedule with the caregiver, discovering Isla's birth certificate with the father's name left blank and a birth date of ten weeks prior. And after placing a call to Trina's mother, Maresa had obtained contact information for the girl's father in Florida, who'd been able to give her a number for Trina herself. The girl had tearfully confirmed everything she said in her note—promising to give custody of the child to Rafe's family since she wasn't ready to be a mother and she didn't trust her own mother to be a good guardian.

The young woman had been so distraught, Maresa had felt sorry for her. All the more so because Trina had tried to handle motherhood alone when she'd been so conflicted about having a baby in the first place.

Now, Maresa wanted to see Rafe for herself to make sure he was okay. What if Jaden had mentioned Isla to him? Or even just mentioned Trina leaving town? Rafe hadn't asked about his girlfriend since regaining consciousness. She suspected Rafe would have been walking onto the ferry that morning the same time as Jaden was walking off.

Earlier that day, she'd left him a to-do list when she'd had an appointment to keep with the on-site restaurant's chef. She'd given Rafe only two chores, and they were both jobs he'd done before so she didn't think he'd have any trouble. He had to pick up some supplies at the gift shop and deliver flowers to one of the guests' rooms.

"I saw him about an hour ago." Nancy rang out a customer's check. "He brought me this." She pointed to the tiny purple wildflowers stuffed behind the engraved silver pin with her name on it. "He really is the sweetest."

"Thank you for being so kind to him." Maresa had witnessed enough people be impatient and rude to him that he'd become her barometer for her measure of a person. People who were nice to Rafe earned her respect.

"Kind to *him*?" Nancy tossed her head back and laughed, her long ponytail swishing. "That boy should earn half my tips since it's Rafe who makes me smile when I feel like strangling some of my more demanding customers—like that Mr. Holmes." She straightened the purple blooms with one hand and shoved the cash drawer closed with her hip. "These flowers from your brother are the nicest flowers any man has ever given me."

Reassured for the moment, Maresa felt her heart squeeze at the words. Her brother had the capacity for great love despite the frustrations of his injury. Maybe he'd come to accept his daughter as part of his life down the road.

Until then, she needed to keep them both safely employed and earning benefits to take care of their family.

"It makes me happy to hear you say that." Maresa turned on her heel, leaving Nancy to her job. "If you see him, will you let him know I'm having lunch down by the croquet field?"

"Sure thing." Nancy lifted a tray full of drinks to take to another table. "Sometimes he hangs out in the break room if the Yankees are on the radio, you know. You might check if they play today."

"Okay. Thanks." She knew her brother liked listening to games on the radio. Being able to listen on his earbuds was always soothing for him.

Maresa hitched her knapsack with the insulated cooler onto her shoulder to carry out to the croquet area. The field didn't officially open again until late afternoon when it cooled down, so no one minded if employees sat under the palm trees there for lunch. There were a handful of places like that on the private island—spots where guests didn't venture that workers could enjoy. She needed a few minutes to collect herself. Come up with a plan for what she was going to do with a ten-week-old infant after work. And what she would tell Rafe about the baby since his counselor hadn't yet returned her phone call.

Her phone vibrated just then as her sandals slapped

along the smooth stone path dotted with exotic plantings on both sides. Her mother's number filled the screen.

"Mom?" she answered quietly while passing behind the huge pool and cabanas that surrounded it. The area was busy with couples enjoying outdoor meals or having cocktails at the swim-up bar and families playing in the nearby surf. Seeing a mother share a bite of fresh pineapple with her little girl made Maresa's breath catch. She'd once dreamed of being a mother to Jaden's children until he betrayed her.

Now, she might be a single mother to her brother's baby if Trina truly relinquished custody.

She scuttled deeper into the shade of some palms for her phone conversation, knowing she couldn't blurt out Isla's existence to her mom on the phone even though, in the days before her mother's health had taken a downhill spiral, she might have been tempted to do just that.

"No need to worry." Her mother's breathing sounded labored. From stress? Or exertion? She tired so easily over the past few months. "I just wanted to let you know your brother came home."

Maresa's steps faltered. Stopped.

"Rafe is there? With you?" Panic tightened her shoulders and clenched her gut. She peered around the path to the croquet field, half hoping her brother would come strolling toward her anyhow, juggling some pilfered deck cushions for her to sit on for an impromptu picnic the way he did sometimes.

"He showed up about ten minutes ago. I would have called sooner, but he was upset and I had to calm him down. I guess the florist gave him a pager—"

"Oh no." Already, Maresa could guess what had happened. "Those are really loud." The devices vibrated and blinked, setting off obnoxious alarms that would startle anyone, let alone someone with nervous tendencies. The floral delivery must not have been prepared when Rafe arrived to pick it up, so they gave him the pager to let him know when it was ready.

"He got scared and dropped it, but I'm not sure where—" Her mother stopped speaking, and in the background, Maresa heard Rafe shouting "I don't know, I don't know, I don't know" in a frightened chorus.

Her gut knotted. How could she bring a ten-week-old into their home tonight, knowing how loud noises upset her brother?

"Tell him everything's fine. I'll find the pager." Turning on her heel, she headed back toward the hotel. She thought the device turned itself off after a few minutes anyhow, but just in case it was still beeping, she'd rather find it before anyone else on staff. "I can probably retrace his steps since I sent him on those errands. I'll deliver the flowers myself."

"Honey, you're taking on too much having him there with you. You don't want to risk your job."

And the alternative? They didn't have one. Especially now with little Isla's care to consider.

"My job will be fine," she reassured her mother as she tugged open a door marked Employees Only that led to the staff room and corporate offices. She needed to sign Rafe out for the day before she did anything else.

Blinking against the loss of sunlight, Maresa felt the blast of air conditioning hit her skin, which had gone clammy with nervous sweat. She picked at the neckline of her thin silk camisole beneath her linen jacket.

"Ms. Delphine?" a familiar masculine voice called to her from the other end of the corridor.

Even before she turned, she knew who she would see. The tingling that tripped over her skin was an unsettling mix of anticipation and dread.

"Mom, I'll call you back." Disconnecting quickly, she dropped the phone in her purse and turned to see Cameron Holmes striding out of the hotel director's office, her boss at his side.

"Mr. Holmes." She forced a smile for both men, wondering why life was conspiring so hard against her today. What on earth would a guest be doing in the hotel director's office if not to complain? Unless maybe he had something extremely valuable he wanted to place in the hotel safe personally.

Highly unorthodox, but that's the only other reason she could think of to explain his presence here.

"Maresa." Her hotel director nodded briefly at her before shaking hands with Cameron Holmes. "And sir, I appreciate you coming to me directly. I certainly understand the need for discretion."

Aldo Ricci turned and re-entered his office, leaving Maresa with a racing heart in the presence of Cameron Holmes, who looked far more intimidating in a custom navy silk suit and a linen shirt open at the throat than he had in his board shorts this morning.

The level of appeal, however, seemed equal on both counts. She couldn't forget his unexpected kindness on the beach no matter how demanding he'd been as a hotel guest.

"Just the woman I was hoping to see." His even white teeth made a quick appearance in what passed for a smile. "Would you join me for a moment in the conference room?"

No.

Her brain filled in the answer even as her feet wisely followed where he led. She didn't want to be alone with him anywhere. Not when she entertained completely inappropriate thoughts about him. She couldn't let her attraction to a guest show.

Furthermore? She needed to sign her brother out of work, locate the pager he'd lost and deliver those flowers before the florist got annoyed and reported Rafe for not doing his job. Now was not the time for fantasizing about a wealthy guest who could afford to shape the world to his liking, even if he had the body of a professional surfer underneath that expensive suit.

As she crossed the threshold into the Carib Grand's private conference room full of tall leather chairs around an antique table, Maresa realized she couldn't do this. Not now.

"Actually, Mr. Holmes," she said, spinning around to face him and misjudging how close he followed behind her.

Suddenly, she stood nose-to-nose with him, her thigh grazing his, her breast brushing his strong arm. She stepped back fast, heat flooding her cheeks. The contact was so brief, she could almost tell herself it hadn't happened, except that her body hummed with awareness where they'd touched.

And then, there was the fact that he gripped her elbow when she wobbled.

"Sorry," she blurted, tugging away from him completely as the door to the conference room closed automatically behind them.

Sealing them in privacy.

Sunlight spilled in behind her, the Caribbean sun the only illumination in the room that hadn't been in use yet today. The quiet was deep here, the carpet muffling his step as he shifted closer.

"Are you all right?" His forehead creased with concern. "Are you comfortable with the caregiver for Isla?"

She glanced up at him, surprised at the thoughtful question. He really had been supportive this morning, giving her courage during an impossible situation. Right now, however, it was difficult to focus on his kind side when the man was simply far too handsome. She wished fervently he had that adorable little dog with him so she could pet Poppy instead of thinking about how hot Mr. Holmes could be when he wasn't scowling.

"I'm fine. I have everything under control." *Um, if only.* Clearly, she needed to date more often so she didn't turn into a babbling idiot around handsome men during work hours. "It's just that you caught me on my lunch hour, so I'm not technically working."

"Unfortunately, Maresa, I am." He folded his arms across his chest before he paced halfway across the room.

Confused, she watched him. He was not an easy man to look away from.

"I don't understand." She wondered how it happened that being around him made her feel like there wasn't enough air in the room. Like she couldn't possibly catch her breath.

"I'm doing some work for the hotel," he explained, pacing back toward her. "Secretly."

Confusion filled her as she tried to sort through his words that didn't make a bit of sense.

"So you're not actually on vacation at all? What kind of work?" She could think better now that he was on the opposite side of the room. "Is that why you were in the hotel director's office?"

"Yes. My real name is Cameron McNeill and I'm investigating why guest satisfaction has been declining over the last two months." He kept coming toward her, his blue eyes zeroing in on her. "And now I'm beginning to think you're the only person who can help me figure out why."

Cameron could feel her nervousness as clearly as if it was his own.

She stood, alert and ready to flee, her tawny eyes wide. She bit her full lower lip.

"McNeill? As in McNeill Resorts?" She blinked slowly.

"The same."

"Why do you think I can help you?" She smoothed the cuff of her ivory-colored linen jacket and then swiped elegant fingers along her forehead as if perspiring in spite of the fact she looked cool. So incredibly smooth and cool.

He hated doing this to her today of all days. The woman had just found out her brother had a child who would—he suspected—become her financial and familial dependent. What he'd gathered about Rafe Delphine's health suggested the man wouldn't be in any position to care for a newborn, and Aldo Ricci had made it clear Maresa put her family before herself.

"Preliminary data indicates the Carib is floundering in performance reviews and customer satisfaction." That was true enough. "You have a unique perspective on the hotel and everyone who works here. I'd like to know your views on why that might be?"

"And my boss told you I would talk to you about those issues?" Her gaze flitted to the door behind him and then back to him as if she would rather be anywhere else than right here.

Truth be told, he was a little uncomfortable being alone with her under these circumstances himself. She was far too tempting to question in the privacy of an empty conference room when the attraction was like a live wire sending sparks in all directions.

How could he ignore that?

"Your hotel director assured me you would be discreet."

She'd garnered the respect of her peers. The praise of superiors. All of which only made Cameron more curious about her. He stopped in front of her. At a respectable distance. He held her gaze, not allowing his eyes to wander.

"Of course, Mr. McNeill." She fidgeted with a bracelet—a shiny silver star charm—partially hidden by the sleeve of her jacket. "But what exactly did he hope I could share with you?"

"Call me Cam. And I hope you will share any insights about the staff and even some of the guests." He knew the data could be skewed by one or two unhappy visitors, particularly if they were vocal about their displeasure with the hotel.

"A difficult line to walk considering how much a concierge needs to keep her guests happy. It doesn't serve me—or McNeill Resorts—to betray confidences of valued clients."

Cameron couldn't help the voice in his head that piped up just then, wanting to know what she might have done to keep *him* happy as her guest.

Focus, damn it.

"And yet, you'll want to please the management as well," he reminded her. "Correct?"

"Of course." She nodded, letting go of the silver star so the bracelet slipped lower on her wrist.

"So how about if I buy you lunch and we'll begin our work together? I'll speak to Mr. Ricci about giving you the afternoon off." He needed to take her somewhere else. A place where the temptation to touch her wouldn't get the better of him. "We can bring Isla."

Nothing stifled attraction like an infant, right?

"Thank you, Mr. Mc—er, Cam." Maresa's face lit up with a glow that damn near took his breath away; her relief and eagerness to be reunited with the little girl were all too obvious. "That would be really wonderful."

Her pleasure affected him far more than it should, making him wonder how he could make that smile return to her face again and again. Had he really thought a baby would dull his desire for Maresa?

Not a chance.

Chapter 4

"You rented a villa here," Maresa observed as she held the ends of her hair in one hand to keep it from flying away in the open-top Jeep Cameron McNeill used for tooling around the private island. "In addition to the hotel suite."

The Jeep bounced down a long road through the lush foliage to a remote part of the island. In theory, she knew about the private villas that the Carib Grand oversaw on the extensive property, but the guests who took those units had their own staff so she didn't see them often and she'd never toured them. She turned in her seat to peer back at Isla, in the car seat she'd procured from the hotel. The baby faced backward with a sunshade tilted over the seat, but Maresa could see the little girl was still snoozing contentedly.

The caregiver had fed and changed her, and before

Maresa could compensate her, Cameron had taken care of the bill, insisting that he make the day as easy as possible for Maresa to make up for the inconvenience of working with him. Spending the day in a private villa with yet another caregiver—this one a licensed nurse from the hospital in Saint Thomas who would meet them there—was hardly an inconvenience. Truth be told, she was grateful to escape the hotel for the day after the stress of discovering Isla and finding out that Rafe had left work without authorization. Luckily, she'd signed him out due to illness and found the pager he dropped on her way to pick up Isla from the caregiver. Maresa had assigned the flower delivery to another runner before leaving.

Now, all she had to do was get through an afternoon with her billionaire boss who'd only been impersonating a pain-in-the-butt client. But what if Cameron McNeill turned out to be even more problematic than his predecessor, Mr. Holmes?

"The villas are managed by a slightly different branch of the company," Cameron informed her, using a remote to open a heavy wrought-iron gate that straddled the road ahead. "My privacy is protected here. I'll return to the hotel suite later tonight to continue my investigation work under Mr. Holmes's name. Unless, of course, you and I can figure out the reason behind the declining reviews before then."

The ocean breeze whipped another strand of Maresa's hair free from where she'd been holding it, the wavy lock tickling against her cheek and teasing along her lips. What was it about Cameron's physical presence that made her so very aware of her own? She'd never felt so on edge around Jaden even when they'd been wildly in love. Cameron's nearness made her feel…anxious. Expectant.

"From my vantage point, everything has been running smoothly at the Carib." Maresa didn't need a poor performance review. What if Cameron McNeill thought that the real reason for the declining ratings was her? A concierge could make or break a customer's experience of any hotel. Maybe this meeting with the boss wasn't to interview her so much as to interrogate her.

But damn it, she knew her performance had been exemplary.

"We'll figure it out, one way or another," Cameron assured her as the Jeep climbed a small hill and broke through a cluster of trees.

The most breathtaking view imaginable spread out before her. She gasped aloud.

"Oh wow." She shook her head at the sparkling expanse of water lapping against White Shoulders Beach below them. On the left, the villa sat at the cliff's edge, positioned so that the windows, balconies and infinity pool all faced the stunning view. "I grew up here, and still—you never grow immune to this."

"I can see why." He pulled the Jeep into a sheltered parking bay beside a simple silver Ford sedan. "It looks like the sitter has already arrived. We can get Isla settled inside with some air conditioning and then get to work."

Unfastening her gaze from the view of Saint John's in the distance, and a smattering of little islands closer by, Maresa turned to take in the villa. The Aerie was billed as the premiere private residence on the island; she thought she recalled the literature saying it was almost twenty thousand square feet. It was a palatial home decorated in the Mediterranean style. The white-sashed stucco and deep bronze roof tiles were an understated color combination, especially when accented with weathered gray doors. The landscaping dominated the home from the outside, but there were balconies everywhere to take advantage of the views.

Sliding out of the Jeep, she smoothed a hand over her windblown hair to try to prepare herself for what was no doubt the most important business meeting of her life. She couldn't allow her guard to slip, not even when Cameron McNeill spared a kind smile for Baby Isla as he carefully unbuckled her from the car seat straps.

"Need any help?" she asked, stepping closer to the Jeep again.

"I've got it." He frowned slightly, reaching beneath the baby to palm her head in his big hand. He supported her back with his forearm, cradling her carefully until he had her tucked against his chest. "There." He grinned over at Maresa. "Just like carrying a football. You take the fall yourself before you fumble."

"Ideally, there's no falling involved for anyone." She knew he was teasing, but she wondered if she should have offered to carry Isla just the same.

She couldn't deny she was a bit overwhelmed, though. She didn't know much about babies, and now she would be lobbying for primary custody of Rafe's little girl, even if Trina changed her mind. Maresa knew Rafe would have wanted to exercise his parental rights, and she would do that in his place. Still, it was almost too much to get her brain around in just a few hours, and she had no one she could share the news with outside of Rafe's counselor. Oddly, having Cameron McNeill beside her today had anchored her when she felt most unsteady, even as she knew she had to keep her guard up around him.

Half an hour later, Maresa finally managed to walk out of the makeshift nursery—a huge suite of rooms adapted for the purpose with the portable crib the hospital nurse had brought with her. The woman had packed a bag full of other baby supplies for Maresa including formula, diapers, fresh clothes and linens, a gift funded by Cameron McNeill, she'd discovered. And while Maresa understood that the man could easily afford such generosity, she couldn't afford to accept any more after this day.

Today, she told herself, was an adjustment period. Tomorrow, she would have a plan.

Clutching the baby monitor the caregiver had provided, Maresa followed the scent of grilled meat toward the patio beside the pool. A woman in a white tuxedo shirt and crisp black pants bustled through the kitchen, her blond ponytail bobbing with her step. She nodded toward the French doors leading outside.

"Mr. McNeill said to tell you he has drinks ready right out here, unless you'd like to swim first, in which case there are suits in the bathhouse." She pointed to the left where a small cabana sat beside a gazebo.

"Thank you." Maresa's gaze flicked over the food the woman was assembling on the kitchen island—tiny appetizers with flaked fish balanced on thin slices of mango and endive, bright red crabmeat prepped for what looked like a shellfish soup and chopped vegetables for a conch salad. "It all looks delicious."

Her stomach growled with a reminder of how long it had been since her usual lunch hour had come and gone. Now, stepping outside onto the covered deck, Maresa spotted Cameron seated at a table beneath the gazebo, a bottled water in hand as he stared down at his laptop screen. Tropical foliage in colorful clay pots dotted the deck. The weathered teak furniture topped by thick cream-colored cushions was understated enough to let the view shine more than the decor. The call of birds and the distant roll of waves on the beach provided the kind of soundtrack other people piped in using a digital play-list in order to relax.

Seeing her, Cameron stood. The practice wasn't un-common in formal business meetings, and happened more often when she'd worked in Europe. But the ges-ture here, in this private place, felt more intimate since it was for her alone.

Or maybe she was simply too preoccupied with her boss.

"Did you find everything you needed?" he asked, tug-ging off the aviators he'd been wearing to set them on the graying teak table.

It was cool in the shade of the pergola threaded with bright pink bougainvillea, yet just being close to him made her skin warm. Her gaze climbed his tall height, stalling on his well-muscled shoulders before reaching his face. She took in the sculpted jaw and ice-blue eyes before shifting her focus to his lips. She hadn't kissed a man since her broken engagement.

A fact she hadn't thought about even once until right this moment.

"I'm fine," she blurted awkwardly, remembering she was there to work and not to catalog the finer masculine traits of the man whose family owned the company she worked for. "Ready to work."

Beneath the table, a dog yapped happily.

Maresa glanced down to see Poppy standing on a bright magenta dog bed. Beside the bed, a desk fan os-cillated back and forth, blowing through the dog's long white fur at regular intervals.

"Hello, Poppy." She leaned down to greet the fluffy

pooch. "That's quite a setup you have there." She let the dog sniff her hand for a moment before she scratched behind the ears, not sure if Poppy would remember her.

"I had the dog walker pick up a few things to be sure she was comfortable. Plus, with a baby in the house, I thought she might be…you know. Jealous."

She looked up in time to see him shrug as if it was the most natural thought in the world to consider if his dog would be envious of an infant guest.

"That's adorable." She knew then that the Cameron Holmes character she'd met the day before had been all for show. Cameron McNeill was another man entirely. Although his jaw tightened at the "adorable" remark. She hurried to explain. "I mean, the dog bed and all of Poppy's matching accessories. Your mom found a lot of great things to coordinate the wardrobe."

Maresa rose to her feet, knowing she couldn't use the pup as a barrier all day.

"Actually, I borrowed Poppy from my brother's administrative assistant." He gestured to the seat beside him and turned the laptop to give her a better view. "I figured a fussy white show dog was a good way to test the patience and demeanor of the hotel staff. But I'll admit, she isn't nearly as uptight as I imagined." He patted the animal's head; the Maltese was rubbing affectionately against his ankles while he talked about her. "She's pretty great."

Coming around to his side of the table, Maresa took the seat he indicated. Right beside him. He'd changed into more casual clothes since she'd last seen him, his white cotton T-shirt only slightly dressed up by a pair of khakis and dark loafers. He wore some kind of brightly colored socks—aqua and purple—at odds with the rest of his outfit.

"The Carib is pet friendly, but I understand why you thought there might be pushback on demands like natural grass for the room." She glanced down at the laptop to see he'd left open a series of graphs with performance rankings for the Carib.

The downturn in the past two months was small, but noticeable.

"Ryegrass only," he reminded her. "I don't enjoy being tough on the staff, but I figured that playing undercover boss for a week or two would still be quicker and less painful for them than if I hire an independent agency to do a thorough review of operations."

"Of course." She gestured to the laptop controls. "May I look through this?"

At his nod, Maresa clicked on links and scrolled through the files related to the hotel's performance. Clearly, Cameron had been doing his homework, making margin notes throughout the document about the operations. Her name made frequent appearances, including a reference to an incident of misplaced money by a guest the week before.

"I remember this." Maresa's finger paused on the comment from a post-visit electronic survey issued to the guest. "An older couple reported that their travelers' checks had gone missing during a trip to the beach." She glanced up to see Cameron bent over the screen to read the notes, his face unexpectedly close to hers.

"The guy left the money in his jacket on the beach. It was gone when he returned." Cameron nodded, his jaw tense. "Definitely a vacation-ruiner."

She bristled. "But not the staff's fault. Our beach employees are tasked with making sure there are pool chairs and towels. We serve drinks and even bring food down to the cabanas. But we can't police everyone's possessions."

"On a private island where everyone should either be a guest or a staff member?" he asked with a hint of censure in his voice.

"That amounts to quite a few people," she pointed out, without hesitation. "And don't forget, many of our guests feel comfortable indulging in extra cocktails while vacationing."

"A few drinks won't make you think you had a thousand dollars in your pocket when you only had ten."

"Maybe not." She thrummed her fingernails on the teak table, remembering some of the antics she'd seen on the beach. Even before her work at the Carib, she'd seen plenty of visitors to Saint Thomas behave like springbreakers simply because they were far from home. Her father included. "However, a few drinks could make you think you put your money in your jacket when you actually had it in the pocket of the shorts you wore into the water, where you lost it while you tried to impress your trophy wife by doing backflips off a Jet Ski."

"And is that what happened in this case?" He glanced over at her, the woodsy scent of his aftershave teasing her senses.

"No." She shook her head, regretting the candid speech as much as the memory of her father's easy transition of affection from Maresa's mother to a wealthy female colleague. Today had rattled her. Her mind kept drifting back to Isla and what she would do tonight to keep her comfortable. "I'm sure it wasn't. I only meant to point out that the staff can't guard against some of the questionable decisions that guests make while vacationing."

Cam regarded her curiously. "I don't suppose your ex-fiancé has a trophy wife?"

"Jaden is still happily single from what I hear." She couldn't afford to share any more personal confidences with this man—her boss—who already knew far too much about her. To redirect their conversation, she tapped a few keys on his laptop. "These other incidents that guests wrote about on their comment forms—slow bar service, a disappointing gallery tour off-site—I assume you've looked into them?"

Both were news to her.

"The bar service, yes. The gallery tour, no. I don't suppose you know which tour they're referencing?"

"No one has asked me to arrange anything like this." She might not remember every hotel recommendation, but she certainly recalled specialty requests. "I can speak to some of the other staff members. Some guests like to ask the doormen or the waiters for their input on local sites."

"Good." He cleared a space in front of them on the table as a server came onto the patio with covered trays. "That's one of the drawbacks of maintaining a presence as a demanding guest—I can't very well quiz the staff for answers about things that happened last month."

Maresa watched as the server quickly set the table, filled their water glasses and left two platters behind along with a wine bottle in a clay pot to maintain the wine's temperature. The final thing the woman did was set out a fresh bowl of water for Poppy before she left them to their late lunch.

"I'm happy to help," Maresa told him honestly, relieved to know that the downturn in performance at the Carib was nothing tied to her work. Or her brother's.

Their jobs were more important than ever with a baby to support.

"For that matter, I can't reveal the positive feedback we've received about the staff members either." Cameron lifted the wine bottle from the cooling container and inspected the label before pouring a pale white wine into her glass. "But I can tell you that Rafe received some glowing praise from a guest who referenced him by name."

"Really?" Pleased, Maresa helped herself to some of the appetizers she'd seen inside, arranging a few extra pieces of mango beside the conch salad. "Did the guest say what he did?"

Cameron loaded his plate with ahi tuna and warm plantain chips with some kind of spicy-looking dipping sauce.

"Something about providing a 'happy escort' to the beach one day and lifting the guest's spirits by pointing out some native birds."

Rafe? Escorting a guest somewhere?

Maresa realized she'd been quiet a beat too long.

"Rafe loves birds," she replied truthfully, hating that she needed to mask her true thoughts with Cameron after he'd trusted her to give him honest feedback on the staff. "He does know a lot about the local plants and animals, too," she rushed to add. "That's one area of knowledge that his accident left untouched."

"Does it surprise you that he was escorting a guest to the beach?" Cameron studied her over his glass as he tasted the wine.

His blue eyes missed nothing.

Clearly, he would know Rafe's job description—something he'd have easy access to in his research of the performance reviews. There was no sense trying to deny it. Still, she hated feeling that she needed to defend her brother for doing a good job.

"A little," she admitted, her shoulders tense. Wary.

Before she could explain, however, a wail came through the baby monitor.

Cam hung back, unsure how to help while Maresa and the nurse caregiver discussed the baby's fretful state. Maresa held the baby close, shifting positions against her shoulder as the baby arched and squirmed.

Over half an hour after the infant's initial outburst, the little girl still hadn't settled down. Her face was mottled and red, her hands flexing and straining, as if she fought unseen ghosts. Cam hated hearing the cries, but didn't have a clue what to offer. The woman he'd hired for the day was a nurse, after all. She would know if there was anything they needed to worry about, wouldn't she?

Still. He didn't blame Maresa for questioning her. Cameron had done some internet searches himself, one of the few things he knew to contribute.

A moment later, Maresa stepped out of the nursery and shut the door behind her, leaving Isla with Wendy. The cries continued. Poppy paced nervously outside the door.

"I should leave." Worry etched her features. She scraped back her sun-lightened curls behind one ear. "You've been so kind to help me manage my first day of caring for an infant, finding Wendy and the baby supplies, but I really can't impose any longer—"

"You are not anywhere close to an imposition." He didn't want her to leave. "I'm trying to help with Isla because I want to."

Maresa's hands fisted at her side, her whole body rigid. "She's my responsibility."

Her stubborn refusal reminded him of his oldest brother. Quinn never wanted anyone to help him either—a trait Cam respected, even when Quinn became too damn overbearing.

"You've know about her for less than twenty-four hours. Most families get nine months to prepare." He settled a hand on Maresa's shoulder, wanting to ease some of the weight she insisted on putting there.

"That doesn't make her any less my obligation." She folded her arms across her chest in a gesture that hovered between a defensive posture and an effort to hold herself together.

Another shriek from the nursery sent an answering spike of tension through Maresa; he could feel it under his fingertips. He'd have to be some kind of cretin not to respond to that. Still, he dropped his hand before he did something foolish like thread his fingers through her brown hair and soothe away the tension in her neck. Her back.

"Maybe not, but it gives you a damn good reason to accept some help until you get the legalities sorted out and come up with a game plan going forward." He extended his arms to gesture to the villa he'd taken for two weeks. "This place is going to be empty all evening once I head back to the hotel to put the Carib staffers through their paces. Stay put with Isla and the nurse. Have something to eat. Follow up with your lawyer. Poppy and I can sleep at the hotel tonight."

She shook her head. "I can't possibly accept such an offer. Even if you didn't own the company I work for, I couldn't allow you to do that."

"Ethics shouldn't rule out human kindness." Cameron wasn't going to rescind the offer because of some vague notion about what was right or proper. She needed help, damn it.

He drew her into a study down the hallway where indoor palm trees grew in a sunny corner under a series of skylights. Poppy trailed behind them, her collar jingling. Even here, the view of the water and the beach below was breathtaking. It made him want to cliff dive or wind surf. Or kiteboard.

He ground his teeth together on the last one. He hadn't been kiteboarding since the accident that ensured he'd never have children of his own. As if the universe had conspired to make sure he didn't repeat his father's mistakes.

"Is that what this is?" She stared up at him with questioning eyes. Worried. "Kindness? Because to be quite honest, this day has felt like a bit more than that, starting down at the beach this morning."

Starting yesterday for him, actually.

So he couldn't pretend not to know what she meant.

"There may be an underlying dynamic at work, yes. But that doesn't mean I can't offer to do something kind for you on an impossibly hard day." He had that ability, damn it. He wasn't totally self-absorbed. "And it's not just for you. It's for your brother, who might need more time to deal with this. And for Isla, who is clearly unhappy. Why not make their day easier, too?"

Maresa was quiet a long moment.

"What underlying dynamic?" she asked finally.

"It's not obvious?" He turned on his heel, needing a minute to weigh how much he wanted to spell things

out. Go on the record. But he did, damn it. He liked this
woman. He liked her fearless strength for her family,
taking on their problems with more fierceness than she
exercised for herself. Who took care of her? "I'm attracted to you."

He wasn't sure what kind of reaction he expected.
But if he had to guess, he wouldn't have anticipated an
argument.

"No." Her expression didn't change, the unflappable
concierge facade in full play. "That's not possible."

There was a flash of fire in her tawny eyes, though.
He'd bank on that.

"For all of my shortcomings, I'm pretty damn sure I
know what attraction feels like."

"I didn't mean that. It's just—" She closed her eyes for
a moment, as if she needed that time in the dark to collect her thoughts. When she opened them again, she took
a deep breath. "I don't think I have the mental and emotional wherewithal to figure out what that means right
now and what the appropriate response should be." She
tipped two fingers to the bridge of her nose and pressed.
"I can't afford to make a decision I'll regret. This job
is…everything to me. And now I need it more than ever
if I'm going to take proper care of Isla and my brother."

"I understand." Now that he'd admitted the attraction,
he realized how strong it was, and that rattled him more
than a little. He was here for business, not pleasure. "And
I'm not acting on those feelings because I don't want to
add to the list of things you need to worry about."

"Okay." She eyed him warily. "Thank you."

"So here's what I propose. I'm going to need your help
on this project. It's important to me." He couldn't afford
trouble at the Carib with so much riding on the Carib-

bean expansion program. The McNeills had their hands full with their grandfather's failing health and three more heirs on the horizon to vie for the family legacy. "Take a couple of days off from the hotel. Stay here with Isla and get acquainted with her while you prepare your family and plan your next steps. I'll stay at the hotel with Poppy."

"Cam—"

"No arguments." He really needed to leave her be so she could settle in and connect with the baby. He understood the crying and the newness of the situation would upset anyone, especially a woman accustomed to running things smoothly. "You can review those files I showed you earlier in more detail. I'd like your assessment of a variety of hotel personnel."

Finally, she nodded. It felt like a major victory. And no matter what he'd said about ignoring the attraction, he couldn't help but imagine what it would be like to have her agree to other things he wanted from her. Having dinner with him, for instance. Letting him taste her full lips. Feeling her soft curves beneath his palms.

"Isla and I can't thank you enough." She backed away from him and reached for the door. "I should really go check on her."

"Don't wear yourself out," he warned. "Share the duties with the nurse."

"I will." She smiled, her hand pausing on the doorknob, some of the tension sliding off her shoulders.

"And that Jeep we used to get here actually goes with the property. I'll leave the keys on the kitchen counter and have a plate sent up from the kitchen for you." He wasn't going out of his way, he told himself. It was easy enough to do that for her.

Or was he deluding himself? He wanted Maresa—

pure and simple. But he knew it was more than that. Something about her drew him. Made him want to help her. He could do this much, at least, with a clear conscience. It benefitted McNeill Resorts to have her review those reports. He was simply giving her the time and space to do the job.

"But how will you get back to the hotel?"

"Poppy is ready for a walk." He could use a long trek to cool off. Remind himself why he had no business acting on what he was feeling for Maresa. "We'll take the scenic route along the beach." He held up his phone. "I'll leave my number with the keys downstairs. Call if you need anything."

"Okay." She nodded, then tipped her head to one side, her whole body going still. "Oh wow. Do you hear that?"

"What?" He listened.

"She stopped crying." Maresa looked relieved. Happy. So it was a total surprise that she burst into tears.

Chapter 5

If Maresa hadn't needed her job so badly, she would have seriously considered resigning.

Never in her life had she done anything so embarrassing as losing control in front of an employer. But the day had been too much, from start to finish. After the intense stress of listening to Isla cry for forty minutes, she'd been so relieved to hear silence reign in the nursery. The sudden shift of strong emotions had tipped something inside her.

Now, much to her extreme mortification, Cameron McNeill's arms were around her as he drew her onto a cushioned gray settee close to the door. Even more embarrassing? How much she wanted to sink into those arms and wail her heart out on his strong chest. She cried harder.

"It's okay," he assured her, his voice beside her ear

and his woodsy aftershave stirring a hunger for close-
ness she could not afford.

"No, it's really not." She shook her head against his
shoulder, telling herself to get it together.

"As your boss, I order you to stop arguing with me."

She couldn't stop a watery laugh. "I don't know what's
the matter with me."

"Anyone would be overwhelmed right now." His arms
tightened, drawing her closer in a way that was undeni-
ably more comfortable. "Don't fight so damn hard. Let
it out."

And for a moment, she did just that. She didn't let
herself think about how deeply she'd screwed up by sob-
bing in his arms. She just let the emotions run through
her, the whole great big unwieldy mess that her life had
become. She hadn't cried like this when the doctor told
her Rafe might not live. Day after day, she'd sat in that
hospital and willed him to hang on and fight. Then, by
the time he finally opened his eyes again, she couldn't
afford to break down. She needed to be strong for him.
To show him that she was fighting, too.

She'd helped him relearn to walk. Had that really been
just six months ago? He'd come so far, so fast. But she
knew there were limits to what he could do.

Limits to how much he could do because she willed it.
She knew, in her heart, he would not be able to handle a
crying baby even if she could make him understand that
Isla was his. It wouldn't be right to thrust this baby into
his life right now. Or fair.

She didn't need the counselor to tell her that, even
though the woman had finally returned her call and left
a message to come by the office in the morning. Maresa
knew that the woman was trying to find a way to tell her

the hard truth—this baby could upset him so much he could have a setback.

And she cried for that. For him. Because there had been a time in Rafe's life when the birth of his daughter would have been a cause for celebration. It broke her heart that his life had to be so different now.

With one last shuddering sigh, she felt the storm inside her pass. As it eased away, leaving her drained but more at peace, Maresa became aware of the man holding her. Aware of the hard plane of his chest where her forehead rested. Of the warm skin beneath the soft cotton T-shirt that she'd soaked with her tears. Amidst all the other embarrassments of the day she was at least grateful that her mascara had been waterproof. It would have been one indignity too many to leave her makeup on his clothes.

His arm was around her shoulders, his hand on her upper arm where he rubbed gentle circles that had soothed her a moment before. Now? That touch teased a growing awareness that spread over her skin to make her senses sing. With more than a little regret, she levered herself up, straightening.

"Cameron." Her voice raspy from the crying, his name sounded far too intimate when she said it that way.

Then again, maybe it seemed more intimate since she was suddenly nose-to-nose with him, his arm still holding her close. She forgot to think. Forgot to breathe. She was pretty sure her heart paused, too, as she stared up at him.

A sexy, incredibly appealing man.

Without her permission, her fingers moved to his face. She traced the line of his lightly shadowed jaw, surprised at the rough bristle against her fingertips. His blue eyes hypnotized her. There was simply no other explanation for what was happening to her right now. Her brain told her to extricate herself. Walk away.

Her hands had other ideas. She twined them around his neck, her heart full of a tenderness she shouldn't feel. But he'd been so good to her. So thoughtful. And she wanted to kiss him more than she wanted anything.

"Maresa." Her name on his lips was a warning. A chance to change her mind.

She understood that she was pushing a boundary. Recognized that he'd just drawn a line in the sand.

"I didn't mind giving up my dream job in Paris to care for Rafe and help my mother recover," she confided, giving him absolutely no context for her comment and hoping he understood what she was saying. "And I will gladly give eighteen years to raise my niece as my own daughter." She'd known it without question the moment Jaden handed her Isla. "But I'm not sure I can sacrifice the chance to have this kiss."

She'd crossed the boundary. Straight into "certifiable" territory. She must have cried out all her good sense.

His blue eyes simmered with more heat than a Saint Thomas summer. He cupped her chin, cradling her face like she was something precious.

"If I thought you wouldn't regret it tomorrow, I'd give you all the kisses you could handle." The stroke of his thumb along her cheek didn't begin to soothe the rejection.

Her eyes burned again, reminding her just how jumbled her emotions were right now. Knowing he had a point did nothing to salvage her pride.

"You told me you were attracted to me." She unwound her hands from his neck.

"Too much," he admitted. "That's why I'm trying to

be smart about this. I'm willing to wait to be with you until a time when you won't have any regrets about it."

"You say that like it's a foregone conclusion." She straightened, her cheeks heating.

"Or maybe it's using the power of positive thinking." His lips kicked up in a half smile, but she needed air. Space.

"You should go." She wanted time to clear her head.

Tipping her head toward him, he kissed her forehead with a gentle tenderness that made her ache for all she couldn't have.

"I'll see you in the morning," he told her, shoving to his feet.

"I thought I was taking time off?" She tucked her disheveled hair behind one ear, eager to call her mother and figure out what to do about Isla.

"From the hotel. Not from me." He shoved his hands in his pockets, and something about the gesture made her think he'd done it to keep from touching her.

She knew because she felt the same need to touch him.

"When will I see you?"

"Text me when you and Isla are ready in the morning and I'll come get you. I'm traveling to Martinique tomorrow and I'd like you with me."

She arched an eyebrow. "You need a tour guide with an infant in tow?"

"We could talk through some of the data in those reports a bit more. You could help give me a bigger picture of what's going on here." He opened the door into the quiet hallway of the expansive vacation villa. "Besides, I want to be close by if you decide you want to share kisses you won't regret down the road."

He strode away, whistling softly for Poppy as he

headed toward the main staircase. He left Maresa alone in the extravagant house with a baby, a nurse and all kinds of confused feelings for him. One thing was certain, though.

A man like Cameron McNeill might tempt her sorely. But he was a fantasy. A temporary escape from the reality of a life full of obligations she would never walk away from. So until her heart understood how thoroughly off-limits he was, Maresa needed to put all thoughts of kisses out of her head.

An hour later, Maresa had her mother in the Jeep with her as she pulled up to the gated vacation villa. She'd calmly explained the Isla situation on a phone call on the way over to her house, arranging for their retired neighbor to visit with Rafe for a couple of hours while Maresa brought her mom to meet her grandchild.

After hearing back from Rafe's counselor that a mention of his daughter could trigger too much frustration and a possible memory block, Maresa had simply told her brother she wanted to bring their mother to meet a girlfriend's new baby.

She'd kept the story simple and straightforward, and Rafe didn't mind the visit time with Mr. Leopold, who was happy to play one of Rafe's video games with him and keep an eye on him. The paperwork requesting temporary legal custody of the baby would be filed in the morning by her attorney, so she'd taken care of that, too.

Now, driving through the gates, Maresa enjoyed her mother's startled gasp at the breathtaking view of the Caribbean.

"I had the same reaction earlier," she admitted, halting the Jeep in the space beside the nurse's sedan. "But this isn't half as beautiful as Isla."

"I cannot wait to meet her." Analise Delphine opened the car door slowly, the neuropathy in her hands one of many nerve conditions caused by her MS. "But I'm still so angry at Trina for not telling us sooner. Can you imagine what happiness it would have given us in those dark hours with your brother if we had only known about his daughter?"

Maresa hurried around the car to help her mother out since it did no good to tell her to wait. Analise had struggled more with her disease ever since the car crash that injured Rafe. Maresa worried about her since her mother seemed to blame herself—and her MS—for the injury to her beloved son, and some days it appeared as if she wanted to suffer because of her guilt. For months, Maresa had encouraged her mother to get into some more family counseling, but Analise would only go to sessions that were free through a local clinic, not wanting to "be a burden."

Maresa had tread lightly around the topic until now, but if they were going to be responsible for this baby, she needed her mother to be strong emotionally even if her physical health was declining.

"Trina is young," Maresa reminded her as she helped her up the white stone walkway to the main entrance of the villa. "She must have been scared and confused between finding out she was pregnant and then learning Rafe wasn't going to make a full recovery."

Analise breathed heavily as she leaned on Maresa's arm. Analise had always been the most beautiful girl on the block, according to their neighbor Mr. Leopold. She'd worked as a dancer in clubs and in street perfor-

mances for tourists, earning a good living for years before the MS hit her hard. Her limber dancer's body had
thickened with her inability to move freely, but her careful makeup and her eye for clothing meant she always
looked stage-ready.

"She is old enough to make better choices." Her
mother stopped abruptly, squinting into the sunlight as
she peered up at the vacation home. "Speaking of which,
Maresa, I hope you are making wise choices by staying
here. You said your boss is allowing you to do this?"

"Yes, Mom." She tugged gently at her mother's arm,
drawing her up the wide stone steps. "He was there when
Jaden handed me Isla, so he knew I had a lot to contend
with today."

She wasn't sure about the rest of his motives. She was
still separating Cameron McNeill from surly Mr. Holmes,
trying to understand him. He'd walked out on her today
when she would have gladly lost herself in the attraction.
Some of her wounded pride had been comforted by his
assurance that he wanted her.

So where did that leave them for tomorrow when he
expected her to accompany him to a neighboring island?

"Most men don't share their expensive villas without
expectations, Maresa. Be smarter than that," her mother
chastised her while Maresa unlocked the front door with
the key Cameron had left behind. "You need to come
home."

Before she could argue, Wendy appeared in the foyer,
a pink bundle in her arms. Her mother oohed and aahed,
mesmerized by her new grandchild as she happily cata-
loged all the sleeping baby's features. Maresa paid scant
attention, however, as Analise declared the hairline was
Rafe's and the mouth inherited was from Analise herself.

Maresa still smarted from her mother's insistence that she wasn't "being smart" to stay in the villa with Isla tonight. Perhaps it stung all the more because that had been Maresa's first instinct, as well. But damn it, Cameron had a point about the practicality of it. The Carib did indeed comp rooms to special guests who provided services. Why couldn't she enjoy the privilege while she helped Cameron McNeill investigate the operations of his luxury hotel?

Putting aside her frustration, she tried to enjoy her mother's pleasure in the baby even as Maresa worried about the future. It was easy for her mom to tell her that she should simply bring Isla home, but it would be Maresa who had to make arrangements for caregiving and Maresa who would wake up every few hours to look after the child. All of their lives were going to change dramatically under the roof of her mother's tiny house.

Maybe she needed to look for a larger home for all of them. She'd thought she couldn't afford it before, but now she wondered how she could afford *not* to buy something bigger. She would speak to her mother about it, but first, it occurred to her she could speak to Cameron. He was a businessman. His brother—she'd once read online— was a hedge fund manager. Surely a McNeill could give sound financial advice.

Besides, talking about the Caribbean housing market would be a welcome distraction in case the conversation ever turned personal tomorrow. If ever she was tempted to kiss him again, she'd just think about interest rates. That ought to cool her jets in a hurry.

"Look, Maresa!" Her mother turned the baby on her lap to show her Isla's face as they sat on the loveseat of a sprawling white family room decorated with dark leather furnishings and heavy Mexican wood. The little girl's eyes were open now, blinking owlishly. "She has your father's eyes! We need to call him and tell him. He won't believe it."

"Mom. No." She reached for the baby while Analise dug in her boho bag sewn out of brightly colored fabric scraps and pulled out a cell phone. "Dad never likes hearing from us."

She'd been devastated by her father's furious reaction to her phone call the night of Rafe's accident.

I've moved on, Maresa. Help your mother get that through her head.

"Nonsense." Analise grinned as she pressed the screen. "He'll want to hear this. Isla is his first grandchild, too, you know."

In Maresa's arms, the infant kicked and squirmed, her back arching as if she were preparing for a big cry. Maresa resisted the urge to call to Wendy, needing the experience of soothing the little girl. So she patted her back and spoke comforting words, shooting to her feet to walk around the room while her mother left a message on her father's voice mail. No surprise he hadn't picked up the call.

"I bet he'll book a flight down here as soon as he can," Analise assured her. "I should be getting home so I can make the house ready for company. And a baby, too!"

She levered slowly out of her chair to her feet, her new energy and excitement making her wince less even though the hurt had to be just the same as it was an hour ago.

"I don't think Dad will come down here," Maresa warned her quietly, not wanting her mom's hopes raised to impossible levels.

Jack Janson hadn't returned once since moving overseas. He hadn't even visited Maresa in Paris; she'd briefly hoped that since he lived in the UK, he might make the effort to see her. But no.

"Could you let me be excited about just this one thing? We have enough to worry us, Maresa. Let's look for things to be hopeful about." She put her hand on Maresa's shoulders, a touch that didn't comfort her in the least.

If anything, Maresa remembered why she needed to be all the more careful with Cameron McNeill. Like her father, he was only here on business. Like her father, he might think it was fun to indulge himself with a local woman while he was far from his home and his real life.

But once he left Saint Thomas and solved the problems at the Carib Grand, Maresa knew all too well that he wasn't ever coming back.

Cameron had new respect for the running abilities of Maltese show dogs.

He sprinted through the undergrowth on the beach the next morning, about an hour after sunrise, trying to keep up with the little pooch.

"Poppy!" he called to her, cursing himself for giving her a moment off the leash. He'd scoped the beach and knew they were alone on the Carib Grand's private stretch of shore, so he'd figured it was okay.

He could keep up with the little dog on her short legs after all. But Poppy was small and shifty, darting and zigzagging through the brush where Cam couldn't fit. The groomer was going to think he'd gotten the pup's fur tangled on purpose, but damn it, he was just trying to let her have some fun. She seemed so happy chasing those terns.

If only it was as easy to tell what would make Maresa Delphine happy. He'd spent most of the day with her and still wasn't sure how to make her smile again. The concierge had the weight of the world on her straight shoulders.

Catching sight of muddy white fur, Cameron swooped low to scoop up the dog in midstride.

"Gotcha." He held on to the wriggling, overexcited bundle of wet canine while she tried her best to lick his face.

He'd have to shower again before his day in Martinique with Maresa since he was now covered with beach sand and dog fur, but it was tough to stay perturbed with the overjoyed animal. Chiding her gently while he attached the leash, Cam turned to go back up the path to the hotel.

Only to spot Rafe Delphine walking toward the beach beside a well-dressed, much older woman.

Surprised that Rafe had come in to work with Maresa taking the day off, Cameron watched the pair from a hidden vantage point in the bushes.

"Do you know this painter I'm meeting, young man?" the woman asked, her accent sounding Nordic, maybe. Or Finnish.

The woman was probably in her late sixties or early seventies. She had a sleek blond bob and expensive-looking bag. Even the beach sandals she wore had the emblem of an exclusive designer Cam recognized because a long-ago girlfriend had dragged him to a private runway show.

"Jaden paints." Rafe nodded his acknowledgement of the question but his eye was on the ground where a bird flapped its damp wings. "Look. A tern."

Poppy wriggled excitedly. The movement attracted the

older woman's attention, giving up Cam's hiding place
She smiled at him.

"What a precious little princess!" she exclaimed, eyes
on Poppy. "She looks like she's been having fun today."

Rafe's tawny eyes—so like his sister's—turned his
way. He gave Cam a nod of recognition, or maybe it was
just politeness. Effectively called out of his spot in the
woods, Cameron stepped into the sunlight and let the
woman meet Poppy, who was—as always—appropri-
ately gracious for the attention.

After a brief exchange with the dog, Cameron continued toward the hotel. He'd known that Jaden Torries was
probably trolling for work at the Carib, so it shouldn't be
a huge surprise that one of the hotel guests was meeting him at the beach. But why was Rafe bringing her to
meet him?

Given how much Maresa disliked her ex-fiancé, it
seemed unlikely she would be the one facilitating Jaden
doing any kind of work with hotel patrons. Especially
since she wasn't even working today. Then again, what
if she had found a way to make a little extra income by
helping Jaden find patrons? Would she set aside her dis-
taste for him if it made things easier for her?

Deep in thought, Cam arrived at the pool deck. He
didn't want to think his attraction to Maresa would influence his handling of the situation, but his first instinct
was to speak to her directly. He would ask her about it
when he picked her up at the villa, he decided.

Except then he spotted her circulating among the
guests by the pool. She'd been here all along?

Suspicion mounted. Grinding his teeth, he charged
toward her, more than ready for some answers.

Chapter 6

Morning sun beating down on her head, Maresa noticed Cameron McNeill heading her way and she braced herself for the resurrection of Mr. Holmes. She knew he needed to be undercover to learn more about the hotel operations, but did he have to be quite so convincing in his "difficult guest" role? The hard set of his jaw and brooding glare were seriously intimidating even knowing how kind he could be.

She straightened from a conversation with one of her seasonal guests from Quebec who rented a suite for half the year. Pasting on a professionally polite smile to greet Cameron, she told herself she should be grateful to see this side of him so she wouldn't be tempted to throw herself at him again.

Even if his bare chest and low-slung board shorts drew every female eye.

"Good morning, Mr. Holmes." She reached to smooth

her jacket sleeves, only to remember she'd worn a sundress today for the trip into Martinique. *Oh, my.* Her skin had goose bumps of awareness just from standing this close to him.

"May I speak to you privately?" He handed off Poppy to the dog groomer who scurried over from where he'd been waiting by the tiki bar.

Cameron certainly couldn't have any complaints about the service he was receiving, could he? People seemed to hurry to offer him assistance.

"Of course." She excused herself from the other guests, following him toward the door marked Employees Only.

He didn't slow his step until they were in the same conference room where they'd spoken yesterday. The cool blast of air almost matched the ice chips in his blue eyes. He shoved the door shut behind them before he turned to face her.

"I thought you were taking the day off from the hotel." His jaw flexed and he crossed his arms over his bare chest, the board shorts riding low on his hips.

She tried not to stare, distracting herself by focusing on the hint of confrontation in his tone.

"I am." She gestured to her informal clothing. "I only stopped by this morning to see my brother and make sure he felt comfortable about his workday."

"And is he comfortable escorting guests to the beach?" Cameron's arctic glare might have made another woman shiver. Maresa straightened her spine.

"I never give him jobs like that. Why do you ask?" Defensiveness for her brother roared through her.

"Because I just saw him walking one of our overseas guests to the shore to meet Jaden Torries."

Surprised, she quickly guessed he must be mistaken. He had to be. Still a hint of tension tickled her gut. "Rafe doesn't even arrive until the next ferry." She checked her watch just to be sure the day hadn't slipped away from her. "He should be walking in the employee locker rooms any minute to punch his time card."

"He's already here." Cameron pulled out one of the high-backed leather chairs for her, all sorts of muscles flexing as he moved, distracting her when she needed to be focused. "I saw him myself at the beach with one of the hotel guests just a few minutes ago."

"I don't understand." Ignoring the seat, she paced away from all that tempting male muscle to peer out the windows overlooking the croquet lawn near the pool, hoping to get a view of the path to the beach. How could she relax, wondering if her brother might be doing jobs around the Carib without her knowing? She was supposed to watch over him during his first few months of employment. She'd promised the hotel director as much. "I got here early so I wouldn't miss him when he came to work. I want everything to go smoothly for him if I'm not here to supervise him myself."

Cameron joined her at the window, his body warm beside hers as he peered out onto the mostly empty side lawns. A butterfly garden near the window attracted a handful of brightly colored insects. His shoulder brushed hers, setting off butterflies inside, too. She hated feeling this way—torn between the physical attraction and the mental frustration.

"Did you know Jaden was soliciting business from hotel guests?" Cameron's question was quiet. Dispassionate.

And it offended her mightily. How dare he question her integrity? Her work record was impeccable and he should know as much if he was even halfway doing *his* job.

Anger burned through her as she whirled to face him, her skirt brushing his leg he stood so close to her. She took a step back.

"Absolutely not. Until yesterday, I hadn't seen Jaden since I left for Paris two years ago." She frowned, not understanding why Cameron would think she'd do such a thing. "And while I don't wish him ill, my relationship with him is absolutely over. I certainly don't have any desire to risk my job to help a man I dislike profit off our guests."

"I see." Cameron nodded slowly, as if weighing whether or not to believe her.

Worry balled in her stomach and she reined in her anger. She couldn't afford to be offended. She needed him to believe her.

"Why would you think I'd do such a thing?" She didn't want to be here. She wanted to find her brother and ask him what was going on.

Did Rafe even understand what he was doing by helping Jaden meet potential clients for his artwork? Was Jaden asking him for that kind of help?

"That type of business is probably lucrative for him—"

Understanding dawned. Indignation flared, hot and fast. "And you thought I would be a part of some sordid scheme with my ex-fiancé for the sake of extra cash? Even twisting my brother's arm into setting up meetings when I do everything in my power to protect him?"

If it had been anyone else, she would have stormed out of the meeting room. But she needed this job too much and, at the end of the day, Cameron McNeill was still an owner of the Carib.

He held all the cards.

"I don't know what to think. That's why I wanted to speak to you privately." He picked up a gray T-shirt from the back of a chair in the conference room and pulled it over his head.

She watched in spite of herself, realizing he must have been doing work in the conference room earlier that morning since a laptop and phone sat on the table.

"I won't have any answers until I speak to my brother." She was worried about him. For him. For the baby. Oh God, when had life gotten so complicated?

What had her brother gotten into?

"You realize this isn't the first time he's done it." Cameron's voice softened as he headed toward her again. "That customer review that I shared with you yesterday was from someone who said he provided a 'happy escort' to the beach." Cameron's blue eyes probed hers, searching for answers she didn't have.

As much as she longed to share her fears with him, she couldn't do that. Not when he was in charge of her fate at the hotel, and Rafe's, too.

"I remember." She itched to leave, needing to see Rafe for herself. "And now that you've put that comment in context, I'm happy to speak to my brother and clear this up."

She turned toward the door, desperate to put the complicated knot of feelings her boss inspired behind her.

"Wait." Cameron reached for her hand and held it,

his touch warm and firm. "I realize you want to protect him, Maresa, but we need to find out what's going on."

"And we will," she insisted, wishing he didn't make her heart beat faster. "Just as soon as I speak to him."

Cameron studied her for a long moment with searching eyes, then quietly asked, "What if he doesn't have a clear answer?"

Some of the urgency eased from her. She couldn't deny that was a possibility.

"I can only do my best to figure out what's going on." She couldn't imagine who else would be giving him extra chores to do around the hotel. Rafe had never particularly liked Jaden. Then again, her brother was a different man since the accident.

"I know that. And what if we learn more by observing him for a few days? Maybe it would be better to simply keep a closer eye on him now that we know he's carrying out duties for the hotel—or someone else—that you haven't authorized." His tone wasn't accusing. "Maybe you shouldn't upset him unnecessarily."

She wanted to tell him she already spent hours supervising her brother. More than others on her staff. But she bit her lip, refusing to reveal a piece of information that could get Rafe terminated from his position.

"I don't want him getting hurt," she argued, worried about letting her brother's behavior continue unchecked. "And I don't know who he's speaking to that would advise him to take risks like this with his job."

The day had started out so promising, with Isla sleeping for five hours straight and waking up with a drooly baby smile, only to take this radical nosedive. Anxiety spiked. Rafe was going to lose this job, damn it. She would never be able to afford a caregiver for Isla and a companion to supervise Rafe, too. Especially not once they lost Rafe's income. Heaven only knew how much he would recover from the brain injury. What kind of future he would have? How much he could provide for himself, much less a child? All the fears of the unknown jumped up inside her.

Cameron hissed a low, frustrated breath between his teeth. "What if we compromise? You confront him now, but if you don't get a direct answer or if you sense there's more to his answer than what he shares, you back off. Then, we can keep a closer eye on him for the next week and see who is setting up these meetings."

She didn't like the idea of waiting. She knew there was a good chance Rafe wouldn't give her a direct answer. But what choice did she really have? She wouldn't be able to push him anyhow, since his health and potential recovery were more important than getting answers to any mystery going on at the Carib.

"Fine." She turned to the door, eager to see her brother, but she paused when Cameron followed her. "I'd prefer to speak to him alone."

He followed her so closely that she needed to tilt her head to peer up at him.

"Of course." He stood near enough that she could see the shades of blue in his eyes, as varied as the Caribbean. "I'm going to change for our trip. I'll have a car meet you out front in fifteen minutes."

She wondered if it was wise to risk being seen leaving the hotel with surly Mr. Holmes. But then, that wasn't her problem so much as his. She had enough to worry about waiting for the DNA tests to come back so she could finally tell Rafe about Isla. Her lawyer and his psychologist had advised her and her mother to wait until then.

Hurrying away from all that distracting masculine appeal, Maresa rushed into the employee lounge to look for her brother. She'd already called in a favor from Big Bill, the head doorman, to help keep an eye on Rafe for the next few days. Bill was a friend of her mother's from their old neighborhood and he'd been kind enough to agree, but Maresa knew the man could only do so much.

Inside the lounge, the scent of morning coffee mingled with someone's too-strong perfume. A few people from the maintenance staff gossiped around the kitchen table where a box of pastries sat open. Moving past the kitchen, Maresa peered into the locker area between the men's and women's private lounges. Rafe sat in the middle row of lockers, carefully braiding the stems of yellow buttercups into a chain. Flowers spilled over the polished bench as he straddled it, his focus completely absorbed in the task.

Any frustration she felt with him melted away. How could Cameron think for a moment that her brother would knowingly do anything unethical at work? It was only because Cameron didn't know Rafe. If he did, he'd never think something like that for a moment.

"Hey, Rafe." She took a seat on the bench nearby, wishing with all her heart he could be in a work program designed for people with his kinds of abilities. He had so much to offer with his love of nature and talent with green and growing things. Even now, his affinity for plants was evident, the same as before the accident when he'd had his own landscaping business. "What are you making?"

He glanced up at her, his eyes so like the ones she saw in the mirror every day.

"Maresa." He smiled briefly before returning his attention to the flowers. "I'm making you a bracelet."

"Me?" She had worried he was heaping more gifts on Nancy. And while she liked the server, she didn't want Rafe to have any kind of romantic hopes about the woman. Hearing the flowers were for her was a relief.

"I felt bad I left work." He lifted the flower chain and laid it on her wrist, his shirt cuffs brushing her skin as he carefully knotted the stems together. "I'm sorry."

Her heart knotted up like the flowers.

"Thank you. I love it." She kissed him on the cheek, smiling at the way his simple offering looked beside the silver star bracelet he'd given her two years ago before she left for Paris.

He was as thoughtful as ever, and his way of showing it hadn't changed all that much.

"Rafe?" She drew a deep breath, hating to ruin a happy moment with questions about Jaden. But this was important. The sooner she helped Cameron McNeill figure out what was going on at the Carib Grand, the sooner their jobs would be secure and they could focus on a new life with Isla—if Isla was in fact his child. And even though their lives would be less complicated without the child, Maresa couldn't deny that the thought of Isla leaving made her stomach clench. "Why did you go to the beach this morning?"

She kept the question simple. Direct.

"Mr. Ricci asked." Rafe rose to his feet, dusting flower petals off his faded olive cargoes. "Time to go to work. Mom said I don't work with you today."

She blinked at the fast change of topic. "Mr. Ricci asked you to bring a guest to the beach?"

"It's eight thirty." Rafe pointed to his watch. "Mom said I don't work with you today."

Damn it. Damn it. She didn't want to throw his whole workday off for the sake of a conversation that might lead nowhere. Maybe Cameron was right and they were better off keeping an eye on the situation.

"Right. I have to work off-site today. You'll be helping Glenna at the concierge stand, but Big Bill is on duty today. If you need help with anything, ask Bill, okay?"

"Ask Big Bill." Rafe gave her a thumbs-up before he stalked out of the locker room and into the hotel to start work.

Watching him leave, Maresa's fingers went to the bracelet he'd made her. He was thoughtful and kind. Surely he would have so much to give Isla. She needed to speak to his counselor in more detail so they could brainstorm ideas for the right way to introduce them. It seemed wrong to deprive the little girl of a father when her mother had already given up on her.

For now, however, she needed to tell Cameron that Rafe was escorting guests to the beach because the hotel director told him to. Would Cameron believe her? Or would he demand to speak to her brother himself?

Cameron's seductive promise floated back to her. *If I thought you wouldn't regret it tomorrow, I'd give you all the kisses you could handle.* She'd replayed those words again and again since he'd said them.

She walked a tightrope with her compelling boss— needing him to allow Rafe to stay in his job, but needing her own secured even more. Which meant she had to help him in his investigation.

Most of all, to keep those objectives perfectly clear, she had to ignore her growing attraction to him. His kindness with Isla might have slid past her defenses, but in order to protect the baby's future, Maresa would have to set aside her desire to find out what "all the kisses she could handle" would feel like.

The flight to Martinique was fast and efficient. They took off from the private dock near the Carib Grand's beach and touched down in the Atlantic near Le Francois on the east coast of Martinique. The pilot landed the new seaplane smoothly, barely jostling Baby Isla's carrier where she sat beside Maresa in the seats facing Cameron.

Cameron tried to focus on the baby to keep his mind off the exotically gorgeous woman across from him. The task had been damn near impossible for the hour of flight time between islands. Maresa's bright sundress was so different from the linen suits he'd seen her in for work. He liked the full skirt and vibrant poppy print, and he admired that she wore the simple floral bracelet around one wrist. With her hair loose and sun-tipped around her face, she looked impossibly beautiful. Her movements with Isla were easier today and her fascination with the little girl was obvious every time she glanced Isla's way.

Before she unbuckled the baby's carrier, she pressed a kiss to the infant's smooth forehead. A new pink dress with a yellow bunny on the front had been a gift from Maresa's mother, apparently. They'd spoken about that much on that flight. Maresa had given him an update on the custody paperwork with the lawyer, the paternity test she'd ordered using Rafe's hair and a cheek swab of Isla's, and she'd told him about her mother's reaction to her granddaughter. They'd only discussed Rafe briefly, agreeing not to confront him any further about bringing guests to meet Jaden Torries. They would watch Rafe more carefully when they returned to Saint Thomas. Until then, Bill the doorman knew to keep a close eye on him.

Cameron hadn't pushed her to discuss her theory about what might be going on, knowing that she was already worried about her brother's activities at the hotel. But at some point today, they would have to discuss where to go next with Rafe, and Jaden, too. For now, Cameron simply wanted to put her at ease for a few hours while he gathered some information about this secret branch of his family. The Martinique McNeills had a home in Le Francois, an isolated compound that was the equivalent of Grandfather Malcolm's home in Manhattan—a centrally located hub with each of the brothers' names on the deed. The family had other property holdings, but their mother had lived here before her death and the next generation all spent time there.

Cameron had done his homework and was ready to check out this group today. Later, after Maresa had time to relax and catch her breath from the events of the last few days, he would talk to her about a plan for the future. For her and for Isla, too. The little girl in the pink dress tugged at his heart.

"So you have family here?" Maresa passed the baby carrier to him while the pilot opened the plane door.

Fresh air blew in, toying lightly with Maresa's hair.

"In theory. Yes." He wasn't happy about the existence of the other McNeills. "That is—they don't know we're related yet. My father kept his other sons and mistress a secret. When his lover tired of being hidden, she sold the house he'd bought her and left without a forwarding address. He didn't fight her legally because of the scandal that would create." As he said it aloud, however, he realized that didn't sound like his father. "Actually, he was probably just too disinterested to try and find them. He never paid us much attention either."

Liam McNeill had been a sorry excuse for a father. Cameron refused to follow in those footsteps.

Cam lifted the baby carrier above the seats, following Maresa to the exit. They'd parked at a private dock for the Cap Est Lagoon, a resort hotel in Le Francois close to the McNeill estate.

"But at least he's still a part of your life, isn't he?" Maresa held her full skirt with one hand as she descended the steps of the plane. A gusty breeze wreaked havoc with the hem.

The view of her legs was a welcome distraction during a conversation about his dad.

"He is part of the business, so I see him at company meetings. But it's not like he shows up for holidays to hang out. He's never been that kind of father." Even Cameron's grandfather hadn't quite known what to do to create a sense of family. Sure, he'd taken in Quinn, Ian and Cameron often enough as teens. But they were more apt to travel with him on business, learning the ropes from the head of the company, than have fun.

Luckily, Cam had had his brothers.

And, later, his own reckless sense of fun.

Maresa held her hair with one hand as they walked down the dock together, the baby between them in her seat. Behind them, the hotel staff unloaded their bags from the seaplane. Not that they'd travelled with much, but Cam had taken a suite here so Maresa would have a place to retreat with Isla. The Cap Est spread out on the shore ahead of them, the red-roofed buildings ringing the turquoise lagoon. Birds called and circled overhead. A few white sailing boats dotted the blue water.

"A disinterested father is a unique kind of hurt," Maresa observed empathetically—so much so it gave him pause for a moment. But then he was distracted by a hint of her perfume on the breeze as she followed him to the villa where their suite awaited. A greeter from the hotel had texted him instructions on the location so they could proceed directly there. "Do you think your half brothers will be glad to see him again? Has it been a long time that they've been apart?"

"Fifteen years. The youngest hasn't seen his father—my father—since the kid was ten." Cameron hadn't thought about that much. He'd been worried about what the other McNeills might ask from them in terms of the family resort business. But there was a chance they'd be too bitter to claim anything.

Or so bitter that they'd want revenge.

Cameron wouldn't let them hurt his grandfather. Or the legacy his granddad had worked his whole life to build.

"Wow, fifteen? That's not much older than I was the last time I saw my dad." Maresa's words caught him by surprise as they reached the villa where a greeter admitted them.

Cameron didn't ask her about it until the hotel representative had shown them around the two-floor suite with a private deck overlooking the lagoon. When the woman left and Maresa was lifting Isla from the carrier, however, Cameron raised the question.

"Where's your father now?" He watched her coo and

comfort the baby, rubbing the little girl's back through her pink dress, the bowlegs bare above tiny white ankle socks.

The vacation villa was smaller than the one near the Carib Grand, but more luxuriously appointed, with floor-to-ceiling windows draped in white silk that fluttered in the constant breeze off the water. Exotic Turkish rugs in bright colors covered alternating sections of dark bamboo floors. Paintings of the market at Marigot and historic houses in Fort-de-France, the capital of Martinique, hung around the living area, providing all the color of an otherwise quietly decorated room. Deep couches with white cushions and teak legs and arms were positioned for the best views of the water. There was even a nursery with a crib brought in especially for their visit.

"He lives outside London with his new wife. I spoke to him briefly after Rafe's accident, but his only response was a plea that I tell my mother he's *moved on* and not to bother him again." She stressed the words in a way that suggested she would never forget the tone of voice in which they'd been spoken. Shaking her head, she walked Isla over to the window and stared out at the shimmering blue expanse. "I won't be contacting him anymore."

Cameron sifted through a half dozen responses before he came up with one that didn't involve curses.

"I don't blame you. The man can't be bothered to come to his critically injured son's bedside? He doesn't deserve his kids." Cameron knew without a doubt that he'd suck as a father, but even he would never turn his back like that on a kid.

Maresa's burden in caring for her whole family became clearer, however. Her mother wasn't working because of her battle with MS, her father was out of the picture and her brother needed careful supervision. Maresa was supporting a lot of people on her salary.

And now, an infant, too. That was one helluva load for a person to carry on her own. Admiration for her grew. She wasn't like his dad, who disengaged from responsibilities and the people counting on him.

"What will you do if your half brothers don't want to see your father?" she asked him now, drifting closer to him as she rubbed her cheek against the top of Isla's downy head.

Cameron was seized with the need to wrap his arms around both of them, a protective urge so strong he had to fight to keep his hands off Maresa. He jammed his fists in the pocket of his khakis to stop himself. Still, he walked closer, wanting to breathe in her scent. To feel the way her nearness heated over his skin like a touch.

"I'll convince them that my grandfather is worth ten of my father and make sure they understand the importance of meeting him." He lowered his voice while he stood so close to her, unable to move away.

Fascinated, he watched the effect he had on her. The goose bumps down her arm. The fast thrum of a tiny vein at the base of her neck. A quick dart of her tongue over her lips that all but did him in.

He wanted this woman. So much that telling himself to stay away wasn't going to help. So much that the baby in her arms wasn't going to distract him, let alone dissuade him.

"I should change," Maresa said suddenly, clutching Isla tighter. "Into something for the trip to your brothers' house. That is, if you want me to accompany you there? I'm not sure what you want my role to be here."

His gaze roamed over her, even knowing it was damned unprofessional. But they'd passed that point in this relationship the day before when Maresa had wrapped her arms around him. He'd used up all his restraint then. Time for some plain talk.

"Your role? First, tell me honestly what you think would happen between us this week if I wasn't your boss." He couldn't help the hoarse hunger in his voice, and knew that she heard it. He studied her while she struggled to answer, envious of the way Isla's tiny body curved around the soft swell of Maresa's breast.

"What good does it do to wonder what if?" Frustration vibrated through her, her body tensing. "The facts can't be changed. I'd never quit this job. It's more important to me than ever."

Right. He knew that. She'd made that more than clear. So why couldn't he seem to stay away? Stifling a curse at himself, he stepped back. Swallowed.

"I need to visit my brothers' place. You can relax here with Isla and review the files I started to show you yesterday. Make whatever notes you can to help me weed through what's important." He had to get some fresh air in his lungs if he was going to keep his distance from Maresa until the time was right.

"Okay. Thank you." She nodded, relief and regret both etched in her features.

"When I get back, I'll have dinner ordered in. We can eat on the upstairs deck before we fly back tonight, unless of course, you decide you'd like to stay another day."

Her eyes widened, a flush of heat stealing along the skin bared by the open V of her sundress. He couldn't look away.

"I'm sure that won't be necessary." She clung to her professional reserve.

"Nevertheless, I'll keep the option open." He reached for her, stroking the barest of touches along her arm. "Just in case."

Chapter 7

Just in case.

Hours later, Cameron's parting words still circled around in Maresa's brain. She'd been ridiculously productive in spite of the seductive thoughts chasing through her mind, throwing herself into her work with determined intensity. Still, Cameron's suggestion of spending the night together built a fever in her blood, giving her a frenetic energy to make extensive notes on his files, research leads on Carib Grand personnel, and review her and Rafe's performance in depth. She hadn't found any answers about Rafe's additional activities, but at least she'd done the job Cameron asked of her to the best of her ability.

Now, walking away from the white-spindled crib where she'd just laid Isla for a nap with a nursery monitor by the bedside, Maresa was drawn across the hallway into the master bedroom while she waited for Cameron to return.

What would happen between us if I wasn't your boss?

Why had he asked that? Hadn't she already made it painfully clear when she'd confided how much she wanted a kiss in those heated moments in his arms yesterday? She'd relived that exchange a million times already and it had happened just twenty-four hours ago.

Now, lowering herself to a white chaise longue near open French doors, Maresa settled the nursery monitor on the hardwood floor at her feet. She would hear Isla if the baby needed anything. For just a few moments at least, she would enjoy overlooking the terrace and the turquoise lagoon below while she waited for Cameron to return. She would inhale the flower-scented sea air of her home, savor the caress of that same breeze along her skin. When was the last time she'd sat quietly and simply enjoyed this kind of beauty, let herself just soak in sensations? Sure, the beach around the Cap Est hotel in Martinique was more upscale than the Caribbean she'd grown up with—public beaches where you brought your own towels from home. But the islands were gorgeous everywhere. No one told the beach morning glory where to grow. It didn't discriminate against the public beaches any more than the yellow wedelia flowers or the bright poinciana trees.

It felt as if she hadn't taken a deep breath all year, not since she'd returned from Paris. There'd been days on the Left Bank when she'd sat at Café de Flore and simply enjoyed the scenery, indulged in people-watching, but since coming home to Charlotte Amalie? Not so much. And now? She had an infant to care for.

If Trina didn't want her baby back—and given the way

she'd abandoned Isla, Maresa vowed to block any effort to regain custody—Maresa would have eighteen years of hard work ahead. Her time to stare out to sea and enjoy a few quiet moments would be greatly limited. Given the responsibilities of her brother, mother and now the baby, she couldn't envision many—if any—men who would want to take on all of that to be with her. This window of time with Cameron McNeill might be the last opportunity she had to savor times like this.

To experience romantic pleasure.

Closing her eyes against the thought, she rested her head on the arm of the chaise, unwilling to let her mind wander down that sensual road. She was just tired, that was all.

She'd nap while Isla napped and when she woke up she'd feel like herself again—ready to be strong in the face of all that McNeill magnetism...

"Maresa?"

She awoke to the sound of her name, a whisper of sound against her ear.

Cameron's voice, so close, made her shiver in the most pleasant way, even as her skin warmed all over. The late afternoon sun slanted through the French doors, burnishing her skin to golden bronze—or so it felt. She refused to open her eyes and end the languid sensation in her limbs. The scent of the sea and Cam's woodsy aftershave was a heady combination, a sexy aphrodisiac that had her tilting her head to one side, exposing her neck in silent invitation.

"Mmm?" She arched her back, wanting to be closer to him, needing to feel his lips against her ear once more.

It'd been so long since she'd known a man's touch.

And Cameron McNeill was no ordinary man. She bet he kissed like nobody's business.

"Are you hungry?" he asked, the low timbre of his voice turning an everyday question into a sexual innuendo.

Or was it just her imagination?

"Starving," she admitted, reaching up to touch him. To feel the heat and hard muscle of his chest.

She hooked her fingers along the placket of his button-down, next to the top button, which was already undone. She felt his low hiss of response, his heart pumping faster against the back of her knuckles where she touched him. He lowered his body closer, hovering a hair's breadth away.

Breathing him in, she felt the kick of awareness in every nerve ending, her whole body straining toward his.

"Are you sure?" His husky rasp made her skin flame since he still hadn't touched her.

Her throat was dry and she had to swallow to answer. "So sure. So damn certain—"

His lips captured hers, silencing the rest of her words. His chest grazed her breasts, his body covering hers and setting it aflame. Still she craved more. She'd only known him for days but it felt as though she'd been waiting years for him to touch her. His leg slid between hers, his thigh flexing against where she needed him most. A ragged moan slid free…

"Maresa?" He chanted her name in her ear once more, and she thought she couldn't bear it if she didn't start pulling his clothes off.

And her clothes off. She needed to touch more of him.

"Please," she murmured softly, her eyes still closed. She gripped his heavy shoulders. "Please."

"Maresa?" he said again, more uncertainly this time. "Wake up."

Confused, her brain refused to acknowledge that command. She wanted him naked. She did not want to wake up.

Then again…wasn't she awake?

Her eyes wrenched open.

"Cameron?" His name was on her lips as she slid to a sitting position.

Knocking heads with the man she'd been dreaming about.

"Ow." Blinking into the dim light in the room now that the sun had set, Maresa came fully—painfully—awake, her body still on fire from her dream.

"Sorry to startle you." Cameron reached for her, cradling the spot where his forehead had connected with her temple. "Are you okay?"

No. She wasn't okay. She wanted things to go back to where they'd been in her dream. Simple. Sensual.

"Fine." Her breathing was fast. Shallow. Her heartbeat seemed to thunder louder than the waves on the shore. "Is there a storm out there?" she asked, realizing the wind had picked up since she'd fallen asleep. "Is Isla okay?"

The white silk curtains blew into the room. The end of one teased along her bare foot where she'd slid off her shoes. She spotted the nursery monitor on the floor. Silent. Reassuring.

"I just checked on her. She's fine. But there's some heavy weather on the way. The pilot warned me we might want to consider leaving now or—ideally—extending our stay. This system came out of nowhere."

She appreciated the cooler breeze on her overheated skin, and the light mist of rain blowing in with it. Only now did she realize the strap of her sundress had fallen off one shoulder, the bodice slipping precariously down on one side. Before she could reach for it, however, Cameron slid a finger under the errant strap and lifted it into place.

Her skin hummed with pleasure where he touched her.

"Sorry." He slid his hand away fast. "The bare shoulder was…" He shook his head. "I get distracted around you, Maresa. More than I should when I know you want to keep things professional."

The room was mostly dark, except for a glow from the last light of day combined with a golden halo around a wall sconce near the bathroom. He must have turned that on when he'd entered the master suite and found her sleeping.

Dreaming.

"What about you?" Her voice carried the sultriness of sleep. Or maybe it was the sound of desire from her sexy imaginings. Even now, she could swear she remembered the feel of his strong thigh between hers, his chest pressed to aching breasts. "I can't be the only one who wants to keep some professional objectivity."

She slid her feet to the floor, needing to restore some equilibrium with him. Some distance. They sat on opposite sides of the chaise longue, the gathering storm stirring electricity in the air.

"Honestly?" A flash of lightning illuminated his face in full color for a moment before returning them to black-and-white. "I would rather abdicate my role as boss where you're concerned, Maresa. Let my brother Quinn make any decisions that involve you or Rafe. My professional judgment is already seriously compromised."

She breathed in the salty, charged air. Her hair blew

silky caresses along her cheek. The gathering damp sat
on her skin and she knew he must feel it, too. She was
seized with the urge to lean across the chaise and lick
him to find out for sure. If she could choose her spot,
she'd pick the place just below his steely jaw.

"I don't understand." She shook her head, not following what he was saying. She was still half in dreamland,
her whole body conspiring against logic and reason. Re-
belling against all her workplace ethics. "We haven't done
anything wrong."

Much. They'd talked about a kiss. But there hadn't
been one.

His eyes swept her body with unmistakable want.

"Not yet. But I think you know how much I want to."
He didn't touch her. He didn't need to.

Her skin was on fire just thinking about it.

"What would your brother think of me if he knew
we…" Images of her body twined together with this incredibly sexy man threatened to steal the last of her defenses. "How could he be impartial?"

Another flash of lightning revealed Cam in all his
masculine deliciousness. His shirt was open at the collar, just the way it had been in her dream. Except now,
his shirt was damp with raindrops, making the pale cotton cling like a second skin.

Cameron watched her steadily, his intense gaze as stirring as any caress. "You know the way you have faith in
your brother's good heart and good intentions? No matter what?"

She nodded. "Without question."

"That's how I feel about Quinn's ability to be fair.
He can tick me off sometimes, but he is the most level-
headed, just person I know."

She weighed what he was saying. Thought about what it meant. "And you're suggesting that if we acted on this attraction...you'd step out of the picture. Your brother becomes my boss, not you."

"Exactly." Cameron's assurance came along with a roll of ominous thunder that rumbled right through the villa.

Right through her feet where they touched the floor.

Maresa felt as if she were standing at the edge of a giant cliff, deciding whether or not to jump. Making that leap would be terrifying. But turning away from the tantalizing possibilities—the lure of the moment—was no longer an option. Even before she'd fallen asleep, she'd known that her window for selfish pleasures was closing fast if Isla proved to be Rafe's daughter and Maresa's responsibility.

How could she deny herself this night?

"Yes." She hurled herself into the unknown and hoped for the best. "I know that you're leaving soon, and I'm okay with that. But for tonight, if we could be just a man and a woman..." The simple words sent a shiver of longing through her.

Even in the dim light, she could see his blue eyes flare hotter, like the gas fireplace in the Antilles Suite when you turned up the thermostat.

"You have no idea how much I was hoping you'd say that." His words took on a ragged edge as his hands slid around her waist. He drew her closer.

Crushed her lips to his.

On contact, fireworks started behind her eyelids and Maresa gave herself up to the spark.

Cameron was caught between the need to savor this moment and the hunger to have the woman he craved like no other. He'd never felt a sexual need like this one. Not as a teenager losing it for the first time. Not during any of the relationships he'd thought were remotely meaningful in his past.

Maresa Delphine stirred some primal hunger different than anything he'd ever experienced. And she'd said *yes*.

The chains were off. His arms banded around her, pressing all of those delectable curves against him. He ran his palms up her sides, from the soft swell of her hips to the indent of her waist. Up her ribs to the firm mounds of beautiful breasts. Her sundress had tortured him all damn day and he was too glad to tug down the wide straps, exposing her bare shoulders and fragrant skin.

Any hesitation about moving too fast vanished when she lunged in to lick a path along his jaw, pressing herself into him. A low growl rumbled in his chest and he hoped she mistook it for the thunder outside instead of his raw, animal need.

"Please," she murmured against his heated flesh, just below one ear. "Please."

The words were a repeat of the sensual longing he'd heard in her voice when he had first walked into the room earlier. He'd hoped like hell she'd been dreaming about him.

"Anything," he promised her, levering back to look into her tawny eyes. "Name it."

Her lips were swollen from his kiss; she ran her tongue along the top one. He felt a phantom echo of that caress in his throbbing erection that damn near made him light-headed.

"I want your clothes off." She held up her hands to show him. "But I think I'm shaking too badly to manage it."

He cradled her palms in his and kissed them before rising to stand.

"Don't be nervous." He raked his shirt over his head; it was faster than undoing the rest of the buttons.

"It's not that. It's just been such a long time for me." She stood as well, following him deeper into the room. Closer to the bed. "Everything is so hypersensitive. I feel so uncoordinated."

The French doors were still open, but no one would be able to look in unless they were on a boat far out in the water. And then, it would be too dark in the room for anyone out there to see inside. He liked the feel of the damp air and the cool breeze blowing harder.

"Then I'd better unfasten your dress for you." He couldn't wait to have her naked. "Turn around."

She did as he asked, her bare feet shifting silently on the Turkish rug. Cameron found the tab and lowered it slowly, parting the fabric to reveal more and more skin. The bodice dipped forward, falling to her hips so that only a skimpy black lace bra covered the top half of her.

He released the zipper long enough to grab two fistfuls of the skirt and draw her backward toward him. Her head tipped back against his shoulder, a beautiful offering of her neck. Her body. Her trust. He wanted to lay her down on the bed right now and lose himself inside her, but she deserved better than that. All the more so since it had been a long time for her.

"Can I ask you a question?" He nipped her ear and kissed his way down her neck to the crook of her shoulder. There, he lingered. Tasting. Licking.

"Anything. As long as you keep taking off some clothes." She arched backward, her rump teasing the hard length of him until he had to grind his teeth to keep from tossing her skirt up and peeling away her panties.

A groan of need rumbled in his chest as the rain picked up intensity outside. He cupped her breasts in both hands, savoring the soft weight while he skimmed aside the lace bra for a better feel.

"What were you dreaming when I first walked in here?" He rolled a taut nipple between his thumb and forefinger, dying to taste her. "The soft sighs you were making were sexy as hell."

Her pupils widened with a sensual hint of her answer before she spoke.

"I was dreaming about this." She spun in his arms, pressed her bare breasts to his chest. Her hips to his. "Exactly this. And how much I wanted to be with you."

Her hands went to work on his belt buckle, her trembling fingers teasing him all the more for their slow, inefficient work. He tipped her head up to kiss her, learning her taste and her needs, finding out what she liked best. He nipped and teased. Licked and sucked. She paid him in kind by stripping off his pants and doing a hip shimmy against his raging erection. Heat blasted through him like a furnace turned all the way up.

Single-minded with new focus, he laid her on the bed and left her there while he sorted through his luggage. He needed a condom. Now.

Right. Freaking. Now.

He ripped open the snap on his leather shaving kit and found what he was looking for. When he turned back to the bed, Maresa was wriggling out of her dress, leaving on nothing but a pair of panties he guessed were black lace. It was tough to tell color in the dim light from the wall sconce near the bathroom. The lightning flashes had slowed as the rain intensified. He stepped out of his boxers and returned to the bed.

And covered her with his body.

Her arms went around him, her lips greeting him with hungry abandon, as though he'd been gone for two days instead of a few seconds. His brain buzzed with the need to have her. Still, he laid the condom to one side of her on the bed, needing to satisfy her first. And thoroughly.

She cupped his jaw, trailing kisses along his cheek. When he reached between them to slip his hand beneath the hem of her panties, her head fell back to the bed, turning to one side. She gave herself over to him and that jacked him up even more. She was impossibly hot. Ready. So ready for him. He'd barely started to tease and tempt her when she convulsed with her release.

The soft whimpers she made were so damn satisfying. He wanted to give that release to her again and again. But she wasn't going to sit still for him any longer. Her long leg wrapped around his, aligning their bodies for what they both craved.

He tried to draw out the pleasure by turning his attention to her breasts, feasting on them all over again. But she felt around the bed for the condom and tore it open with her teeth, gently working it over him until he had to shoo her hand away and take over the task. He was hanging by a thread already, damn it.

She chanted sweet words in his ear, encouraging him to come inside her. To give her everything she wanted. He had no chance of resisting her. He thrust inside her with one stroke, holding himself there for a long moment to steel himself for this new level of pleasure. She wrapped her legs around him and he was lost. His eyes crossed. He probably forgot his own name.

It was just Maresa now. He basked in the feel of her body around his. The scent of her citrusy hair and skin. The damp press of her lips to his chest as she moved her hips, meeting his thrusts with her own.

The rain outside pelted harder, faster, cooling his skin when it caught on the wind blowing into the room. He didn't care. It didn't come close to dousing the fire inside him. Maresa raked her nails up his back, a sweet pain he welcomed to balance the pleasure overwhelming him and…

He lost it. His release pounded through him fast and hot, paralyzing him for a few seconds. Through it all, Maresa clung to him. Kissed him.

When the inner storm passed, he sagged into her and then down on the bed beside her, listening to the other storm. The one picking up force outside. He lay beside her in the aftermath as their breathing slowed. Their heartbeats steadied.

He should feel some kind of guilt, maybe, for bringing her here. For not being able to leave her alone and give her that professional distance she'd wanted. But he couldn't find it in himself to regret a moment of what had just happened. It felt fated. Inevitable.

And if that sounded like him making excuses, so be it.

"Should I shut those?" he asked, kissing her damp forehead and stroking her soft cheek. "The doors, I mean?"

"Probably. But I'm not sure I can let you move yet." A wicked smile kicked up the corner of her lips.

"What if I promise to come back?" He wanted her again. Already.

That seemed physically impossible. And yet…damn.

"In that case, you can go. I'll check on Isla." She untwined her legs from his and eased toward the edge of the bed.

He wanted to ask her if they were okay. If she was upset about what had happened, or if she regretted it.

Then again, did he really want to know if she was already thinking about ways to back off? Now more than ever, he wanted to help her figure out a plan for her future and for Isla's, too. He could help with that. A pragmatic plan to solve both their problems had been growing in his head all day, but now wasn't the time to talk to her about it.

The morning—and the second-guessing that would come with it—was going to happen soon enough. He didn't have any intention of ruining a moment of this night by thinking about what would happen when the sun came up.

Chapter 8

A loud crack of thunder woke Maresa later that night.

Knifing upright in bed, she saw that the French doors in the master bedroom had been closed. Rain pelted the glass outside while streaks of lightning illuminated the empty spot in the king-size bed beside her. Reaching a hand to touch the indent on the other pillow, she felt the warmth of Cameron McNeill's body. The subtle scent of him lingered on her skin, her body aching pleasantly from sex on the chaise longue before a private catered dinner they'd eaten in bed instead of on the patio. Then, there'd been the heated lovemaking in the shower afterward.

And again in the bed before falling asleep in a tangle just a few hours ago. It was after midnight, she remembered. Close to morning.

Isla.

Her gaze darted to the nursery monitor that she'd

placed on the nightstand, but it was missing. Cameron must have it, she thought, and be with the baby. But it bothered her that the little girl hadn't been the first thought in her head when she'd opened her eyes.

Dragging Cam's discarded T-shirt from the side of the bed, she pulled it over her head. The hem fell almost to her knees. She hurried out of the master bedroom across the hall to the second room where the hotel staff had brought in a portable crib. There, in a window seat looking out on the storm, lounged Cameron McNeill, cradling tiny Isla against his bare chest.

The little girl's arms reached up toward his face, her uncoordinated fingers flexing and stretching while her eyes tracked him. He spoke to her softly, his lips moving. No. He was singing, actually.

"Rain, rain, go away," he crooned in a melodic tenor that would curl a woman's toes. "Little Isla wants to play—" He stopped midsong when he spotted Maresa by the door. "Hey there. We tried not to wake you."

Her emotions puddled into a giant, liquid mass of feelings too messy to identify. She knew that her heart was at risk because she'd just given this man her body. Of course, that was part of it. But the incredible night aside, she still would have felt her knees go weak to see this impossibly big, strong man cradling a baby girl in his arms so tenderly.

Not just any baby girl, either. This was Rafe's beautiful daughter, given into Maresa's care. Her heart turned over to hear Cameron singing to her.

"It was the storm that woke me, not you." She dragged in a deep breath, trying to steady herself before venturing closer.

He propped one foot on the window seat bench, his

knee bent. The other leg sprawled on the floor while his back rested against the casement.

"I gave her a bottle and burped her. I think I did that part all right." He held up the little girl wrapped in a light cotton blanket so Maresa could see. "Not sure how I did on my swaddle job, though."

Maresa smiled, stepping even nearer to take Isla from him. Her hands brushed his chest and sensual memories swamped her. She'd kissed her way up and down those pecs a few hours ago. She shivered at the memory.

"Isla looks completely content." She admired the job he'd done with the blanket. "Although I'm not sure she'll ever break free of the swaddling." She loosened the wrap just a little.

"I wrapped her like a baby burrito." He rose to his feet, scooping up an empty bottle and setting it on the wet bar. "You may be surprised to know I worked in the back of a taco truck one summer as a teen."

"I would be very surprised." She paced around the room with the baby in her arms, taking comfort from the warm weight. Earlier, Maresa had put Isla to bed in a blue-and-white-striped sleeper. Now, she wore a yellow onesie with cartoon dragons, so Cameron must have changed her. "Did your grandfather make you all take normal jobs to build character?"

"No." Cameron shook his head, his dark hair sticking up on one side, possibly from where she'd dragged her fingers through it earlier. He tugged a blanket off the untouched double bed and pulled it over to the window seat. "Come sit until she falls asleep."

She followed him over to the wide bench seat with thick gray cushions and bright throw pillows. The sides were lined with dark wooden shelves containing a few artfully arranged shells and stacks of books. She sat with her back to one of the shelves so she could look out at the storm. Cameron sat across from her, their knees touching. He pulled the blanket over both of their laps.

"You were drawn to the taco truck for the love of fine cuisine?" she pressed, curious to know more about him. She rocked Isla gently, leaning down to brush a kiss across the top of her downy forehead.

"Best tacos in Venice Beach that summer, I'll have you know." He bent forward to tug Maresa's feet into his lap. He massaged the balls of her feet with his big hands. "I was out there to surf the southern California coast that year and ended up sticking around Venice for a few months. I learned everything I know about rolling burritos from Senor Diaz, the dude who owned the truck."

"A skill that's serving you well as a stand-in caregiver," she teased, allowing herself to enjoy this blessedly uncomplicated banter for now. "You'll have to show me your swaddling technique."

"Will do."

"How did your visit to the McNeill family home go?" she asked, regretting that she hadn't done so earlier. "I was so distracted when you got back." She got tingly just thinking about all the ways he'd distracted her over the past few hours.

"You won't hear any complaints from me about how we spent our time." He slowed his stroking, making each swipe of his hands deliberate. Delectable. "And I didn't really visit anyone today. I just wanted to see the place with my own eyes before we contact my half brothers."

"But you will contact them?" She couldn't help but identify with the "other" McNeills. Her mother had been the forgotten mistress of a wealthy American business-man. She knew how it felt to be overlooked.

"My grandfather is insistent we bring them into the fold. I just want to be sure we can trust them."

She nodded, soothed by the pleasure of the impromptu foot massage. "You're proceeding carefully," she observed. "That's probably wise. I want to do the same with Isla—really think about a good plan for raising her." She wanted to ask him what he thought about buying a house, but she didn't want to detract from their personal conversation with business. "I have a lot to learn about caring for a baby."

"Are you sure you want to go for full custody?" His hands stilled on her ankles, his expression thoughtful while lightning flashed in bright bolts over the lagoon. "There's no grandparent on the mother's side that might fight for Isla?"

"I spoke to both of them briefly while I was trying to track down Trina. Trina's mother is an alcoholic who never acknowledged she has a problem, so she's not an option. And the father told me it was all he could do to raise Trina. He's not ready for a newborn." Maresa hadn't even asked him about Isla, so the man must have known that Trina was looking for a way out of being a parent.

"Rafe doesn't know yet?" he said, with a hint of surprise, and perhaps even censure in his voice. He resumed work on her feet, stroking his long fingers up her ankles and the backs of her calves.

"His counselor said we can tell him once paternity is proven, which should be next week. She said she'd help me break the news, and I think I'll take her up on that offer. I know I was floored when I heard about the baby, so I can't imagine how he might feel." She peered down at Isla, watching the baby's eyelids grow heavy. "I'm not sure that Rafe will participate much in Isla's care, but I'll have my mother's help, for as long as she stays healthy."

"You've got a lot on your plate, Maresa," he observed quietly.

"I'm lucky I still have a brother." She remembered how close they'd been to losing him those first few days. "The doctors performed a miracle saving his life, but it took Rafe a lot of hard work to relearn how to walk. To communicate as well as he does. So whatever obstacles I have to face now, it's nothing compared to what Rafe has already overcome."

She brushed another kiss along Isla's forehead, grateful for the unexpected gift of this baby even if her arrival complicated things.

"Does your mother's house have enough room for all of you?" Cameron pressed. "Have you thought about who will care for Isla during the day while you and Rafe are working? If your mother is having more MS attacks—"

"I'll figure out something." She had to. Fast.

"If it comes to a custody hearing, you might need to show the judge that you can provide for the baby with adequate space and come up with a plan for caregiving."

Maresa swallowed past the sudden lump of fear in her throat. She hadn't thought that far ahead. She'd been granted the temporary custody order easily enough, but she hadn't asked her attorney about the next steps.

A bright flash of lightning cracked through the dark horizon, the thunder sounding almost at the same time.

She slid her feet out of Cameron's lap and stood, pacing over to the crib to draw aside the mosquito netting so she could lay Isla in it.

"I'll have to figure something out," she murmured

to herself as much as him. "I can't imagine that a judge would take Isla away when Trina herself wants us to raise her."

"Trina could change her mind," he pointed out. His level voice and pragmatic concern reminded her that his business perspective was never far from the surface. "Or one of her parents could decide to sue for custody."

An idea that rattled Maresa.

She whirled on him, her bare feet sticking on the hardwood.

"Are you trying to frighten me?" Because it was working. She'd had Isla in her care for a little less than forty-eight hours and already she couldn't imagine how devastated she would be to lose her. It was unthinkable.

"No, the last thing I want to do is upset you." He stood from the window seat, the blanket sliding off him. "I'm trying to help you prepare because I can see how much she means to you. How much your whole family means to you."

"They're everything," she told him simply, stepping out of the baby's room with the nursery monitor in hand. When her father left Charlotte Amalie, she had been devastated. But her mother and her brother were always there for her, cheering her on when she yearned to travel, helping her to leave Saint Thomas and take the job in Paris when Jaden dumped her. "I won't let them down."

"And I know you'd fight for them to the end, Maresa, but you might need help this time." Cameron closed the door of the second bedroom partway before following Maresa downstairs into the all-white kitchen.

She was wide-awake now, tense and hungry. She'd been more focused on Cameron than eating during dinner, and she was feeling the toll of an exhausting few days. Arriving in the eat-in kitchen with a fridge full of leftovers from the catered meal that they'd only half eaten, she slid a platter of fruits and cheeses from the middle shelf, then grabbed the bottle of sparkling water.

"What kind of help?" she asked, pouring the water into two glasses he produced from a high cabinet lit from within so that the glow came through the frosted-glass front.

Cameron peeled the plastic covering off the fruit and put the platter down in the breakfast nook.

"I have a proposition I'd like to explain." He found white ceramic plates in another cabinet and held out one of the barstools for her to take a seat. "A way we might be able to help one another."

She tucked her knees under the big T-shirt of his that she'd borrowed.

"I'm doing everything I can to help you figure out why the Carib's performance reviews are declining." She couldn't imagine what other kind of help he would need.

"I realize that." He dropped into the seat beside her and filled his plate with slices of pineapple and mango. He added a few shrimp from another tray. "But I've got a much bigger idea in mind."

She tore a heel of crusty bread from the baguette they hadn't even touched earlier. "I'm listening."

"A few months ago, I proposed to a woman I'd never met."

"Seriously?" She put down the bread, shocked. "Why would anyone do that?"

"It was impulsive of me, I'll admit. I was irritated with my grandfather because he rewrote his will with a dictate that his heirs could only inherit after they'd been married for twelve months."

"Why?" Maresa couldn't imagine why anyone would attach those kinds of terms to a will. Especially a rich corporate magnate like Malcolm McNeill. She knew a bit about him from reading the bio on the McNeill Resorts website.

"We're still scratching our heads about it, believe me. I was mad because he'd told me he'd change the terms over his dead body—which is upsetting to hear from an eighty-year-old man—and then he cackled about it like it was a great joke and I was too much of a kid to understand." Cameron polished off the shrimp and reached for the baguette. "So I worked with a matchmaker and picked a woman off a website—a woman who I thought was a foreigner looking for a green-card marriage. Sounded perfect."

"Um. Only if you're insane." Maresa had a hard time reconciling the man she knew with the story he was sharing. Although, when she thought about it, maybe he had shown her his impulsive side with the way he'd taken on her problems like they were his own—giving her the villa while he stayed in the hotel, paying for the caregiver for Isla while Maresa worked. "That's not the way most people would react to the news that they need a bride."

"Right. My brothers said the same thing." Cameron poured them both more water and flicked on an overhead light now that the storm seemed to be settling down a little. "And anyway, I backed out of the marriage proposal when I realized the woman wasn't looking to get married anyhow. My mistake had unexpected benefits, though, since—surprise—my oldest brother is getting married to the woman I proposed to."

Maresa's fork slid from her grip to jangle on the granite countertop. "You're kidding me. Does he even *want* to marry her, or is this just more McNeill maneuvering for the sake of the will?"

"This is the real deal. Quinn is big-time in love." Cameron grinned and she could see that he was happy for his brother. "And Ian is, too, oddly. It's like my grandfather waved the marriage wand and the two of them fell into line."

As conflicted as Cameron's relationships might be with his father and grandfather, it was obvious he held his siblings in high regard.

"Which leaves you the odd man out with no bride."

"Right." He shoved aside his plate and swiveled his stool in her direction. "My grandfather had a heart attack last month and we're worried about his health. From a financial standpoint, I don't need any of the McNeill inheritance, but keeping the company in the family means everything to Gramps."

She wondered why he thought so if the older man hadn't made his will more straightforward, but she didn't want to ask. Tension crept through her shoulders.

"So you still hope to honor the terms of the will." Even as she thought it, she ground her teeth together. "You know, I'm surprised you didn't mention you had plans to marry when you wooed me into bed with you. That's not the kind of thing I take lightly."

"Neither do I." He covered her hand with his. "I am not going to march blindly into a marriage with someone I don't know. That was a bad idea." He stroked his thumb over the back of her knuckles. "But I know you."

Her mouth went dry. A buzzing started in her ears.

Surely she wasn't understanding him. But she was too dumbfounded to speak, let alone ask him for clarification.

"Maresa, you need help with Isla and your family.

Rafe needs the best neurological care possible, something he could get in New York where they have world-
class medical facilities. Likewise, for your mother—she
needs good doctors to keep her healthy."

"I don't understand." She shook her head to clear it
since she couldn't even begin to frame her thoughts.
"What are you saying?"

"I'm saying a legal union between the two of us would
be a huge benefit on both sides." He reached below her
to turn her seat so that she faced him head-on. His blue
eyes locked on hers with utter seriousness. "Marry me,
Maresa."

Cameron knew his brothers would accuse him of being
impulsive all over again. But this situation had nothing
in common with the last time he'd proposed to a woman.

He knew Maresa and genuinely wanted to help her.
Hell, he couldn't imagine how she could begin to care
for a baby with everything she was already juggling. He
could make her life so much easier.

She stared at him now as if he'd gone off the deep end.
Her jaw unhinged for a moment. Then, she snapped it
shut again.

"Maybe we've both been working too hard," she said
smoothly, trotting out her competent, can-do concierge
voice. "I think once we've gotten some rest you'll see
that a legal bond between us would complicate things
immeasurably."

Despite the cool-as-you-please smile she sent his way,
her hand trembled as she retrieved her knife and cut a
tiny slice of manchego from a brick of cheese. With her
sun-tipped hair brushing her cheek as she moved and
her feminine curves giving delectable shape to his old

T-shirt, Maresa looked like a fantasy brought to life. Her lips were still swollen from his kisses, her gorgeous legs partially tucked beneath her where she sat. Yet seeing her hold Isla and tuck the tiny girl into bed had been...

Touching. He couldn't think of any other way to describe what he'd felt, and it confused the hell out of him since he'd never wanted kids. But Maresa and Isla brought a surprise protectiveness out of him, a kind of caring he wasn't sure he'd possessed. And while he wasn't going to turn into a family man anytime soon, he could certainly imagine himself playing a role to help with Isla for the next year. That was worth something to Maresa, wasn't it? Besides, seeing Maresa's tender side assured him that she wasn't going to marry him just for the sake of a big payout. She had character.

"I appreciate you trying to give me a way out." He smoothed a strand of hair back where it skimmed along her jaw. "But I'm thinking clearly, and I believe this is a good solution to serious problems we're both facing."

"Marriage isn't about solving problems, Cam." She set down the cheese without taking a single bite. "Far from it. Marriage *causes* problems. You saw it in your own family, right?"

She was probably referring to his parents' divorce and how tough that had been for him and his brothers, but he pushed ahead with his own perspective.

"But we're approaching this from a more objective standpoint." It made sense. "You and I like each other, obviously. And we both want to keep our families safe. Why not marry for a year to secure my grandfather's legacy and make sure your brother, mother and niece have the best health benefits money can buy? The best doctors and care? A home with enough room where you're not worried about Rafe being upset by the normal sounds of life with an infant?"

"In New York?" She spread her arms wide, as if that alone proved he was crazy. "My work is here. Rafe's job is here. How could we move to New York for the health care? And even if we wanted to, how would we get back here—and find work again—twelve months from now?"

"By focusing on the wheres and hows, I take it you're at least considering it?" He would have a lot of preparations to make, but he could pull it off—he could relocate all of them to Manhattan next week. He just needed to finish up his investigation into the Carib Grand and then he could return to New York.

With the terms of his grandfather's will fulfilled. It would be a worry off his mind and it would be his pleasure to help her family. It would be even more of a pleasure to have her in his bed every night.

The more he thought about it, the more right it seemed.

"Not even close." She slid off the barstool to stand. "By focusing on the wheres and hows, I'm trying to show you how unrealistic this plan is. I'm more grateful to you than I can say for trying to help me, but I will figure out a way to support my family without imposing on the McNeills for a year."

"What about your brother?" Cam shoved aside his plate. "In New York, Rafe could work in a program where he'd be well supervised by professionals who would respect his personal triggers and know how to challenge him just enough to move his recovery forward."

She folded her arms across her breasts, looking vulnerable in the too-big shirt. "You've been doing your research."

"I read up on his injury to be sure you had him doing

work he could handle." Cam wouldn't apologize for looking into Rafe's situation. "You know that's why I came to the Carib in the first place—to make sure everyone was doing their job."

"It hardly seems fair to use my brother's condition to convince me."

"Isn't it less fair to deny him a good program because you wouldn't consider a perfectly legitimate offer? I'm no Jaden Torries. I'm not going to back out on you, Maresa." And she would be safe from the worry of having children with him since he would never have any of his own. That would be a good thing in a temporary marriage, right? "We'll sign a contract that stipulates what will happen after the twelve months are up—"

"I don't want a contract," she snapped, raising her voice as she cut him off. "I've already got a failed engagement in my past. Do you think I want a failed marriage, too?" Her eyes shone too bright and he realized there were unshed tears there.

She didn't want to hear all the reasons why they would work well together on a temporary basis.

He'd hurt her.

By the time he'd figured that out, however, he was standing in the kitchen by himself. The thunder had stopped, but it seemed the storm in the villa wasn't over.

Chapter 9

Two days later, Maresa sat behind the concierge's desk typing an itinerary for the personal assistant of an aging rock-and-roll star staying at the Carib. The guitar legend was taking his entourage on a vacation to detox after his recent stay in rehab. Maresa's job had been to keep the group occupied and away from drugs and alcohol for two weeks. With her help, they'd be too busy zip-lining, kayaking and Jet Skiing to think about anything else.

The project had been a good diversion for her since she'd returned from her trip to Martinique with Cameron. She still couldn't believe he'd proposed to her for the sake of a mutually beneficial one-year arrangement and not out of any romantic declaration of interest. Great sex aside, a proposal of a marriage of convenience really left her gut in knots.

Leaning back in her desk chair, she blinked into the afternoon sun slanting through the lobby windows and hit the send button on the digital file. She wished she could have stretched out the project a bit longer to help her from thinking about Cam. He'd been kind to her since she'd turned down his proposal, promising her that the marriage offer would remain open until he returned to New York. She shouldn't be surprised that his engagement idea had an expiration date since he wasn't doing it because he'd fallen head over heels for her. It was just business to him. Whereas for her? She had no experience conducting affairs for the sake of expedience. It sounded tawdry and wrong.

Shoving to her feet, she tried not to think about how helpful the arrangement would be for her family. For her, even. He'd dangled incredible enticement in front of her nose by promising the best health care for her brother. Her mom, too. Maresa felt like an ogre for not accepting for those reasons alone. But what was the price to her heart over the long haul? Her self-respect? Maybe it would be different if they hadn't gotten involved romantically. If they'd remained just friends. But he'd waited to spring the idea on her until after she'd kissed him. Peeled off all her clothes with him and made incredible love.

Of course her heart was involved now. How could she risk it again after the way Jaden had shredded her? Things were too murky with Cameron. There were no boundaries with him now that they'd slept together. She could too easily envision herself falling for him and then she would be devastated a year from now when he bought her a first-class ticket back to Saint Thomas. She sagged back in the office chair, the computer screen blurring because of the tears she just barely held back.

Foot traffic in the lobby was picking up as it neared five o'clock. Guests were returning from day trips. New visitors were checking in. A crowd was gathering for happy hour at the bar before the dinner rush. Maresa smiled and nodded, asking a few guests about their day as they passed her. When her phone rang, she saw Cameron's number and her stomach filled with unwanted butterflies. Needing privacy, she stepped behind the concierge stand to take the call. Her heart ached just seeing his number, wishing her brief time with him hadn't imploded so damn fast.

"Hello?" She smoothed a hand over her hair and then caught herself in the middle of the gesture.

"Rafe is on the move with a guest," Cameron spoke quietly. "Meet me on the patio and we'll follow him."

Fear for her brother stabbed through her. What was going on with him? Would this be the end of his job? She might not want to be involved with Cameron personally, but she needed him to support her professionally. She hoped it wouldn't come down to calling in the oldest McNeill brother, Quinn, to decide Rafe's fate, but they'd agreed that Cameron couldn't supervise her after what had happened between them.

"On my way." Her feet were already moving before she disconnected the call. She hurried through the tiki bar where a steel drum band played reggae music for the happy hour crowd. Dodging the waitstaff carrying oversize drinks, Maresa also avoided running into a few soaked kids spilling out onto the pool deck with inflatable rings and toys.

Another time, she would gently intervene to remind the parents they needed to be in the kids' pool. But she wouldn't let Cameron confront Rafe alone. She needed to be there with him.

And then, there he was.

The head of McNeill Resorts waited on the path to the beach for her, his board shorts paired with a T-shirt this time, which was a small favor considering how much the sight of his bare chest could make her forget all her best resolve. He really was spectacularly appealing.

"Where's Rafe?" she asked, gaze skipping past him to the empty path ahead.

"They just turned the corner. Rafe and a young mother who checked in two days ago with her husband for a long weekend."

Maresa wondered how he'd found that out so quickly. She fell into step beside him. "How did you know Rafe was with a guest? I sent him on an errand to the gift shop about twenty minutes ago."

"I hired a PI to keep tabs on things here for a few days."

Her heeled sandal caught on a tree root in the sand. "You're having someone spy on Rafe?"

"I can't assign the task to anyone in the hotel, especially if Aldo Ricci really has anything to do with assigning Rafe the extra duties." Cameron's hand snaked out to hold her back, his attention focused on the beach ahead. "Look."

Maresa peered after her brother and the petite brunette. Her short ponytail swung behind her as she walked. Rafe didn't bring her to the regular beach, but waved her through a clearing to the east. Maresa wanted to charge over there and split them up. Ask Rafe who told him to bring the woman to a deserted beach.

"What's the plan?" she asked, fidgeting with an oversize flower hanging from a tropical bush.

"We see who he's meeting and confront him when he turns back."

"We'll make too much noise tramping through there." She pointed to the overgrown foliage. "I can't believe that woman is following a total stranger into the unknown." Why didn't vacationers have more sense?

"He's a hotel employee at one of the most exclusive resorts in the world," Cameron reminded her, his jaw tensing as he drew her into the dense growth. "She paid a lot of money to feel safe here."

Right. Which meant Rafe was so fired. Panic weighted down her chest. Today, every penny of Rafe's check would go to extra care for Isla—an in-home sitter to help Maresa's mom with the baby. What would they do when they lost that money?

She would have to marry Cameron.

The truth stared her in the face as surely as Rafe waved at Jaden Torries on the beach right now. Her ex-fiancé stood by the water's edge with his easel already set up—a half-baked artist trolling for clients at the Carib and using Rafe to deliver them off-site so he could paint them. Rafe was risking his job for…what? He never made any money from this scheme.

"I'm going to strangle Jaden," she announced, fury making her ready to launch through the bushes to read him the riot act.

"No." Cameron's arm slid around her waist, holding her back. He pressed her tightly to him so he could speak softly in her ear. "Say nothing. Follow me and we'll ask Rafe about it when we're farther away so Jaden can't hear."

She wanted to argue. But Cameron must have guessed as much because he covered her lips with one finger.

"Shh." The sound was far more erotic than it should have been since she was angry.

Her body reacted to his nearness without her permission, a fever crawling over her skin until she wanted to turn in his arms and fall on him. Right here.

Thankfully, he let her go and tugged her back to the hotel's main beach where they could wait for Rafe.

"Someone is using him," she informed Cameron while they waited. "He didn't orchestrate this himself, and he doesn't receive any money. I would know if someone was paying him."

"That woman he just took down to the beach is partners with the investigator I hired," Cameron surprised her by saying. "We'll find out what's going on. But for now, ask him who sent him and see what he says. Do you want me to stay with you or do you want to speak to him alone?"

"Um." She bit her lip, her anger draining away. He was helping Rafe. And her. The PI was a good idea and could prove her brother's innocence. "It might be better if I speak to him privately. And thank you."

Cameron's blue eyes held her gaze. His hand skimmed along her arm, setting off a fresh heat inside her. "We'd make a great team if you'd give us a chance."

Would they? Could she trust him to look out for her and her family if she gave in and helped him to secure his family legacy? Sure, Cameron could help her family in ways she couldn't. He already had. But what would it be like to share a home with him for a year while they fulfilled the terms of the marriage he needed? Still, while she worried about all the ways a legal union would be risky for her, she hadn't really stopped to consider that he was already holding up his end of the promised bargain—helping all the Delphines—while she'd given him nothing in return.

Maybe she already owed him her help for all that he'd done for her. Even if the fallout twelve months from now was going to hurt far more than Jaden's betrayal.

"You're right." She squeezed Cameron's hand briefly, then let go as she saw her brother step onto the beach. "If you're still serious about that one-year deal, I'll take it."

"Maresa?" Rafe stopped when he spotted her standing underneath a date palm tree.

She was nervous about confronting him, wishing she could talk to him about everything at once. His secret meeting on the beach. His daughter. His future.

But she worried about how he would handle the news of Isla and she wanted his counselor there. The paternity results were in, and the woman had agreed to meet them at the Delphine residence after work today, so at least Maresa would be able to share that with him soon. For now, she just needed to ask who sent him here. Keep it simple. Nonthreatening.

He got confused and agitated so easily. Which was understandable, considering the long-and short-term memory loss that plagued him. She'd be agitated too if she couldn't remember what she was doing.

"Hi, Rafe." Forcing herself to smile, she hurried over to him. Slipped an arm through his. "Gorgeous day, isn't it?"

"Nancy says, 'another day in paradise.' Every day she says that." Rafe grinned at her.

His work uniform—mostly khaki, but the short sleeves of his staff shirt were white—was loose on him, making her worry that Rafe had lost weight without her noticing. She needed to care for him more and worry about his job less. Maybe, assuming Rafe agreed, a move to

New York could be a real gift for their family right now. She needed to focus on how much Cameron was trying to help her brother, mother and niece, instead of thinking about how this growing attachment to him was only going to hurt in the end.

Cameron McNeill was a warmhearted, generous man, and he'd been that way before she agreed to help him, so it wasn't as though he was self-serving. She admired the careful way he'd gone about investigating the happenings at the Carib. It showed a decency and respect for his employees that she'd bet most billionaire corporate giants wouldn't feel.

"We're lucky like that." Maresa tipped her head to his shoulder for a moment as they walked together, wanting to feel that connection to him. "What brought you down to the beach?"

Overhead, a heron flew low, casting a shadow across her brother's face before landing nearby.

"A guest wanted her picture painted. Mr. Ricci said so."

Again with the hotel director?

Maresa found that hard to believe. The man had been extremely successful in the industry for years. Why would he undermine his position by promoting solicitation on the Carib's grounds? Why would he allow his guests to think they were receiving some kind of luxury experience through a session with Jaden, whose talents were…negligible.

"Rafe." She paused her step, tugging gently on his arm to stop him, too. She needed to make sure, absolutely sure, he understood what she was asking. "Did Mr. Ricci himself tell you to escort that woman here, or did someone else tell you that Mr. Ricci said so?"

She'd tried to keep the question simple, but as soon as she asked it, she could see the furrow between Rafe's brows. The confusion in his eyes, which were so like Isla's. Ahead on the path, she could hear the music from the tiki bar band, the sound carrying on the breeze as the sun dipped lower in the sky.

"Mr. Ricci said it." A storm brewed in Rafe's blue gaze, turning the shade from sapphire to cold slate. "Why don't you believe me?"

"I do believe you, Rafe."

He shook off her hand where she touched him.

"You don't believe me." He raised his voice. He walked faster up the path, away from her. "Every day you ask me the same things. Two times. Everything. Everyday."

He muttered a litany of disjointed words as he stomped through the brush. She closed her eyes and followed him without speaking, not wanting to upset him more. Maybe she should have asked Cameron to stay with her for this.

She craved Cameron's warm touch. His opinion and outside perspective. He'd become important to her so quickly. Was she crazy to let him draw her even more deeply into his world? All the way to New York?

But as she followed Rafe up the path toward the Carib, watching the way his shoulders tensed with agitation, she knew that his job wouldn't have lasted much longer here anyway. She'd wanted this to be the answer for him—for them—until they caught up on the medical bills and she could get him in a different kind of program to support TBI sufferers. Now, she knew she'd been deceiving herself that she could make it work. In truth, she'd been unfair to her brother, setting him up to fail.

No matter how much she loved Rafe, she needed to face the fact that he would never be the brother she once knew. For his own good, she needed to start protecting him and his daughter, too. Tonight, she'd give her notice to the hotel director.

For her family's sake, she would become Mrs. Cameron McNeill. She just hoped in twelve months' time, she'd be able to resurrect Maresa Delphine from the wreckage.

Back in the Antilles Suite rented out to his alter-ego, Mr. Holmes, Cameron reread Maresa's text.

Rafe said Mr. Ricci sent him on the errand. Became agitated when I asked a second time but stuck to the same facts.

Turning off the screen on his phone, Cam stroked Poppy's head. The Maltese rested on the desk where he worked. She liked being by his laptop screen when they were indoors, maybe because he tended to pet her more often. He was going to hate returning her to Mrs. Trager when they went back to New York and his stint as an undercover boss was over.

His stint as a temporary groom was up next. He'd been surprised but very, very pleased that Maresa had said yes to his proposal. He needed to make it more official, of course. And more romantic, too, now that he thought about it. Hell, a few months ago, he'd proposed to a woman he'd never met before with flowers and a ring. Maresa, on the other hand, had gotten neither and he intended to change that immediately.

He needed to romance her, not burden her with every nitnoid detail that was going into the marriage contract. She hadn't been interested in thinking about the business details, so he would put them in writing only. It didn't matter that she didn't know about his inability to father children. She was focused on her own family. Her own child. And for his part, Cameron would make sure she didn't regret their arrangement for a moment by making it clear she had twelve incredible months ahead.

He dialed his brother Quinn to give him an update on the situation at the Carib, wanting to lay some ground-work for his hasty nuptials.

"Cam?" His brother answered the phone with a wary voice. "Before you ask, the answer is no. You don't get to fly the seaplane yourself."

Quinn was messing with him, of course. A brotherly jab about his piloting skills—which were actually excellent. But the fact that they were the first words out of his brother's mouth made Cam wonder about the way the rest of the world perceived him. Reckless. Impulsive.

And his quickie engagement wouldn't do anything to change that.

"I'm totally qualified, and you know it," he returned, straightening Poppy's topknot that she'd scratched side-wise. He'd gotten his sport pilot certification years ago and he kept it updated.

"Technically, yes," Quinn groused, the sound of clas-sical music playing in the background. "But I know the first thing you'll do is test the aerial maneuvering or see how she handles in a barrel roll, so the controls are off-limits."

Funny, that had never occurred to him. But a few years ago, it might have. Yeah. It would have. He'd totaled Ian's titanium racing bike his first time on, seeing how fast it would go. He'd felt bad about that. Ian replaced it, but Cameron knew the original had been custom-built by a friend.

He hated being like his father.

"If I stay out of the cockpit, will you do me a favor?" He thought about bringing Maresa to New York and introducing her to his family. Would she look at him the same way when she discovered that he was considered the family screwup, or would she take the first flight back to Saint Thomas?

"Possibly." Quinn lowered his voice as the classical music stopped in the background. "Sofia's just finishing up a rehearsal, though. Want me to call you back?"

"No." The less time Quinn had to protest the move, the better. "I'm bringing my new fiancée home as soon as possible," he announced, knowing he had a long night ahead to make all the necessary arrangements.

"Not again." His brother's quick assumption that Cameron was making another mistake grated on Cam's last nerve.

Straightening, he moved away from the desk to stare out the window at the Caribbean Sea below.

"This time it's for real." He trusted Maresa to follow through with the marriage for the agreed-upon time. "Maresa deserves a warm welcome from the whole family and I want your word that she'll receive it."

"Cam, you've been in Saint Thomas for just a few days—"

"Your word," Cam insisted. "And I'll need Ian's cooperation, too."

For a moment, all he heard was Vivaldi's "Spring" starting up in the background of the call. Then, finally, Quinn huffed out a breath.

"Fine. But the plane better damn well be in one piece."

Cameron relaxed his shoulders, realizing now how tense he'd been waiting for an answer. "Done. See you soon, Brother, and I'll give you a full report on the Martinique McNeills plus an update on the Carib."

Disconnecting the call, Cameron went through a mental list of all he needed to do in order to leave for a few days. He had to have the PI take a close look at Aldo Ricci, no matter how stellar the guy's reputation was in the industry. Cameron needed to make arrangements for a ring, flowers and a wedding. He had to find a nanny, narrow down some options for good programs for Rafe and research the best neurosurgeon to have a consultation with Analise Delphine. He could farm out some of those tasks to his staff in New York. But before anything else, he needed to phone his lawyer to draw up the contracts that would protect his interests and Maresa's, too. He felt a sense of accomplishment that he'd be able to help someone he'd come to care about. This was surprisingly easy for him. As long as they both went into this marriage with realistic expectations, it could all work.

Only when that was done would he allow himself to return to Maresa's place and remind her why marrying him was going to be the best decision of her life. He might have his impulsive and reckless side, but he could damn well take good care of her every need for the upcoming year.

With great pleasure for them both.

Chapter 10

I need to see you tonight.

Standing in her mother's living room, Maresa read the text from Cameron, resisting the urge to hug the phone to her chest like an adolescent.

She stared out the front window onto the street, reminding herself he wanted a business arrangement, not a romantic entanglement. If she was going to commit herself to a marriage in name only, she needed to stop spending so much time thinking about him. How kind he'd been to her. How good he could make her feel. How sweet he was with Isla.

Because Cameron McNeill didn't spend his free hours dreaming about her in those romantic ways. He was too busy investigating business practices at the Carib Grand and fulfilling the legal terms of his grandfather's will. Those things were important to him. Not Maresa.

The scent of her mother's cooking lingered in the air—plantains and jerk chicken that she'd shared with Mr. Leopold earlier. Her mom had warmed up a plate for Rafe when they returned from work, but Maresa's stomach was in too many knots to eat. Huffing out a sigh of frustration, Maresa typed out a text in response to Cameron.

The counselor just arrived. Any time after nine is fine.

She shut off her phone as soon as the message went through to stop herself from looking for a reply. If she wasn't careful, she'd be sending heart emojis and making an idiot of herself with him the way she had with Jaden. At least with this marriage, she knew the groom would really go through with it since he wanted to secure his millions. Billions? She had no clue. She only knew that the McNeills lived on a whole other level from the Delphines.

Here, they were a family of four crowded into her mother's two-bedroom apartment. For now, Isla's portable crib was in Analise's bedroom so they could shut the door if she started to cry. They'd told Rafe the little girl was a friend's daughter and that Maresa was babysitting for the night, but he'd barely paid any attention since he was still upset with his sister.

"Mom?" Maresa called as she opened the door for their guest—Tracy Seders, the counselor who would help them tell Rafe about his daughter. "She's here."

Analise Delphine shuffled out of the kitchen, dropping an old-fashioned apron behind a chair on her way out. The house was neat and clean, but their style of housekeeping meant you needed to be careful when opening closets or junk drawers. The mess lurked dangerously below the surface. How would they merge their lifestyle with Cameron's for the next year? Maresa would speak to him in earnest tonight, to make sure he knew what he was getting into by taking on a whole, chaotic family and not just one woman.

"Thank you for coming." Maresa ushered Tracy Seders inside, showing her to a seat in the living area where Maresa had slept since returning from Paris. She'd tucked away the blanket and pillow for the visit.

The three women spent a few minutes talking while Rafe finished his dinner and Isla bounced in a baby seat on the floor, her blue eyes wide and alert. She wore a pastel yellow sleeper with an elephant stitched on the front, one of a half dozen outfits that had arrived from the hotel gift shop that morning, according to Analise. The card read, "Congratulations from McNeill Resorts."

More thoughtfulness from Cameron that made it difficult to be objective about their arrangement.

Now, the counselor turned to Analise. "As I told Maresa on the phone, there's a good chance Rafe doesn't remember his relationship with Trina. He's never once mentioned her to me in our sessions." She smoothed a hand through her windblown auburn hair. The woman favored neat shirtdresses and ponytails most days, and made Maresa think of a kindergarten teacher. Today, the reason for the ponytail was more apparent: her red curls were rioting. "If that's the case, we'll have a difficult time explaining about Isla."

Analise nodded as she frowned, her eyes turned to where Rafe sat alone at the kitchen table, listening to a Yankees game on an old radio and adjusting the antennae.

Maresa repositioned the crochet throw pillow behind her back, fidgeting in her nervousness. "But we don't need to press, right? We can always just end the discussion and reinforce the relationship down the road when he's less resistant."

"Exactly." Tracy Seders tucked her phone in her purse and sat forward on the love seat. "Rafe, would you like to join us for a minute?" she called.

Maresa's stomach knotted tighter. She hadn't told her mother about Cam's proposal yet, but she'd mentioned it to the counselor on the phone in the hopes the woman would help her feel out Rafe about a move to New York. She feared it was too much at once, but the counselor hadn't seemed concerned, calling it a potential diversion from the baby news if Rafe didn't react well to that.

Now her brother ambled toward them. He'd changed out of his work clothes. In his red gym shorts and gray T-shirt, he looked much the same as he had as a teen, only now there were scattered scars in his hair from the surgery that had saved his life. More than the scars though, it was the slow, deliberate movements that gave away his injury. He used to dart and hurry everywhere, a whirling force of nature.

"Ms. Seders. You don't belong here." He grinned as he said it and the counselor didn't take offense.

"You aren't used to me in your living room, are you, Rafe?" She laughed and patted the seat beside her. "I heard your family has exciting news for you."

"What?" He lowered himself beside her, watching her intently.

Maresa held her breath, willing the woman to take the reins. She didn't know how to begin. Especially after she'd hurt his feelings earlier.

"They heard from your old girlfriend, Rafe. Trina?" She waited for any show of recognition.

There was none.

The counselor plowed ahead. "Trina had a baby this spring, Rafe. Your baby." The woman nodded toward Maresa, gesturing for her to show him Isla.

She bent to lift the little girl from the carrier.

"No." Rafe said, shaking his head. "No. No girlfriend. No baby."

He got to his feet and would have walked away if Tracy hadn't taken his hand.

"Rafe, your sister will watch over Isla for you. But the baby is your daughter. One day, when you feel better—"

"No baby." Rafe looked at Maresa. Was it her imagination, or did his eyes narrow a bit? Was he still angry with her? "No."

He stalked out of the room this time and Analise made a strangled cry. Of disappointment? Maresa couldn't be sure. She'd been so focused on Rafe and trying to read his reaction she hadn't paid attention to her mother. Gently, Maresa returned Isla to the baby carrier, buckling her in to keep her safe.

"Rafe?" the counselor called after him. "I have a friend in New York City I would like you to meet. Another counselor. She lives near where the Yankees play."

Maresa's mother drew a breath as if to interrupt, but Maresa put her hand on her mom's arm to stop her. Analise's eyes went wide while Rafe spun around, his eyes bright.

"The Yankees?" He stepped toward them again, irresistibly drawn. "I could go to New York?" He looked at Maresa, and she realized how much she'd become a parent figure to him in the last months.

"Maresa." Her mother's voice was stern, although she kept her words low enough that Rafe wouldn't hear. "You know that's not possible."

Maresa squeezed her mom's hand, while she kept her eyes on Rafe. "We could all go if you don't mind seeing a new doctor."

Rafe raised his arm above his head and it took Maresa a moment to realize he was pumping his fist.

"Yankees." He smiled crookedly. "Yankees! Yes."

The counselor shared a smile with Maresa while Rafe went to turn up the radio louder, a happy expression lingering on his face as he sank into a chair at the table.

"Maresa?" Analise asked. "What on earth?"

They both rose to their feet to walk the counselor to the door, and Maresa gave her mother an arm to lean on. Thanking the woman for her help that had gone above and beyond her job description, Maresa waved to her while she walked to her car. Only then did she face her mother, careful to keep Analise balanced on her unsteady feet.

"I'm getting married, Mom." The announcement lacked the squealing joy she'd had when she told her mother about Jaden's proposal. But at least now, with a contract sure to come that would document what she was agreeing to, Maresa knew the marriage would happen as surely as she knew the divorce would, too. "He cares, Mom, and wants to help with Rafe however he can."

Analise bit her lip. "Maresa. Baby." She shook her head. "After everything I went through with your daddy? You ought to know men don't mean half of what they say."

Maresa couldn't have said what surprised her more—

that her mother recognized her father had played her false, or that Analise sounded protective on Maresa's behalf.

"I know, Mom." Maresa watched as the counselor sped away from the curb. "But this is different, trust me. I don't have any illusions that he loves me."

"No love?" Her mother grabbed her hand and squeezed—probably as hard as her limited mobility allowed. "There is no other reason to marry, Maresa Delphine, and you know it."

Right. And fairy tales came true.

But Maresa wasn't going to argue that with her mother right now. Instead, she hugged her gently.

"It's going to be okay. And this is going to be good for Rafe. I want us all to move to New York where he can get into a supervised care program that will really help him." She remained on the front step, breathing in the hot air as the moon came out over the Caribbean. Palm trees rustled in the breeze.

"Honey, once you get your heart broke, you can't just unbreak it." Her mother's simple wisdom was a good reminder for her.

She would be like Cameron and look at this objectively. They could be a good team. And just maybe, she could keep her heart intact. But in order to do that, she really shouldn't be sleeping with her charismatic future husband. It was while she was in his arms, kissing him passionately and sharing her body with him, that her emotions got all tangled up.

"I understand," she promised, just as Isla let out a small cry. Her mother insisted on being the one to check on the baby. Before Maresa could follow, a pair of headlights streaked across her as a vehicle turned up her street.

A warm tingle of anticipation tripped over her skin, telling her who it was. What kind of magic let her know when Cameron McNeill was nearby? It was uncanny.

Yet sure enough, on the road below, a dark Jeep slid into the spot that Rafe's counselor had vacated just a short time ago.

Maresa's fiancé had arrived.

Half an hour later, Cameron had Maresa in the passenger seat of the Jeep. They'd left Isla at her mother's house since the women agreed the baby was out for the night after a final feeding. Or at least until the 3:00 a.m. bottle feeding, which had been her pattern the last few nights.

He'd kept silent in front of Maresa's mom about the fact that he'd been the one to provide that bottle to the baby two nights before. Analise Delphine had been cordial but not warm, unmoved by the bouquets of tropical wildflowers he'd brought for each of them. No doubt Maresa's mother was concerned about the quick engagement, the same way Quinn had been concerned. Both women were worried about Rafe's reaction to his daughter, which had been adamant denial that she belonged to him. Just hearing as much made Cameron's heart ache for the little girl. He knew Maresa would be a good mother figure to her. But how hard must it be for a girl to grow up without a father? Or worse, a father who was a presence but didn't care to acknowledge her?

Of course, one day, she would know that Rafe suffered an injury that changed his personality. But still…he hated that for Isla, who deserved to grow up with every advantage. With a lot of love. Cameron didn't know why he felt so strongly about that. About her. Was it because of the baby's connection to Maresa? Or did he simply have a soft spot for kids that he'd never known about? He'd never questioned his comfort with giving up fatherhood before, but he wondered if he'd always feel as adamant about that.

Now, the breeze whipped through the Jeep since he'd taken the top down. With the speed limit thirty-five everywhere, they were safe enough. Poppy was buckled into her pet carrier in the backseat, her nose pressed to the grates for a better view.

Maresa had shown him how to leave the city and climb the winding road at the center of the island to get to Crown Mountain where he'd rented a place for the night. He hadn't mentioned the destination because they weren't staying there for long, but he didn't want to give her a ring on the doorstep of her mother's home. They might be marrying for mutual benefit, but that didn't mean the union had to be devoid of romance.

She'd had a rough year with her brother's injury and now the surprise baby. And he could tell she'd had a rough evening, the stress of the day apparent in her quietness. The tension in her movements. He wanted to do something nice for her. The first of many things.

"You're very mysterious tonight," she observed as she pointed to another turn he needed to take.

"I don't mean to be." He ignored her directions now that they were close to the cottage he'd rented. He recalled how to get there from here. "But I do have a surprise for you."

She twisted in her seat, her hair whipping across her cheek as she looked backward. "It will be a surprise if we don't get lost since you didn't follow my directions."

"I've got my bearings now." He used the high beams to search for a road marker the owner of the secluded property had mentioned. "There it is." He spotted a bent and rusted road work sign that looked like it had been there for a decade.

Behind the sign lurked a driveway and he turned the Jeep onto the narrow road.

"I'm sure this is private property," Maresa ducked when he slowed for a low tree limb.

"It is." He could see the house now in the distance high up the mountainside. "And I have a key."

"Of course you do." She slouched back in her seat. "I'm sleeping on a couch while you have a seemingly infinite number of places to lay your head at night."

"It helps to own a resort empire." He wouldn't apologize for his family's hard work. "And soon you'll be a part of it. We've got properties all over the globe."

"Including a mountain cottage in Saint Thomas?" She folded her arms, edgy and tense.

"No. I rented this one." He turned a corner and spotted the tropical hideaway that promised amazing views from the terraces. "Come on. I'm anxious to show you your surprise."

"There's more?" She unbuckled her seatbelt as he parked the Jeep in the lighted driveway surrounded by dense landscaping.

Night birds called out a welcome, the scent of fragrant jasmine in the air. The white, Key West-style home was perched on stilts, the dense forest growing up underneath it, although he spotted some kayaks and bikes stored down there. The main floor was lit up from within. Visible through the floor-to-ceiling window, the simple white furnishings and paint contrasted with dark wood floors and ceiling fans.

"Yes and I'm hoping you're more impressed with the

next one than you are with the cottage." He stepped down from the Jeep and went around to free Poppy, attaching her leash so she didn't run off after a bird.

"I'm impressed," Maresa acknowledged, briefly brushing against him as she hopped out, unknowingly tantalizing the hell out of him. "I'm just frazzled after the way I upset Rafe down by the beach tonight and then again when we tried to tell him about Isla." She blinked up at Cameron in the moonlight, her shoulders partly bared by the simple navy blue sundress she wore. "It hurts to be the one causing him so much distress after all the months I've tried to take care of him and help his recovery."

The pain in her words was so tangible it all but reached out to sucker punch him. He wanted to kiss her. To offer her the comfort of his arms and his touch, but he didn't want to take anything for granted when the parameters of their relationship had shifted. He settled for brushing a hair from her forehead while Poppy circled their legs.

"They say we often lash out at the people we feel most comfortable with. The people who make us feel safe." His hand found the middle of her back and he palmed it, rubbing gently for a moment. Then he ushered her ahead on the path to the house where he punched in the code he'd been given for the alarm system.

A few minutes later, they'd found enough lights to illuminate the way to the back terrace, which was the main feature he'd brought her here for.

Poppy claimed a chair at the back of the patio and Cam added an extension to the leash to give her lots of freedom to explore. She looked as though she was done for the night, however, settling into the lounger with a soft dog sigh.

"Oh, wow. It's so beautiful here." Maresa paused at the low stone wall that separated them from the brush and trees of the mountainside.

Peering down Crown Mountain, they could see into the harbor and the islands beyond. With a cruise ship docked in the harbor and a hundred other smaller boats in the water nearby, the area looked like a pirate's jewel box, lit up with bright colors.

"Would you like to swim?" He pointed to the pool that overlooked the view, the water lit up to show the natural stone surround and a waterfall feature.

"No, thank you." She wrapped her arms around herself. "It's a beautiful night. I'm happy to just sit and enjoy this." Her tawny eyes flipped up to his. "But I'm curious why you texted me. You said you needed to see me tonight?"

It occurred to him now that part of the reason she'd been tense and edgy on the ride was because she'd been nervous. Or at least, that's how he read her body language now. Wary. Worried.

He wanted to banish every worry from her pretty eyes. And he wanted it with a fierceness that caught him off guard.

"Only because I wanted to make sure we were on the same page about this marriage." He dragged two chairs to the edge of the stone wall so they could put their feet up and look out over the view. "That you felt comfortable about it. That if you had any worries or concerns, I could address them."

Also, he just plain wanted to see her again. Spend time with her when they weren't working. When the whole of the Carib Grand hotel wasn't looking over their shoulders. He didn't want her to feel like he was rushing her into something she wasn't ready for.

"I'm not worried for my sake." She tipped her chin at him as she took her seat and he did the same. "But I'd be lying if I said I wasn't worried about my family. My brother seems excited to go to New York, but my mother thinks it's crazy, of course." She wrapped her arms around herself. "And Isla... I worry that a year is a long time for a baby. How can she help but get attached to you in that time?"

It was a question that had never crossed his mind. But even as he wanted to deny that such a thing would happen, how could he guarantee it? The truth was, he was already growing attached to the little girl and he'd known her less than a week.

"She'll have a nanny," he offered, not sure how else to address the concern. "I've already asked my staff to arrange for candidates for you to interview when we get to New York. And whoever you choose will have the option of returning to Saint Thomas with you if you want to return next year."

"Where else would I go?" She frowned.

"Maybe you'll decide to stay in New York." He couldn't imagine why she'd want to leave. "I've already found a program for Rafe that he's going to love. There's a group of gardeners who work in Central Park under excellent supervision—"

"Don't." She cut him off, shaking her head. Her eyes were over-bright. "We'll never be able to afford to stay there after the year is up and—"

"Maresa." Hadn't he made this clear? The guilt that he might have contributed to her stress by not explaining himself stung. Yes, he'd kept quiet about his inability

to father children since they were entering a marriage
of convenience, and it wouldn't be a factor anyway.
But there were plenty of other things—positive, happy
things—he could have shared with her to reassure her
about this union. "I'll provide for you afterward. And
your whole family. I'm having my attorney work on a fair
settlement for you to review, but I assure you that you'll
be able to stay in New York if you choose." Maybe the
time had come to make things more concrete. He dug in
his pocket and found the ring box.

A jingle sounded behind them as Poppy leaped down
from her perch and dragged her leash over to see what
was happening. She sat at his feet, expectant. The animal was too smart.

"That's kind of you," Maresa said carefully, not seeing the ring box while she looked down at the harbor.
The hem of her navy blue sundress blew loosely around
her long legs where she had them propped. "But when
you say the marriage will be real, how exactly do you
mean that?"

He cracked open the black velvet and leaned closer to
show her what was inside.

"I mean this kind of real." He pulled out the two carat
pear-shaped diamond surrounded by a halo of smaller
diamonds in a platinum band. It was striking without
being overdone, just like Maresa. "Will you marry me,
Maresa Delphine?"

He heard her breath catch and hoped she liked the
surprise, but her eyes remained troubled as she took in
the ring.

"I don't understand." Sliding her feet to the stone terrace, she stood. She paced away from him, her blue dress
swirling around her calves. "Is it a business arrangement?

Or are we playing house and pretending to care about one another as part of some deal?" She spun to face him, her hands fisting on her hips. "Because I don't think I can do both."

Carefully, he tucked the ring back in its box and set it on the seat before he followed her.

"I'm not sure we'll be *playing* at anything," he replied, weighing his words. "My house is real enough. And I care about you or I wouldn't have asked you to do this with me in the first place."

He studied her, looking for a hint of the woman who'd come apart in his arms not once, but three times on that night they'd spent together in Martinique. He'd felt their connection then. She had, too. He'd bet his fortune on it.

"You might think you care about me, but I'm not the efficient and organized concierge that you met when you were pretending to be Mr. Holmes." She folded her arms over her chest. "Maybe I was pretending then, too. I fake that I'm super capable all day to make up for the fact that I keep failing my family every time I turn around. The real me is much messier, Cameron. Much less predictable."

He weighed her rapid-fire words. *O-kay.* She was worried about this. Far more than she'd let on initially. But he was glad to know it now. That's why they were here. To talk about whatever concerned her. To make a plan for tomorrow.

For their future.

"The real you is fascinating as hell." Maybe it was his own impulsive streak responding, but a little straight talk never scared him off. "No need to hide her from me." He reached to touch her, his hands cupping her shoulders, thumbs settling on the delicate collarbone just beneath the straps of her dress.

"Then answer one thing for me, because I can't go into this arrangement without knowing."

"Anything."

"Why me?"

Chapter 11

It was all too much.

The moonlight ride to this beautiful spot. A fairytale proposal from a man who promised to take care of her struggling family. A man who wasn't scared off by the fact that she'd just inherited a baby.

With her mother's warning still ringing in her ears—that there was no other reason to marry if not for love—Maresa needed some perspective on what was happening between them before she signed a marriage certificate to be Cameron's wife.

"Are you asking me what I find appealing about you?" He lifted a dark eyebrow at her, his gaze simmering as it roamed over her. "I must not have done my job the other night in Martinique."

"Not that." She understood the chemistry. It was hot enough to make her forget all her worries. Hot enough to make her lose herself. "I mean, with all the women in the world who would give their right arm to marry a McNeill, why would you ever choose a bride with a new baby, an ailing mother and a brother who will need supervision for the rest of his adult life? Why go for the woman with the most baggage imaginable?"

As she said the words aloud, they only reinforced how ludicrous the notion seemed. Women like her didn't get the fairytale ending. Women like Maresa just put their heads down and worked harder.

He never stopped touching her, even at her most agitated, his fingers smoothing over her shoulders, brushing aside her hair, rubbing taut muscles she didn't know were so tense. "Let's pretend for a moment that Rafe had never been injured and he was just a regular, twenty-two-year-old brother. How disappointed would you be in him if he chose who to date—who to care about—based on a woman's family life? Based on, as you call it, who had the least baggage?"

Was it Cam's soothing hands that eased some of her tension? Or were his words making a lot of sense? Listening to him made her feel that she'd denigrated her own worth—and damn it, she knew better than that.

"All I'm saying is that you could have made your life a lot simpler by dating someone else." She edged closer to him, drawn by the skillful work of his fingers. He smelled good. And she'd missed him these last two days. "Is that what we're doing, by the way? Dating?"

She wished she didn't need so much assurance. But she'd been jilted before. And she would be making a big leap to follow him to New York, leaving her job behind.

"Married people can date," he assured her, his voice whispering over her ear in a way that made her shiver. "And much more. The two aren't mutually exclusive."

Closing her eyes, she leaned into him, soaking up his hard male strength. She inhaled the woodsy pine scent of his aftershave, not fighting the chemistry that happened every time he came near her. He tilted her face up to his and she closed her eyes. Waiting.

Wanting.

His thumb traced the outline of her jaw. Brushed her cheek. Trailed delicious shivers in its wake.

When his lips covered hers she almost felt faint. Her knees were liquid and her legs were shaky. She wound her arms around his neck, savoring the brush of five o'clock shadow against her cheek when he kissed her. The gentle abrasion tantalized her, reminding her of the places on her body where she'd found tiny patches of whisker burn after the night they'd spent together.

"You rented this house for the night," she reminded him, her thoughts already retreating to the bedroom indoors.

"I did." He plucked her off her feet, lifting her higher against him so their bodies realigned in new and delicious ways.

"And you haven't even asked me inside." She arched her neck for him to kiss her there, inhaling sharply as he ran his tongue behind her ear.

"I didn't want to be presumptuous." His fingers found the zipper in the back of her dress and tugged the tab down, loosening the soft cotton.

"Gallant." She kissed his jaw. "Chivalrous, even." She kissed his cheek. "But right now, you should start presuming."

He chuckled quietly as he lowered Maresa to her feet again and whistled for Poppy, unhooking the pup's leash where he'd fastened it earlier.

"Let me just grab the chairs." He opened the door for Maresa and then jogged back to return the furniture to where they'd found it.

Cam was back at her side in no time, hauling her toward the bedroom that he must have scoped out earlier. As if walking on a cloud of hope, she followed him into the large, darkened room where pale blue moonlight streamed through open blinds overlooking the ocean, spotlighting the white duvet of a king-size bed.

It smelled like cypress wood and lemon polish and possibility. Then Cameron's arms were around her again. He slid his hands into her dress, watching with hungry eyes as the fabric slid to the floor and all the possibilities became reality. She hadn't worn much underneath and he made quick work of it now, peeling down the red satin bra and bikini panties that had been her one splurge purchase in Paris. She'd liked the feel of that decadent lace against her skin, but Cameron's hands felt better. Much, much better.

He cupped between her thighs and stroked her with long fingers until she was mindless with want. Need. She felt a deep ache for them to connect in any way possible to help alleviate the nerves in her belly. To ease her reservations about marriage that she desperately didn't want to think about.

Especially not now.

She tugged at his shirt, wanting it gone. But the longer he touched her, the less her limbs cooperated. She couldn't think. She could only feel. Or there was something inherently perfect about only feeling, about abandoning concerns and taking this moment for the two of them, only them, the rest of the world be damned for now.

When the first shudders began, he covered her mouth

with a kiss, catching her cries of release. He was so gen-erous. So good to her. He held her while she recovered from the last aftershock. She wanted to return all that generosity with her hands and lips, but he was already lifting her, depositing her where he wanted her on the bed while he stripped off his clothes.

Another time, she would ask him to strip slower so she could savor the ways his muscles worked together on his sculpted body. But right now, she craved the feel of him inside her. Deeply. Sooner rather than later. She waited until he'd found a condom, then sat up on the bed, pull-ing him down to her.

With unsteady hands, she stroked him, exploring the length and texture of him, wanting to provide the same pleasure he'd given her. He cupped her breasts, molding them in his hands. Teasing the sensitive tips with his tongue. Sensation washed through, threatening to draw her under again. He reached for the condom and passed it to her, letting her roll it into place.

He spanned her thighs with his palms, making room for himself before he thrust into her deeply, fully. She stared up at him and found his gaze on her. He lined up their hands and fit his fingers between each of hers be-fore drawing her arms over her head, holding them there as she took in the moment of them, connected, as one, and a shimmer rippled along her skin.

With the moonlight spilling over their joined bod-ies, she had to catch her breath against a wave of emo-tion. Hunger. Want. Tenderness. A whole host of feelings surged and she had to close her eyes against the power of the moment.

He started a rhythm that took her higher. Higher. She

lifted her hips, meeting his thrusts, relishing the feel of him as the tension grew taut. Hot.

He still held her hands, her body stretched beneath his, writhing. He didn't touch her anywhere else. He only leaned close to speak into her ear.

"All mine." The words were a rasp. A breath.

And her total undoing.

Her back arched, every nerve ending tightening for a moment before release came in one wrenching wave after another. She squeezed his hands tight and she felt the answering shock in his body as he went utterly still. His shout mingled with her soft cries while the sensations wrapped around them both.

Replete, Maresa splayed beneath him, waiting to catch her breath. Eventually he rolled to her side but he kissed her shoulder as he went. He brushed her damp hair from her face, smoothing it, pulled the white duvet over her cooling skin and fluffed her pillow. Her body was utterly content. Sated. Pleasurable endorphins frolicked merrily in her blood.

But her heart was already heading back toward wariness. The sex had been powerful. Far more than just chemistry. And she wasn't ready to think about that right now. Not by a long shot.

Yet how long could she delay? Not more than a moment apparently. She didn't have a choice when all too soon she felt Cameron lean over the bed and dig in the pile of clothes. When he came back, he slid something cold along her hand and then onto her left ring finger.

"You should wear this." He left the diamond there and tugged her hand from the covers so they could see the brilliant glint of the stones in the moonlight.

The engagement ring.

She swallowed hard, trying not to think about what it would have been like to have him slide it into place for real, kissing her fingers to seal the moment.

Maresa turned to look at his handsome profile in the dark, his face so close to hers. He must have felt her stare because he turned toward her, too.

"It's beautiful," she told him honestly, feeling that he deserved some acknowledgement of all his hard work to make this night special for her, even if this marriage might very well break her heart in a million pieces. "Of course I love it. Who wouldn't?"

The words were out of her mouth before she could rethink them. Cameron smiled and kissed her, pleased with her assessment.

But Maresa feared she wasn't just talking about the ring. She was talking about the night and what they'd just shared. Her emotions were too raw and this was all happening way too fast. But somehow, in spite of her better judgment and the mistakes of her past, she was developing deep feelings for him. Very real feelings.

How on earth was she going to hide it from him for the next twelve months? He'd brought her here tonight to discuss their plans for a future. A move to New York. A union that would benefit both of them on paper.

If she had any hope of holding up her end of the agreement to walk away in twelve months, she needed to do a better job of shoring up her defenses.

Starting right now.

Chapter 12

Two weeks after he first placed a rock on Maresa's finger, Cameron prepared to introduce her to his family. Seated in the third-floor library of his grandfather's house on Manhattan's Upper East Side, Cam sipped the Chivas his brother Ian had just handed him. The three brothers had gathered in the late afternoon to discuss the other McNeill situation before a dinner with their wives, their father and grandfather. He hadn't wanted Maresa to arrive at the house unescorted this evening but she'd been excited to visit Rafe on-site at his new work program during his first full day. It was the first sign of genuine happiness Cameron had seen from her since they'd signed the marriage certificate.

He was trying to give her time to get acclimated to New York before meeting the McNeills, not wanting to make her transition more stressful with the added pressure of a family meeting. He'd even kept the courthouse marriage a secret for the first week—a ceremony conducted by a justice of the peace in Saint Thomas to help keep the McNeill name out of the New York papers. But he could keep things quiet for only so long. Quinn had known a marriage was in the works and finally harassed the truth out of him—that Cam had relocated all the Delphines, including baby Isla, to his place in Brooklyn. Rafe was so excited to see his favorite baseball team play that Cameron had finagled a friend's corporate box for the season, an extravagance Maresa had chided him about, but not for too long after seeing how happy it made Rafe. She didn't know it yet, but Cameron was flying in Bruce Leopold, the Delphines' neighbor in Charlotte Amalie, to attend the team's next home series with Rafe.

Cameron ran a finger over one of the historic Chinese lacquer panels between the windows overlooking the street while he waited for his brothers to finish up a conversation about a hotel Ian had been working on. Cameron felt good about where things stood with all of Maresa's family now. Analise had warmed to him considerably after seeing the in-law suite, thanking him personally for the modifications he'd made so she could get around more easily. It hadn't taken a construction crew long to add handrails to the tub and a teak bench to the shower stall, along with new easier-to-turn doorknobs in all the rooms and an intercom system in case she needed anything.

Isla was sleeping longer stretches at night and Maresa had personally hired a live-in nanny and a weekend caregiver who were settling in well. She seemed pleased with them, and her legal suit for permanent custody of the baby should be settled within the week now that Cameron had gotten his legal team involved to expedite things. Trina wasn't interested in visitation, which made Maresa sad, but Cameron told her she might change her mind one day. For his part, he enjoyed spending time with a twelve-week-old far more than he ever would have imagined. He liked waving off the nanny at 5:00 a.m. and walking around his house with the baby, showing her the view from the nursery window and discussing his plans for the day. Sometimes, when she stared up at him with her big blue eyes, Cameron would swear she was really listening.

If only his new wife seemed as content. She'd been pulling away from him ever since the night he'd slid the ring onto her finger and he wanted to know why.

"Earth to Cam?" Ian waved his own glass of dark amber Scotch in front of Cameron's nose. "You ready to join us or are you too busy dreaming of the new bride?"

Cam shook his head. "I'm waiting for you to quit talking business so we can figure out our next move with Dad's secret sons."

He wasn't going to talk about Maresa when she wasn't around. He would introduce his brothers to her soon enough and they would be impressed. Hell, they'd be downright envious of him if they hadn't recently scooped up impressive women themselves.

Lowering himself into a leather club chair near one of the built-in bookshelves full of turn-of-the-century encyclopedias that had amused him as a kid, Cameron waited for his brothers to grill him on his fact-finding mission to Martinique.

Quinn took the couch across from Cam and Ian paced. One of them must have hit the button on the entertainment system because an Italian aria played in the background. Quinn must be refining his musical tastes now that he was marrying a ballerina.

"You didn't give us much to go on," Ian noted, pausing by an antique globe. "You said all three of them—Damon, Gabe and Jager—keep a presence in Martinique?"

Cameron remembered that day of sleuthing well. The only thing that had kept him from feeling resentful as hell about seeing the McNeill doppelgängers had been knowing that Maresa was waiting for him back at the Cap Est Lagoon villa. They'd shared an incredible night together.

"Correct. Jager runs the software empire." They'd all read the report from the PI who'd found the brothers in the first place. "Damon actually founded the company, but he's been noticeably absent over the last six months since his wife disappeared shortly after their wedding." From all accounts, the guy was shredded about the loss, even though he hadn't made the disappearance public. Talking to a few people close to the family about it had made Cameron all the more determined to figure things out with Maresa. "And Gabe, the youngest, runs a small resort property. Ironic coincidence or a deliberate choice to mirror the McNeill business, I can't say."

Frowning, Quinn set down his glass on a heavy stone coaster with a map of Brazil—a gift from their mother. "I thought they were all involved in software? Didn't the PI's report say as much?"

"They are. But they each have outside specialties and interests," Cameron clarified.

Ian took a seat on the arm of the couch at the opposite end from Quinn. He picked up a backgammon piece from a set that remained perpetually out and flipped it in his hand. "Just like us."

Quinn leaned forward. "One obvious way to bring

them into the fold is to see if the one who has a resort—Gabe?" He looked to Cam for confirmation before continuing. "We ask him if he's interested in stepping into Aldo Ricci's spot at the Carib now that Cam ousted him. With good reason, I might add." He lifted his Scotch in a toast.

Ian did the same. "Here, here. Good job figuring that one out, Cam."

Enjoying a rare moment of praise from his brothers, Cam lifted the glass in acknowledgement and took a sip along with them. With the help of another investigator, Cameron had confirmed that Aldo Ricci had been taking kickbacks from low-end artists passing their work off as far more valuable than it was to the guests. With Ricci's worldly demeanor and contacts around the globe, he was someone that guests trusted when he assured them a sitting with a famous artist was difficult to procure.

But for a fee, he could arrange it.

Ricci hadn't just done so with Jaden Torries, but a whole host of artists at the Carib Grand and at properties he worked for before coming to McNeill Resorts. Cameron had released him from his contract and the company lawyers would decide if it was worth a lawsuit. Certainly, there would be public relations damage control. But at least the Carib was free of a man who gladly preyed on employees like Rafe to facilitate meetings—employees who were working on a trial basis and could be terminated easily. Cameron was certain the performance reviews would improve with the manipulative director out of the picture.

Good riddance to Aldo Ricci. The arrogant ass.

"You want to ask Gabe McNeill to take Aldo Ricci's

job?" Cameron went on to explain that the youngest Mc-Neill's resort was on a much smaller scale.

"All the more reason to get him accustomed to the way we do business," Quinn insisted. "You know Gramps insists we bring them in—"

A scuffle at the library door alerted them to a newcomer's arrival. Malcolm McNeill pushed his way through the door with his polished mahogany walking stick before Ian could reach him to help.

"I heard my name," the gray-haired, thinning patriarch called without as much bluster as he would have even a few months ago. "Don't think you can conduct family business without me."

Cameron worried to see the toll his grandfather's heart attack had taken on him in the past months. Malcolm had booked a trip to China after initially changing his will, saying he didn't want to discuss the new terms. But having his heart attack while abroad had meant the family couldn't see him for weeks afterward, and they hadn't been able to find out much about treatments or the extent of damage until he was well enough to travel home. It had really scared them.

More than ever, Cam was grateful to Maresa for agreeing to this marriage. Crappy relationship with his father notwithstanding, Cam's family meant everything to him. And even though he'd resented having his grandfather dictate his personal life, it seemed like a small thing compared to the possibility of losing him. For most of Cameron's life, he wouldn't have been able to imagine a world without Malcolm McNeill in it. Now, he sure didn't want to, but he could envision it all too well when he saw how unsteady Gramps was on his feet as Quinn helped him into a favorite recliner.

"We need the women, I think, to really make this a party," Gramps observed once he caught his breath. He peered around the room, piercing blue eyes assessing each the brothers. "Family business needs a woman's touch."

Ian lifted his phone before speaking. "Lydia just texted me. She and Maresa are waiting for Sofia downstairs before they join us."

Cameron resisted the urge to bolt to his feet, strongly suspecting Maresa would rather meet the other women on her own terms. She was great with people, after all. It was part of what made her so good at her job. Still, it bothered him that he wasn't with her to make the introductions himself.

"Good." Gramps underscored the sentiment by pounding his walking stick on the floor. "In the meantime, Cameron, you can give me the update you already shared with these two." He nodded to Quinn and Ian. "When are the rest of my grandsons coming to New York to meet me?"

Cameron was secretly relieved when Ian stepped in to field the question for him. Maybe, as a recently married man himself, Ian knew that Cam was nervous about tonight. Finishing off the Scotch more quickly than he'd intended, he got to his feet and prowled around the room, looking at antique book spines on the walls without really seeing them.

He was uneasy for a lot of reasons tonight. One reason was that discussion of the other McNeills stirred old anger about his father's faithlessness to the woman he'd married. Cam resented that his father's selfish actions resulted in three other sons and a whole life they'd known nothing about. But, as he now watched his grandfather listen to Ian with obvious interest, Cam had to respect the old man for refusing to limit his idea of family. Gabe, Damon and Jager were all as important to Gramps as Ian, Quinn and Cameron.

It didn't matter that he'd never met them.

For the first time, it occurred to Cam that he had more in common with his grandfather than he'd realized. All his life, Cam had been compared to his reckless, impulsive father. But Cameron would never be the kind of man who cheated on his wife. More importantly, he was the kind of man who could—like his grandfather Malcolm—embrace a wider definition of family.

Because Rafe was Cam's brother now. And Analise's health and safety were as important to him as his own mother's.

As for Isla?

Could he adore that little girl more if he'd fathered her himself? Like Malcolm McNeill, Cameron would never let go of the Delphines. He would use all his resources to protect them. Most of all, he would love them.

The insight hit him with resounding force, as sudden and jarring as the impact of that old kiteboarding crash that had stolen his ability to father children of his own. He didn't need to avoid having a real family for fear of repeating his father's mistakes. He already had a real family and he needed to start treating all of them—especially Maresa—like more than contractual obligations.

Because twelve months weren't ever going to be enough time to spend with her. Twelve years weren't going to cover it, in fact. He needed to make this marriage last and now that he knew as much, he didn't want to wait another second to let her know. Because, yes, he'd always have some of that impulsiveness in his character.

Only now he knew he'd never let it hurt the woman—the family—he loved.

"Will you excuse me?" he said suddenly, stalking toward the library door. "I need to see my wife."

"We've been dying to meet you," Sofia Koslov told Maresa in the foyer of the impressive six-story Italianate mansion that Malcolm McNeill called home.

Maresa tried not to be intimidated by the tremendous wealth of her surroundings and the elegance of the beautiful women who had greeted her so warmly. Dark-haired Lydia McNeill, a pale-skinned, delicate nymph of a woman who worked in interior design, was married to Cam's brother Ian. The blonde ballerina Sofia was engaged to Quinn and due to marry within the month.

Both of them appeared completely at home on the French baroque reproduction benches situated underneath paintings Maresa was pretty sure she'd seen in art history books. Cushions of bright blue picked up the color scheme shared by the two huge art pieces. Dark wooden banisters curled around the dual stone staircases leading up to the second floor. A maid had told her the men were on the third floor and they were welcome to take the elevator.

Un-freaking-believable. Maresa had been overwhelmed by Cameron's generosity ever since arriving in New York, but seeing the roots of his family wealth, she began to understand how easy it was for him to reorder the world to his liking. He might have grown his own fortune with his online gaming company, but he'd been raised in a world of privilege unlike anything she'd ever known.

"Thank you." Maresa hoped she was smiling with the

same kind of genuine warmth that her sister-in-law and soon-to-be sister-in-law demonstrated. But it was difficult to be so out of her element. Knowing she was going to be a part of this family for only eleven and a half more months hurt, too. "I will confess I've been nervous to meet Cameron's family."

Lydia nodded in obvious empathy. She wore a smartly cut sheath dress in a pink mod floral. "Who wouldn't be nervous? They are the *McNeills*—practically a New York institution." She gestured vaguely to the painting above her head. "This is a Cézanne, for crying out loud. I was a wreck my first time here."

Sofia slanted a glance at Lydia. "With good reason, since we witnessed our first McNeill brawl." She shook her head and tugged an elastic band from her long blond hair, releasing the pretty waves from the ballerina bun. She wore dark leggings with a gray lace top, but her style was definitely understated. No makeup in sight and still incredibly lovely. Sofia turned to Maresa and winked. "Your husband is a man of intense passion, we discovered."

"Cam?" Maresa asked, since she couldn't imagine him getting into a physical fight with anyone, least of all his family. He'd been incredibly good to hers, after all.

Lydia opened her purse and found a roll of breath mints, offering them each one before explaining, "It wasn't really a brawl. But Quinn, Ian and Cameron were devastated to learn that their father had a whole other family he'd kept secret for twenty-plus years. Cam landed a fist on his dad's jaw before they all settled down."

Maresa found it impossible to reconcile her knowledge of Cameron with the image they painted. But then again, he had proposed to Sofia mere months ago in a moment of impulsiveness. Maresa knew he'd gone on to extend the offer of marriage to Maresa because he thought he knew her much better. Because they had a connection. But was she really just another impulsive choice on his part?

Her stomach sank at the thought. No matter how hard she struggled to keep her feelings a secret from him these past two weeks, she feared they'd only gotten deeper. Seeing him walk around Isla's nursery with the little girl in his arms at the crack of dawn the past few mornings chinked away at the defenses she needed around him. How effective were those defenses when just the idea that he'd chosen her in a moment of rashness was enough to rattle her?

Drawing a fortifying breath, she sat up straighter on the bench seat. "He's been incredibly good to me and to my family," she said simply.

From somewhere down the hall she thought she heard the swish of an elevator door opening. Maybe the maid was returning to call them in for dinner?

Sofia flexed her feet and pointed her toes, stretching her legs while she sat. "That doesn't surprise me. We were all glad to hear that he's so taken with your little girl."

Lydia leaned forward to lower her voice. "And for a man who swore he'd never have kids, that's incredible." She reached to squeeze Maresa's hand. "His brothers are relieved you've changed his mind."

Footsteps sounded nearby. But Maresa was too distracted by the revelation to pay much attention. Her world had just shifted. Cameron had never said anything about his stance on children.

"Cam doesn't want kids?" She thought about him singing to Isla in the temporary nursery he'd outfitted for her personally while his construction crew worked to remodel an upstairs suite for her that would be ready the following week.

Had his show of caring been as fake as their marriage?

A male shadow fell over her right as her eyes began to burn. "Maresa."

Cameron stood in the foyer at the foot of the stairs, his face somber. Lydia and Sofia greeted him briefly but he didn't so much as flick a gaze their way before the other women excused themselves.

Maresa stood too quickly, feeling suddenly lightheaded at the news that she was being carefully deceived. He'd never wanted children. Did that mean he'd also never wanted a wife? That their marriage was even more of a pure necessity than she'd realized? She felt duped. Betrayed.

And just how many other secrets was her husband keeping from her in order to secure the McNeill legacy?

She cleared her throat. "I don't feel well. If you can make my excuses to your family, I need to be leaving." Picking up her purse, she took a half step toward the massive entryway.

Cameron sidestepped, blocking her path. "We need to talk."

Even at a soft level, their voices echoed off all the marble in the foyer.

"What is there to talk about? Your wish not to have children? Too late. I already heard about it." Hurt tore through her to think she was letting Isla grow attached to him.

"I should have told you sooner—" he began, but she

couldn't listen. Couldn't hear him explain how or why he'd decided he didn't enjoy kids.

"Please." She brushed past him. "I spent so many hours interviewing potential nannies and caregivers. I should have devoted more time to interviewing my husband." She couldn't help but remember all the ways he'd stepped into a fatherly role.

All those little betrayals she hadn't seen coming.

"It's not that I don't like children, Maresa." He cupped her shoulders with gentle hands. "I had an accident as a stupid twenty-year-old kid. And as a result—medically speaking—I can't father children."

Chapter 13

Cameron was losing her.

He could tell by the way Maresa's face paled at the news. He should have told her about this sooner. He'd disclosed his net worth and offered her a prenup with generous financial terms and special provisions for her family.

Yet it had never crossed his mind to share this part of his past. A part that would have had huge implications for a couple planning a genuine future together. A real marriage. He'd been so focused on making a sound plan for the short-term, he hadn't thought about how much he might crave something more.

Something deeper.

"Please." He shifted his grip on her shoulders when she seemed to waver on her feet. "There's a private sitting room over here. Just have a seat for a minute, and let me get you a glass of water."

She looked at him with such naked hurt in her tawny eyes that it felt like a blow to him, too.

"Isla has to be my highest priority. Now and always." Her words were firm. Stern. But, thankfully, her feet followed him as he led her to the east parlor where they could close a door and speak privately.

"I understand that." He drew her into the deep green room with a marble fireplace and windows looking out onto Seventy-Sixth Street. The blinds were tilted to let in sunlight but blocked any real view. Cameron flicked on the sconces surrounding the fireplace while he guided her to a chair near the fireplace. "I admire that more than I can say."

He wanted to tell her about the realization he'd had upstairs with his grandfather. That he was more like Malcolm McNeill than he'd realized. But that would have to wait and he'd be damn lucky if she even stayed and listened to him for that long. He had the feeling the only reason she'd followed him in here was because she was too shell-shocked to decide what to do next.

He needed to talk fast before that wore off. He made quick work of pouring the contents of a chilled water bottle from a hidden minifridge into a cut-crystal glass he pulled off the tea cart.

"It's not fair to Isla to let her grow attached to you." Maresa closed her eyes as he brought over the cold drink, opening them only when he sat down in the chair next to her. "Even if what you say is true—that you like kids—I should have been thinking about it more before I agreed to this marriage." She accepted the drink and took a sip. "Not that I'm backing out since we signed a binding agreement, but maybe we need to reconsider how much time you spend with her, given that you won't be a part of her life twelve months from now."

The hits just kept coming. And feeling the full brunt of that one made him realize how damned unacceptable he found this temporary arrangement. He needed to help her see that they could have a real chance at something more.

"I hope you will change your mind about that, Maresa, but I understand if you can't." He wanted to touch her. To put his hands on her in any way possible while he made his case to her, but she sat with such brittle posture in the upholstered eighteenth-century chair that he kept his hands to himself. "I never knew how much I would enjoy a baby until I met you and Isla. I never had any experience with kids and told myself it was just as well because my father sucked at fatherhood and everyone has always compared me to him."

She looked down at the glass she balanced on one knee but made no comment. Was she waiting? Listening?

Hell, he sure hoped so.

He plowed ahead. "Liam McNeill is reckless and impulsive, and even my brothers said I was just like him. I've always had a lot of restless energy and I channeled it into the same kind of stuff he did—skydiving and hang gliding. Whitewater rafting and surfing big waves. It was a rush and I loved it. But when a kiteboarding accident nearly killed me I had to rethink what I was doing."

Her gaze flew up to meet his. She had been listening. "How did it happen?"

"Too much arrogance. Not enough sense I wanted to catch big air. I jumped too high and got caught in a crosswind that slammed me into some trees." He'd been lucky he remained conscious afterward or he might have died hanging there. "The harness I was wearing got wrapped around my groin." He pantomimed the constriction. "The pain was excruciating, but I needed to cut myself down to alleviate the pressure threatening to cut off all circulation to my leg."

"Wasn't anyone else there to help?" Her eyes were wide. She set her glass aside, turning toward him as she listened.

"Not even close. That crosswind blew me a good half mile out of the water. My friends had to boat to shore and then drive and search for me. They called 911 and the paramedics found me first." He felt the warmth of her leg close to his. He wanted to touch her but he held back because he had to get this right.

"Thank God. You could have lost a limb." She frowned, shaking her head slowly, empathy in her eyes.

For the moment, anyway, it seemed as though she was too caught up in the tale to think about how much distance she wanted to put between the two of them. Between him and Isla. His chest ached with the need to fix this, because losing his new family was going to hurt worse than if he'd lost that leg. If she chose to stay with him, she needed to make that decision for the right reasons. Because he'd told her everything.

"Right. And that's how I always looked at it." He took a deep breath. "A lifetime of compromised sperm count seemed like I got off easy—at the time. I lost my option of being a father since my own father sucked at it and I was already too much like him. Right down to the daredevil stupidity."

She eased her hand from under his, twisting her fingers together as if restraining herself from touching him again. "Do you do things like that anymore?"

"Hell no." He realized he still clutched the water bottle

in his hand. He took a sip from it now, needing to clear his thoughts as much as his mind. "I channeled all that restless energy into building the gaming company. I designed virtual experiences that were almost as cool as the real thing. But safer. I know life is too precious to waste."

"Then you're not all that much like your father, after all," she surprised him by saying. She set down the cut-crystal glass and stood, walking across the library to the fireplace where she studied a photo on the mantle.

It was an image from one of the summers in Brazil with his brothers and their mother. They all looked tan and happy. He'd had plenty of happy times as a kid and he wanted to make those kinds of memories with Maresa and Isla. Maybe he'd convinced himself he didn't care about having a family because he'd never met Maresa. He'd been holding on to his heart, waiting for the right person.

"That's what I came down from the library to tell you tonight." He crossed to stand beside her, reaching to lay his hand over hers. "It's taken me a lifetime to realize it, but I've got plenty of my grandfather's influence at work in me, too."

"How so?" She turned to face him. Listening. Dialed in.

She was so damned beautiful to him, her warmth and caring apparent in everything she did. In every expression she wore. He wanted to be able to see her face every day, forever. To see how she changed as they grew older. Together.

Cameron prayed he got the words right that would make her understand. He couldn't lose this woman who'd become so important to him in a short span of time. Couldn't afford to lose the little girl that he wanted to raise with as much love as he'd give his own child. In fact, he wanted Isla to be his child.

"Because Gramps would never turn his back on family." He gathered up her hands and held them. "He insists we bring my half brothers to New York and cut them in on the McNeill inheritance, even though he's never met any of them. I was upset about that at first, mostly because I'm still mad at my father for keeping such a hurtful secret from Mom."

"I don't like hurtful secrets." Maresa's eyes still held traces of that pain he'd put there and he needed to fix that.

"I didn't withhold that information about my accident on purpose," he told her honestly. "I didn't give it any thought. And that's still my fault for being too concerned about the physical whys and wherefores of making the move to New York work instead of thinking about the intangibles of sharing…our hearts."

"Our what?" She blinked at him as though she'd misunderstood. Or hadn't heard properly.

"I got too caught up in making this a business arrangement without thinking about how much I would come to care about you and your whole family, Maresa." He tugged her closer, trapped her hands between his and his chest so that her palm rested on his heart. "I'm in love with you. And I don't care about the business arrangement anymore. I want you in my life for good. Forever."

For a long moment, Maresa couldn't hear anything outside of her heart pounding a thunderous answer to Cameron's words. But she wasn't sure she could trust her feelings. She didn't plan to let her guard down long enough for him to shatter her far worse than Jaden could have ever dreamed of doing.

Except, when her heart quieted a tiny bit and she began to hear the traffic sounds out on Seventy-Sixth Street—the shrill whistle of someone hailing a cab and the muted laughter of a crowd passing the windows—Maresa realized that Cameron was still here. Still clutching her hands tight in his. And the last words he'd said to her had been that he wanted her to be a part of his life forever.

That hadn't changed.

And since he'd done everything else imaginable to make her happy these last two weeks, she wondered if maybe she ought to let down her guard long enough to at least check and see if he could be serious about a future together.

Her mind reeled as her heart started that pounding thing all over again.

"Cameron, as tempting as it might be to just believe that—"

"You think I would deceive you about being in love?" He sounded offended. He angled back to get a clear view of her eyes.

"No." She didn't mean to upset him when he'd just said the most beautiful things to her. "But I wonder if you're interpreting the emotions correctly. Maybe you simply enjoy the warmth of a family around you and it doesn't have much to do with me."

"It has everything to do with you." He released her hands to wrap one arm around her waist. He slid the other around her shoulders. "I want every night to be like that last night we spent in Saint Thomas when we made love in the villa at Crown Mountain. Do you remember?"

She remembered all right. That was the night she'd understood she was falling for him and decided she needed to be more careful with her heart. As much as she'd treasured their nights together since then, she'd been holding back a part of herself ever since. Her heart. "I do."

"Even if it was just us, I would want you in my life forever. But it's a bonus that I get your mom and your brother and your niece." His touch warmed her while his words wound around her heart and squeezed. "Getting to be a part of Isla's life would be an incredible gift for me since I can't have children of my own. But I understand that could be enough reason alone for you to want to walk away. I don't want to deny you the chance to be a biological mother."

She could see the pain in his eyes at the thought. And the love there, too. He wasn't pushing her away, but he loved her enough that he would be willing to give her up so she could have that chance. That level of love—for her—stunned her. And she knew, without question, she didn't need a child of her own to find fulfillment as a mother. She was lucky to have a baby who already shared her family's DNA, something she was reminded of every time she peered down into Isla's sweet face. If they wanted more children, she felt sure they could open their hearts to more through adoption. If Cameron could already love Isla so completely, Maresa knew he could expand his sense of family to other children who needed them.

"I have a lifetime of mothering ahead of me no matter what since Isla isn't going anywhere." She would make sure Rafe's daughter grew up loved and happy, even if Rafe never fully understood his connection to her. He smiled now when he saw Isla, and that counted as beautiful progress. "Isla is going to fill my life and bring me a lot of joy so I'm not thinking about other children down the road. If I was, however, I agree with your grandfather that we can stretch the definition of what makes a family. We could reach out to a child who needs a home."

"We?" His eyes were the darkest shade of blue as they tracked hers. "Are you considering it then? A real marriage?"

The hope in his voice could never be faked. Any worries she'd had about him deceiving her in order to secure his family legacy melted away. He might act on instinct, but he did so with honest intentions. With integrity. She'd seen the love in his gaze when he'd held Isla. She should have trusted it. He was so different from Jaden, and she'd already let her past rob her of enough happiness. Time to take a chance on this incredible man.

Even when he'd been masquerading as Mr. Holmes, she'd seen the real man beneath the facade. She'd known there was someone worthy and good, someone noble and kind inside.

"Cameron." She pulled in a deep breath to steady herself. "I've been holding back from loving you because I've been terrified of how much it would hurt to let you go a year from now."

He tipped his head back and seemed to see her with new eyes. "That's why you've pulled away. Ever since—"

"That night on Crown Mountain." She nodded, knowing that he'd seen the difference in her since then. The way she'd been holding herself tightly so she didn't fall the rest of the way in love.

She was failing miserably. Magnificently.

"I'm so sorry if I hurt you that night," he began, stroking her face, threading his fingers into her hair tenderly.

"You did nothing wrong." She cupped his beard-stubbled cheeks in both hands. "I just couldn't afford to love a man who didn't love me back. Not again. I went halfway around the world to get over the hurt and humiliation of Jaden, so I couldn't begin to imagine how much a truly incredible guy like you could hurt me."

For her honesty, she was rewarded with a hug that left her breathless. Cameron's arms wrapped around her tight. Squeezed. He lifted her against him, burying his face in her hair.

"I love you, Maresa Delphine. So damn much the thought of losing you was killing me inside." His heart-felt confession mirrored her own emotions so perfectly she felt her every last defense fall away.

She closed her eyes, swallowed around the lump in her throat. And hugged him back, so tightly, her body tingling with happiness.

"I love you, Cam. And I'm not going anywhere in twelve months." She arched back to see his face, loving the happiness she saw in his eyes. "I'm going to stay right here with you and be as much a part of your family as you already are of mine."

He grinned, setting her on her feet again and sweeping her hair back from her face. "You have to meet them first."

She laughed, her heart bubbling with joy instead of nerves. With this man at her side, the future stretched out beautifully before her. It wouldn't necessarily be perfect or have no bumps along the way, but it was a real-life fairy tale because they would take on life together. "I do."

"And that's not happening today." He kissed her cheek and temple and her closed eyes.

"It isn't?" She wondered how she got so lucky to find a man who loved her the way Cameron did. A man who would do anything to protect his family.

A man who extended that protectiveness to her and everyone important to her.

"No." He cupped her face in his hand and brushed a kiss over her lips, sending a shiver of want through her. "Or at least, it's not happening until the dessert course."

"We can't leave them all waiting and wondering what's happened."

"They'll get hungry. They'll eat." He nipped her bottom lip, driving her a little crazy with the possessive sweep of his tongue over hers. "I have a whole private suite on the fifth floor, you know."

"Of course you do." She wound her arms around him as heat simmered all through her. "Maybe it would be a good time to celebrate this marriage for real."

"The lifetime one," he reminded her, drawing her out of the parlor and toward the elevator. "Not the twelve-month one."

"Or we could wait until we got home tonight," she reminded him. "And we could celebrate it after we tuck Isla in after her last feeding, when we are at home."

"Our home," he reminded her as he stepped inside the elevator cabin. "So you really want to go meet the McNeills?"

"Every last one of them." She didn't feel nervous at all now. She felt like she belonged.

Cameron had given her that, and it was one of many things she would treasure about him.

About their marriage.

"As my wife wishes." He stabbed at the button for the third floor. "But don't be surprised when I announce a public wedding ceremony to the table."

She glanced up at him in surprise. "Even though we're already married?"

"A courthouse wedding isn't nearly enough of a party to kick off the best marriage ever." He lifted their clasped hands and kissed her ring finger right over the diamond set. "We're going to make a great team, Maresa."

He'd told her that once before and she hadn't believed him nearly enough. With his impulsive side tempered by his loving nature, he was going to make this marriage fun every day.

"I know we will." Squeezing his hand, she felt like a newlywed for the first time and knew in her heart that feeling would last a lifetime. "We already are."

* * * * *

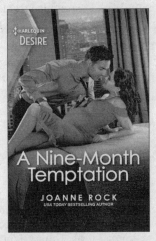

*Sable Cordero's dream job as a celebrity stylist is
upended after she spends one sexy night with fashion
CEO Roman Zayn. When he learns Sable is pregnant,
he promises to take care of his child, nothing more. But
neither anticipated the attraction still between them...*

Read on for a sneak peek at
A Nine-Month Temptation
by USA TODAY bestselling author Joanne Rock.

"Okay." Roman let his fingers dip between her knees. But
when she sucked in a rapid breath, he pulled back again. Forced
his hand to stay in one place. "Clearly we need to revisit the
parameters of our original deal. Things didn't cool off after
two months. If anything, I want you more than ever."

"Same." Sable murmured the word in a way that made him
think she'd been saying it to herself. Especially when her hazel
eyes shot to his belatedly, as if gauging his reaction. "That is, I
agree about the heat level. Still...hot."

The sticky drawl of her words teased over him while she
wrapped a dark curl around her finger. With another woman,
Roman might have thought the move was a deliberate flirtation.
But Sable's gaze had left his while her teeth worked her lower
lip. Nervous. Uneasy.

And that, he couldn't abide.

"Hey." He cupped her jaw to turn her face toward him. "We
don't have to act on it just because it's there. I'm going to be

right there with you through this pregnancy whether you want to share my bed again or not. You know that, don't you?"

"I do." She nodded as if she'd understood that all along, but it unsettled him that some of her tension seemed to slide off her shoulders with his reassurance. "It's just the chemistry is so strong, I almost can't think when you're near me. What if a return to intimacy makes it all the more difficult to be objective about what happens next? And the stakes are higher than ever now, so I don't want to make a bad call about what happens between us."

"I'm man enough to admit that while I don't like that answer, I respect the hell out of you for it." He appreciated her honesty, too. Because the attraction had the power to flatten both of them, and it was easy to prove with one kiss.

"You do?" Letting go of the lock of hair, she glanced up at him, her intelligent eyes tracking his.

"Hell yes. You're being protective of our future relationship as parents. I want you to have strong opinions about that. To trust your instincts." Even though his body was already threatening a mutiny at the prospect of not being with her tonight. "The only answer is that we wait."

Hell, even saying it out loud hurt.

"We wait." She exhaled the words on a breathy sigh, sounding about as enthused for the plan as he felt, which tugged a smile from his lips.

Don't miss what happens next in...
A Nine-Month Temptation
by USA TODAY *bestselling author Joanne Rock,*
the first book in her new Brooklyn Nights series!

Available soon wherever
Harlequin Desire books and ebooks are sold.

Harlequin.com

HDJREXP0521

From *New York Times* bestselling author

LORI FOSTER

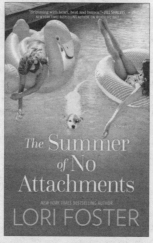

comes the heartwarming story of two best friends who cross paths with a pair of new-in-town brothers with one angry ten-year-old boy in tow. A stand-alone story of second chances at life and love, with found family and rescued animals.

"Brimming with heart, heat and humor."
—Jill Shalvis, *New York Times* bestselling author,
on *Worth the Wait*

Order your copy today!

PHLFBPAO721

Love Harlequin romance?

DISCOVER.

Be the first to find out about promotions, news and exclusive content!

 Facebook.com/HarlequinBooks

 Twitter.com/HarlequinBooks

 Instagram.com/HarlequinBooks

 Pinterest.com/HarlequinBooks

You Tube YouTube.com/HarlequinBooks

ReaderService.com

EXPLORE.

Sign up for the Harlequin e-newsletter and download a free book from any series at **TryHarlequin.com**

CONNECT.

Join our Harlequin community to share your thoughts and connect with other romance readers! **Facebook.com/groups/HarlequinConnection**

HSOCIAL2021

HARLEQUIN

Heartfelt or thrilling, passionate or uplifting—Harlequin is more than just happily-ever-after.

With twelve different series to choose from and new books available every month, you are sure to find stories that will move you, uplift you, inspire and delight you.

HNEWS2021